The spell was cast...

"River Spider, black and strong,
Folks 'bout here have done me wrong.
Here's a gif' I send to you,
Got some work for you to do.

"If Anjy-woman miss the flood,
River Spider, drink her blood.
Little one was good to me,
Drown her quick and let her be.

"River Spider, Jon you know,
Kill that man,
*   and—kill—him—slow..."*

—from "The Hag Séleen"
by Theodore Sturgeon

Magic Tales Anthology Series From Ace Fantasy Books

SORCERERS!

EDITED BY
JACK DANN & GARDNER DOZOIS

ACE FANTASY BOOKS
NEW YORK

For
three generations
of
Haldemans

SORCERERS!

An Ace Fantasy Book/published by arrangement with
the editors

PRINTING HISTORY
Ace Fantasy edition/October 1986
Second printing / November 1986

ISBN: 0-441-77532-2

Ace Fantasy Books are published by
The Berkley Publishing Group,
200 Madison Avenue, New York, New York 10016.
PRINTED IN THE UNITED STATES OF AMERICA

Acknowledgment is made for permission to print the following material:

"The Bleak Shore" by Fritz Leiber. Copyright © 1970 by Fritz Leiber.

"O Ugly Bird!" by Manly Wade Wellman. Copyright © 1951 by Mercury Press, Inc. First appeared in *The Magazine of Fantasy and Science Fiction*, December 1951. Reprinted by permission of the author.

"The Power of the Press" by Richard Kearns. Copyright © 1983 by Richard Kearns. First appeared in *Isaac Asimov's Science Fiction Magazine*, Mid-December 1983. Reprinted by permission of the author.

"The Finger" by Naomi Mitchison. Copyright © 1980 by Naomi Mitchison. First published in *Edges* (Pocket Books). Reprinted by permission of the author and the author's agent, Richard Curtis Associates.

"The Word of Unbinding" by Ursula K. Le Guin. Copyright © 1964, 1975 by Ursula K. Le Guin. Reprinted by permission of the author and the author's agent, Virginia Kidd.

"His Coat So Gay" by Sterling E. Lanier. Copyright © 1970 by Mercury Press, Inc. First published in *The Magazine of Fantasy and Science Fiction*, July 1970. Reprinted by permission of the author and the author's agent, Curtis Brown Associates.

"Narrow Valley" by R. A. Lafferty. Copyright © 1966 by Mercury Press, Inc. First published in *The Magazine of Fantasy and Science Fiction*, September 1966. Reprinted by permission of the author and the author's agent, Virginia Kidd.

"Sleep Well of Nights" by Avram Davidson. Copyright © 1978 by Mercury Press, Inc. First appeared in *The Magazine of Fantasy and Science Fiction*, October 1978. Reprinted by permission of the author and the author's agent, John Silbersack.

"Armaja Das" by Joe Haldeman. Copyright © 1976 by Joe W. Haldeman. First published in *Frights* (St. Martin's Press). Reprinted by permisison of the author.

"My Boat" by Joanna Russ. Copyright © 1976 by Mercury Press, Inc.; copyright © 1981 by Joanna Russ. First published in *The Magazine of Fantasy and Science Fiction*, January 1976. Reprinted by permission of the author.

"The Hag Séleen" by Theodore Sturgeon. Copyright © 1941 by The Condé Nast Publications, Inc. First appeared in *Unknown*, December 1942. Reprinted by permission of the author.

"The Last Wizard" by Avram Davidson. Copyright © 1972 by Davis Publications, Inc. From *Ellery Queen's Mystery Magazine*, December 1972. Reprinted by permission of the author and the author's agent, John Silbersack.

"The Overworld" by Jack Vance. Copyright © 1965 by Mercury Press, Inc.; © 1966 by Ace Books; © 1977 by Jack Vance for the Underwood-Miller version of *Eyes of the Overworld*. First appeared in *The Magazine of Fantasy and Science Fiction*, December 1965. Reprinted by permission of the author.

The editors would like to thank the following people for their help and support:

Michael Swanwick, Bob Walters, Trina King, Susan Casper, Jeanne Dann, Bernie Sheredy, Stu Schiff, Perry Knowlton, Adam Deixel, Virginia Kidd, John Silbersack, Tom Whitehead of the Special Collections Department of the Paley Library at Temple University (and his staff, especially John Betancourt and Connie King), Shawna McCarthy, Edward Ferman, Brian Perry and Tawna Lewis of Fat Cat Books (263 Main St., Johnson City, New York 13790), and special thanks to our editors, Susan Allison and Ginjer Buchanan.

CONTENTS

PREFACE

Rival claims to the contrary, the world's oldest profession is probably sorcerer. Shaman, witch, medicine man, seer . . . the origins of the magic-user, the-one-who-intercedes-with-the-spirits, almost certainly go back to the very beginnings of humanity—and beyond. Fascinating traces of ritual sorcery have been unearthed at various Neanderthal sites: the ritual burial of the dead, laid to rest with their favorite tools and food, and sometimes covered with flowers; a low-walled stone enclosure containing seven bear heads, all facing forward; a human skull on a stake in a ring of stones. . . . Neanderthal magic. A few tens of thousands of years later, in the deep caves of Lascaux and Pech-Merle and Rouffignac, the Cro-Magnons were practicing magic, too; perhaps they had learned it from their hairy Neanderthal cousins. Deep in the darkest hidden depths of the caves at La Mouthe and Combarelles and Altamira, in the most remote and isolate galleries, the Cro-Magnons filled wall after wall with vivid, emblematic paintings of Ice Age animals. There is little doubt that these cave paintings—and their associational phenomena: realistic clay sculptures of bison, carved ivory horses, the enigmatic and non-representational "Venus" figurines, the abstract and interlacing "Macaronis," the paint-outlined handprints—were magic, designed to be used in sorcerous rites (although there is some recent debate in anthropological circles as to *how* the cave paintings were magically employed; the old symbolically-kill-the-painting-to-ensure-success-in-the-hunt theory may turn out to have been too simple an answer to fit a multiplex and probably multipurposed cultural phenomenon). So Magic predates Art. In fact, Art may have been invented as a tool to *express* Magic, to give Magic a practical means of execution —to make it *work*. So that, if you go back far enough, artist and sorcerer are indistinguishable, one-and-the-same . . . a claim that can *still* be made with a good deal of validity, in fact, to this very day.

For the last couple of decades, the most common public image of the sorcerer, at least in America, has probably been that of the benign, white-bearded, slouch-hatted, staff-wielding wizard—an image which almost certainly owes most of its ubiquity to the enormous success of J. R. R. Tolkien's *Lord of the Rings* trilogy, an image primarily composed of a large measure of Gandalf the Grey, with perhaps a jigger of T. H. White's Merlin thrown in for flavor. Throughout history, however, the sorcerer has worn *many* faces—sometimes benevolent and wise, sometimes evil and malign, sometimes—ambiguously—both. To the ancient Greeks, it was the Great Science; Paracelsus called it "a great hidden wisdom," and the famous mystic Agrippa considered it to be the true path of communion with God. Conversely, to medieval European society, the sorcerer was one who collaborated with the Devil in the spreading of evil throughout the world, in the corruption and ruination of Christian souls, and the smoke of thousands of burning witches and warlocks filled the chilly autumn air for a hundred years or more. To some Amerind tribes, the magic-user was either sorcerer *or* magician depending on the *use*—either malevolent or benign—to which he put his magic. In fact, nearly every human society has its own image of the sorcerer. In Mexico, the sorcerer is *curandero, brujo,* or *bruja;* in Haiti, he is *houngan* or *quimboiseur;* in Amerind lore, the Shaman or Medicine Man or Singer; in Jewish mysticism, the kabbalist; in Gypsy circles, the *chóvihánni,* the witch; in parts of today's rural America, the hoodoo or conjure man; to the Maori of New Zealand, the *tghunga makutu . . .* and so on, throughout the world, in the most "progressive" societies no less than the most "primitive." The fact is, we are all still sorcerers under the skin, and magic seems to be part of the intuitive cultural heritage of most human beings. Whenever you cross your fingers to ward off bad luck, or knock wood, or insure the health of your mother's back by not step-ping on the cracks in the sidewalk—or, for that matter, when you deliberately *step* on them, with malice aforethought—you are putting on the mantle of sorcerer... then you are practic-ing magic, as surely as the medieval alchemist puttering with his alembics and pestles, as surely as the bear-masked, stag-horned Cro-Magnon shaman making ritual magic in the dark-ness of the deep caves at Rouffignac.

In this anthology, we have endeavored to cover the whole world of magic, the sorcerer in every mask and role. Here you will find benevolent white wizards, and the blackest of black magicians. Sorcerers who can kill with a touch, or the point of a finger. Sorcerers who encyst their enemies in crystal spheres forty-five miles beneath the surface of the earth. Whimsical sorcerers who make magic with newspapers and beer cans, grim sorcerers who whisper of death in the still of night in the most chill and terrible of voices. Sorcerers who rule your dreams and shape them to their own ends. Sorcerers who command the forces of Hell. Sorcerers who guard the very world of life itself against vast implacable Powers from beyond the dry vales of death. Here you'll drink and dice at the Silver Eel tavern, and sample the dangerous wares of Azenomei Fair.... Cross the black and measureless Outer Sea, sail aboard the *Night Bird,* or with the fabulous ship *My Boat,* whose ports of call include Knossos and Atlantis, Ka-dath in the Cold Waste, and Celephais the Fair.... Meet Iu-counu the Laughing Magician, General Jack, and Silver John... squint-eyed Mr. Onselm and the fearsome Hag Séleen.... Encounter, if you dare, the monstrous Dead Horse ... the Ugly Bird... the sinister River Spider.... Visit worlds outside the time and space we know, the mythic lands of Earthsea and Newhon and The Dying Earth... Lankhmar and Almery... and then return home to find that magic is also afoot in the remote hills of Appalachia... in the deep bayou country of Louisiana... in post-colonial Africa... in a sleepy little Central American nation... in a big-city park at night ... in the stuffy environs of a Long Island high school in the fifties... amidst the whir and clatter of an ultramodern com-puter room...

... and perhaps you will find that magic is afoot in your *own* heart, as well....

The Bleak Shore

by

Fritz Leiber

There are only a few real giants in the heroic fantasy field;
once you have made the obligatory bow to past masters like
Robert E. Howard, Clark Ashton Smith, E. R. Eddison, C. L.
Moore, and Lord Dunsany, you come very quickly to Fritz
Leiber. Even among contemporary heroic fantasy writers,
Leiber is seriously rivaled for excellence only by Jack Vance
(and, to a somewhat lesser degree, by Michael Moorcock and
Poul Anderson), but Leiber's roots go all the way back to
1939, when he began publishing the first of a long series of
stories and novels about that swashbuckling pair of rogues,
Fafhrd and the Gray Mouser. Not content to rest on his
laurels as an Ancestral Figure, Leiber has continued to add to
this canon over the last forty-five years, building it into probably the most complex and intelligent body of work in the entire
sub-genre of "Sword & Sorcery" (which term Leiber himself
is usually credited with coining). The Fafhrd-Gray Mouser
stories have been published in six volumes, the most essential
of which are probably The Swords of Lankhmar and Swords
in the Mists.

Here, in one of the strangest and most evocative of their
adventures, Fafhrd and the Gray Mouser encounter a small,
pale, black-robed man with a white, bulging forehead and
cold cavernous eyes . . . and learn that, though death has
many voices, sometimes it may call by saying "the Bleak

1

*Shore." ... Nothing more than that. "The Bleak Shore." ...
And you would have to go....*

*Born in Chicago in 1910, the multitalented Fritz Leiber is
also a towering Ancestral Figure in the science fiction field—
being one of the major writers of both Campbell's "Golden
Age" Astounding of the forties and H. L. Gold's Galaxy in the
fifties, for instance—and is also considered to be perhaps the
finest practitioner of the supernatural horror tale—especially
updated "modern" or "urban" horror—since Poe and Lovecraft. He has won six Hugos, four Nebulas, two World Fantasy Awards—one of them the prestigious Life Achievement
Award—and a Grand Master of Fantasy Award. His other
books include* The Big Time, The Wanderer, Our Lady of
Darkness, Gather, Darkness, *and* The Green Millennium, *and
the collections* The Best of Fritz Leiber, The Book of Fritz
Leiber, *and* The Ghost Light.

*   *   *

"SO YOU THINK A MAN CAN CHEAT DEATH AND OUTWIT
doom?" said the small, pale man, whose bulging forehead was
shadowed by a black cowl.

The Gray Mouser, holding the dice box ready for a throw,
paused and quickly looked sideways at the questioner.

"I said that a cunning man can cheat death for a long time."

The Silver Eel bustled with pleasantly raucous excitement.
Fighting men predominated and the clank of swordsmen's
harness mingled with the thump of tankards, providing a deep
obbligato to the shrill laughter of the women. Swaggering
guardsmen elbowed the insolent bravos of the young lords.
Grinning slaves bearing open wine jars dodged nimbly between. In one corner a slave girl was dancing, the jingle of her
silver anklet bells inaudible in the din. Outside the small,
tight-shuttered windows a dry, whistling wind from the south
filled the air with dust that eddied between the cobblestones
and hazed the stars. But here all was jovial confusion.

The Gray Mouser was one of a dozen at the gaming table.
He was dressed all in gray—jerkin, silken shirt, and mouse-
skin cap—but his dark, flashing eyes and cryptic smile made
him seem more alive than any of the others, save for the huge
copper-haired barbarian next to him, who laughed immoder-
ately and drank tankards of the sour wine of Lankhmar as if it
were beer.

"They say you're a skilled swordsman and have come close

to death many times," continued the small, pale man in the black robe, his thin lips barely parting as he spoke the words.

But the Mouser had made his throw, and the odd dice of Lankhmar had stopped with the matching symbols of the eel and serpent uppermost, and he was raking in triangular golden coins. The barbarian answered for him.

"Yes, the gray one handles a sword daintily enough—almost as well as myself. He's also a great cheat at dice."

"Are you, then, Fafhrd?" asked the other. "And do you, too, truly think a man can cheat death, be he ever so cunning a cheat at dice?"

The barbarian showed his white teeth in a grin and peered puzzledly at the small, pale man whose somber appearance and manner contrasted so strangely with the revelers throng the low-ceilinged tavern fumy with wine.

"You guess right again," he said in a bantering tone. "I am Fafhrd, a Northerner, ready to pit my wits against any doom." He nudged his companion. "Look, Mouser, what do you think of this little black-coated mouse who's sneaked in through a crack in the floor and wants to talk with you and me about death?"

The man in black did not seem to notice the jesting insult. Again his bloodless lips hardly moved, yet his words were unaffected by the surrounding clamor, and impinged on the ears of Fafhrd and the Gray Mouser with peculiar clarity.

"It is said you two came close to death in the Forbidden City of the Black Idols, and in the stone trap of Angarngi, and on the misty island in the Sea of Monsters. It is also said that you have walked with doom on the Cold Waste and through the Mazes of Klesh. But who may be sure of these things, and whether death and doom were truly near? Who knows but what you are both braggarts who have boasted once too often? Now I have heard tell that death sometimes calls to a man in a voice only he can hear. Then he must rise and leave his friends and go to whatever place death shall bid him, and there meet his doom. Has death ever called to you in such a fashion?"

Fafhrd might have laughed, but did not. the Mouser had a witty rejoinder on the tip of his tongue, but instead he heard himself saying: "In what words might death call?"

"That would depend," said the small man. "He might look at two such as you and say the Bleak Shore. Nothing more than that. The Bleak Shore. And when he said it three times you would have to go."

This time Fafhrd tried to laugh, but the laugh never came. Both of them could only meet the gaze of the small man with the white, bulging forehead, stare stupidly into his cold, cavernous eyes. Around them the tavern roared with mirth at some jest. A drunken guardsman was bellowing a song. The gamblers called impatiently to the Mouser to stake his next wager. A giggling woman in red and gold stumbled past the small, pale man, almost brushing away the black cowl that covered his pate. But he did not move. And Fafhrd and the Gray Mouser continued to stare—fascinatedly, helplessly—into his chill, black eyes, which now seemed to them twin tunnels leading into a far and evil distance. Something deeper than fear gripped them in iron paralysis. The tavern became faint and soundless, as if viewed through many thicknesses of glass. They saw only the eyes and what lay beyond the eyes, something desolate, dreary, and deadly.

"The Bleak Shore," he repeated.

Then those in the tavern saw Fafhrd and the Gray Mouser rise and without sign or word of leave-taking walk together to the low oaken door. A guardsman cursed as the huge Northerner blindly shoved him out of the way. There were a few shouted questions and mocking comments—the Mouser had been winning—but these were quickly hushed, for all perceived something strange and alien in the manner of the two. Of the small, pale, black-robed man none took notice. They saw the door open. They heard the dry moaning of the wind and a hollow flapping that probably came from the awnings. They saw an eddy of dust swirl up from the threshold. Then the door was closed and Fafhrd and the Mouser were gone.

No one saw them on their way to the great stone docks that bank the east side of the River Hlal from one end of Lankhmar to the other. No one saw Fafhrd's north-rigged, red-sailed sloop cast off and slip out into the current that slides down to the squally Inner Sea. The night was dark and the dust kept men indoors. But the next day they were gone, and the ship with them, and its Mingol crew of four—these being slave prisoners, sworn to life service, whom Fafhrd and the Mouser had brought back from an otherwise unsuccessful foray against the Forbidden City of the Black Idols.

About a fortnight later a tale came back to Lankhmar from Earth's End, the little harbor town that lies farthest of all towns to the west, on the very margin of the shipless Outer

Sea; a tale of how a north-rigged sloop had come into port to take on an unusually large amount of food and water—unusually large because there were only six in the crew; a sullen, white-skinned Northern barbarian; an unsmiling little man in gray; and four squat, stolid, black-haired Mingols. Afterward the sloop had sailed straight into the sunset. The people of Earth's End had watched the red sail until nightfall, shaking their heads at its audacious progress. When this tale was repeated in Lankhmar, there were others who shook their heads, and some who spoke significantly of the peculiar behavior of the two companions on the night of their departure. And as the weeks dragged on into months and the months slowly succeeded one another, there were many who talked of Fafhrd and the Gray Mouser as two dead men.

Then Ourph the Mingol appeared and told his curious story to the dockmen of Lankhmar. There was some difference of opinion as to the validity of the story, for although Ourph spoke the soft language of Lankhmar moderately well, he was an outsider, and, after he was gone, no one could prove that he was or was not one of the four Mingols who had sailed with the north-rigged sloop. Moreover, his story did not answer several puzzling questions, which is one of the reasons that many thought it untrue.

"They were mad," said Ourph, "or else under a curse, those two men, the great one and the small one. I suspected it when they spared our lives under the very walls of the Forbidden City. I knew it for certain when they sailed west and west, never reefing, never changing course, always keeping the star of the ice fields on our right hand. They talked little, they slept little, they laughed not at all. Ola, they were cursed! As for us four—Teevs, Larlt, Ouwenyis, and I—we were ignored but not abused. We had our amulets to keep off evil magics. We were sworn slaves to the death. We were men of the Forbidden City. We made no mutiny.

"For many days we sailed. The sea was stormless and empty around us, and small, very small; it looked as if it bent down out of sight to the north and the south and the awful west, as if the sea ended an hour's sail from where we were. And then it began to look that way to the east, too. But the great Northerner's hand rested on the steering oar like a curse, and the small gray one's hand was as firm. We four sat mostly in the bow, for there was little enough sail-tending, and diced our destinies at night and morning, and gambled for our amulets and clothes—we would have played for our hides and bones, were we not slaves.

"To keep track of the days, I tied a cord around my right thumb and moved it over a finger each day until it passed from right little finger to left little finger and came to my left thumb. Then I put it on Teev's right thumb. When it came to his left thumb he gave it to Larlt. So we numbered the days and knew them. And each day the sky became emptier and the sea smaller, until it seemed that the end of the sea was but a bowshot away from our stem and sides and stern. Teevs said that we were upon an enchanted patch of water that was being drawn through the air toward the red star that is Hell. Surely Teevs may have been right. There cannot be so much water to the west. I have crossed the Inner Sea and the Sea of Monsters—and I say so.

"It was when the cord was around Larlt's left ring finger that the great storm came at us from the southwest. For three days it blew stronger and stronger, smiting the water into great seething waves; crags and gullies piled mast-high with foam. No other men have seen such waves nor should see them; they are not churned for us or for our oceans. Then I had further proof that our masters were under a curse. They took no notice of the storm; they let it reef their sails for them. They took no notice when Teevs was washed overboard, when we were half swamped and filled to the gunwales with spume, or bailing buckets foaming like tankards of beer. They stood in the stern, both braced against the steering oar, both drenched by the following waves, staring straight ahead, seeming to hold converse with creatures that only the bewitched can hear. Ola! They were accursed! Some evil demon was preserving their lives for a dark reason of his own. How else came we safe through the storm?

"For when the cord was on Larlt's left thumb, the towering waves and briny foam gave way to a great black sea swell that the whistling wind rippled but did not whiten. When the dawn came and we first saw it, Ouwenyis cried out that we were riding by magics upon a sea of black sand; and Larlt averred that we were fallen during the storm into the ocean of sulphurous oil that some say lies under the earth—for Larlt has seen the black, bubbling lakes of the Far East; and I remembered what Teevs had said and wondered if our patch of water had not been carried through the thin air and plunged into a wholly different sea on a wholly different world. But the small gray one heard our talk and dipped a bucket over the side and soused us with it, so that we knew our hull was still in water and that the water was salt—whatever that water might be.

"And then he bid us patch the sails and make the sloop shipshape. By midday we were flying west at a speed even greater than we had made during the storm, but so long were the swells and so swift did they move with us that we could only climb five or six in a whole day. By the Black Idols, but they were long!

"And so the cord moved across Ouwenyis' fingers. But the clouds were as leaden dark above us as was the strange sea heavy around our hull, and we knew not if the light that came through them was that of the sun or of some wizard moon, and when we caught sight of the stars they seemed strange. And still the white hand of the Northerner lay heavy on the steering oar, and still he and the gray one stared straight ahead. But on the third day of our flight across that black expanse the Northerner broke silence. A mirthless, terrible smile twisted his lips, and I heard him mutter 'the Bleak Shore.' Nothing more than that. The gray one nodded, as if there were some portentous magic in the words. Four times I heard the words pass the Northerner's lips, so that they were imprinted on my memory.

"The days grew darker and colder, and the clouds slid lower and lower, threatening, like the roof of a great cavern. And when the cord was on Ouwenyis' pointing finger we saw a leaden and motionless extent ahead of us, looking like the swells, but rising above them, and we knew that we were come to the Bleak Shore.

"Higher and higher that shore rose, until we could distinguish the towering basalt crags, rounded like the sea swell, studded here and there with gray boulders, whitened in spots as if by the droppings of gigantic birds—yet we saw no birds, large or small. Above the cliffs were dark clouds, and below them was a strip of pale sand, nothing more. Then the Northerner bent the steering oar and sent us straight in, as though he intended our destruction; but at the last moment he passed us at mast length by a rounded reef that hardly rose above the crest of the swell and found us harbor room. We sent the anchor over and rode safe.

"Then the Northerner and the gray one, moving like men in a dream, accoutered themselves, a shirt of light chain mail and a rounded, uncrested helmet for each—both helmets and shirts white with salt from the foam and spray of the storm. And they bound their swords to their sides, and wrapped great cloaks about them, and took a little food and a little water, and bade us unship the small boat. And I rowed them ashore and they stepped out onto the beach and walked toward the cliffs. Then, although I was much frightened, I cried out after them, 'Where are you going? Shall we follow? What shall we do?' For several moments there was no reply. Then, without turning his head, the gray one answered, his voice a low, hoarse, yet far-carrying whisper. And he said, 'Do not follow. We are dead men. Go back if you can.'

"And I shuddered and bowed my head to his words and rowed out to the ship. Ouwenyis and Larlt and I watched them climb the high, rounded crags. The two figures grew smaller and smaller, until the Northerner was no more than a tiny, slim beetle and his gray companion almost invisible, save when they crossed a whitened space. Then a wind came down from the crags and blew the swell away from the shore, and we knew we could make sail. But we stayed—for were we not sworn slaves? And am I not a Mingol?"

"As evening darkened, the wind blew stronger, and our desire to depart—if only to drown in the unknown sea—became greater. For we did not like the strangely rounded basalt crags of the Bleak Shore; we did not like it that we saw no gulls or hawks or birds of any kind in the leaden air, no seaweed on the beach. And we all three began to catch glimpses of something shimmering at the summit of the cliffs. Yet it was not until the third hour of night that we upped anchor and left the Bleak Shore behind.

"There was another great storm after we were out several days, and perhaps it hurled us back into the seas we know. Ouwenyis was washed overboard and Larlt went mad from thirst, and toward the end I knew not myself what was happening. Only I was cast up on the southern coast near Quarmall and. after many difficulties, am come here to Lankhmar. But my dreams are haunted by those black cliffs and by visions of the whitening bones of my masters, and their grinning skulls staring empty-eyed at something strange and deadly."

Unconscious of the fatigue that stiffened his muscles, the Gray Mouser wormed his way past the last boulder, finding shallow handholds and footholds at the juncture of the granite and black basalt, and finally stood erect on the top of the rounded crags that walled the Bleak Shore. He was aware that Fafhrd stood at his side, a vague, hulking figure in whitened chain-mail vest and helmet. But he saw Fafhrd vaguely, as if through many thicknesses of glass. The only things he saw clearly—and it seemed he had been looking at them for an eternity—were two cavernous, tunnel-like black eyes, and beyond them something desolate and deadly, which had once been across the Outer Sea but was now close at hand. So it had been, ever since he had risen from the gaming table in the low-ceilinged tavern in Lankhmar. Vaguely he remembered the staring people of Earth's End, the foam, and fury of the storm, the curve of the black sea swell, and the look of terror on the face of Ourph the Mingol; these memories, too, came to him as if through many thicknesses of glass. Dimly he realized that he and his companion were under a curse, and that they were now come to the source of that curse.

For the flat landscape that spread out before them was without sign of life. In front of them the basalt dipped down to form a large hollow of black sand—tiny particles of iron ore. In the sand were half embedded more than two score of what seemed to the Gray Mouser to be inky-black, oval boulders of various sizes. But they were too perfectly rounded, too regular in form to be boulders, and slowly it was borne in on the Mouser's consciousness that they were not boulders, but monstrous black eggs, a few small, some so large that a man could not have clasped his arms around them, one big as a tent.

Scattered over the sand were bones, large and small. The Mouser recognized the tusked skull of a boar, and two smaller ones—wolves. There was the skeleton of some great predatory cat. Beside it lay the bones of a horse, and beyond them the rib case of a man or ape. The bones lay all around the huge black eggs—a whitely gleaming circle.

From somewhere a toneless voice sounded, thin but clear, in accents of command, saying: "For warriors, a warrior's doom."

The Mouser knew the voice, for it had been echoing in his ears for weeks, ever since it had first come from the lips of a pale little man with a bulging forehead, wearing a black robe and sitting near him in a tavern in Lankhmar. And a more whispering voice came to him from within, saying, *He seeks always to repeat past experience, which has always been in his favor.*

Then he saw that what lay before him was not utterly life-

less. Movement of a sort had come to the Bleak Shore. A
crack had appeared in one of the great black eggs, and then in
another, and the cracks were branching, widening as bits of
shell fell to the black, sandy floor.

The Mouser knew that this was happening in answer to the
first voice, the thin one. He knew this was the end to which
the thin voice had called him across the Outer Sea. Powerless
to move farther, he dully watched the slow progress of this
monstrous birth. Under the darkening leaden sky he watched
twin deaths hatching out for him and his companion.

The first hint of their nature came in the form of a long,
swordlike claw which struck out through a crack, widening it
farther. Fragments of shell fell more swiftly.

The two creatures which emerged in the gathering dusk
held enormity even for the Mouser's drugged mind. Sham-
bling things, erect like men but taller, with reptilian heads
boned and crested like helmets, feet clawed like a lizard's,
shoulders topped with bony spikes, forelimbs each terminating
in a single yard-long claw. In the semidarkness they seemed
like hideous caricatures of fighting men, armored and bearing
swords. Dusk did not hide the yellow of their blinking eyes.

Then the voice called again: "For warriors, a warrior's
doom."

At those words the bonds of paralysis dropped from the
Mouser. For an instant he thought he was waking from a
dream. But then he saw the new-hatched creatures racing toward them, a shrill, eager screeching issuing from their long
muzzles. From beside him he heard a quick, rasping sound as
Fafhrd's sword whipped from its scabbard. Then the Mouser
drew his own blade, and a moment later it crashed against a
steel-like claw which thrust at his throat. Simultaneously,
Fafhrd parried a like blow from the other monster.

What followed was nightmare. Claws that were swords
slashed and stabbed. Not so swiftly that they could not be
parried, though there were four against two. Counter-thrusts
glanced off impenetrable bony armor. Both creatures suddenly
wheeled, striking at the Mouser. Fafhrd drove in from the
side, saving him. Slowly the two companions were driven
back toward where the crag sheered off. The beasts seemed
tireless, creatures of bone and metal rather than flesh. The
Mouser foresaw the end. He and Fafhrd might hold them off
for a while longer, but eventually fatigue would supervene;

their parries would become slower, weaker; the beasts would have them.

As if in anticipation of this, the Mouser felt a claw nick his wrist. It was then that he remembered the dark, cavernous eyes that had drawn them across the Outer Sea, the voice that had loosed doom upon them. He was gripped with a strange, mad rage—not against the beasts but their master. He seemed to see the black, dead eyes staring at him from the black sand. Then he lost control of his actions. When the two monsters next attempted a double attack on Fafhrd he did not turn to help, but instead dodged past and dashed down into the hollow, toward the embedded eggs.

Left to face the monsters alone, Fafhrd fought like a madman himself, his great sword whistling as his last resources of energy jolted his muscles. He hardly noticed when one of the beasts turned back to pursue his comrade.

The Mouser stood among the eggs, facing one of a glossier hue and smaller than most. Vindictively he brought his sword crashing down upon it. The blow numbed his hand, but the egg shattered.

Then the Mouser knew the source of the evil of the Bleak Shore, lying here and sending its spirit abroad, lying here and calling men to doom. Behind him he heard the scrabbling steps and eager screeching of the monster chosen for his destruction. But he did not turn. Instead, he raised his sword and brought it down whirring on the half-embryonic creature gloating in secret over the creatures he had called to death, down on the bulging forehead of the small pale man with the thin lips.

Then he waited for the finishing blow of the claw. It did not come. Turning, he saw the monster sprawled on the black sand. Around him, the deadly eggs were crumbling to dust. Silhouetted against the lesser darkness of the sky, he saw Fafhrd stumbling toward him, sobbing out vague words of relief and wonder in a deep, throaty voice. Death was gone from the Bleak Shore, the curse cut off at the root. From out of the night sounded the exultant cry of a sea bird, and Fafhrd and the Mouser thought of the long, trackless road leading back to Lankhmar.

O Ugly Bird!

by

Manly Wade Wellman

*Although we like to compliment ourselves—rather smugly—
on the brightness and rationality of our modern world, the
Old Ways still exist, and often a drive of only a few hours from
the biggest of cities will take you to isolated little hamlets deep
in the mountains and woods ... places where time seems to
have stood still, good folks keep inside of nights, and the
witch and the Hoodoo Man still hold sway. ...*

*The late Manly Wade Wellman was one of the finest modern
practitioners of the "dark fantasy" or "supernatural horror"
tale. He was probably best known for his stories about John
the Minstrel or "Silver John," scary and vividly evocative
tales set against the background of a ghost-and-demon
haunted rural Appalachia that, in Wellman's hands, is as bi-
zarre and beautiful as many another writer's entirely imagi-
nary fantasy world. "O Ugly Bird!" is perhaps the best of the
"Silver John" stories, which have been collected in* Who
Fears the Devil?—*generally perceived as Wellman's best
book; it was certainly his most influential. In recent years,
there were "Silver John" novels as well:* The Old Gods
Waken, After Dark, The Lost and the Lurking, The Hanging
Stones, *and, most recently,* Voice of the Mountain. *Wellman's
non-"Silver John" stories were assembled in the mammoth
collection* Worse Things Waiting, *which won a World Fantasy
Award as the Best Anthology/Collection of 1975. Wellman*

himself has won the prestigious World Fantasy Award for Life Achievement. He died in 1986 at the age of 82.

* * *

I SWEAR I'M LICKED BEFORE I START, TRYING TO TELL YOU ALL what Mr. Onselm looked like. Words give out sometimes. The way you're purely frozen to death for fit words to tell the favor of the girl you love. And Mr. Onselm and I pure poison hated each other from the start. That's a way that love and hate are alike.

He's what folks in the country call a low man, meaning he's short and small. But a low man is low other ways than in inches, sometimes. Mr. Onselm's shoulders didn't wide out as far as his big ears, and they sank and sagged. His thin legs bowed in at the knee and out at the shank, like two sickles put point to point. His neck was as thin as a carrot, and on it his head looked like a swollen-up pale gourd. Thin hair, gray as tree moss. Loose mouth, a little bit open to show long, straight teeth. Not much chin. The right eye squinted, mean and dark, while the hike of his brow stretched the left one wide open. His good clothes fitted his mean body as if they were cut to its measure. Those good clothes of his were almost as much out of match to the rest of him as his long, soft, pink hands, the hands of a man who'd never had to work a tap's worth.

You see now what I mean? I can't say just how he looked, only that he looked hateful.

I first met him when I was coming down from that high mountain's comb, along an animal trail—maybe a deer made it. I was making to go on across the valley and through a pass, on to Hark Mountain where I'd heard tell was the Bottomless Pool. No special reason, just I had the notion to go there. The valley had trees in it, and through and among the trees I saw, here and there down the slope, patchy places and cabins and yards.

I hoped to myself I might could get fed at one of the cabins, for I'd run clear out of eating some spell back. I didn't have any money, nary coin of it; just only my hickory shirt and blue jeans pants and torn old army shoes, and my guitar on its sling cord. But I knew the mountain folks. If they've got anything to eat, a decent-spoken stranger can get the half part of it. Town folks ain't always the same way about that.

Down the slope I picked my way, favoring the guitar just in

case I slipped and fell down, and in an hour I'd made it to the first patch. The cabin was two rooms, dog-trotted and open through the middle. Beyond it was a shed and a pigpen. In the yard was the man of the house, talking to who I found out later was Mr. Onselm.

"You don't have any meat at all?" Mr. Onselm inquired him, and Mr. Onselm's voice was the last you'd expect his sort of man to have, it was full of broad low music, like an organ in a big town church. But I decided not to ask him to sing when I'd taken another closer glimpse of him—sickle-legged and gourd-headed, and pale and puny in his fine-fitting clothes. For, small as he was, he looked mad and dangerous; and the man of the place, though he was a big, strong-seeming old gentleman with a square jaw, looked scared.

"I been right short this year, Mr. Onselm," he said, and it was a half-begging way he said it. "The last bit of meat I done fished out of the brine on Tuesday. And I'd sure enough rather not to kill the pig till December."

Mr. Onselm tramped over to the pen and looked in. The pig was a friendly-acting one; it reared up with its front feet against the boards and grunted up, the way you'd know he hoped for something nice to eat. Mr. Onselm spit into the pen.

"All right," he said, granting a favor. "But I want some meal."

He sickle-legged back toward the cabin. A brown barrel stood out in the dog trot. Mr. Onselm flung off the cover and pinched up some meal between the tips of his pink fingers. "Get me a sack," he told the man.

The man went quick indoors, and quick out he came, with the sack. Mr. Onselm held it open while the man scooped out enough meal to fill it up. Then Mr. Onselm twisted the neck tight shut and the man lashed the neck with twine. Finally Mr. Onselm looked up and saw me standing there with my guitar under my arm.

"Who are you?" he asked, sort of crooning.

"My name's John," I said.

"John what?" Then he never waited for me to tell him John what. "Where did you steal that guitar?"

"This was given to me," I replied him. "I strung it with the silver wires myself."

"Silver," said Mr. Onselm, and he opened his squint eye by a trifle bit.

"Yes, sir." With my left hand I clamped a chord. With my

right thumb I picked the silver strings to a whisper. I began to make up a song:

> "Mister Onselm,
>   They do what you tell 'em—"

"That will do," said Mr. Onselm, not so singingly, and I stopped with the half-made-up song. He relaxed and let his eye go back to a squint again.

"They do what I tell 'em," he said, halfway to himself. "Not bad."

We studied each other, he and I, for a few ticks of time. Then he turned away and went tramping out of the yard and off among the trees. When he was gone from sight, the man of the house asked me, right friendly enough, what he could do for me.

"I'm just a-walking through," I said. I didn't want to ask him right off for some dinner.

"I heard you name yourself John," he said. "Just so happens my name's John, too. John Bristow."

"Nice place you got here, Mr. Bristow," I said, looking around. "You cropping or you renting?"

"I own the house and the land," he told me, and I was surprised; for Mr. Onselm had treated him the way a mean-minded boss treats a cropper.

"Oh," I said, "then that Mr. Onselm was just a visitor."

"Visitor?" Mr. Bristow snorted out the word. "He visits ary living soul here around. Lets them know what thing he wants, and they pass it to him. I kindly thought you knew him, you sang about him so ready."

"Oh, I just got that up." I touched the silver strings again. "Many a new song comes to me, and I just sing it. That's my nature."

"I love the old songs better," said Mr. Bristow, and smiled; so I sang one:

> "I had been in Georgia
>   Not a many more weeks than three
>   When I fell in love with a pretty fair girl
>   And she fell in love with me.
>
> "Her lips were red as red could be,
>   Her eyes were brown as brown,

> Her hair was like a thundercloud
> Before the rain comes down."

Gentlemen, you'd ought to been there, to see Mr. Bristow's face shine. He said: "By God, John, you sure enough can sing it and play it. It's a pure pleasure to hark at you."

"I do my possible best," I said. "But Mr. Onselm doesn't like it." I thought for a moment, then I inquired him: "What's the way he can get ary thing he wants in this valley?"

"Shoo, can't tell you what way. Just done it for years, he has."

"Doesn't anybody refuse him?"

"Well, it's happened. Once, they say, Old Jim Desbro refused him a chicken. And Mr. Onselm pointed his finger at Old Jim's mules, they was a-plowing at the time. Them mules couldn't move nary hoof, not till Mr. Onselm had the chicken from Old Jim. Another time there was, Miss Tilly Parmer hid a cake she'd just baked when she seen Mr. Onselm a-coming. He pointed a finger and he dumbed her. She never spoke one mumbling word from that day on to the day she laid down and died. Could hear and know what was said to her, but when she tried to talk she could only just gibble."

"Then he's a hoodoo man," I said. "And that means, the law can't do a thing to him."

"No sir, not even if the law worried itself up about anything going on this far from the country seat." He looked at the meal sack, still standing in the dog-trot. "Near about time for the Ugly Bird to come fetch Mr. Onselm's meal."

"What's the Ugly Bird?" I asked, but Mr. Bristow didn't have to tell me that.

It must have been a-hanging up there over us, high and quiet, and now it dropped down into the yard, like a fish hawk into a pond.

First out I could see it was dark, heavy-winged, bigger by right much than a buzzard. Then I made out the shiny gray-black of the body, like wet slate, and how the body looked to be naked, how it seemed there were feathers only on the wide wings. Then I saw the long thin snaky neck and the bulgy head and the long crane beak. And I saw the two eyes set in the front of the head—set man-fashion in the front, not bird-fashion one on each side.

The feet grabbed for the sack and taloned onto it, and they showed pink and smooth, with five grabby toes on each one.

Then the wings snapped, like a tablecloth in a high wind, and it went churning up again, and away over the tops of the trees, taking the sack of meal with it.

"That's the Ugly Bird," said Mr. Bristow to me, so low I could just about hear him. "Mr. Onselm's been companioning with it ever since I could recollect."

"Such a sort of bird I never before saw," I said. "Must be a right scared-out one. Do you know what struck me while I was a-watching it?"

"Most likely I do know, John. It's got feet look like Mr. Onselm's hands."

"Could it maybe be," I asked, "that a hoodoo man like Mr. Onselm knows what way to shape himself into a bird thing?"

But Mr. Bristow shook his gray head. "It's known that when he's at one place, the Ugly Bird's been sighted at another." He tried to change the subject. "Silver strings on your guitar; I never heard tell of aught but steel strings."

"In the olden days," I told him, "silver was used a many times for strings. It gives a more singy sound."

In my mind I had it made sure that the subject wasn't going to be changed. I tried a chord on my guitar, and began to sing:

> "You all have heard of the Ugly Bird
> So curious and so queer,
> It flies its flight by day and night
> And fills folks' hearts with fear."

"John—" Mr. Bristow began to butt in. But I sang on:

> "I never came here to hide from fear,
> And I give you my promised word
> That I soon expect to twist the neck
> Of the God damn Ugly Bird."

Mr. Bristow looked sick at me. His hand trembled as it felt in his pocket.

"I wish I could bid you stop and eat with me," he said, "but—here, maybe you better buy you something."

What he gave me was a quarter and a dime. I near about gave them back, but I saw he wanted me to have them. So I thanked him kindly and walked off down the same trail through the trees Mr. Onselm had gone. Mr. Bristow watched me go, looking shrunk up.

Why had my song scared him? I kept singing it:

> "O Ugly Bird! O Ugly Bird!
> You spy and sneak and thieve!
> This place can't be for you and me,
> And one of us got to leave."

Singing, I tried to recollect all I'd heard or read or guessed that might could help toward studying out what the Ugly Bird was.

Didn't witch folks have partner animals? I'd read, and I'd heard tell, about the animals called familiars. Mostly they were cats or black dogs or such matter as that, but sometimes they were birds.

That might could be the secret, or a right much of it. For the Ugly Bird wasn't Mr. Onselm, changed by witching so he could fly. Mr. Bristow had said the two of them were seen different places at one and the same time. So Mr. Onselm could no way turn himself into the Ugly Bird. They were close partners, no more. Brothers. With the Ugly Bird's feet looking like Mr. Onselm's pink hands.

I was ware of something up in the sky, the big black V of something that flew. It quartered over me, half as high as the highest scrap of woolly white cloud. Once or twice it made a turn, seemingly like wanting to stoop for me like a hawk for a rabbit; but it didn't do any such. Looking up at it and letting my feet find the trail on their own way, I rounded a bunch of mountain laurel and there, on a rotten log in the middle of a clearing, sat Mr. Onselm.

His gourd head was sunk down on his thin neck. His elbows set on his crooked knees, and the soft, pink, long hands hid his face, as if he felt miserable. The look of him made me feel disgusted. I came walking close to him.

"You don't feel so brash, do you?" I asked him.

"Go away," he sort of gulped, soft and tired and sick.

"What for?" I wanted to know. "I like it here." Sitting on the log next to him, I pulled my guitar across me. "I feel like singing, Mr. Onselm."

I made it up again, word by word as I sang it:

> "His father got hung for hog stealing,
> His mother got burnt for a witch,

> And his only friend is the Ugly Bird,
> The dirty son—"

Something hit me like a shooting star, a-slamming down from overhead.

It hit my back and shoulder, and it knocked me floundering forward on one hand and one knee. It was only the mercy of God I didn't fall on my guitar and smash it. I crawled forward a few quick scrambles and made to get up again, shaky and dizzy, to see what had happened.

I saw. The Ugly Bird had flown down and dropped the sack of meal on me. Now it skimmed across the clearing, at the height of the low branches. Its eyes glinted at me, and its mouth came open like a pair of scissors. I saw teeth, sharp and mean, like the teeth of agar fish. Then the Ugly Bird swooped for me, and the wind of its wings was colder than a winter tempest storm.

Without thinking or stopping to think, I flung up my both hands to box it off from me, and it gave back, it flew back from me like the biggest, devilishest humming bird you'd ever see in a nightmare. I was too dizzy and scared to wonder why it pulled off like that; I had barely the wit to be glad it did.

"Get out of here," moaned Mr. Onselm, not stirring from where he sat.

I take shame to say, I got. I kept my hands up and backed across the clearing and to the trail on the far side. Then I halfway thought I knew where my luck had come from. My hands had lifted my guitar up as the Ugly Bird flung itself at me, and some way it hadn't liked the guitar.

Reaching the trail again, I looked back. The Ugly Bird was perching on the log where I'd been sitting. It slaunched along close to Mr. Onselm, sort of nuzzling up to him. Horrible to see, I'll be sworn. They were sure enough close together. I turned and stumbled off away, along the trail down the valley and off toward the pass beyond the valley.

I found a stream, with stones making steps across it. I followed it down to where it made a wide pool. There I got on my knee and washed my face—it looked pale as clabber in the water image—and sat down with my back to a tree and hugged my guitar and had a rest.

I was shaking all over. I must have felt near about as bad for a while as Mr. Onselm had looked to feel, sitting on that rotten log to wait for his Ugly Bird and—what else?

Had he been hungry near to death? Sick? Or maybe had his own evil set back on him? I couldn't rightly say which.

But after a while I felt some better. I got up and walked back to the trail and along it again, till I came to what must have been the only store thereabouts.

It faced one way on a rough gravelly road that could carry wagon traffic, car traffic too if you didn't mind your car getting a good shakeup, and the trail joined on there, right across from the doorway. The building wasn't big but it was good, made of sawed planks, and there was paint on it, well painted on. Its bottom rested on big rocks instead of posts, and it had a roofed open front like a porch, with a bench in there where folks could sit.

Opening the door, I went in. You'll find many such stores in back country places through the land, where folks haven't built their towns up too close. Two-three counters. Shelves of cans and packages. Smoked meat hung up in one corner, a glass-fronted icebox for fresh meat in another. Barrels here and there, for beans or meal or potatoes. At the end of one counter, a sign says U.S. POST OFFICE, and there's a set of maybe half a dozen pigeonholes to put letters in, and a couple of cigar boxes for stamps and money order blanks. That's the kind of place it was.

The proprietor wasn't in just then. Only a girl, scared and shaky back of the counter, and Mr. Onselm, there ahead of me, a-telling her what it was he wanted.

He wanted her.

"I don't care a shuck if Sam Heaver did leave you in charge here," he said with the music in his voice. "He won't stop my taking you with me."

Then he heard me come in, and he swung round and fixed his squint eye and his wide-open eye on me, like two mismatched gun muzzles. "You again," he said.

He looked right hale and hearty again. I strayed my hands over the guitar's silver strings, just enough to hear, and he twisted up his face as if it colicked him.

"Winnie," he told the girl, "wait on this stranger and get him out of here."

Her round eyes were scared in her scared face. I thought inside myself that seldom I'd seen as sweet a face as hers, or as scared a one. Her hair was dark and thick. It was like the thundercloud before the rain comes down. It made her paleness look paler. She was small and slim, and she cowered there, for fear of Mr. Onselm and what he'd been saying to her.

"Yes, sir?" she said to me, hushed and shaky.

"A box of crackers, please, ma'am," I decided, pointing to where they were on the shelf behind her. "And a can of those little sardine fish."

She put them on the counter for me. I dug out the quarter Mr. Bristow had given me up the trail, and slapped it down on the counter top between the scared girl and Mr. Onselm.

"Get away!" he squeaked, shrill and sharp and mean as a bat. When I looked at him, he'd jumped back, almost halfway across the floor from the counter. And for just once, his both eyes were big and wide.

"Why, Mr. Onselm, what's the matter?" I wondered him, and I purely was wondering. "This is a good quarter."

I picked it up and held it out for him to take and study.

But he flung himself around, and he ran out of that store like a rabbit. A rabbit with dogs running it down.

The girl he'd called Winnie just leaned against the wall as if she was bone tired. I asked her: "Why did he light out like that?"

I gave her the quarter, and she took it. "That money isn't a scary thing, is it?" I asked.

"It doesn't much scare me," she said, and rang it up on the old cash register. "All that scares me is—Mr. Onselm."

I picked up the box of crackers and sardines. "Is he courting you?"

She shivered, although it was warm in the store. "I'd sooner be in a hole with a snake than be courted by Mr. Onselm."

"Then why not just tell him to leave you be?"

"He wouldn't hark at that," she said. "He always just does what pleasures him. Nobody dares to stop him."

"So I've heard tell," I nodded. "About the mules he stopped where they stood, and the poor old lady he struck dumb." I returned to the other thing we'd been talking. "But what made him squinch away from that money piece? I'd reckon he loved money."

She shook her head, and the thundercloud hair stirred. "Mr. Onselm never needs any money. He takes what he wants, without paying for it."

"Including you?" I asked.

"Not including me yet." She shuddered again. "He reckons to do that later on."

I put down my dime I had left from what Mr. Bristow had gifted me. "Let's have a coke drink together, you and me."

She rang up the dime, too. There was a sort of dried-out chuckle at the door, like a stone flung rattling down a deep dark well. I looked quick, and I saw two long, dark wings flop away outside. The Ugly Bird had come to spy what we were doing.

But the girl Winnie hadn't seen, and she smiled over her coke drink. I asked her permission to open my fish and crackers on the bench outside. She said I could. Out there, I worried open the can with that little key that comes with it, and had my meal. When I'd finished I put the empty can and cracker box in a garbage barrel and tuned my guitar.

Hearing that, Winnie came out. She told me how to make my way to the pass and on beyond to Hark Mountain. Of the Bottomless Pool she'd heard some talk, though she'd never been to it. Then she harked while I picked the music and sang the song about the girl whose hair was like the thundercloud before the rain comes down. Harking, Winnie blushed till she was pale no more.

Then we talked about Mr. Onselm and the Ugly Bird, and how they had been seen in two different places at once. "But," said Winnie, "nobody's ever seen the two of them together."

"I have," I told her. "And not an hour back."

And I related about how Mr. Onselm had sat, all sick and miserable, on that rotten log, and how the Ugly Bird had lighted beside him and crowded up to him.

She was quiet to hear all about it, with her eyes staring off, the way she might be looking for something far away. When I was done, she said: "John, you tell me it crowded right up to him."

"It did that thing," I said again. "You'd think it was studying how to crawl right inside him."

"Inside him!"

"That's the true fact."

She kept staring off, and thinking.

"Makes me recollect something I heard somebody say once about hoodoo folks," she said after a time. "How there's hoodoo folks can sometimes put a sort of stuff out, mostly in a dark room. And the stuff is part of them, but it can take the shape and mind of some other person—and once in a while, the shape and mind of an animal."

"Shoo," I said, "now you mention it, I've heard some talk of the same thing. And somebody reckoned it might could explain those Louisiana stories about the werewolves."

"The shape and mind of an animal," she repeated herself. "Maybe the shape and mind of a bird. And that stuff, they call it echo—no, ecto—ecto—"

"Ectoplasm." I remembered the word. "That's it. I've even seen a book with pictures in it, they say were taken of such stuff. And it seems to be alive. It'll yell if you grab it or hit it or stab at it or like that."

"Couldn't maybe—" Winnie began, but a musical voice interrupted.

"I say he's been around here long enough," Mr. Onselm was telling somebody.

Back he came. Behind him were three men, Mr. Bristow was one, and there was likewise a tall, gawky man with wide shoulders and a black-stubbly chin, and behind him a soft, smooth-grizzled old man with an old fancy vest over his white shirt.

Mr. Onselm was like the leader of a posse. "Sam Heaver," he crooned at the soft grizzled one, "do you favor having tramps come and loaf around your store?"

The soft old storekeeper looked at me, dead and gloomy. "You better get going, son," he said, as if he'd memorized it.

I laid my guitar on the bench beside me, very careful of it. "You men ail my stomach," I said, looking at them, from one to the next to the next. "You come at the whistle of this half-born, half-bred witch-man. You let him sic you on me like dogs, when I'm hurting nobody and nothing."

"Better go," said the old storekeeper again.

I stood up and faced Mr. Onselm, ready to fight him. He just laughed at me, like a sweetly played horn.

"You," he said, "without a dime in your pocket! What are you a-feathering up about? You can't do anything to anybody."

Without a dime . . .

But I had a dime. I'd spent it for the coke drinks for Winnie and me. And the Ugly Bird had spied in to see me spend it, my silver money, the silver money that scared and ailed Mr. Onselm . . .

"Take his guitar, Hobe." Mr. Onselm said an order, and the gawky man moved, clumsy but quick and grabbed my guitar off the bench and backed away to the inner door.

"There," said Mr. Onselm, sort of purring, "that takes care of him."

He fairly jumped, too, and grabbed Winnie by her wrist. He pulled her along out of the porch toward the trail, and I heard her whimper.

"Stop him!" I yelled out, but the three of them stood and looked, scared to move or say a word. Mr. Onselm, still holding Winnie with one hand, faced me. He lifted his other hand and stuck out the pink forefinger at me, like the barrel of a pistol.

Just the look his two eyes, squint and wide, gave me made me weary and dizzy to my bones. He was gong to witch me, as he'd done the mules, as he'd done the woman who'd tried to hide her cake from him. I turned away from his gaze, sick and—sure, I was afraid. And I heard him giggle, thinking he'd won already. I took a step, and I was next to that gawky fellow named Hobe, who held my guitar.

I made a quick long jump and started to wrestle it away from him.

"Hang onto that thing, Hobe!" I heard Mr. Onselm sort of choke out, and, from Mr. Bristow:

"Take care, there's the Ugly Bird!"

Its big dark wings flapped like a storm in the air just behind me. But I'd shoved my elbow into Hobe's belly-pit and I'd torn my guitar from his hands, and I turned on my heel to face what was being brought upon me.

A little way off in the open, Mr. Onselm stood stiff and straight as a stone figure in front of an old court house. He still held Winnie by the wrist. Right betwixt them came a-swooping the Ugly Bird at me, the ugliest ugly of all, its long sharp beak pointing for me like a sticky knife.

I dug my toes and smashed my guitar at it. I swung the way a player swings a ball bat at a pitched ball. Full-slam I struck its bulgy head, right above that sharp beak and across its two eyes, and I heard the loud noise as the polished wood of my music-maker crashed to splinters.

Oh, gentlemen, and down went that Ugly Bird!

Down it went, falling just short of the porch.

Quiet it lay.

Its great big feathered wings stretched out either side, without any flutter to them. Its beak was driven into the ground like a nail. It didn't kick or flop or stir once.

But Mr. Onselm, where he stood holding Winnie, screamed out the way he might scream if something had clawed out his all insides with one single tearing dig and grab.

He didn't move. I don't even know if his mouth came rightly open to make that scream. Winnie gave a pull with all the strength she had, and tottered back, loose from him. Then, as if only his hold on her had kept him standing, Mr. Onselm slapped right over and dropped down on his face, his arms flung out like the Ugly Bird's wings, his face in the dirt like the Ugly Bird's face.

Still holding onto my broken guitar by the neck, like a club, I walked quick over to him and stooped. "Get up," I bade him, and took hold of what hair he had and lifted up his face to look at it.

One look was a plenty. From the war, I know a dead man when I see one. I let go Mr. Onselm's hair, and his face went back into the dirt the way you'd know it belonged there.

The other men moved at last, slow and tottery like old men. And they didn't act like my enemies now, for Mr. Onselm who'd made them act thataway was down and dead.

Then Hobe gave a sort of shaky scared shout, and we looked where he was looking.

The Ugly Bird looked all of a sudden rotten and mushy, and while we saw that, it was soaking into the ground. To me, anyhow, its body had seemed to turn shadowy and misty, and I could see through it, to pebbles on the ground beneath. I moved close, though I didn't relish moving. The Ugly Bird was melting away, like dirty snow on top of a hot stove; only no wetness left behind.

It was gone, while we watched and wondered and felt bad all over, and at the same time glad to see it go. Nothing left but the hole punched in the dirt by its beak. I stepped closer yet, and with my shoe I stamped the hole shut.

Then Mr. Bristow kneeled on his knee and turned Mr. Onselm over. On the dead face ran lines across, thin and purple, as though he'd been struck down by a blow from a toaster or a gridiron.

"Why,' said Mr. Bristow. "Why, John, them's the marks of your guitar strings." He looked up at me. "Your silver guitar strings."

"Silver?" said the storekeeper. "Is them strings silver? Why, friends, silver finishes a hoodoo man."

That was it. All of us remembered that at once.

"Sure enough," put in Hobe. "Ain't it a silver bullet that it takes to kill a witch, or hanging or burning? And a silver knife to kill a witch's cat?"

"And a silver key locks out ghosts, doesn't it?" said Mr. Bristow, getting up to stand among us again.

I looked at my broken guitar and the dangling strings of silver.

"What was the word you said?" Winnie whispered to me.

"Ectoplasm," I replied her. "Like his soul coming out of him—and getting itself struck dead outside his body."

Then there was talk, more important, about what to do now. The men did the deciding. They allowed to report to the county seat that Mr. Onselm's heart had stopped on him, which was what it had done, after all. They went over the tale three-four times, to make sure they'd all tell it the same. They cheered up while they talked it. You couldn't ever call for a bunch of gladder folks to get shed of a neighbor.

Then they tried to say their thanks to me.

"John," said Mr. Bristow, "we'd all of us sure enough be proud and happy if you'd stay here. You took his curse off us, and we can't never thank you enough."

"Don't thank me," I said. "I was fighting for my life."

Hobe said he wanted me to come live on his farm and help him work it on half shares. Sam Heaver offered me all the money he had in his old cash register. I thanked them. To each I said, no, sir, thank you kindly, I'd better not. If they wanted their tale to sound true to the sheriff and the coroner, they'd better help it along by forgetting that I'd ever been around when Mr. Onselm's heart stopped. Anyhow, I meant to go look at that Bottomless Pool. All I was truly sorry about was my guitar had got broken.

But while I was saying all that, Mr. Bristow had gone running off. Now he came back, with a guitar he'd had at his place, and he said he'd be honored if I'd take it instead of mine. It was a good guitar, had a fine tone. So I put my silver strings on it and tightened and tuned them, and tried a chord or two.

Winnie swore by all that was pure and holy she'd pray for me by name each night of her life, and I told her that that would sure enough see me safe from any assault of the devil.

"Assault of the devil, John!" she said, almost shrill in the voice, she meant it so truly. "It's been you who drove the devil from out this valley."

And the others all said they agreed her on that.

"It was foretold about you in the Bible," said Winnie, her voice soft again. "There was a man sent from God, whose name was John—"

But that was far too much for her to say, and she dropped her sweet dark head down, and I saw her mouth tremble and two tears sneak down her cheeks. And I was that abashed, I said goodbye all around in a hurry.

Off I walked toward where the pass would be, strumming my new guitar as I walked. Back into my mind I got an old, old song. I've heard tell that the song's written down in an old-timey book called *Percy's Frolics*, or *Relics*, or some such name:

> "Lady, I never loved witchcraft,
>   Never dealt in privy wile,
>   But evermore held the high way
>   Of love and honor, free from guile. . . ."

And though I couldn't bring myself to look back yonder to the place I was leaving forever, I knew that Winnie was a-watching me, and that she listened, listened, till she had to strain her ears to catch the last, faintest end of my song.

The Power of the Press

by

Richard Kearns

In the wry and poignant story that follows, we meet the debonair Gideon Upton, who picks up the evening paper and then takes a stroll through the park . . . a typical urban park, filled with walking trees and living fountains, where two powerful sorcerers wage war with newspaper, buttons, and beer cans. . . .

A former editor of the SFWA Bulletin, *Richard Kearns has published stories in* Orbit 21, Dragons of Light, *and* Isaac Asimov's Science Fiction Magazine. *He lives in Beverly Hills, California.*

* * *

OLD WILLIE HAD ONE NEWSPAPER LEFT TO SELL BEFORE HE closed up his stand for the night.

It had been a clear, pleasant spring day, and all the smell of lilacs blooming in the park behind his newsstand had lingered in the air long after sundown, becoming somehow sweeter and fresher because of the chill that crept across town once the sun was gone. The stars overhead had come out quickly, putting on a spectacular display—red and blue-white and glittering like they hadn't done this side of winter. Nights like this Willie didn't mind waiting to sell the last paper, though most of the theatre crowd had been and gone by now. It was more of an excuse to stay out late and enjoy the evening.

So he had another swig of whiskey from his flask—just to keep the cold away—and continued to wait, huddled in the warmth of his overcoat and draped in the thin yellow light that fell from an old-fashioned granite-pillared streetlamp next to his stand. He listened to the quiet settle in around town, and heard different church bells toll ten, off in the distance.

"Good evening, Willie."

Willie jumped. "Ho, it's you, sir. Gave me quite a start there for a minute. I didn't hear you come up."

"I'm sorry," said the second man. He was tall—well over six feet—and youngish. He wore what appeared to be a black overcoat which was unbuttoned at the front and revealed a tuxedo within; but where the overcoat ended and night and shadow began was a difficult thing to say. There was a shapeless black hat sitting on his head, and the shadow of its brim cut across the man's face diagonally, making the one green eye that was left in the pale lamplight seem more alive than it should be. "Have you got a paper?" he asked.

"Just one, sir. I shoulda known it would be you that came for it."

The second man smiled—not a normal smile, mind you, but a smile that was bright and wide and had good quantities of white teeth and sunlight in it. He took off his hat and pulled out a crisp new twenty dollar bill, handing it to Willie. His hair was blond and curly and fairly long. "Keep the change," he said, putting his hat on again. "Use it to buy whiskey for cold evenings."

Willie took the bill, chuckled, folded it in half, and stuck it in his overcoat pocket. "That I will, sir, and thank you very much." He gave the man the paper. "*Evening Sun*, too, just the way you like it, sir. You don't have to unfold four miles of paper to find out what's in the news, if you take my meaning. Not like the *Trib*."

The second man took the paper, hefted it to determine its weight, flipped through the pages, and smiled again. "This will do fine, thank you," he said. Then he turned and walked toward the park entrance, his boots making crisp, gritty sounds against the quiet of the night.

"I would be careful about going through the park if I was you, sir," Willie called out as he went about closing up.

The second man stopped. "Really?" he asked.

"Sure enough," said Willie. "It's been vandals and muggings something terrible this past month. Course, there's a park patrol now," and here the hinges of the stand groaned as he swung the big metal doors shut, "for what good they're worth."

"A park patrol?"

"Yes, sir. Just started last week." Willie snapped the padlock shut and wiped his hands on his coat. "But they're new at it," he added, "and I don't know as I would trust 'em to keep me safe."

"I shall remember that. Thank you."

"Good night to you, then, sir."

"Good night, Willie."

They headed in opposite directions.

Now the second man's name was Gideon Upton, and he had been around, to say the least. He had certainly been to the park after dark before, although his purpose here tonight was quite different from his usual one. He was a very capable individual and managed to get himself into and out of more trouble than Old Willie could ever imagine.

Still, the information about the vandals and the park patrol disturbed him. He was thoughtful as he walked along the broad sidewalk that served as one of the park's main thoroughfares. Rows of elm trees on either side of him stretched their newly leaf-clad branches over his head; their boughs met and meshed halfway across to form pointed archways, shutting out the moon and the stars above and creating a cathedral hallway down the length of the walk.

He passed streetlamps, like the one next to Willie's newsstand. These filled the avenue with a weak light, painting the scene in tones of yellow and gray and heightening the shadows. The wrought-iron park benches that lived along the way were dour, and disinclined to comment on the current situation.

So Gideon kept walking.

At first there were other footsteps. Then, a discreet cough. Gideon ignored both of these.

What came next wasn't much of a surprise.

"That will be far enough, Mr. Gideon Upton," a voice bellowed out from behind him. "That is you, isn't it?"

Gideon stopped but didn't turn around. "Supposing it was," he said. "What then?"

"Why, then I would hope you'd come along peaceably,"

the voice answered. "You know better than to fight me in my own territory."

Gideon laughed and turned where he stood. "But you hardly go anywhere else lately," he explained. In his left hand he held the *Evening Sun*, rolled up. But from the fingers of his right hand now dangled a double page of the newspaper, hanging loosely in an upside down V. "Hello, Jack," Gideon said.

Jack was dressed in a military uniform, though there was hardly a square inch of cloth to be seen on him. His chubby form was covered, head to toe, hat to boots, with brass buttons, gold braid, and a host of bright ribbons and medals that made him look like a cross between a lost galaxy and a sterling silver tea service. "It's General Jack tonight," he said, and saluted Gideon with a drawn sword. His paraphernalia clinked and clattered pleasantly in accompaniment to his motions.

Gideon laughed again and returned the salute with his rolled up newspaper. "General Jack of the Park Patrol. I'm impressed. What is it that you want with me?"

"You're under arrest," said General Jack, visibly irritated. "I can't have you wandering all around the park like some vagrant, now, can I?"

"But I'm not wandering aimlessly," Gideon replied, gesturing with his arms, the darkness clinging to his coat and gathering behind him. "I've come to save the Lady Alice."

"Ha, then it's treason you're here for!"

"Well, I'd hardly call it that."

"There's but one penalty for treason," cried General Jack, raising his sword over his head. "Death!" he screamed, and charged toward Gideon.

Gideon had been waiting for that. He tossed the double page of newspaper into the air, and it beat its wings and screeched, raucously, its print-filled pinions cutting through the night in furious flight, its black eyes glistening, its beak sharp, its taloned feet strong and eager for pieces of the General's face.

They didn't quite collide.

The General stopped his headlong rush just in time, narrowly avoiding the eagle's inky claws on its first attack. His sword was in position and he was ready as the bird made its second dive.

General Jack swung his sword and cursed, the eagle swooped and screamed and ripped, and the air was quickly filled with metal buttons and shreds of newsprint. While the buttons fell to the ground, the pieces of newsprint formed themselves into tiny eagles and joined the fight, which put the General at quite a disadvantage.

But he batted the eagle gnats aside with his free arm, and kept slicing at the big eagle until he succeeded in cutting it nearly in half, at which point it fluttered helplessly to the ground, squawking. Its tiny companions rushed to its aid.

Before they could join together and make themselves whole again, General Jack, dark blood oozing from scratches on his cheeks and forehead, quietly spoke a Word. The paper burst into bright orange flames, spewing bits of ash that drifted aimlessly up and down the sidewalk. He didn't take his eyes off the pile until the fire went out, and twin streams of blue smoke curled up into the chilly night air.

"Well," he said, to no one in particular, since Gideon was gone, "I can see I'm going to need some help with this one." He slid his sword back into its scabbard, hitched up his pants, dabbed at his face with a handkerchief, and began to pick up the buttons that had been torn from his uniform during the fight.

Gideon came trotting up to Bastille Fountain with two freshly-made newspaper panthers flanking him. They growled when he stopped and lashed their tails back and forth, standing guard. Overhead the flapping of newspaper wings could be heard. Gideon felt safe for the moment. He turned his attention to the fountain.

Bastille Fountain wasn't fancy, but it was big—the main pool was a good twenty feet across. In the center, cement figures representing the four seasons, their features blurred and rust-stained held a second basin suspended in midair. A lazy four-foot waterjet burbled and splashed inside of that, spilling wet curtains over the basin edge and sending slick streams down the fingers that gripped its ornamental rim, drenching the arms, faces, and dresses of the seasons below.

Gideon leaned over the waters. "Alice!"

There was no answer, though strange ripples raced across the surface.

He called a second time, slightly louder: "Alice!"

Nothing.

Gideon stood up straight. "Alice!" he yelled. "Damn you, woman, wake up!" He dug into his coat pocket, pulled out a thick handful of coins, tossed them all at the raised pool. Some of them rang out briefly as they hit cement; others—the majority, actually—plopped as they fell into the water in both basins, a sound hardly distinguishable from the gurgle of the fountain.

But the pillar of water moved now, turning, weaving, not quite stumbling, raising her hands gracefully to cover her face, while her hair, with a life of its own, cascaded out and down her back in black, starlit ribbons. Her robe was a thing of sparkling white foam that tumbled into the waters of the inner pool; when she tried to gather up its skirts, she found them caught in the unyielding cement fingers of the seasons below.

"Gideon!" Her voice was clear and sweet, and her bright blue eyes stared at him in surprise and distress.

"Alice."

"Gideon, help! I can't get out!"

"I know, my dear. I'm here to save you." He took a sheet of newspaper, folded it lengthwise, and changed it into a set of parapeted stairs that telescoped across the main pool and came to rest on the edge of Lady Alice's basin.

General Jack finished pinning a scarlet cross for bravery above and beyond the call of duty during the Crimean War on the last of the hundred and forty-two elm trees that lined the main walk. It had been a tedious task, making sure the correct button or medal was properly affixed to each trunk. The knowledge that Gideon was loose in the park and looking for the Lady Alice hadn't made things go any faster, either.

He took his hat off, tucked it under his arm, and walked slowly to the center of the walk. In spite of the cool night air, a thin film of sweat covered his bald, egg-shaped head, and yellow highlights from the streetlamps played across his features. He mopped at his face and the back of his neck with his handkerchief, then replaced his hat and drew his sword.

"Troops!" he screamed. "Attention!"

There were shadowy stirrings among the trees, and they untangled their branches over the walk, one from the other, destroying the leafy roof and letting the sky peep in overhead.

"Fall in!"

Now there was a rumbling and churning among the tree

roots as knobby feet dug their way out of the ground, scattering black clods of dirt in every direction. The trees clambered onto the sidewalk slowly, but without any hint of clumsiness; the main impressions they gave off were ones of strength and immense weight. Their buttons and medals glittered balefully in the night.

General Jack, his arms crossed over his chest, the unsheathed sword held upright in his right hand, waited patiently until they formed four straight rows on the sidewalk. "At ease, trees," he said. "Now listen up. There's an enemy in the park. Your mission tonight is to find him and keep him from doing any mischief. Take whatever measures you think necessary, but I want him alive—" and here the General paused, and ran his thumb across his sword blade to check its sharpness, "—so I can deal with him myself." He paused again, and then yelled out: "Do you understand that, trees?"

"Yes, sir!" the trees yelled back.

"I can't hear you!" screamed the General.

"Yes, sir!" the trees screamed back.

"I still can't hear you!" he shouted.

"YES SIR!"

"All right! Now, who is your leader?"

"GENERAL JACK!"

"And who do you fight for?"

"GENERAL JACK!"

"And who do you die for?"

"GENERAL JACK!"

"And who do we fight?"

"THE ENEMY, SIR!"

"And what is his name?"

"GIDEON, SIR!"

"Let's hear it again!"

"GIDEON, SIR!"

"One more time!"

"GIDEON, SIR!"

"And what do we do to him—kill him?"

"NO!"

"Maim him?"

"YES!"

"Torture him, bruise him, and scrape him?"

"YES!"

"Tie him up, stop him, detain him?"

"YES!"

"Forward!"
"MARCH!"
"Forward!"
"MARCH!"
"Forward!"
"MARCH!"
They shrumphed off into the distance.

"Oh Gideon!" said the Lady Alice, "Hurry, please! I can't bear it any longer!" She frantically tugged at the section of her glowing dress still pinned by a last cement hand; this only made Gideon stop working with his newspaper crowbar because the material got in the way.

"I'm not going to save you if you keep acting like this," he told her in an even tone, trying not to succumb to the tension he felt. General Jack should have shown up a good fifteen minutes ago, or at least run into one of the traps Gideon had set along the way. But he had done neither, and Gideon could feel tremors of his magic at work in the park.

Dismayed, Alice let fall the skirts she had gathered up in her arms, and they splashed in the fountain waters, nearly dousing Gideon. "I'm sorry," she said.

"It's all right." He went back to work on the fingers, muttering spells—or at least something that sounded like spells —and prying with the crowbar.

Alice knelt and hugged her knees, wanting to watch his work more closely. But she ended up studying Gideon's face: his delicate, fine-boned features; his lips, normally thin and now compressed into a determined line; the three blonde curls that had crept out from under his hat to become stuck in the sweat on his forehead; the way his green eyes glittered with spell-kindled fires.

She reached out and took his hat off. "I really am sorry," she said.

"I said it was all right," he snarled back, snatching his hat from her and putting it on again. He started pushing harder on the crowbar, trying to ignore her.

"Now you're angry with me," she said, taking his hat away again.

"No!" he roared, loosening two of the cement fingers but dropping the crowbar in the water at the same time, where it reverted to a sheet of wet newspaper. He grabbed at the hat, but Alice hid it behind her back.

"Tell me you're not angry with me," she said.

Gideon glared at her. "I'm not angry with you," he said between clenched teeth. "Now give me back my hat."

She kissed him instead.

Her kiss was cool and sweet and fresh, and Gideon, after his initial surprise, drank deeply of it. In it, he could taste the bubbling cold of far-off mountain streams, hints of peppermint and clove and sassafras, the elusive flavor of honeysuckle rose, and the darker, heavier essences of wild blackberry and grape.

He had been furious with Alice at first, but then he quickly abandoned himself in her kiss. And once he did that, he felt the fear and worry drain out of him, leaving behind only confidence, composure, and a renewed strength.

It took him a second to realize the kiss had ended. When he did, he threw back his head and laughed loud and long, until the tears dripped out of his eyes.

The Lady Alice smiled when she saw Gideon had recovered his senses, and put his hat on her own head. "That's much more like it," she told him.

Gideon wiped the tears away with his coat sleeve. "Ah! You should have done that sooner, Alice!"

She grinned at him. His hat was far too large for her, and made her look like a thin pixie. "Everything has its moment, I suppose." Her blue eyes sparkled with amusement.

"I've missed you, Alice."

"And I you. Make me a promise."

"What?"

"When we get out of here—"

"You mean *if* we get out of here." He gingerly fished the piece of newspaper out of the water, turned it back into a soggy crowbar, and began wringing water from it.

"*When* we get out of here," she said firmly. She pushed the hat back on her forehead and rested her hands on her knees, her elbows jutting out at odd angles. "*When* we get out of here, let's go away together."

Gideon frowned. "Where?"

"Does it matter?"

"Well, it's just that we've *been* everywhere there is to go away to."

"Really?"

"Gideon applied the crowbar to the remaining cement

fingers, but it bent because it was still too wet. "Try thinking of a place we haven't been," he said, forcing the crowbar back into its proper shape.

"Paris."

"We were there last fall."

"But I like Paris."

"Everybody goes to Paris." He changed the crowbar into a bicycle pump. "Pick someplace else."

"How about Egypt?"

"It's flooding along the Nile now," he said, working the pump vigorously and sending a weak stream of water out the end of the hose and into the pool below. "The peasants are all busy being farmers, and we'd only get in the way."

"New Orleans?"

"Too late—we'll have missed the Mardi Gras this year, and that's the only time it's worth going."

"Tibet, then."

"Nope." He shook the pump, heard water sloshing inside it still, and examined the open end of the air tube. "We went there at the turn of the century. You hated it—it was either too hot or too cold. The only reason you don't remember is you caught Tibetan fever, and I had to haul you all the way to Ceylon before you recovered."

"Oh." She stood up.

"But don't let that stop you. Try some other places." Gideon changed the bicycle pump into a walking stick, unscrewed the cap, and poured more water out.

"Why don't you just make a new one?" she asked him, grumpily. "You've got enough fresh paper."

"Waste not, want not," he answered. "And I'm not sure I have enough to waste—we still have to make an exit once I get you loose." He looked up at her and smiled. "You're not giving up so quickly, are you?"

"No."

"Then let me help," he told her, screwing the top back on the cane and sticking it under his arm so he could count on his fingers. "Should I start with continents or bodies of water?"

"Oh, stop being so boring."

"All right. Continents then. That would be Africa, Asia, Australia—"

"I have it!"

"Australia?"

"No, no, not there." She knelt and took his hands in hers.

"I've heard it said that the night is an uncharted ocean," she began.

Gideon looked at the sky doubtfully. "You're mad," he mumbled, shaking his head. "Stark, raving mad."

"But Gideon, just think of it—if the night is an ocean, then the moon must surely be a beautiful island," she said, standing up and beginning a dance of delight, whirling in slow circles, her arms outstretched, "and the stars like fishes—"

"Fishes?"

"Oh, yes, Gideon, and we'll bring the purple ones back with us to Avalon—" and here she became so tangled in her dress where the cement fingers held it that she stopped dancing and started tugging again. But even as she did so, a horrified look came over her face.

"All right, all right, I'll get it loose—"

"Gideon!"

"What?"

"Gideon, the trees are moving!"

Gideon looked over his shoulder, saw the burnt pavement and drifting ash that marked what was left of his sentinels, and then swore.

The southern half of the square around Bastille Fountain was quickly filling with cold, silent, walking elm trees. At the back of their ranks Gideon spotted a small, shining figure that could only have been General Jack; he threw his walking stick at the figure, and the stick swiftly whizzed through the air as if it had been shot from a bow, hitting the General with a satisfying thud and an accompanying oof.

Gideon leapt from the inner pool and hit the ground rolling so he could dodge the clutching branches of the nearest trees. He sprinted toward the open end of the square and, holding what remained of the *Evening Sun* perpendicular to the ground, wrapped newspaper castle walls around himself, walls that seemed to leap into the sky, reaching for the stars, towering over the turmoil.

It is unfortunate that Gideon wasn't inside when the transformation was complete.

It wasn't his fault, of course. It was the fault of one particularly surly elm tree, pinned with the scarlet cross for bravery above and beyond the call of duty during the Crimean War, a potent medal to be sure. This crafty, battlewise tree had entered the open square on the northern side, crept up behind Gideon unnoticed as he jumped from the fountain, and plucked him off his castle ramparts as they shot heavenward.

The other trees were quick to grasp the situation, and, since each tree wanted to be the one to turn the enemy over to General Jack, they all converged on Gideon and began a tug-of-war with him. General Jack, downed as he was by the flying cane, couldn't get to the scene in time to take control of the situation, so what followed wasn't strictly his fault.

Different contingents of trees had a hold of different parts of Gideon—his arms, his legs, his head—and when the General came hobbling up, bellowing commands indiscriminately, they all gave one last tug, one final effort to lay victory at the feet of their beloved leader.

Gideon came apart in their hands.

He came apart in dusty reams, in chunks of faded yellow *Tribunes*, in heaps of brittle *Post-Dispatches*, in wads of *Manchester Guardians*, *Philadelphia Bulletins*, *Miami Heralds* and *New York Times*, most of them early morning editions. When this happened, Gideon's castle wavered and fell, snowing pages of the *Evening Sun* everywhere.

Silence set in, broken only by the sound of water splashing in Lady Alice's fountain.

The trees lined up in awkward, embarrassed rows, trying not to notice the sea of paper in which they were wading but looking very guilty all the same. General Jack just stood there, leaning on Gideon's cane. He stared at the trees, stared at the litter of papers, glanced briefly but contemptuously at the Lady Alice, and then stared at the paper some more. He poked at the mess with the cane and cleared his throat.

"Listen up, trees," he said. "There's nothing that can be done about this now." He stuck his chin out proudly and surveyed his troops. "But there is one big job we've got to finish before we can quit for the night."

The trees murmured excitedly among themselves. General Jack pulled a brass button off his uniform. "I want it all cleaned up," he told them, tossing the button to one side, where it exploded in a puff of smoke and left a green wire-meshed trash can. "Every scrap, every shred," and another button produced another can, "every page, every tiny piece, even if it's confetti-sized—I want it all." Two cans at once this time. "We can't afford to miss anything that would let our enemy escape." He tossed off a final three buttons with a flourish, and they thundered in a three-can grand finale. "Got it?"

The trees either mumbled or nodded their assent.

"Then get to it!" he screamed, and the trees immediately bent over to start picking up the paper, the majority of them bumping into one another in the process.

General Jack avoided the ensuing confusion by limping over to the fountain with Gideon's cane. "Good evening," he said, tipping his hat to the Lady Alice. "I must say, you are looking quite beautiful tonight."

Alice ignored him, her arms folded across her chest.

"Look, Alice, I can understand your being upset about all this, but it was really for the best."

Still no answer.

"He was beneath you, Alice."

Alice stared down at the General, her eyes a chill, icy blue. "Really?" she said.

The General smiled. "Why, yes, of course. He never would have been good enough for you. He just couldn't cut it, I guess."

"And I suppose you are good enough for me."

"The best, Alice." He thumped his chest. "Solid brass."

"Well let me tell you something, Jack. I will kill you for what you've done to Gideon tonight."

"Oh?"

"Yes, oh. I will call my beasts from the pits of the ocean, have them hunt you down, and then cheerfully throttle you with my own hands."

The General chuckled, thinly, nasally, and conceitedly. "I think not, my dear," he said, twirling Gideon's cane in his fingers. "You will come around to my way of seeing things eventually. In fact," he added, debonairely thumping the cane on the pavement, "I was hoping this little episode tonight would make you realize how untenable your situation is." He leaned on the cane with both hands, his right leg jauntily crossed over his left, his foot balanced toe-first on the ground. "You are beginning to realize that, aren't you?"

A large wave rose suddenly from the bottom basin and doused the General. "I hope you rust," she told him.

"You know, Alice," the General said, dripping, "I am rapidly losing my patience with you."

"Not rapidly enough," Alice answered.

"Perhaps you are right." General Jack studied Gideon's cane thoughtfully for a moment. Suddenly, he tossed it into the air, making it spin with a flick of his wrist. Alice lunged for it desperately as it passed her, missing and falling to her knees.

The General caught the cane just before it fell into the bottom pool. "Missed!" he said, staring straight at her; he smiled, and without turning his gaze from her face, let the cane drop into the water, where it was transformed into a sheet of newspaper again.

The Lady Alice struggled to her feet.

"There is nothing left to change him back with now," the General told her. "You could have bargained for his life, you know. Nothing to say to that?" He smiled again. "Good. Very good. Perhaps you *are* beginning to realize the futility of your position."

He turned his back on her and rejoined his trees, although he still favored one leg slightly as he went. He spoke briefly to the elm with the scarlet cross, tossed a button toward the fountain, where it exploded into a waste can, and watched as the tree fished the newspaper out of the fountain waters.

The tree looked as if he might have said something to Alice, but evidently thought better of it when he saw the stern look on her face. He shrugged and continued to help with the cleanup.

The moon set, leaving the stars to fend for themselves.

After carefully collecting the last scraps of Gideon they could find, the elm troops had lined up all eight trash cans in a row and then marched off victoriously with General Jack in the lead.

The Lady Alice, of course, was neither fooled nor amused by this tactic. She had waited a good three hours, patiently watching the shadows in the foliage behind the trash cans, before the shadow that didn't belong stepped out into the square, its scarlet cross for bravery above and beyond the call of duty during the Crimean War glowing softly in the dark.

"Seen enough?" Alice asked.

The tree regarded her for a moment, apparently considering her question. Then he lumbered over to the trash cans, and mashed down the paper in each one securely. When he finished that, he looked back at Alice, grinned at her arrogantly, stretched his scrawny-leafed spring green limbs, and shuffled down the west walk to join his squadron.

As soon as he was out of sight, Alice knelt and whispered five words: "Now—bring him to me!"

The water at her feet and in the basin below boiled strangely, sending clouds of steam drifting in the night air. Crabs came scuttling out—hundreds of copper-colored fiddler crabs, none of them more than three inches across. They either flung themselves over the edge of the top pool, or crept quietly out of the bottom pool, moving across the fountain square with remarkable speed for their size.

Alice had made them out of the coins Gideon had tossed in her fountain, the first workable materials she'd had since the General had trapped her in the fountain. She watched, her heart pounding, as the first wave of crabs reached the trash cans and began climbing; clutched to her breast was Gideon's hat, warm and dry and hidden by the folds of her gown. It was his last chance, the hat. The crabs were to bring enough newspaper over to the fountian for her to restore him with it.

The plan would have worked, too, except that the trash cans were enchanted.

Or perhaps it would be more accurate to say the trash cans were singularly devoid of enchantment. As soon as the first crabs passed over the rim of a can, they would fall inside, pennies once again.

The crabs following what were now pennies were nobody's fools. As soon as they saw what had happened to their fellow crustaceans, they stopped in their tracks and began to warn the others in high-pitched rasping voices. In no time at all, confusion, accompanied by miniature squeals of consternation, spread through the ranks.

Crabs began leaping and falling off the trash cans into the masses below. Waves of crabs, still coming up from the rear, folded over waves of crabs that were milling and arguing with one another, until there were crabs five layers thick in some places. Little crab leaders stood on the tops of little shifting crab hills and screamed for attention over the rising tide of shrill babble.

The Lady Alice swore. "This isn't the time for a debate," she said. "Bring him to me!"

The crabs' response was immediate. They attacked two of the trash cans, trying to knock them over. Their actions were not very well coordinated, however: as often as one group of crabs would get a can rocking, another group, working at cross purposes to the first, would negate the momentum the first group had set up.

Alice endured this as long as she could. She watched the

empty walks, half expecting to see dark shapes moving through the shadows toward her. "Hurry up!" she whispered, stamping her foot in frustration. "Get him over here now!"

A contingent of crabs—maybe a third of the entire group —broke away from the flurry of activity around the first two cans, and headed for a third can. The wishes of the Lady Alice were clear to them. If they couldn't get Gideon's papers to her, they would have to get a canful of Gideon to her.

The screech of metal on cement ripped through the quiet night, two, three, four times, every time the crabs moved the can forward. Alice wailed unhappily. Before, there had been a chance to quietly restore Gideon and escape without the General or any of his trees the wiser. Now, though—

Now the General and whatever else was awake in the park would be sure to come and investigate the strange noise. It was almost as if they had set off an alarm.

There was nothing else they could do now. Alice drew out Gideon's hat, half afraid it would revert to newspaper as soon as the night air hit it. The hat held, and she got ready to throw it.

The seconds drained away slowly, punctuated by the shrieking can. The crabs managed to get it more than halfway across the fountain square, still a good twenty feet away from Alice.

The first two cans were rocking violently.

That was when Alice heard footsteps to her left: giant, pavement-shuddering footsteps; smaller, quicker, pattering footsteps; and an accompanying military bellow that was very familiar to her.

She didn't even look to confirm what she knew; she threw the hat.

And everything began to happen very quickly.

Even as she threw Gideon's hat, the first set of cans tipped over like dominoes, one making the other fall, both of them sending papers scattering across a wider area than seemed possible, had they been normal papers.

General Jack and the elm with the crimson cross entered Bastille Square from the east. They both saw Gideon's hat wafting through the air on a slow, perfect arc; the General slowed down, pointed, and screamed a command, while the tree moved quickly to intercept the hat.

He missed. His twigs whipped through empty air as the hat landed in the trash can, sitting there for a second before the papers underneath it started quivering.

The elm got two steps closer.

A reconstituted Gideon shot out of the garbage can, past the arms of the surprised elm, and landed, rolling, in the litter of papers that the crabs had managed to spill out of the first two trash cans.

He sat there, dazed, for perhaps another second, then scrambled to his feet, raised his hands, and sang out his own Words of power in a melodious voice.

A sail arched up before him, fifty feet tall, triangular, paisley patterned, purple, gold and translucent, and billowing and snapping as it filled with a sudden wind. The varnished brown bows of a wooden ship surrounded Gideon, the crabs, and the now empty waste cans, carrying all of them forward and up, up, slowly and inexorably up.

They knocked the elm tree over and sent him rolling, and still they climbed up, their rounded keel almost ten feet in the air, their timbers creaking as they gained speed and altitude.

General Jack chanted counter spells, making orange sparks swirl all around the ship. Gideon looked for a weapon; his magic was invested in the rising ship, and there was nothing left for fighting. Desperate, he took two steps aft, picked up an empty trash can, and heaved it over the side.

The General was caught completely by surprise. The trash can came falling over him, top down, and pinned him flat. There was an electric flash, and his torso reverted to aluminum beer cans; his arms and legs were splayed outside the can after it came to rest upside down, and his hatless head went slowly rolling away from the site of his body.

And that was that.

Gideon brought the golden bulk of the *Night Bird* to rest three feet away from the edge of the inner pool. The ship's single giant sail ripped serenely in the quieted wind; it cast faint shadows in starlight on the ground below.

He dropped an anchor into the bottom pool, placed a boarding plank between the boat and the edge of the fountain, picked out a particularly sturdy-looking stave, and walked over to Alice.

"Shall we?" he asked, holding his arm out for her after he had broken the final cement fingers of winter.

Alice smiled at him, kissed him on the cheek, took his arm, and said, "I believe we shall." They boarded the ship.

"Well," she said, seeing all the stacks of newspaper neatly bundled and stored on the deck, "I see you're provisioned for a long escape."

"Actually, I had hoped we could go away together."

"Really?"

"Of course. I wouldn't fib about something like that."

Alice giggled. "Where then?" she asked, stroking the *Night Bird*'s balustrade.

"I'm not sure," said Gideon. "But there are these rumors."

"Rumors?"

"Yes. I've heard it said that the night is an uncharted ocean."

"And that the moon must be like a beautiful island?"

"Yes."

"And the stars like fishes?"

"Yes, yes."

The Lady Alice played with Gideon's lapels. "You can't believe everything you hear, you know."

"No. But it seems to me we ought to find out the truth of the matter for ourselves."

She hugged him. "I love you, Gideon."

"I love you too, Alice. Otherwise—"

"Help!" cried a voice from below. "Help! Help!"

Gideon and Alice furrowed their eyebrows at each other, slightly puzzled, then ran to the starboard bow to investigate.

It was General Jack's head that had cried out for help. It lay face up in the middle of a constellation of bright copper pennies, ten feet away from the reach of the fallen elm.

"You can't leave me here like this," pleaded the head.

Gideon laughed. "I do believe you're right," he said, and then jumped over the side. Once on the ground, he righted the trash can, threw in General Jack's arms and legs, and then walked over to the head.

"What are you going to do?" asked the head.

"What do you think I ought to do?" asked Gideon in return. "You were perfectly willing to finish me off."

The head didn't answer. Gideon frowned at it, and then looked up at the *Night Bird*. "Alice?"

There was silence for a space. "Let him go, Gideon," she said, softly. "I wish I could tell you to get rid of him. But let him go."

Gideon glared at Jack's head in his hand. "And I, for my part," he said, "wish she wasn't right." Tossing the head into the waiting arms of the elm tree, he then walked over to the trash can, dumped out the clattering beer cans and swept them into a neat pile with his feet. The trash can went into the fountain next, where it sizzled, popped, and turned into a brass button. "Goodbye, Jack," said Gideon, waving at the tree. "See you around sometime."

Jack didn't answer.

Alice lowered a rope for Gideon to climb back to the ship. They weighed anchor and disappeared quickly into the darkness.

"Well," said the head, after the *Night Bird* was gone, "let's not just sit here. Hurry up and toss me on my pile of cans. There's work that needs doing before the morning gets here."

The elm took aim as best it could, and Jack made it after only one bounce. He buried himself in cans quickly, huffing and puffing and rattling with exertion once he was out of sight. He finally came crawling out from under the far side of the pile, whole once more but changed. He was shorter, and his uniform, while still a tribute to the timelessness of brass and chrome and glitter, was of a decidedly different cut.

Jack seated himself on the ground, legs askew, his back against the cement rim of Bastille Fountain, took a deep breath and blew it out in relief. He picked up a stray beer can, negligently changed it into a handkerchief, and mopped his face, forehead and neck. Stuffing the handkerchief up his sleeve, he leaned back and looked around him.

The General's cap lay a couple of feet to his right. He stared at it a bit, grunted, leaned on his elbow, and stretched over to it, barely able to reach it and draw it to him. He held the cap up in front of his face and studied it.

"The Army was a good life," he said, glancing at the elm tree and then back at the cap. "Pity it wasn't good enough." He tossed the cap, which went rolling across Bastille Square, coming to a stop when it bumped up against an overturned trash can.

Jack leaned to his left and dug into what remained of his pile of cans. "The Navy, though," he said, pulling a three-cornered Admiral's hat out of the pile, "offers many, many more possibilities." He frowned at the hat a moment. "We'll have to raid a junkyard or two," he said, grabbing a can and changing it into a brilliant purple feather, "until we have enough supplies on hand." He stuck the plume on the Admiral's hat, then fitted the hat on his head. "You can never really have enough raw materials."

He struggled to his feet, straightened his jacket, stood up as tall as he could, and then blew the feather out of his face. "But first," he said, turning a critical eye to the elm tree with the crimson cross for bravery above and beyond the call of duty during the Crimean War, "there remains the matter of a proper ship."

Old Willie loved to walk through the park at dawn, before he opened his newsstand for the day.

There was something eerie and beautiful and utterly private about the park when the sun first came up, particularly during the spring. Maybe it was the way the long, golden sunbeams gilded the dew that had collected in all sorts of unlikely places overnight. Or perhaps it was the songs the newly-arrived birds sang, or the fresh smells and colors from different just-opened blossoms and leaves that had been nonexistent the day before. Whatever the circumstances, Willie felt like the park was full of quiet miracles made just for him when he walked through every morning.

Today, though, he saw nothing but ruin when he came through Bastille Square—broken branches, scattered change, and beer cans everywhere. It made the play of water in Bastille Fountain seem harsh and out of place, like it was the wonder that didn't belong, rather than the mess. Well, he thought, there was no help for it. The park patrol would find the vandals eventually, and there was nothing to do but wait until that happened.

Just as he was about to leave the fountain square, he spotted an odd glimmering near a cluster of trash cans on the other side. Investigating, he found an old military hat buried in a pile of yesterday's papers; the hat was covered with pins and medals and badges, most of which Willie had never seen the likes of before. "Well, now," he said, polishing the hat with his coat sleeve and then trying it on, "ain't that something." It wasn't a perfect fit, but it was close enough. He decided to keep the hat.

He whistled a cheerful tune all the rest of the way to his newsstand.

The Finger

by

Naomi Mitchison

In this chilling little story of authentic tribal magic and medicine murder, the Good Man is actually the bad man, one who is busily insinuating his corruption into the modern world of post-colonial Africa, the practitioner of kgogela . . . *sorcery.*

Here a boy must confront implacable evil with nothing more than the vulnerability—and strength—of innocence. . . .

British novelist Naomi Mitchison, sister of physicist J. B. Haldane, was once a tribal advisor to the Bakgatla tribe of southeast Botswana. She is the author of more than ten books, including Memories of a Spacewoman, The Corn King of the Spring Queen, *and* To the Chapel Perilous, *an idiosyncratic retelling of the Arthurian legend, which some critics consider to be an underground classic. At the age of eighty-six, she published a new novel,* Not by Bread Alone.

* * *

KOBEDI HAD A MOTHER BUT NO FATHER. WHEN HE WAS OLD enough to understand such things someone said that his father was the Good Man. By that they meant the Bad Man, because, so often, words, once they are fully known, have meanings other or opposite to their first appearance. Kobedi, however, hoped that his father was the fat man at the store. Sometimes his mother went there and brought back many things, not only the needful meal and oil, but tea and sugar

48

and beautiful tins with pictures, and almost always sweets for himself. Once, when he was a quite little boy, he had asked his mother where she kept the money for this and she answered "Between my legs." So, when she had drunk too much beer and was asleep on her back and snoring, he lifted her dress to see if he could find this money and take a little. But there was nothing there except a smell which he did not like. He had two small sisters, both fat and flat-nosed like the man at the store. But his own nose was thin, and the Good Man also had a thin nose as though he could cut with it.

Kobedi went to school and he thought he now understood what his mother had meant though he did not wish to think of it; at least she paid the school fees, though she grumbled about them. He was in Standard Three and there were pictures on the wall which he liked; now he wrote sentences in his jotter and they were ticked in red because they were correct. That was good. But in a while he became aware that things were happening around him which were not good. First it was the way his mother looked at him, and sometimes felt his arms and legs, and some of her friends who came and whispered. Then came the time he woke in the blackest of the night, for there was a smell which made him feel sick and the Good Man was there, sitting on the stuffed and partly torn sofa under the framed picture of white Baby Jesus. He was wearing skins of animals over his trousers, and his toes, which had large nails, clutched and burrowed in the rag rug Kobedi's mother made. The Good Man saw that Kobedi was awake because his eyes were open and staring; he pointed one finger at him. That was the more frightening because his other hand was under the skirt of a young girl who was sitting next to him, snuggling. The pointing finger twitched and beckoned and slowly Kobedi unrolled himself from his blanket and came over naked and shaking.

The Good Man now withdrew his other hand and his dampish fingers crawled over Kobedi. He took out two sinews from a bundle, rubbing them in the sweat of his own skin until they became thin and hard and twisted and dipped them into a reddish medicine powder he had and spat on them and he pointed the finger again and Kobedi slunk back and pulled the blanket over his head.

The next day the tied-on sinews began to make his skin itch. He tried to pull them off but his mother slapped him, saying they were strong medicine and he must keep them on.

He could not do any arithmetic that day. The numbers had lost their meaning and his teacher beat him.

The next time he became aware of that smell in the night he carefully did not move nor open his eyes, but pulled the blanket slowly from his ears so that he could hear the whispering. Again it was the Good Man and his mother and perhaps another woman or even two women. They were speaking of a place and a time, and at that place and time, a happening. The words were so dressed as to mean something else, as when speaking of a knife they called it a little twig, when they spoke of the heart it was the cooking pot, when they spoke of the liver it was the red blanket, and when they spoke of the fat it was the beer froth. And it became clear to Kobedi that when they spoke of the meal sack it was of himself they were speaking. Death, death, the whispers said, and the itching under the sinews grew worse.

The next morning all was as always. The little sisters toddled and played and their mother pounded meal for the porridge and called morning greetings to her neighbors across the walls of the lapa. Then she said to him: "After the school is finished you are to go to the store and get me one packet tea. Perhaps he will give you sweets. Here is money for tea."

It was not much money, but it was a little and he knew he had to go and fast. He passed by the school and did not heed the school bell calling to him and he walked to the next village and on to the big road. He waited among people for a truck and fear began to catch up on him; by now he was hungry and he bought fatty cakes for five cents. Then he climbed in at the back of the truck with the rest of the people. Off went the truck, north, south, he did not know. Only there was a piece of metal in the bottom of the truck, some kind of rasp, and he worked with this until he had got the sinew off his ankle and he dropped it over the side so that it would be run over by many other trucks. It was harder to get at the arm one and he only managed to scrape his own skin before the truck stopped in a big town.

Now it must be said that Kobedi was lucky; after a short time of hunger and fear he got a job sweeping out a small shop and going with heavy parcels. He was also allowed to sleep on a pile of sacks under the counter, though he must be careful to let nobody know, especially not the police. But under the sacks was a loose board and below it he had a tin, and into this he put money out of his wages, a few cents at a time. He heard about a school that was held in the evenings after work; he did not speak to anyone about it, and indeed he had no friends in the big town because it seemed to him that friends meant losing one's little money at playing dice games or taking one's turn to buy a coke; and still his arm itched.

When he had enough money he went one evening to the school and said he had been in Standard Three and he wanted to go on with education and had money to buy it. The white man who was the head teacher asked him where he came from. He said from Talane, which was by no means the name of his village, and also that his father was dead and there was no money to pay for school. The truth is too precious and dangerous to be thrown anywhere. So the man was sorry for him and said well, he could sit with the others and try how he did.

At this time Kobedi worked all day and went to classes in the evening and still he was careful not to become too friendly, in case the friend was an enemy. There was a knife in the shop, but it was blunt, and though he sawed at the sinew on his arm he could not get it off. Sometimes he dreamed about whispering in the night and woke frozen. Sometime he thought his mother would come suddenly through the door of the shop and claim him. If she did, could the night school help him?

One of the Botswana teachers took notice of him and let him come to his room to do homework, since this was not possible in the shop. There were some books in the teacher's room and a photograph of himself with others at the T.T.C.; after a while Kobedi began to like this teacher, Mr. Tshele, and half thought that one day he would tell him what his fears were. But not yet. There came an evening when he was writing out sentences in English, at one side of the table where the lamp stood. Mr. Tshele had a friend with him; they were drinking beer. He heard the cans being opened and smelled the fizzing beer. At a certain moment he began to listen because Mr. Tshele was teasing his friend, who was hoping for a post in the civil service and had been to a doctor to get a charm to help him. "You believe in that!" said Mr. Tshele. "You are not modern. You should go to a cattle post and not to the civil service!"

"Everyone does the same," said his friend, "perhaps it helps, perhaps not. I do not want to take risks. It is my life."

"Well, it is certainly your money. What did he charge

you?" The friend giggled and did not answer; the beer cans chinked again. "I am asking you another thing," said Mr. Tshele, "This you have done at least brings no harm. But what about sorcery? Do you believe?"

The friend hesitated. "I have heard dreadful things," he said, "What they do. Perhaps they are mad. Perhaps it no longer happens. Not in Botswana. Only perhaps—well, perhaps in Lesotho. Who knows? In the mountains."

Mr. Tshele leaned back in his chair. Kobedi ducked his head over his paper and pencil and pretended to be busy writing. "There is a case coming up in the High Court," said Mr. Tshele. "My cousin who is a lawyer told me. A man is accused of medicine murder. The trial will be next week. They are looking for witnesses, but people are afraid to come forward."

"But they must have found—something?"

"Yes, a dead child. Cut in a certain way. Pieces taken out. Perhaps even while the child was alive and screaming for help."

"This is most dreadful," said the friend, "and most certainly the man I went to about my civil service interview would never do such a thing!"

"Maybe not," said Mr. Tshele, "not if he can get your money a safer way! Mind you, I myself went to a doctor who was a registered herbalist when I had those headaches, and he threw the *ditaola* and all that, but most certainly he did not murder."

"Did he cure your headaches?"

"Yes, yes, and it was cheaper than going to the chemist's shop. He rubbed the back of my neck and also gave me a powder to drink. Two things. It was a treatment, a medical treatment, not just a charm. I suppose you also go for love charms?"

Again the friend giggled, and Kobedi was afraid they would now only speak about girls. He wanted to know more, more, about the man who had cut out the heart—and the liver—and stripped off the fat for rubbing, as he remembered the whispering in the night. But they came back to it. "This man, the one you spoke of who is to be tried, he is from where?" the friend asked. And Mr. Tshele carelessly gave the name of the village. His village. The name, the shock, the knowledge, for it must indeed and in truth be the Good Man. Kobedi could not speak, could not move. He stared at the lamp and the light blurred and pulsed with the strong terrible feeling he had in him like the vomiting of the soul.

He did not speak that evening. Nor the next. He wondered if the Good Man was in a strong jail, but if so surely he could escape, taking some form, a vulture, a great crow? And his mother? And the other women, the whisperers? But the evening after that, in the middle of a dusty open space near the school where nobody could be hiding to listen, he touched Mr. Tshele's coat and looked up at him, for he did not yet come to a man's shoulder height. Mr. Tshele bent down, thinking this was some school trouble. It was then that Kobedi whispered the name of his village and when Mr. Tshele did not immediately understand: "Where *that one* who is to be tried comes from. I know him."

"You? How?" said Mr. Tshele and then Kobedi began to tell him everything and the dust blew round them and he began to cry and Mr. Tshele wiped his dusty tears away and took him to a shop at the far side of the open space and gave him an ice lolly on a stick. He had seen boys sucking them, but for him it was the first time and great pleasure.

Then Mr. Tshele said, "Come with me," and took him by the hand and they went together to the house of his cousin the lawyer, which was set in a garden with fruit trees and tomato plants and flowers and a thing which whirled water. Inside it was as light as a shop and Kobedi's bare feet felt a soft and delicious carpet under them. "Here is your witness in the big case!" said Mr. Tshele, and then to Kobedi: "Tell him!" But Kobedi could not speak of it again.

But they gave him a drink that stung a little on the tongue and was warm in the stomach, and in a while Kobedi was able to say again what he had said to his teacher and it came more easily. "Good," said the cousin who was a lawyer. "Now, little one, will you be able to say this in the Court? If you can do it you will destroy a great evil. Modimo will be glad of you." Kobedi nodded and then he whispered to Mr. Tshele, "It will come better if you take this off me," and he showed them the sinew with the medicine. The two men looked at one another and the lawyer fetched a strong pair of scissors and cut through the sinew; then he took it into the kitchen, and before Kobedi's eyes he put it with his own hand into the stove and poked the wood into a blaze so that it was consumed altogether. After that Kobedi told the lawyer the shop where he worked. "So now," said the lawyer, "no word to any other person. This is between us three. *Khudu Thamaga*."

That night Kobedi slept quickly without dreaming. Two days later a big car stopped at the shop where he was sweeping out the papers and dirt and spittle of the customers. The lawyer came to the door and called him: "You have not spoken? Good. But in Court you will speak." Then the lawyer gave some money to the man at the shop to make up for taking his servant, and when they were in the car he explained to Kobedi how it would be. The accused here, the witness there. "I will ask you questions," he said, "and you will answer and it will be only the truth. Look at the Judge in the high seat behind the table where men write. Do not look at the accused man. Never look at him. Do you understand?" Kobedi nodded. The lawyer went on, "Speak in Setswana when I question you, even if you know some English words which my cousin says you have learnt. These things of which you will tell cannot be spoken in English. But show also that you know a little. You can say to the Judge, 'I greet you, Your Honour.' Repeat that. Yes, that is right. Your Honour is the English name for a Judge and this is a most important Judge."

So in a while the car stopped and Kobedi was put into a room and given milk and sandwiches with meat in them and he waited. The time came when he was called into the Court and a man helped him and told him not to be afraid. He kept his eyes down and saw nothing, but the man touched his shoulder and said, "There is His Honour the Judge." So Kobedi looked up bravely and greeted the Judge, who smiled at him and asked if he knew the meaning of an oath. At all times there was an interpreter in the Court and there seemed to be very many people, who sometimes made a rustling sound like dry leaves of mealies, but Kobedi carefully looked only at the Judge. So he took his oath; there was a Bible, such as he had seen at his first school. And then the lawyer began to ask him questions and he answered, so that the story grew like a tree in front of the Judge.

Now it came to the whisperers in the midnight room and what they had shown him of their purpose; the lawyer asked him who there were besides the accused. Kobedi answered that one was his mother. And as he did so there was a scream and it came from his mother herself. "Wicked one, liar, runaway, oh how I will beat you!" she yelled at him until a policewoman took her away. But he had turned towards her, and suddenly he had become dreadfully unhappy. And in his unhappiness he looked too far and in a kind of wooden box half a grown person's height, he saw the Good Man.

Before he could take his eyes away the Good Man suddenly shot out his finger over the top of the box and it was as though a rod of fire passed between him and Kobedi. "It is all lies," shouted the Good Man. "Tell them you have lied, lied, lied!" And a dreadful need came onto Kobedi to say just this thing and he took a shuffling step towards the Good Man, for what had passed between them was *kgogela*, sorcery, and it had trapped him. But there was a great noise from all round and he heard the lawyer's voice and the Judge's voice and other voices and he felt a sharp pain in the side of his stomach.

Now after this Kobedi was not clear what was happening, only he shut his eyes tight, and then it seemed to him that he still wore those sinews which the Good Man had fastened onto him. And the pain in his stomach seemed to grow. But the *kgogela* had been broken and he did not need to undo his words and he was able to open his eyes and look at the Judge and to answer three more questions from his friend the lawyer. Then he was guided back to the room where one waited and he did not speak of the pain, for he hoped it might go.

But it was still there. After a time his friend the lawyer came in and said he had done well. But somehow Kobedi no longer cared. When he was in the car beside the lawyer he had to ask for it to stop so that he could get out and vomit into a bush, for he could not dirty such a shining car. On the way to the Court he had watched the little clocks and jumping numbers in the front of the car, but now they did not speak to him. He had become tired all over and yet if he shut his eyes he saw the finger pointing. "I will take you to Mr. Tshele," said the lawyer and stopped to buy milk and bread and sausage; but Kobedi was only a little pleased and he began less and less to be able not to speak of his pain.

After a time of voices and whirling and doctors, he began to wake up and he was in a white bed and there was a hospital smell. A nurse came and he felt pain, but not of the same deep kind, not so bad. Then a doctor came and said all was well and Mr. Tshele came and told Kobedi that now he was going to live with him and go properly to school in the daytime and have new clothes and shoes. He and the lawyer would become, as it were, Kobedi's uncles. "But," said Kobedi, "tell me—the one—the one who did these things?"

"The Judge has spoken," said Mr. Tshele. "That man will die and all will be wiped out."

"And—the woman?" For he could not now say mother.

"She will be put away until the evil is out of her." Kobedi wondered a little about the small sisters, but they were no longer in his life so he could forget them and forget the house and forget his village forever. He lay back in the white bed.

After a while a young nurse came in and gave him a pill to swallow. Kobedi began to question her about what happened, for he knew by now that the doctors had cut the pain out of his stomach. The young nurse looked round and whispered: "They took out a thing like a small crocodile, but dead," she said.

"That was the sorcery," said Kobedi. Now he knew and was happy that it was entirely gone.

The young nurse said, "We are not allowed to believe in sorcery."

"I do not believe in it any longer," said Kobedi, "because it is finished. But that was what it was."

The Word of Unbinding

by

Ursula K. Le Guin

Ursula K. Le Guin was possibly the most talked-about SF writer of the seventies—rivaled for that position only by Robert Silverberg, James Tiptree, Jr., and Philip K. Dick—and is probably one of the best-known and most universally respected SF writers in the world today. Her famous novel The Left Hand of Darkness *may have been the most influential SF novel of its decade, and shows every sign of becoming one of the enduring classics of the genre—it won both the Hugo and Nebula awards, as did Le Guin's monumental novel* The Dispossessed, *a few years later. She has also won two other Hugo Awards and a Nebula Award for her short fiction, and the National Book Award for Children's Literature for her novel* The Farthest Shore, *part of her acclaimed Earthsea trilogy. Her other novels include* Planet of Exile, The Lathe of Heaven, City of Illusions, Rocannon's World, The Beginning Place, *and the other two Earthsea novels,* A Wizard of Earthsea *and* The Tombs of Atuan. *She has had three collections:* The Wind's Twelve Quarters, Orsinian Tales, *and* The Compass Rose. *Her most recent book is the novel* Always Coming Home.*

Here, in an early visit to the world of Earthsea, the evocative and starkly beautiful world of the Archipelago, she depicts the travail of a sorcerer trying to defend his home island against the depredations of a vast, implacable Power...a

*sorcerer whose duty leads him to the very shore of death—
and beyond.*

* * *

WHERE WAS HE? THE FLOOR WAS HARD AND SLIMY, THE AIR
black and stinking, and that was all there was. Except a head-
ache. Lying flat on the clammy floor Festin moaned, and then
said, "Staff!" When his alderwood wizard's staff did not come
to his hand, he knew he was in peril. He sat up, and not
having his staff with which to make a proper light, he struck a
spark between finger and thumb, muttering a certain Word. A
blue will o' the wisp sprang from the spark and rolled feebly
through the air, sputtering. "Up," said Festin, and the fireball
wobbled upward till it lit a vaulted trapdoor very high above,
so high that Festin projecting into the fireball momentarily
saw his own face forty feet below as a pale dot in the darkness. The light struck no reflections in the damp walls; they
had been woven out of night, by magic. He rejoined himself
and said, "Out." The ball expired. Festin sat in the dark,
cracking his knuckles.

He must have been overspelled from behind, by surprise;
for the last memory he had was of walking through his own
woods at evening talking with the trees. Lately, in these lone
years in the middle of his life, he had been burdened with a
sense of waste, of unspent strength; so, needing to learn patience, he had left the villages and gone to converse with
trees, especially oaks, chestnuts, and the grey alders whose
roots are in profound communication with running water. It
had been six months since he had spoken to a human being.
He had been busy with essentials, casting no spells and bothering no one. So who had spellbound him and shut him in this
reeking well? "Who?" he demanded of the walls, and slowly a
name gathered on them and ran down to him like a thick black
drop sweated out from pores of stone and spores of fungus:
"Voll."

For a moment Festin was in a cold sweat himself.

He had heard first long ago of Voll the Fell, who was said
to be more than wizard yet less than man; who passed from
island to island of the Outer Reach, undoing the works of the
Ancients, enslaving men, cutting forests and spoiling fields,
and sealing in underground tombs any wizard or Mage who
tried to combat him. Refugees from ruined islands told always

the same tale, that he came at evening on a dark wind over the sea. His slaves followed in ships; these they had seen. But none of them had ever seen Voll. . . . There were many men and creatures of evil will among the Islands, and Festin, a young warlock intent on his training, had not paid much heed to these tales of Voll the Fell. "I can protect this island," he had thought, knowing his untried power, and had returned to his oaks and alders, the sound of wind in their leaves, the rhythm of growth in their round trunks and limbs and twigs, the taste of sunlight on leaves or dark groundwater around roots.—Where were they now, the trees, his old companions? Had Voll destroyed the forest?

Awake at last and up on his feet, Festin made two broad motions with rigid hands, shouting aloud a Name that would burst all locks and break open any man-made door. But these walls impregnated with night and the name of their builder did not heed, did not hear. The name re-echoed back, clapping in Festin's ears so that he fell on his knees, hiding his head in his arms till the echoes died away in the vaults above him. Then, still shaken by the backfire, he sat brooding.

They were right; Voll was strong. Here on his own ground, within this spell-built dungeon, his magic would withstand any direct attack; and Festin's strength was halved by the loss of his staff. But not even his captor could take from him his powers, relative only to himself, of Projecting and Transforming. So, after rubbing his now doubly aching head, he transformed. Quietly his body melted away into a cloud of fine mist.

Lazy, trailing, the mist rose off the floor, drifting up along the slimy walls until it found, where vault met wall, a hairline crack. Through this, droplet by droplet, it seeped. It was almost all through the crack when a hot wind, hot as a furnace-blast, struck at it, scattering the mist-drops, drying them. Hurriedly the mist sucked itself back into the vault, spiralled to the floor, took on Festin's own form and lay there panting. Transformation is an emotional strain to introverted warlocks of Festin's sort; when to that strain is added the shock of facing unhuman death in one's assumed shape, the experience becomes horrible. Festin lay for a while merely breathing. He was also angry with himself. It had been a pretty simple-minded notion to escape as a mist, after all. Every fool knew that trick. Voll had probably just left a hot wind waiting. Festin gathered himself into a small black bat, flew up to the ceiling, retransformed into a thin stream of plain air, and seeped through the crack.

This time he got clear out and was blowing softly down the hall in which he found himself towards a window, when a sharp sense of peril made him pull together, snapping himself into the first small, coherent shape that came to mind—a gold ring. It was just as well. The hurricane of arctic air that would have dispersed his air-form in unrecallable chaos merely chilled his ring-form slightly. As the storm passed he lay on the marble pavement, wondering which form might get out the window quickest.

Too late, he began to roll away. An enormous blank-faced troll strode cataclysmically across the floor, stopped, caught the quick-rolling ring and picked it up in a huge limestone-like hand. The troll strode to the trapdoor, lifted it by an iron handle and a muttered charm, and dropped Festin down into the darkness. He fell straight for forty feet and landed on the stone floor—clink.

Resuming his true form he sat up, ruefully rubbing a bruised elbow. Enough of this transformation on any empty stomach. He longed bitterly for his staff, with which he could have summoned up any amount of dinner. Without it, though he could change his own form and exert certain spells and powers, he could not transform or summon to him any material thing—neither lightning nor a lamb chop.

"Patience," Festin told himself, and when he had got his breath he dissolved his body into the infinite delicacy of volatile oils, becoming the aroma of a frying lamb chop. He drifted once more through the crack. The waiting troll sniffed suspiciously, but already Festin had regrouped himself into a falcon, winging straight for the window. The troll lunged after him, missed by yards, and bellowed in a vast stony voice, "The hawk, get the hawk!" Swooping over the enchanted castle towards his forest that lay dark to westward, sunlight and sea-glare dazzling his eyes, Festin rode the wind like an arrow. But a quicker arrow found him. Crying out, he fell. Sun and sea and towers spun around him and went out.

He woke again on the dank floor of the dungeon, hands and hair and lips wet with his own blood. The arrow had struck his pinion as a falcon, his shoulder as a man. Lying still, he mumbled a spell to close the wound. Presently he was able to sit up, and recollect a longer, deeper spell of healing. But he had lost a good deal of blood, and with it, power. A chill had settled in the marrow of his bones which even the healing-spell could not warm. There was darkness in his eyes, even when he struck a will o' the wisp and lit the reeking air: the same dark mist he had seen, as he flew, overhanging his forest and the little towns of his land.

It was up to him to protect that land.

He could not attempt direct escape again. He was too weak and tired. Trusting his power too much, he had lost his strength. Now whatever shape he took would share his weakness, and be trapped.

Shivering with cold, he crouched there, letting the fireball sputter out with a last whiff of methane—marsh gas. The smell brought to his mind's eye the marshes stretching from the forest wall down to the sea, his beloved marshes where no men came, where in fall the swans flew long and level, where between still pools and reed-islands the quick, silent, seaward streamlets ran. Oh, to be a fish in one of those streams; or better yet to be farther upstream, near the springs, in the forest in the shadow of the trees, in the clear brown backwater under an alder's root, resting hidden . . .

This was a great magic. Festin had no more performed it than has any man who in exile or danger longs for the earth and waters of his home, seeing and yearning over the doorsill of his house, the table where he has eaten, the branches outside the window of the room where he has slept. Only in dreams do any but the great Mages realize this magic of going home. But Festin, with the cold creeping out from his marrow into nerves and veins, stood up between the black walls, gathered his will together till it shone like a candle in the darkness of his flesh, and began to work the great and silent magic.

The walls were gone. He was in the earth, rocks and veins of granite for bones, groundwater for blood, the roots of things for nerves. Like a blind worm he moved through the earth westward, slowly, darkness before and behind. Then all at once coolness flowed along his back and belly, a buoyant, unresisting, inexhaustible caress. With his sides he tasted the water, felt current-flow; and with lidless eyes he saw before him the deep brown pool between the great buttress-roots of an alder. He darted forward, silvery, into shadow. He had got free. He was home.

The water ran timelessly from its clear spring. He lay on the sand of the pool's bottom letting running water, stronger than any spell of healing, soothe his wound and with its coolness wash away the bleaker cold that had entered him. But as he rested he felt and heard a shaking and trampling in the earth. Who walked now in his forest? Too weary to try to change form, he hid his gleaming trout-body under the arch of the alder root, and waited.

Huge grey fingers groped in the water, roiling the sand. In the dimness above water vague faces, blank eyes loomed and vanished, reappeared. Nets and hands groped, missed, missed again, then caught and lifted him writhing up into the air. He struggled to take back his own shape and could not; his own spell of homecoming bound him. He writhed in the net, gasping in the dry, bright, terrible air, drowning. The agony went on, and he knew nothing beyond it.

After a long time and little by little he became aware that he was in his human form again; some sharp, sour liquid was being forced down his throat. Time lapsed again, and he found himself sprawled face down on the dark floor of the vault. He was back in the power of his enemy. And, though he could breathe again, he was not very far from death.

The chill was all through him now; and the trolls, Voll's servants, must have crushed the fragile trout-body, for when he moved, his ribcage and one forearm stabbed with pain. Broken and without strength, he lay at the bottom of the well of night. There was no power in him to change shape; there was no way out, but one.

Lying there motionless, almost but not quite beyond the reach of pain, Festin thought: Why has he not killed me? Why does he keep me here alive?

Why has he never been seen? With what eyes can he be seen, on what ground does he walk?

He fears me, though I have no strength left.

They say that all the wizards and men of power whom he has defeated live on sealed in tombs like this, live on year after year trying to get free. . . .

But if one chose not to live?

So Festin made his choice. His last thought was, If I am wrong, men will think I was a coward. But he did not linger on this thought. Turning his head a little to the side he closed his eyes, took a last deep breath, and whispered the word of unbinding, which is only spoken once.

This was not transformation. He was not changed. His body, the long legs and arms, the clever hands, the eyes that had liked to look on trees and streams, lay unchanged, only still, perfectly still and full of cold. But the walls were gone. The vaults built by magic were gone, and the rooms and towers; and the forest, and the sea, and the sky of evening. They were all gone, and Festin went slowly down the far slope of the hill of being, under new stars.

In life he had had great power; so here he did not forget. Like a candle flame he moved in the darkness of the wider land. And remembering he called out his enemy's name: "Voll!"

Called, unable to withstand, Voll came towards him, a thick pale shape in the starlight. Festin approached, and the other cowered and screamed as if burnt. Festin followed when he fled, followed him close. A long way they went, over dry lava-flows from the great extinct volcanoes rearing their cones against the unnamed stars, across the spurs of silent hills, through valleys of short black grass, past towns or down their unlit streets between houses through whose windows no face looked. The stars hung in the sky; none set, none rose. There was no change here. No day would come. But they went on, Festin always driving the other before him, till they reached a place where once a river had run, very long ago: a river from the living lands. In the dry streambed, among boulders, a dead body lay: that of an old man, naked, flat eyes staring at the stars that are innocent of death.

"Enter it," Festin said. The Voll-shadow whimpered, but Festin came closer. Voll cowered away, stooped, and entered in the open mouth of his own dead body.

At once the corpse vanished. Unmarked, stainless, the dry boulders gleamed in starlight. Festin stood still a while, then slowly sat down among the great rocks to rest. To rest, not sleep; for he must keep guard here until Voll's body, sent back to its grave, had turned to dust, all evil power gone, scattered by the wind and washed seaward by the rain. He must keep watch over this place where once death had found a way back into the other land. Patient now, infinitely patient, Festin waited among the rocks where no river would ever run again, in the heart of the country which has no seacoast. The stars stood still above him; and as he watched them, slowly, very slowly he began to forget the voice of streams and the sound of rain on the leaves of the forests of life.

His Coat So Gay

by

Sterling E. Lanier

Although he has published novels—most notably the well-received Hiero's Journey, *is sequel* The Unforsaken Hiero, *and the recent* Menace Under Marswood—*Sterling E. Lanier is probably best known in the fantasy and science fiction fields for his sequence of stories describing the odd adventures of Brigadier Donald Ffellowes, the bulk of which have been collected in* The Peculiar Exploits of Brigadier Ffellowes.

Unusually well-crafted examples of that curious sub-genre known as the "club story" or "bar story"—whose antecedents in the fantasy field go back at least as far as Lord Dunsany's stories of the clubman Jorkens, and include subsequent work by Arthur C. Clarke and L. Sprague De Camp and Fletcher Pratt—Lanier's Ffellowes stories are erudite, intelligent, witty, fast-paced—and often just plain scary.

In "His Coat So Gay," one of the most suspenseful and chilling of all the Brigadier Ffellowes stories, Ffellowes is invited to a remote mountain valley for a week of hunting, but instead finds himself the prey of a group of very nasty sorcerers—and the monstrous, relentless, clip-clopping black shape of the Dead Horse. . . .

* * *

THERE HAD BEEN A BIG SPREAD IN THE NEWSPAPERS ABOUT A British duke going through bankruptcy proceedings and his third divorce simultaneously. The divorce was contested, the evidence was sordid and those giving it equally so. The nobleman in question came out of the whole thing very badly, it being proved, among other things, that he had run up huge debts to tradesmen, knowing damn well when he did it that he couldn't hope to pay them. There was lots more, though, including secret "orgies," which seem to have been dirty parties of the sort to have passed quite unnoticed in Los Angeles.

One of the members tapped his newspaper. A few of us were sitting upstairs in the library after dinner. It was a hot night in New York, but the club was air-conditioned and very pleasant.

"Good thing," said the man with the paper, "that Mason Williams isn't here to shout about this. He'd love to give General Ffellowes a hard time. Can't you hear him? 'Rotten bunch of degenerates! Lousy overbearing crooks and cadgers! Long line of aristocratic bums and swindlers!' It would be the best opportunity he's had in years for trying to annoy the brigadier."

"I notice you were smart enough to say 'trying'!" said someone else. "He's never managed to annoy Ffellowes yet. I doubt if this would do it either."

"Who wants to annoy me, eh?" came the easy, clipped tones of our favorite English member. He had come up the narrow back stairs at the other end of the room and was now standing behind my own back. He always moved silently, not I feel certain out of a desire to be stealthy, but from a lifetime's training. Ffellowes' years in (apparently) every secret as well as public branch of Her Majesty's service had given him the ability to walk like a cat, and quiet one at that.

I jumped and so did a couple of others, and then there was a moment of embarrassed silence.

Ffellowes is very quick. He saw the newspaper headline in my neighbor's lap and began to chuckle.

"Good heavens, is that supposed to offend me? What a hope! I suppose someone thought our friend Williams might make use of it to savage the British Lion, eh?" He moved from behind my chair and dropped into a vacant seat, his eyes twinkling.

"Item," he said, "the man in question's a Scot, not English. Most important distinction. A lesser and unstable breed." This was said with such dead-pan emphasis that we all started to laugh at once. Ffellowes' smooth, ruddy face remained immobile, but his blue eyes danced.

"If you won't be serious,' he said, when the laughter died

away, "I shall have to explain why Chattan's little peccadilloes are unlikely to move me to wrath. Or anyone else with any real knowledge, for that matter.

"You know, Richard the Lion Heart was a bad debtor on a scale that makes anyone modern look silly. All the Plantagenets were, for that matter. Richard seems to have been a quite unabashed queer as well, of course, and likewise William the Second, called Rufus. When, at any rate, one asked those lads for monies due, one had better have had a fast horse and a waiting ship. They canceled debts rather abruptly. There are thousands more examples, but I mention the kings as quite a fairish sample. Now Chattan's an ass and his sexual troubles are purely squalid, fit only for headlines in a cheap paper. But there are other cases no paper ever got to print. Not so long ago, one of your splashier magazines ran a purely fictional piece about an aged nobleman, Scots again, who was sentenced never to leave his family castle, as a result of an atrocious crime, not *quite* provable. The story happens to be quite true and the verdict was approved by the Lords in a closed session. The last pope but two had a South Italian cardinal locked up in his own palace for the remainder of his life on various charges not susceptible of public utterance. The old man only died ten years ago. So it goes, and there are dozens more cases of a similar nature.

"The fact is, persons in positions of power often abuse that power in the oddest and most unpleasant ways. The extent of caprice in the human mind is infinite. Whenever public gaze, so to speak, is withdrawn, oddities occur, and far worse than illicit sex is involved in these pockets of infection. Once off the highways of humanity, if you care for analogies, one finds the oddest byways. All that's needed is isolation, that and power, economic or physical." He seemed to brood for a moment.

Outside the windows, the haze and smog kept even the blaze of Manhattan at night dim and sultry looking. The garish electricity of New York took on something of the appearance of patches of torch and fire light in the heat and murk.

"Haven't you left out one qualification, sir?" said a younger member. "What about time? Surely, to get these Dracula-castle effects and so on, you have to have centuries to play with a complaisant bunch of peasants, hereditary aristocrats, the whole bit. In other words, a really *old* country, right?"

Ffellowes stared at the opposite wall for a bit before answering. Finally he seemed to shrug, as if he had come to a decision.

"Gilles de Rais," he said, "is perhaps the best example known of your Dracula syndrome, so I admit I must agree with you. In general, however, only in general. The worst case of this sort of thing which ever came to my personal knowledge, and very personal it was, took place in the early 1930's in one of your larger Eastern states. So that while time is certainly needed, as indeed for the formation of any disease, the so-called modern age is not so much of a protection as one might think. And yet there was great age, too."

He raised his hand and the hum of startled comment which had begun to rise died at once.

"I'll tell you the story. But I'll tell it my way. No questions of any sort whatsoever. There are still people alive who could be injured. I shall cheerfully disguise and alter any detail I can which might lead to identification of the family or place concerned. Beyond that, you will simply have to accept my word. If you're interested on that basis . . . ?"

The circle of faces, mine included, was so eager that his iron countenance damned near cracked into a grin, but he held it back and began.

"In the early days of your, and indeed everyone's, Great Depression, I was the most junior military attache of our Washington embassy. It was an agreeable part of my duties to mix socially as much as I could with Americans of my own age. One way of doing this was hunting, fox hunting to be more explicit. I used to go out with the Middleburg Hunt, and while enjoying the exercise, I made a number of friends as well.

"One of them was a man whom I shall call Canler Waldron. That's not even an anagram, but sounds vaguely like his real name. He was supposed to be putting in time as junior member of your State Department, my own age and very good company.

"It was immediately obvious that he was extremely well off. Most people, of course, had been at least affected a trifle by the Crash, if not a whole lot, but it was plain that whatever Can's financial basis was, it had hardly been shaken. Small comments were revealing, especially his puzzlement when, as often happened, others pleaded lack of funds to explain some inability to take a trip or to purchase something. He was, I may add, the most generous of men financially, and without being what you'd call a 'sucker,' he was very easy to leave with the check, so much so one had to guard against it.

"He was pleasant looking, black haired, narrow faced, dark brown eyes, a generalized North European type, and, as I said, about my own age, barely twenty-one. And what a magnificent rider! I'm not bad, or wasn't then, but I've never seen anyone to match Canler Waldron. No fence ever bothered him and he always led the field, riding so easily that he hardly appeared to be conscious of what he was doing. It got so that he became embarrassed by the attention and used to pull his horse in order to stay back and not be first at every death. Of course he was magnificently mounted; he had a whole string of big black hunters, his own private breed he said. But there were others out who had fine 'cattle' too; no, he was simply a superb rider.

"We were chatting one Fall morning after a very dull run, and I asked him why he always wore the black hunting coat of a non-hunt member. I knew he belonged to some hunt or other and didn't understand why he never used their colors.

"'Highly embarrassing to explain to you, Donald, of all people,' he said, but he was smiling. 'My family were Irish and very patriotic during our Revolution. No pink coats ('pink' being the term for hunting red) for us. Too close to the hated redcoat army in looks, see? So we wear light green, and I frankly get damned tired of being asked what it is. That's all.'

"I was amused for several reasons. 'Of course I understand. Some of our own hunts wear other colors, you know. But I thought green coats were for foot hounds, beagles, bassetts and such?'

"'Ours is much lighter, like grass, with buff lapels,' he said. He seemed a little ill at ease for some reason, as our horses shifted and stamped under the hot Virginia sun. 'It's a family hunt, you see. No non-Waldron can wear the coat. This sounds pretty snobby, so again, I avoid questions by not wearing it except at home. Betty feels the same way and she hates black. Here she comes now. What did you think of the ride, Sis?'

"'Not very exciting,' she said quietly, looking around so that she should not be convicted of rudeness to our hosts. I haven't mentioned Betty Waldron, have I? Even after all these years, it's still painful.

"She was nineteen years old, very pale, and no sun ever raised so much as a freckle. Her eyes were almost black, her hair midnight, and her voice very gentle and sad. She was quiet, seldom smiled, and when she did my heart turned over. Usually, her thoughts were miles away and she seemed to walk in a dream. She also rode superbly, almost absentmind-edly, to look at her."

Ffellowes sighed and arched his hands together in his lap, his gaze fixed on the rug before him.

"I was a poor devil of an artillery subaltern, few prospects save for my pay, but I could dream, as long as I kept my mouth shut. She seemed to like me as much, or even more than the gaudy lads who were always flocking about, and I felt I had a tiny, the smallest grain of hope. I'd never said a thing. I knew already the family must be staggeringly rich, and I had my pride. But also, as I say, my dreams.

"'Let's ask Donald home and give him some real sport,' I suddenly heard Can say to her.

"'When?' she asked sharply, looking hard at him.

"'How about the end of the cubbing season? Last week in October. Get the best of both sports, adult and young. Hounds will be in good condition, and it's our best time of year.' He smiled at me and patted his horse. 'What say, limey? Like some real hunting, eight hours sometimes?'

"I was delighted and surprised, because I'd heard several people fishing rather obviously for invitations to the Waldron place at one time or another and all being politely choked off. I had made up my mind never to place myself where such a rebuff could strike me. There was a goodish number of fortune-hunting Europeans about just then, some of them English, and they made me a trifle ill. But I was surprised and hurt, too, by Betty's reaction.

"'Not this Fall, Can,' she said, her face even whiter than usual. 'Not—this—Fall!' The words were stressed separately and came out with an intensity I can't convey.

"'As the head of the family, I'm afraid what I say goes,' said Canler in a voice I'd certainly never heard him use be-fore. It was heavy and dominating, even domineering. As I watched, quite baffled, she choked back a sob and urged her horse away from us. In a moment her slender black back and shining topper were lost in the milling sea of the main body of the hunt. I was really hurt badly.

"'Now look here, old boy,' I said. 'I don't know what's

going on, but I can't possibly accept your invitation under these circumstances. Betty obviously loathes the idea, and I wouldn't dream of coming against her slightest wish.'

"He urged his horse over until we were only a yard apart. 'You must, Donald. You don't understand. I don't like letting out family secrets, but I'm going to have to in this case. Betty was very roughly treated by a man last year, in the Fall. A guy who seemed to like her and then just walked out, without a word, and disappeared. I know you'll never speak of this to her, and she'd rather die than say anything to you. But I haven't been able to get her interested in things ever since. You're the first man she's liked from that time to this, and you've got to help me pull her out of this depression. Surely you've noticed how vague and dreamy she is? She's living in a world of unreality, trying to shut out unhappiness. I can't get her to see a doctor, and even if I could, it probably wouldn't do any good. What she needs is some decent man being kind to her in the same surroundings she was made unhappy in. Can you see why I need you as a friend so badly?' He was damned earnest and it was impossible not to be touched.

"'Well, that's all very well,' I mumbled, 'but she's still dead set against my coming, you know. I simply can't come in the face of such opposition. You mentioned yourself as head of the family. Do I take it that your parents are dead? Because if so, then Betty is my hostess. It won't do, damn it all.'

'Now, look,' he said, 'don't turn me down. By tomorrow morning she'll ask you herself, I swear. I promise that if she doesn't, the whole thing's off. Will you come if she asks you and give me a hand at cheering her up? And we are orphans, by the way, just us two.'

"Of course I agreed. I was wild to come. To get leave would be easy. There was nothing much but routine at the embassy anyway, and mixing with people like the Waldrons was as much a part of my duties as going to any Fort Leavenworth maneuvers.

"And sure enough, Betty rang me up at my Washington flat the next morning and apologized for her behavior the previous day. She sounded very dim and tired but perfectly all right. I asked her twice if she was sure she wanted my company, and she repeated that she did, still apologizing for the day before. She said she had felt feverish and didn't know why she'd spoken as she had. This was good enough for me, and so it was settled.

"Thus, in the last week in October, I found myself hunting the coverts of—well, call it the valley of Waldrondale. What a glorious, mad time it was! The late Indian summer lingered, and each cold night gave way to a lovely misty dawn. The main Waldron lands lay in the hollow of a spur of the Appalachian range. Apparently some early Waldron, an emigrant from Ireland during the '16, I gathered, had gone straight west into Indian territory and somehow laid claim to a perfectly immense tract of country. What is really odd is that the red men seemed to feel it was all fine, that he should do so.

"'We always got along with our Indians,' Canler told me once. 'Look around the valley at the faces, my own included. There's some Indian blood in all of us. A branch of the lost Erie nation, before the Iroquois destroyed them, according to the family records.'

"It was quite true that when one looked, the whole valley indeed appeared to have a family resemblance. The women were very pale, and both sexes were black haired and dark eyed, with lean, aquiline features. Many of them, apparently local farmers, rode with the hunt and fine riders they were, too, well mounted and fully familiar with field etiquette.

"Waldrondale was a great, heart-shaped valley, of perhaps eight thousand acres. The Waldrons leased some of it to cousins and farmed some themselves. They owned still more land outside the actual valley, but that was all leased. It was easy to see that in Waldrondale itself they were actually rulers. Although both Betty and Can were called by their first names, every one of the valley dwellers was ready and willing to drop whatever he or she was doing at a moment's notice to oblige either of them in the smallest way. It was not subservience exactly, but instead almost an eagerness, of the sort a monarch might have got in the days when kings were also sacred beings. Canler shrugged when I mentioned how the matter struck me.

"'We've just been here a long time, that's all. They've simply got used to us telling them what to do. When the first Waldron came over from Galway, a lot of retainers seem to have come with him. So it's not really a strictly normal American situation.' He looked lazily at me. 'Hope you don't think we're too effete and baronial here, not that England's becoming so democratized?'

"'Not at all,' I said quickly and the subject was changed. There had been an unpleasant undertone in his speech, almost jeering, and for some reason he seemed rather irritated.

"What wonderful hunting we had! The actual members of the hunt, those who wore the light green jackets, were only a dozen or so, mostly close relatives of Canler's and Betty's. When we had started the first morning at dawn, I'd surprised them all for I was then a full member of the Duke of Beaufort's pack, and as a joke more than anything else, I had brought the blue and yellow-lapelled hunting coat along. The joke was that I had been planning to show them, the Waldrons, one of our own variant colors all along, ever since I had heard about theirs. They were all amazed at seeing me not only *not* in black, but in 'non-red,' so to speak. The little withered huntsman, a local farmer, named McColl, was absolutely taken aback and for some reason seemed frightened. He made a curious remark, of which I caught only two words, 'Sam Haines,' and then made a sign which I had no trouble at all interpreting. Two fingers at either end of a fist have always been an attempt to ward off the evil eye, or some other malign spiritual influence. I said nothing at the time, but during dinner I asked Betty who 'Sam Haines' was and what had made old McColl so nervous about my blue coat. Betty's reaction was even more peculiar. She muttered something about a local holiday and also that my coat was the 'wrong color for an Englishman,' and then abruptly changed the subject. Puzzled, I looked up, to notice that all conversation seemed to have died at the rest of the big table. There were perhaps twenty guests, all the regular hunt members and some more besides from the outlying parts of the valley. I was struck by the intensity of the very similar faces, male and female, all staring at us, lean, pale and dark eyed, all with that coarse raven hair. For a moment I had a most peculiar feeling that I had blundered into a den of some dangerous creature or other, some pack animal perhaps, like a wolf. Then Canler laughed from the head of the table and conversation started again. The illusion was broken, as a thrown pebble shatters a mirrored pool of water, and I promptly forgot it.

"The golden, wonderful days passed as October drew to a close. We were always up before dawn and hunted the great vale of Waldrondale sometimes until noon. Large patches of dense wood had been left deliberately uncleared here and there and made superb coverts. I never had such a good going, not even in Leicestershire at its best. And I was with Betty, who seemed happy, too. But although we drew almost the entire valley at one time or another, there was one exception, and it puzzled me to the point of asking Can about it one morning.

"Directly behind the Big House (it had no other name) the ground rose very sharply in the direction of the high blue hills beyond. But a giant hedge, all tangled and overgrown, barred access to whatever lay up the slope. The higher hills angled down, as it were, as if to enclose the house and grounds, two arms of high, rocky ground almost reaching the level of the house on either side. Yet it was evident that an area of some considerable extent, a smallish plateau in fact, lay directly behind the house, between it and the sheer slopes of the mountain, itself some jagged outlier of the great Appalachian chain. And the huge hedge could only have existed for the purpose of barring access to this particular piece of land.

"'It's a sanctuary,' Canler said when I asked him. 'The family has a burial plot there, and we always go there on—on certain days. It's been there since we settled the area, has some first growth timber among other things, and we like to keep it as it is. But I'll show it to you before you leave if you're really interested.' His voice was incurious and flat, but again I had the feeling, almost a sixth sense, if you like, that I had somehow managed to both annoy and, odder, amuse him. I changed the subject and we spoke of the coming day's sport.

"One more peculiar thing occurred on that day in the late afternoon. Betty and I had got a bit separated from the rest of the hunt, a thing I didn't mind one bit, and we also were some distance out from the narrow mouth of the valley proper, for the fox had run very far indeed. As we rode toward home under the warm sun, I noticed that we were passing a small, white, country church, wooden, you know, and rather shabby. As I looked, the minister, parson, or what have you, appeared on the porch, and seeing us, stood still, staring. We were not more than thirty feet apart for the dusty path, hardly a road at all, ran right next to the church. The minister was a tired-looking soul of about fifty, dressed in an ordinary suit but with a Roman collar, just like the C. of E. curate at home.

"But the man's expression! He never looked at me, but he stared at Betty, never moving or speaking, and the venom in his eyes was unmistakable. Hatred and contempt mingled with loathing.

"Our horses had stopped and in the silence they fidgeted

and stamped. I looked at Betty and saw a look of pain on her face, but she never spoke or moved either. I decided to break the silence myself.

"'Good day, padre,' I said breezily. 'Nice little church you have here. A jolly spot, lovely trees and all.' I expect I sounded half-witted.

"He turned his gaze on me and it changed utterly. The hatred vanished and instead I saw the face of a decent, kindly man, yes, and a deeply troubled one. He raised one hand and I thought for a startled moment he actually was going to bless me, don't you know, but he evidently thought better of it. Instead he spoke, plainly addressing me alone.

"'For the next forty-eight hours this church will remain open. And I will be here.'

"With that, he turned on his heel and re-entered the church, shutting the door firmly behind him.

"'Peculiar chap, that,' I said to Betty. 'Seems to have a bit of a down on you, too, if his nasty look was any indication. Is he out of his head, or what? Perhaps I ought to speak to Can, eh?'

"'No,' she said quickly, putting her hand on my arm. 'You mustn't; promise me you won't say anything to him about this, not a word!'

"'Of course I won't, Betty, but what on earth is wrong with the man? All that mumbo jumbo about his confounded church being open?'

"'He—well, he doesn't like any of our family, Donald. Perhaps he has reason. Lots of people outside the valley aren't too fond of the Waldrons. And the Depression hasn't helped matters. Can won't cut down on high living and of course hungry people who see us are furious. Don't let's talk any more about it. Mr. Andrews is a very decent man and I don't want Canler to hear about this. He might be angry and do something unpleasant. No more talk now. Come on, the horses are rested, I'll race you to the main road.'

"The horses were *not* rested and we both knew it, but I could never refuse her anything. By the time we rejoined the main body of the hunt, the poor beasts were blown, and we suffered a lot of chaff, mostly directed at me, for not treating our mounts decently.

"The next day was the thirty-first of October. My stay had only two more days to run and I could hardly bear to think of leaving. But I felt glorious too. The previous night, as I had thrown the bedclothes back, preparatory to climbing in, a small packet had been revealed. Opening it, I had found a worn, tiny cross on a chain, both silver and obviously very old. I recognized the cross as being of the ancient Irish or Gaelic design, rounded and with a circle in the center where the arms joined. There was a note in a delicate hand that I knew well, since I'd saved every scrap of paper I'd ever received from her.

"Wear this for me always and say nothing to anyone.

"Can you imagine how marvelous life seemed? The next hunt morning was so fine it could hardly have been exceeded. But even if it had been terrible and I'd broken a leg, I don't think I'd have noticed. I was wearing Betty's family token, sent to *me*, secretly under my shirt, and I came very close to singing aloud. She said nothing to me, save for polite banalities, and she looked tired, as if she'd not slept too well.

"As we rode past a lovely field of gathered shocks of maize, your 'corn,' you know, I noticed all the jolly pumpkins still left lying about in the fields and asked my nearest neighbor, one of the younger cousins, if the local kids didn't use them for Hallowe'en as I'd been told in the papers.

" 'Today?' he said, and then gobbled the same words used by the old huntsman, 'Sam Haines,' or perhaps 'Hayne.'

" 'We don't call it that,' he added stiffly and before I could ask why or anything else, spurred his horse and rode ahead. I was beginning to wonder, in a vague sort of way, if all this isolation really could be good for people. Canler and Betty seemed increasingly moody and indeed the whole crowd appeared subject to odd moods.

"Perhaps a bit inbred, I thought. *I must try and get Betty out of here.* Now apparently I'd offended someone by mentioning Hallowe'en, which, it occurred to me in passing, was that very evening. 'Sam Haines' indeed!

"Well, I promptly forgot all that when we found, located a fox, you know, and the chase started. It was a splendid one and long, and we had a very late lunch. I got a good afternoon rest, since Canler had told me we were having a banquet that evening. 'A farewell party for you, Donald,' he said, 'and a special one. We don't dress up much, but tonight we'll have a sort of hunt ball, eh?'

"I'd seen no preparations for music, but the Big House was so really big that the London Symphony could have been hidden somewhere about.

"I heard the dinner gong as I finished dressing, and when I came down to the main living room, all were assembled, the full hunt, with all the men in their soft-emerald green dress coats, to which my blue made a mild contrast. To my surprise, a number of children, although not small ones, were there also, all in party dress, eyes gleaming with excitement. Betty looked lovely in an emerald evening dress, but also very wrought up, and her eyes did not meet mine. Once again, a tremendous desire to protect her and get her out of this interesting but rather curious clan came over me.

"But Can was pushing his way through the throng and he took me by the elbow. 'Come and be toasted, Donald, as the only outsider,' he said, smiling. 'Here's the family punch and the family punch bowl too, something few others have ever seen.'

"At a long table in a side alcove, stood an extraordinary bowl, a huge stone thing, with things like runes scratched around the rim. Behind it, in his 'greens,' but bareheaded, stood the little withered huntsman, McColl. It was he who filled a squat goblet, but as he did so and handed it to me, his eyes narrowed, and he hissed something inaudible over the noise behind me. It looked like 'watch'! I was alerted, and when he handed me the curious stone cup, I knew why. There was a folded slip of paper under the cup's base, which I took as I accepted the cup itself. Can, who stood just behind me, could have seen nothing.

"I'm rather good at conjuring tricks, and it was only a moment before I was able to pass my hand over my forehead and read the note at the same instant. The message was simple, the reverse of Alice's on the bottle.

"'Drink nothing.' That was all, but it was enough to send a thrill through my veins. I was sure of two things. McColl had never acted this way on his own hook. Betty, to whom the man was obviously devoted, was behind this. And something else too.

"I was in danger. I knew it. All the vague uneasiness I had suppressed during my stay, the peculiar stares, the cryptic remarks, the attitude of the local minister we had seen, all coalesced into something ominous, inchoate but menacing. These cold, good-looking people were not my friends, if indeed they were anyone's. I looked casually about while pretending to sip from my cup. Between me and each one of the three exits, a group of men were standing, chatting and laughing, accepting drinks from trays passed by servants, but *never moving*. As my brain began to race overtime, I actually forgot my warning and sipped from my drink. It was like nothing I have had before or since, being pungent, sweet and at the same time almost perfumed, but not in an unpleasant way. I managed to avoid swallowing all but a tiny bit, but even that was wildly exhilarating, making my face flush and the blood roar through my veins. It must have showed, I expect, for I saw my host half smile and others too, as they raised their cups to me. The sudden wave of anger I felt did not show, but now I really commenced to think.

"I turned and presented my almost full goblet to McColl again as if asking for more. Without batting an eye, he *emptied* it behind the cover of the great bowl, as if cleaning out some dregs, and refilled it. The little chap had brains. As again I raised the cup to my lips, I saw the smile appear on Can's face once more. My back was to McColl, blocking him off from the rest of the room, and this time his rasping, penetrating whisper was easy to hear.

"'After dinner, be paralyzed, stiff, frozen in your seat. You can't move, understand?'

"I made a circle with my fingers behind my back to show I understood, and then walked out into the room to meet Canler who was coming toward me.

"'Don't stand at the punch all evening, Donald,' he said, laughing. 'You have a long night ahead, you know.' But now his laughter was mocking, and his lean, handsome face was suddenly a mask of cruelty and malign purpose. As we moved about together, the faces and manners of the others, both men and women, even the children and servants, were the same, and I wondered that I had ever thought of any of them as friendly. Under their laughter and banter, I felt contempt, yes, and hatred and triumph too, mixed with a streak of pure nastiness. I was the stalled ox, flattered, fattened and fed, and the butchers were amused. They knew my fate, but I would not know until the door of the abattoir closed behind me. But the ox was not quite helpless yet, nor was the door quite slammed shut. I noticed Betty had gone, and when I made some comment or other, Can laughed and told me she was checking dinner preparations, as indeed any hostess might. I played my part as well as I could, and apparently well enough. McColl gave me bogus refills when we were alone, and I tried to seem excited, full of *joie de vivre*, you know. Whatever other effect was expected was seemingly reserved for after dinner.

"Eventually, about nine I should think, we went in to dinner, myself carefully shepherded between several male cousins. These folk were not leaving much to chance, whatever their purpose.

"The great dining room was a blaze of candles and gleaming silver and crystal. I was seated next to Betty at one end of the long table, and Canler took the other. Servants began to pour wine and the dinner commenced. At first, the conversation and laughter were, to outward appearances, quite normal. The shrill laughter of the young rose above the deeper tones of their elders. Indeed the sly, feral glances of the children as they watched me surreptitiously were not the least of my unpleasant impressions. Once again and far more strongly, the feeling of being in a den of some savage and predatory brutes returned to me, nor, this time, did it leave.

"At my side, Betty was the exception. Her face never looked lovelier, ivory white in the candle glow, and calm, as if whatever had troubled her earlier had gone. She did not speak much, but her eyes met mine frankly, and I felt stronger, knowing that in the woman I loved, whatever came, I had at least one ally.

"I have said that as the meal progressed, so too did the quiet. I had eaten a fairish amount, but barely tasted any of the wines from the battery of glasses at my place. As dessert was cleared off, amid almost total silence, I became aware that I had better start playing my other role, for every eye was now trained at my end of the table.

"Turning to the girl, an unmarried cousin, on my other side, my right, I spoke slowly and carefully, as one intoxicated.

"'My goodness, that punch must have been strong! I can scarcely move my hand, d'you know. Good thing we don't have to ride tonight, eh?'

"Whatever possessed me to say *that*, I can't think, but my partner stared at me and then broke into a peal of cold laughter. As she did so, choking with her own amusement, the man on her far side, who had heard me also, repeated it to his neighbors. In an instant the whole table was a-ripple with sinister delight, and I could see Can at the far end, his white teeth gleaming as he caught the joke. I revolved my head slowly and solemnly in apparent puzzlement, and the laughter grew. I could see two of the waiters laughing in a far corner. And then it ceased.

"A great bell or chime tolled somewhere, not too far off, and there was complete silence as if by magic. Suddenly I was aware of Canler, who had risen at his place and had raised his hands, as if in an invocation.

"'The hour returns,' he cried. 'The Blessed Feast is upon us, the Feast of Sam'hain. My people, hence to your duties, to your robes, to the sacred park of the *Sheade!* Go, for the hour comes and passes!'

"It was an effort to sit still while this rigmarole went on, but I remembered the earlier warnings and froze in my seat, blinking stupidly. It was as well, for four of the men servants, all large, now stood behind and beside my chair. In an instant the room was empty, save for these four, myself and my host, who now strode the length of the table to stare down at me, his eyes filled with anger and contempt. Before I could even move, he had struck me over the face with his open hand.

"'You, you English boor, would raise your eyes to the last princess of the Firbolgs, whose stock used yours as the meat and beasts of burden they are before Rome was even a village! Last year we had another one like you, and his polo-playing friends at Hicksville are still wondering where he went!' He laughed savagely and struck me again. I can tell you chaps, I learned real self-control in that moment! I never moved, but gazed up at him, my eyes blank, registering vacuous idiocy.

"'The mead of the *Dagda* keeps its power,' he said. 'Bring him along, you four, the Great Hour passes!'

"Keeping limp, I allowed myself to be lifted and carried from the room. Through the great dark house, following that false friend, its master, we went, until at last we climbed a broad stairway and emerged under the frosty October stars. Before us lay the towering, overgrown hedge, and now I learnt the secret of it. A great gate, overgrown with vines so as to be invisible when shut, had been opened, and before me lay the hidden place of the House of Waldron. This is what I saw:

"An avenue of giant oaks marched a quarter mile to a circular space where towered black tumuli of stone rose against the night sky. As I was borne toward these monoliths, the light of great fires was kindled on either side as I passed, and from them came an acrid, evil reek which caught at the throat.

Around and over them leapt my fellow dinner guests and the
servants, wearing scanty, green tunics, young and old together, their voices rising in a wild screaming chant, unintelli-
gible, but regular and rhythmic. Canler had vanished
momentarily, but now I heard his voice ahead of us. He must
have been gone longer than I thought, for when those carrying
me reached the circle of standing stones, he was standing out-
lined against the largest fire of all, which blazed, newly kindled, behind him. I saw the cause of the horrid stench, for
instead of logs, there were burning white, dry bones, a great
mountain of them. Next to him stood Betty and both of them
had their arms raised and were singing the same wild chant as
the crowd.

"I was slammed to the ground by my guards but held erect
and immovable so that I had a good chance to examine the
two heirs of the finest families in the modern United States.

"Both were barefoot and wore thigh-length green tunics,
his apparently wool, but hers silk or something like it, with
her ivory body gleaming through it almost as if she were
nude. Upon her breasts and belly were marks of gold, like
some strange, uncouth writing, clearly visible through the
gauzy fabric. Her black hair was unbound and poured in
waves over her shoulders. Canler wore upon his neck a massive circular torque, also of gold, and on his head a coronal
wreath, apparently of autumn leaves. In Betty's right hand
was held a golden sceptre, looking like a crude attempt to
form a giant stalk of wheat. She waved this in rhythm as they
sang.

"Behind me the harsh chorus rose in volume, and I knew
the rest of the pack, for that's how I thought of them, were
closing in. The noise rose to a crescendo, then ceased. Only
the crackling of the great, reeking fire before me broke the
night's silence. Then Canler raised his hands again in invocation and began a solitary chant in the strange harsh tongue
they had used before. It was brief, and when it came to an
end, he spoke again, but in English this time.

"'I call to Sam'hain, Lord of the Dead. I, Tuathal, the
Seventieth and One Hundred, of the line of Miled, of the race
of Goedel Glas, last true *Ardr'i* of ancient Erin, Supreme Vate
of the *Corcu Firbolgi*. Oh, Lord from Beyond, who has preserved my ancient people and nourished them in plenty, the
bonefires greet the night, your sacrifice awaits you!' He fell
silent and Betty stepped forward. In her left hand she now

held a small golden sickle, and very gently she pricked my forehead three times, in three places. Then she stepped back and called out in her clear voice.

"'I, Morrigu, Priestess and Bride of the Dead, have prepared the sacrifice. Let the Horses of the Night attend!'

"D'you know, all I could think of was some homework I'd done on your American Constitution, in which Washington advocated separation of church and state? The human mind is a wonderful thing! Quite apart from the reek of the burning bones, though, I knew a stench of a spiritual sort. I was seeing something old here, old beyond knowledge, old and evil. I felt that somehow not only my body was in danger.

"Now I heard the stamp of hooves. From one side, snorting and rearing, a great black horse was led into the firelight by a half-naked boy, who had trouble with the beast, but still held him. The horse was saddled and bridled, and I knew him at once. It was Bran, the hunter I'd been lent all week. Behind him, I could hear other horses moving.

"'Mount him,' shouted Canler, or Tuathal, as he now called himself. With that, I was lifted into the saddle, where I swayed, looking as doped and helpless as I could. Before I could move, my hands were caught and lashed together at the wrists with leather cords, then in turn tied loosely to the head-stall, giving them a play of some inches but no more. The reins were looped up and knotted. Then my host stepped up to my knee and glared up at me.

"'The Wild Hunt rides, Slave and Outlander! You are the quarry, and two choices lie before you, both being death. For if we find you, death by these,' and he waved a curious spear, short and broad in the blade.

"'But *others* hunt on this night, and maybe when Those Who Hunt Without Riders come upon your track, you will wish for these points instead. Save for children's toys, the outside world has long forgotten their Christian Feast of All Hallows. How long then have they forgotten that which inspired it, ten thousand and more years before the Nazarene was slain? Now—ride and show good sport to the Wild Hunt!'

"With that someone gave Bran a frightful cut over the croup, and he bounded off into the dark, almost unseating me in the process. I had no idea where we were going, except that it was not back down the avenue of trees and the blazing fires. But I soon saw that at least two riders were herding me away at an angle down the hill, cutting at Bran's flanks with whips when he veered from the course they had set. Twice the whips caught my legs, but the boots saved me from the worst of it.

"Eventually, we burst out into a glade near the southern spur of the mountain, and I saw that another, smaller gate had been opened in the great hedge. Through this my poor brute was flogged, but once through it, I was alone. The Big House was invisible around a curve of the hill, and no lights marked its presence.

"'Ride hard, Englishman,' called one of my herdsmen. 'Two deaths follow on your track.' With that, they turned back and I heard the gate slam. At the same time, I heard something else. Far off in the night I heard the shrill whinnying of a horse. Mingled with it and nearer was the sound of a horn, golden and clear. The horse cry was like that of no horse I have ever heard, a savage screaming noise which cut into my ear drums and raised the hackles even further on my neck. At the same time I made a new discovery.

"Some sharp thing had been poking into my left thigh ever since I was placed on the horse. Even in the starlight I now could see the reason. The haft of a heavy knife projected under my leg, apparently taped to the saddle! By stretching and bending my body, I could just free it, and once free, I cut the lead which tethered my wrists to the headstall. As I did so, I urged Bran with my knees downhill and to the right, keeping close to the trees which grew unclipt at the base of the mountain spur. I knew there was little time to waste, for the sound of galloping horses was coming through the night, far off, but drawing nearer by the instant! It might be the Twentieth Century outside the valley, but I knew it would be the last of me if that pack of green-clad maniacs ever caught up with me. The Wild Hunt was not a joke at this point!

"As I saw it, I had three secret assets. One, the knife, a sturdy piece of work with an eight-inch blade, which I now held in my teeth and tried to use to saw my wrists free. The other was the fact that I have a good eye for ground and I had ridden the length and breadth of the valley for a week. While not as familiar with the area as those who now hunted me over it like a rabbit, I was, nevertheless, not a stranger and I fancied I could find my way even at night. My third ace was Betty. What she could do, I had no idea, but I felt sure she would do something.

"The damned leather cords simply could not be cut while

Bran moved, even at a walk, and I simply was forced to stop. It only took a second's sawing, for the knife was sharp, and I was free. I was in deep shadows, and I listened intently, while I unknotted the reins.

"The sound of many horses galloping was still audible through the quiet night, but it was no nearer, indeed the reverse. It now came from off to my left and somewhat lower down the valley. I was baffled by this, but only for a moment. Canler and his jolly group wanted a good hunt. Drugged as I was supposed to be, it would never do to follow directly on my track. Instead, they were heading to cut me off from the mouth of the valley, after which they could return at leisure and hunt me down. All of this and much more passed through my mind in seconds, you know.

"My next thought was the hills. In most places the encircling wall of mountain was far too steep for a horse. But I could leave Bran behind, and most of the ground ought to be possible for an active chap on foot. By dawn I could be well out of reach of this murderous gang. As the thought crossed my mind, I urged Bran toward the nearest wall of rock. We crossed a little glade and approached the black mass of the slope, shrouded in more trees at the base, and I kept my eye peeled for trouble. But it was my mount who found it.

"He suddenly snorted and checked, stamping his feet, refusing to go a foot forward. I drew the knife from my belt, also alerted, and by a sudden awakening of a sense far older than anything merely physical. Ahead of us lay a menace of a different sort than the hunters of Waldrondale. I remembered my quondam host, threatening me that something else was hunting that night, and also the men who had driven me through the hedge called after me that *two* deaths were on my track.

"Before me, as I sat, frozen in the saddle, something moved in the shadows. It was large, but its exact shape was not easy to make out. I was conscious of a sudden feeling of intense cold, something I've experienced once or twice. I now know this to mean that one of what I'll call an Enemy from Outside, a foe of the spirit, is about. On my breast there was a feeling of heat, as if I'd been burnt by a match. It was where I wore Betty's gift. The cross, too, was warning me. Then, two dim spots of yellow phosphorescence glowed at a height even with mine. A hard sound like a hoof striking a stone echoed once.

"That was enough for Bran! With a squeal of fright which sounded more like a hare than a blood horse, he turned and bolted. If I had not freed my hands, I would have been thrown off in an instant, and as it was I had the very devil of a time staying on. He was not merely galloping, but bounding, gathering his quarters under him with each stride as if to take a jump. Only sheer terror can make a trained horse so forget himself.

"I did my best to guide him, for through the night I heard the golden questing note of a horn. The Wild Hunt was drawing the coverts. They seemed to be quite far down the valley, and fortunately Bran was running away across its upper part, in the same direction as the Big House.

"I caught a glimpse of its high, lightless gables, black against the stars as we raced over some open ground a quarter mile below it, then we were in the trees again, and I finally began to master the horse, at length bringing him to a halt. Once again, as he stood, sweating and shivering, I used my ears. At first there was nothing, then, well down the vale to my right front came the sound of the questing horn. I was still undiscovered.

"You may wonder, as I did at first, why I had heard no hounds. Surely it would have been easy for this crew to keep some bloodhounds, or perhaps to smear my clothes or horse with anise and use their own thoroughbred foxhounds. I can only say I don't know. At a guess, and mind you, it's only a guess, there were other powers or elements loose that night which might have come into conflict with a normal hunting pack. But that's only a guess. Still, there were none, and though I was not yet sure of it, I was fairly certain, for even the clumsiest hound should have been in full cry on my track by now. The Wild Hunt then, seemed to hunt at sight. Again the clear horn note sounded. They were working up the slope in my direction.

"As quietly as possible, I urged Bran, who now seemed less nervous, along the edge of the little wood we were in and down the slope. We had galloped from the hill spur on the right, as one faced away from the house, perhaps two thirds of the way across the valley, which at this point was some two miles wide. Having tried one slope and met—well, whatever I *had* met, I would now try the other.

"My first check came at a wooden fence. I didn't dare jump such a thing at night, as much for the noise as for the danger of landing badly. But I knew there were gates. I dismounted and led Bran along until I found one, and then shut it carefully behind me. I had not heard the mellow horn note for some time and the click of the gate latch sounded loud in the frosty night. Through the large field beyond I rode at a walk. There was another gate at the far side, and beyond that another dark clump of wood. It was on the edge of this that I suddenly drew rein.

"Ahead of me, something was moving down in the wood. I heard some bulky creature shoulder into a tree trunk and the sound of heavy steps. It might have been another horse from the sound. But at the same moment, up the slope behind me, not too far away came the thud of hooves on the ground, many hooves. The horn note blew, not more than two fields away, by the sound. I had no choice and urged Bran forward into the trees. He did not seem too nervous, and went willingly enough. The sound ahead of me ceased, and then, as I came to a tiny glade in the heart of the little wood, a dim shape moved ahead of me. I checked my horse and watched, knife ready.

"'Donald?' came a soft voice. Into the little clearing rode Betty, mounted on a horse as dark as mine, her great black mare. I urged Bran foward to meet her.

"I've been looking for you for over an hour,' she whispered, her breath warm on my cheek. I was holding her as tightly as I could, our mounts standing side by side, amiably sniffing one another. 'Let me go. Donald, or we'll both be dead. There's a chance, a thin one if we go the way I've thought out.' She freed herself and sat looking gravely at me. My night vision was good and I could see she had changed into a simple tunic of what looked like doeskin and soft, supple, knee boots. Socketed in a sling was one of the short, heavy spears, and I reached over and took it. The very heft of it made me feel better. The glimmering blade seemed red even in the dim tree light, and I suddenly realized the point was bronze. These extraordinary people went in for authenticity in their madness.

"'Come on, quickly,' she said and wheeled her horse back the way she had come. I followed obediently and we soon came to the edge of the forest. Before us lay another gentle slope, but immediately beneath us was a sunken dirt road, which meandered away to the left and downhill, between high banks, their tops planted with hedge. We slid down a sandy slope, and our horses began to walk along the road, raising hardly any dust. Betty rode a little ahead, her white face visible as she turned to look back at intervals. Far away a cock crowed, but I looked at my watch and it was no more than 3 AM. I could hear nothing uphill and the horn was silent. We rode through a little brook, only inches deep. Then, as we had just passed out of hearing of the gurgle of the stream, a new sound broke the quiet night.

"It was somewhere between a whinny and a screech, and I remembered the noise I had heard as the two riders had driven me through the hedge. If one could imagine some unthinkable horse creature screaming at the scent of blood, eagerly, hungrily seeking its prey, well, that's the best I can do to describe it.

"'Come on, we have to ride for our lives!' Betty hissed. 'They have let the Dead Horse loose. No one can stand against that.'

"With that, she urged her mount into a gallop and I followed suit. We tore along the narrow track between the banks, taking each twist at a dead run, always angling somehow downhill and toward the valley mouth.

"Then, the road suddenly went up and I could see both ahead and back. Betty reined up and we surveyed our position. At the same time the horn blew again, but short, sharp notes this time, and a wild screaming broke out. Three fields back up the long gentle slope, the Wild Hunt had seen our black outlines on the little swell where we paused. I could see what looked like a dozen horsemen coming full tilt and the faint glitter of the spears. But Betty was looking back down along our recent track.

"From out of the dark hollows came a vast grunting noise, like that of a colossal pig sighting the swill pail. It was very close.

"Betty struck her horse over the withers and we started to gallop again in real earnest. Bran was tired, but he went on nobly, and her big mare simply flew. The Hunt was silent now, but I knew they were still coming. And I knew too, that something else was coming. Almost, I felt a cold breath on my back, and I held the spear tightly against Bran's neck.

"Suddenly, Betty checked, so sharply that her horse reared, and I saw why as I drew abreast. We had come very close to the mouth of the valley and a line of fires lay before us, not three hundred yards away on the open flat. Around them moved many figures, and even at this distance I could see that a cordon was established, yet from the hats and glint of weapons, I knew they were not the Waldrons or their retainers. Apparently the outside world was coming to Waldrondale, at least this far. We had a fighting chance.

"Between us and the nearest fire, a black horseman rode at us, and he was only a hundred feet off. The raised spear and the bare head told me that at least one of the valley maniacs had been posted to intercept me, in the unlikely event of my getting clear of the rest.

"I spurred the tired hunter forward and gripped the short spear near its butt end, as one might a club. The move was quite instinctive. I knew nothing of spears but I was out to kill and I was a six-goal polo player. The chap ahead, some Waldron cousin, I expect, needed practice which he never got. He tried to stab at me, overhand, but before our horses could touch, I had swerved and lashed out as i would on a long drive at the ball. The heavy bronze edge took him between the eyes and, really, that was that. His horse went off to one side alone.

"Wheeling Bran, I started to call to Betty to come on, and as I did, I saw that which she had so feared had tracked us down.

"I am still not entirely certain of what I saw, for I have the feeling that part of it was seen with what Asiatics refer to as the Third Eye, the inner 'eye' of the soul.

"The girl sat, a dozen yards from me, facing something which was advancing slowly upon us. They had called it the Dead Horse, and its shifting outlines indeed at moments seemed to resemble a monstrous horse, yet at others, some enormous and distorted pig. The click of what seemed hooves was clear in the night. It had an unclean color, an oily shifting, dappling of grey and black. Its pupilless eyes, which glowed with a cold, yellow light, were fixed upon Betty, who waited as if turned to stone. Whatever it was, it had no place in the normal scheme of things. A terrible cold again came upon me and time seemed frozen. I could neither move nor speak, and Bran trembled, unmoving between my legs.

"My love broke the spell. Or it broke her. God knows what it must have cost her to defy such a thing, with the breeding she had, and the training. At any rate, she did so. She shouted something I couldn't catch, apparently in that pre-Gaelic gibberish they used and flung out her arm as if striking at the monster. At the same instant it sprang, straight at her. There was a confused sound or sounds, a sort of *spinning*, as if an incredible top were whirling in my ear, and at the same instant my vision blurred.

"When I recovered myself, I was leaning over Bran's neck, clutching him to stay on, and Betty lay silent in the pale dust of the road. A yard away lay her horse, also unmoving. And there was nothing else.

"As I dismounted and picked her up, I knew she was dead, and that the mare had died in the same instant. She had held the thing from Outside away, kept it off me, but it had claimed a price. The high priestess of the cult had committed treason and sacrilege, and her life was the price. Her face was smiling and peaceful, the ivory skin unblemished, as if she were asleep.

"I looked up at the sound of more galloping hoofbeats. The Wild Hunt, all utterly silent, were rounding a bend below me and not more than a hundred yards away. I lifted Betty easily, for she was very light, and mounted. Bran still had a little go left, and we headed for the fires, passing the dead man lying sprawled in his kilt or whatever on the road. I was not really afraid any longer, and as I drew up at the fire where a dozen gun barrels pointed at me, it all felt unreal. I looked back and there was an empty hill, a barren road. The riders of Waldrondale had vanished, having turned back apparently at the sight of the fires and the armed men.

"'He's not one! Look at the gal! That crowd must have been hunting *him*. Call the parson over or Father Skelton, one of you. Keep a sharp lookout, now!'

"It was a babble of voices and like a dream. I sat staring stupidly down and holding Betty against my heart until I realized a man was pulling at my knees and talking insistently. I began to wake up then, and looking down, recognized the minister I had seen when Betty and I had ridden past a day earlier. I could not remember his name, but I handed Betty down to him when he asked for her, as obediently as a child.

"'She saved me, you know,' I said brightly. 'She left them and saved me. But the Dead Horse got her. That was too much, you see. She was only a girl, couldn't fight *that*. You do see, don't you?' This is what I am told I said at any rate, by Mr. Andrews, the Episcopal minister of the little Church of the Redeemer. But that was later. I remember none of it.

"When I woke, in the spare bed of the rectory the next day, I found Andrews sitting silently by my bed. He was looking at my bare breast on which lay the little Celtic cross. He was fully dressed, tired and unshaven, and he reeked of smoke, like a dead fireplace, still full of coals and wood ash.

"Before I could speak, he asked me a question. 'Did she, the young lady, I mean, give you that?'

"'Yes,' I said. 'It may have saved me. Where is she?'

"'Downstairs, in my late wife's room. I intend to give her a Christian burial, which I never would have dreamt possible. But she has been saved to us.'

"'What about the rest of that crowd?' I said. 'Can nothing be done?'

"He looked calmly at me. 'They are all dead. We have been planning this for three years. That Hell spawn have ruled this part of the country since the Revolution. Governors, senators, generals, all Waldrons, and everyone else afraid to say a word.' He paused. 'Even the young children were not saved. Old and young are in that place behind the house. We took nothing from the house but your clothes. The hill folk, who live to the West, came down on them just before dawn, as we came up. Now there is a great burning, the house, the groves, everything. The State Police are coming, but several bridges are out for some reason, and they will be quite a time.' He fell silent, but his eyes gleamed. The prophets of Israel were not all dead.

"Well, I said a last good-bye to Betty and went back to Washington. The police never knew I was there at all, and I was apparently as shocked as anyone to hear that a large gang of bootleggers and Chicago gangsters had wiped out one of America's first families and got away clean without being captured. It was a six day sensation and then everyone forgot it. I still have the little cross, you know, and that's all."

We sat silent, all brooding over this extraordinary tale. Like all of the brigadier's tales, it seemed too fantastic for human credibility, and yet—and *yet!*

The younger member who had spoken earlier could not resist one question, despite Ffellowes' prestory ban on such things.

"Well, sir," he now said. "Why, this means that one of the oldest royal families in the world, far more ancient than King Arthur's, say, is only recently extinct. That's absolutely amazing!"

Ffellowes looked up from his concentration on the rug and

seemed to fix his gaze on the young man. To my amazement he did not become irritated. In fact, he was quite calm and controlled.

"Possibly, possibly," he said, "but of course they all appear to have been Irish or at least Celts of some sort or other. I have always considered their reliability open to considerable doubt."

Narrow Valley

by

R. A. Lafferty

When all is said, the difficulty of practicing magic may have been overestimated. Here's a casual, part-time, rather slapdash sorcerer who nevertheless manages to achieve some impressive results, in spite of the fact that he uses the wrong word, and throws jack-oak leaves on the fire instead of elder....

R. A. Lafferty started writing in 1960, and throughout the subsequent twenty-six years he has turned out a seemingly endless string of mad and marvelous tall tales, including some of the freshest and funniest short stories ever published: "Thus We Frustrate Charlemagne," "Slow Tuesday Night," "Hog Belly Honey," "Continued on Next Rock," "Land of the Great Horses," and many more. In 1973 he won the Hugo Award for his story "Eurema's Dam." His books include Past Master, The Devil is Dead, The Reefs of Earth, Okla Hannali, The Fall of Rome, Arrive at Easterwine, The Flame Is Green, *and the collections* Nine Hundred Grandmothers, Strange Doings, Does Anyone Else Have Something Further to Add?, Golden Gate and Other Stories, *and* Ringing the Changes. *His most recent books are the novels* Annals of Klepsis *and* Half a Sky.

* * *

IN THE YEAR 1893, LAND ALLOTMENTS IN SEVERALTY WERE made to the remaining eight hundred and twenty-one Pawnee

91

Indians. Each would receive one hundred and sixty acres of land and no more, and thereafter the Pawnees would be expected to pay taxes on their land, the same as the White-Eyes did.

"Kitkehahke!" Clarence Big-Saddle cussed. "You can't kick a dog around proper on a hundred and sixty acres. And I sure am not hear before about this pay taxes on land."

Clarence Big-Saddle selected a nice green valley for his allotment. It was one of the half dozen plots he had always regarded as his own. He sodded around the summer lodge that he had there and made it an all-season home. But he sure didn't intend to pay taxes on it.

So he burned leaves and bark and made a speech:

"That my valley be always wide and flourish and green and such stuff as that!" he orated in Pawnee chant style. "But that it be narrow if an intruder come."

He didn't have any balsam bark to burn. He threw on a little cedar bark instead. He didn't have any elder leaves. He used a handful of jack-oak leaves. And he forgot the word. How you going to work it if you forget the word?

"Petahauerat!" he howled out with the confidence he hoped would fool the fates.

"That's the same long of a word," he said in a low aside to himself. But he was doubtful. "What am I, a White Man, a burr-tailed jack, a new kind of nut to think it will work?" he asked. "I have to laugh at me. Oh well, we see."

He threw the rest of the bark and the leaves on the fire, and he hollered the wrong word out again.

And he was answered by a dazzling sheet of summer lightning.

"Skidi!" Clarence Big-Saddle swore. "It worked. I didn't think it would."

Clarence Big-Saddle lived on his land for many years, and he paid no taxes. Intruders were unable to come down to his place. The land was sold for taxes three times, but nobody ever came down to claim it. Finally it was carried as open land on the books. Homesteaders filed on it several times, but none of them fulfilled the qualification of living on the land.

Half a century went by. Clarence Big-Saddle called his son.

"I've had it, boy," he said. "I think I'll just go in the house and die."

"Okay, Dad," the son Clarence Little-Saddle said. "I'm

going in to town to shoot a few games of pool with the boys. I'll bury you when I get back this evening."

So the son Clarence Little-Saddle inherited. He also lived on the land for many years without paying taxes.

There was a disturbance in the courthouse one day. The place seemed to be invaded in force, but actually there were but one man, one woman, and five children. "I'm Robert Rampart," said the man, "and we want the Land Office."

"I'm Robert Rampart Junior," said a nine-year-old gangler, "and we want it pretty blamed quick."

"I don't think we have anything like that," the girl at the desk said. "Isn't that something they had a long time ago?"

"Ignorance is no excuse for inefficiency, my dear," said Mary Mabel Rampart, an eight-year-old who could easily pass for eight and a half. "After I make my report, I wonder who will be sitting at your desk tomorrow."

"You people are either in the wrong state or the wrong century," the girl said.

"The Homestead Act still obtains," Robert Rampart insisted. "There is one tract of land carried as open in this county. I want to file on it."

Cecilia Rampart answered the knowing wink of a beefy man at the distant desk. "Hi," she breathed as she slinked over. "I'm Cecilia Rampart, but my stage name is Cecilia San Juan. Do you think that seven is too young to play ingenue roles?"

"Not for you," the man said. "Tell your folks to come over here."

"Do you know where the Land Office is?" Cecilia asked.

"Sure. It's the fourth left-hand drawer of my desk. The smallest office we got in the whole courthouse. We don't use it much anymore."

The Ramparts gathered around. The beefy man started to make out the papers.

"This is the land description," Robert Rampart began. "Why, you've got it down already. How did you know?"

"I've been around here a long time," the man answered.

They did the paper work, and Robert Rampart filed on the land.

"You won't be able to come onto the land itself, though," the man said.

"Why won't I?" Rampart demanded. "Isn't the land description accurate?"

"Oh, I suppose so. But nobody's ever been able to get to the land. It's become a sort of joke."

"Well, I intend to get to the bottom of that joke," Rampart insisted. "I will occupy the land, or I will find out why not."

"I'm not sure about that," the beefy man said. "The last man to file on the land, about a dozen years ago, wasn't able to occupy the land. And he wasn't able to say why he couldn't. It's kind of interesting, the look on their faces after they try it for a day or two, and then give it up."

The Ramparts left the courthouse, loaded into their camper, and drove out to find their land. They stopped at the house of a cattle and wheat farmer named Charley Dublin. Dublin met them with a grin which indicated he had been tipped off.

"Come along if you want to, folks," Dublin said. "The easiest way is on foot across my short pasture here. Your land's directly west of mine."

They walked the short distance to the border.

"My name is Tom Rampart, Mr. Dublin." Six-year old Tom made conversation as they walked. "But my name is really Ramires, and not Tom. I am the issue of an indiscretion of my mother in Mexico several years ago."

"The boy is a kidder, Mr. Dublin," said the mother Nina Rampart, defending herself. "I have never been in Mexico, but sometimes I have the urge to disappear there forever."

"Ah yes, Mrs. Rampart. And what is the name of the youngest boy here?" Charley Dublin asked.

"Fatty," said Fatty Rampart.

"But surely that is not your given name?"

"Audifax," said five-year-old Fatty.

"Ah well, Audifax, Fatty, are you a kidder too?"

"He's getting better at it, Mr. Dublin," Mary Mabel said. "He was a twin till last week. His twin was named Skinny. Mama left Skinny unguarded while she was out tippling, and there were wild dogs in the neighborhood. When Mama got back, do you know what was left of Skinny? Two neck bones and an ankle bone. That was all."

"Poor Skinny," Dublin said. "Well, Rampart, this is the fence and the end of my land. Yours is just beyond."

"Is that ditch on my land?" Rampart asked.

"That ditch *is* your land."

"I'll have it filled in. It's a dangerous deep cut even if it is narrow. And the other fence looks like a good one, and I sure have a pretty plot of land beyond it."

"No, Rampart, the land beyond the second fence belongs to Holister Hyde," Charley Dublin said. "That second fence is the *end* of your land."

"Now, just wait a minute, Dublin! There's something wrong here. My land is one hundred and sixty acres, which would be a half mile on a side. Where's my half-mile width?"

"Between the two fences."

"That's not eight feet."

"Doesn't look like it does it, Rampart? Tell you what— there's plenty of throwing-sized rocks around. Try to throw one across it."

"I'm not interested in any such boys' games," Rampart exploded. "I want my land."

But the Rampart children *were* interested in such games. They got with it with those throwing rocks. They winged them out over the little gully. The stones acted funny. They hung in the air, as it were, and diminished in size. And they were small as pebbles when they dropped down, down into the gully. None of them could throw a stone across that ditch, and they were throwing kids.

"You and your neighbor have conspired to fence open land for your own use," Rampart charged.

"No such thing, Rampart," Dublin said cheerfully. "My land checks perfectly. So does Hyde's. So does yours, if we knew how to check it. It's like one of those trick topological drawings. It really is half a mile from here to there, but the eye gets lost somewhere. It's your land. Crawl through the fence and figure it out."

Rampart crawled through the fence, and drew himself up to jump the gully. Then he hesitated. He got a glimpse of just how deep the gully was. Still, it wasn't five feet across.

There was a heavy fence post on the ground, designed for use as a corner post. Rampart up-ended it with some effort. Then he shoved it to fall and bridge the gully. But it fell short, and it shouldn't have. An eight-foot post should bridge a five-foot gully.

The post fell into the gully, and rolled and rolled and rolled. It spun as though it were rolling outward, but it made no progress except vertically. The post came to rest on a ledge of the gully, so close that Rampart could almost reach out and touch it, but it now appeared no bigger than a match stick.

"There is something wrong with that fence post, or with the world, or with my eyes," Robert Rampart said. "I wish I felt dizzy so I could blame it on that."

"There's a little game that I sometimes play with my neighbor Hyde when we're both out," Dublin said. "I've a heavy rifle and I train it on the middle of his forehead as he stands on the other side of the ditch apparently eight feet away. I fire it off then (I'm a good shot), and I hear it whine across. I'd kill him dead if things were as they seem. But Hyde's in no danger. The shot always bangs into that little scuff of rocks and boulders about thirty feet below him. I can see it kick up the rock dust there, and the sound of it rattling into those little boulders comes back to me in about two and a half seconds."

A bull-bat (poor people call it the night-hawk) raveled around in the air and zoomed out over the narrow ditch, but it did not reach the other side. The bird dropped below ground level and could be seen against the background of the other side of the ditch. It grew smaller and hazier as though at a distance of three or four hundred yards. The white bars on its wings could no longer be discerned; then the bird itself could hardly be discerned; but it was far short of the other side of the five-foot ditch.

A man identified by Charley Dublin as the neighbor Hollister Hyde had appeared on the other side of the little ditch. Hyde grinned and waved. He shouted something, but could not be heard.

"Hyde and I both read mouths," Dublin said, "so we can talk across the ditch easy enough. Which kid wants to play chicken? Hyde will barrel a good-sized rock right at your head, and if you duck or flinch you're chicken."

"Me! Me!" Audifax Rampart challenged. And Hyde, a big man with big hands, did barrel a fearsome jagged rock right at the head of the boy. It would have killed him if things had been as they appeared. But the rock diminished to nothing and disappeared into the ditch. Here was a phenomenon: things seemed real-sized on either side of the ditch, but they diminished coming out over the ditch either way.

"Everybody game for it?" Robert Rampart Junior asked.

"We won't get down there by standing here," Mary Mabel said.

"Nothing wenchered, nothing gained," said Cecilia. "I got that from an ad for a sex comedy."

Then the five Rampart kids ran down into the gully. Ran *down* is right. It was almost as if they ran down the vertical face of a cliff. They couldn't do that. The gully was no wider than the stride of the biggest kids. But the gully diminished those children, it ate them alive. They were doll-sized. They were acorn-size. They were running for minute after minute across a ditch that was only five feet across. They were going, deeper in it, and getting smaller. Robert Rampart was roaring his alarm, and his wife Nina was screaming. Then she stopped. "What am I carrying on so loud about?" she asked herself. "It looks like fun. I'll do it too."

She plunged into the gully, diminished in size as the children had done, and ran at a pace to carry her a hundred yards away across a gully only five feet wide.

That Robert Rampart stirred things up for a while then. He got the sheriff there, and the highway patrolmen. A ditch had stolen his wife and five children, he said, and maybe had killed them. And if anybody laughs, there may be another killing. He got the colonel of the State National Guard there, and a command post set up. He got a couple of airplane pilots. Robert Rampart had one quality: when he hollered, people came.

He got the newsmen out from T-Town, and the eminent scientists, Dr. Velikof Vonk, Arpad Arkabaranan, and Willy McGilly. That bunch turns up every time you get on a good one. They just happen to be in that part of the country where something interesting is going on.

They attacked the thing from all four sides and the top, and by inner and outer theory. If a thing measures half a mile on each side, and the sides are straight, there just has to be something in the middle of it. They took pictures from the air, and they turned out perfect. They proved that Robert Rampart had the prettiest hundred and sixty acres in the country, the larger part of it being a lush green valley, and all of it being half a mile on a side, and situated just where it should be. They took ground-level photos then, and it showed a beautiful half-mile stretch of land between the boundaries of Charley Dublin and Hollister Hyde. But a man isn't a camera. None of them could see that beautiful spread with the eyes in their heads. Where was it?

Down in the valley itself everything was normal. It really was half a mile wide and no more than eighty feet deep with a very gentle slope. It was warm and sweet, and beautiful with grass and grain.

Nina and the kids loved it, and they rushed to see what

squatter had built that little house on their land. A house, or a shack. It had never known paint, but paint would have spoiled it. It was built of split timbers dressed near smooth with ax and draw knife, chinked with white clay, and sodded up to about half its height. And there was an interloper standing by the little lodge.

"Here, here what are you doing on our land?" Robert Rampart Junior demanded of the man. "Now you just shamble off again wherever you came from. I'll bet you're a thief too, and those cattle are stolen."

"Only the black-and-white calf," Clarence Little-Saddle said. "I couldn't resist him, but the rest are mine. I guess I'll just stay around and see that you folks get settled all right."

"Is there any wild Indians around here?" Fatty Rampart asked.

"No, not really. I go on a bender about every three months and get a little bit wild, and there's a couple Osage boys from Gray Horse that get noisy sometimes, but that's about all," Clarence Little-Saddle said.

"You certainly don't intend to palm yourself off on us as an Indian," Mary Mabel challenged. "You'll find us a little too knowledgeable for that."

"Little girl, you might as well tell this cow there's no room for her to be a cow since you're so knowledgeable. She thinks she's a short-horn cow named Sweet Virginia. I think I'm a Pawnee Indian named Clarence. Break it to us real gentle if we're not."

"If you're an Indian where's your war bonnet? There's not a feather on you anywhere."

"How you be sure? There's a story that we got feathers instead of hair on—Aw, I can't tell a joke like that to a little girl! How come you're not wearing the Iron Crown of Lombardy if you're a white girl? How you expect me to believe you're a little white girl and your folks came from Europe a couple hundred years ago if you don't wear it? There are six hundred tribes, and only one of them, the Oglala Sioux, had the war bonnet, and only the big leaders, never more than two or three of them alive at one time, wore it."

"Your analogy is a little strained," Mary Mabel said. "Those Indians we saw in Florida and the ones at Atlantic City had war bonnets, and they couldn't very well have been the kind of Sioux you said. And just last night on the TV in the motel, those Massachusetts Indians put a war bonnet on the

President and called him the Great White Father. You mean to tell me that they were all phonies? Hey, who's laughing at who here?"

"If you're an Indian where's your bow and arrow?" Tom Rampart interrupted. "I bet you can't even shoot one."

"You're sure right there," Clarence admitted. "I never shot one of those things but once in my life. They used to have an archery range in Boulder Park over in T-Town, and you could rent the things and shoot at targets tied to hay bales. Hey, I barked my whole forearm and nearly broke my thumb when the bow-string thwacked home. I couldn't shoot that thing at all. I don't see how anybody ever could shoot one of them."

"Okay, kids," Nina Rampart called to her brood. "Let's start pitching this junk out of the shack so we can move in. Is there any way we can drive our camper down here, Clarence?"

"Sure, there's a pretty good dirt road, and it's a lot wider than it looks from the top. I got a bunch of green bills in an old night charley in the shack. Let me get them, and then I'll clear out for a while. The shack hasn't been cleaned out for seven years, since the last time this happened. I'll show you the road to the top, and you can bring your car down it."

"Hey, you old Indian, you lied!" Cecilia Rampart shrilled from the doorway of the shack. "You *do* have a war bonnet. Can I have it?"

"I didn't mean to lie, I forgot about that thing," Clarence Little-Saddle said. "My son Clarence Bare-Back sent that to me from Japan for a joke a long time ago. Sure, you can have it."

All the children were assigned tasks carrying the junk out of the shack and setting fire to it. Nina Rampart and Clarence Little-Saddle ambled up to the rim of the valley by the vehicle road that was wider than it looked from the top.

"Nina, you're back! I thought you were gone forever," Robert Rampart jittered at seeing her again. "What—where are the children?"

"Why, I left them down in the valley, Robert. That is, ah, down in that little ditch right there. Now you've got me worried again. I'm going to drive the camper down there and unload it. You'd better go on down and lend a hand too, Robert, and quit talking to all these funny-looking men here."

And Nina went back to Dublin's place for the camper.

"It would be easier for a camel to go through the eye of a

needle than for that intrepid woman to drive a car down into that narrow ditch," the eminent scientist Dr. Velikof Vonk said.

"You know how that camel does it?" Clarence Little-Saddle offered, appearing of a sudden from nowhere. "He just closes one of his own eyes and flops back his ears and plunges right through. A camel is mighty narrow when he closes one eye and flops back his ears. Besides, they use a big-eyed needle in that act."

"Where'd this crazy man come from?" Robert Rampart demanded, jumping three feet in the air. "Things are coming out of the ground now. I want my land! I want my children! I want my wife! Whoops, here she comes driving it. Nina, you can't drive a loaded camper into a little ditch like that! You'll be killed or collapsed!"

Nina Rampart drove the loaded camper into the little ditch at a pretty good rate of speed. The best of belief is that she just closed one eye and plunged right through. The car diminished and dropped, and it was smaller than a toy car. But it raised a pretty good cloud of dust as it bumped for several hundred yards across a ditch that was only five feet wide.

"Rampart, it's akin to the phenomenon known as looming, only in reverse," the eminent scientist Arpad Arkabaranan explained as he attempted to throw a rock across the narrow ditch. The rock rose very high in the air, seemed to hang at its apex while it diminished to the size of a grain of sand, and then fell into the ditch not six inches of the way across. There isn't anybody going to throw across a half-mile valley even if it looks five feet. "Look at a rising moon sometimes, Rampart. It appears very large, as though covering a great sector of the horizon, but it only covers one-half of a degree. It is hard to believe that you could set seven hundred and twenty of such large moons side by side around the horizon, or that it would take one hundred and eighty of the big things to reach from the horizon to a point overhead. It is also hard to believe that your valley is five hundred times as wide as it appears, but it has been surveyed, and it is."

"I want my land, I want my children. I want my wife," Robert chanted dully. "Damn, I let her get away again."

"I tell you, Rampy," Clarence Little-Saddle squared on him, "a man that lets his wife get away twice doesn't deserve to keep her. I give you till nightfall; then you forfeit. I've taken a liking to the brood. One of us is going to be down there tonight."

After a while a bunch of them were off in that little tavern on the road between Cleveland and Osage. It was only half a mile away. If the valley had run in the other direction, it would have been only six feet away.

"It is a psychic nexus in the form of an elongated dome," said the eminent scientist Dr. Velikof Vonk. "It is maintained subconsciously by the concatenation of at least two minds, the stronger of them belonging to a man dead for many years. It has apparently existed for a little less than a hundred years, and in another hundred years it will be considerably weakened. We know from our checking out folk tales of Europe as well as Cambodia that these ensorceled areas seldom survive for more than two hundred and fifty years. The person who first set such a thing in being will usually lose interest in it, and in all worldly things, within a hundred years of his own death. This is a simple thanato-psychic limitation. As a short-term device, the thing has been used several times as a military tactic.

"This psychic nexus, as long as it maintains itself, causes group illusion, but it is really a simple thing. It doesn't fool birds or rabbits or cattle or cameras, only humans. There is nothing meteorological about it. It is strictly psychological. I'm glad I was able to give a scientific explanation to it or it would have worried me."

"It is a continental fault coinciding with a noospheric fault," said the eminent scientist Arpad Arkabaranan. "The valley really is half a mile wide, and at the same time it really is only five feet wide. If we measured correctly, we would get these dual measurements. Of course it is meteorological! Everything including dreams is meteorological. It is the animals and cameras which are fooled, as lacking a true dimension; it is only humans who see the true duality. The phenomenon should be common along the whole continental fault where the earth gains or loses half a mile that has to go somewhere. Likely it extends through the whole sweep of the Cross Timbers. Many of those trees appear twice, and many do not appear at all. A man in the proper state of mind could farm that land or raise cattle on it, but it doesn't really exist. There is a clear parallel in the Luftspiegelungthal sector in the Black Forest of Germany which exists, or does not exist, ac-

cording to the circumstances and to the attitude of the beholder. Then we have the case of Mad Mountain in Morgan
County, Tennessee, which isn't there all the time, and also the
Little Lobo Mirage south of Presidio, Texas, from which
twenty thousand barrels of water were pumped in one two-
and-a-half-year period before the mirage reverted to mirage
status. I'm glad I was able to give a scientific explanation to
this or it would have worried me."

"I just don't understand how he worked it," said the eminent scientist Willy McGilly. "Cedar bark, jack-oak leaves,
and the word 'Petahauerat.' The thing's impossible! When I
was a boy and we wanted to make a hideout, we used bark
from the skunk-spruce tree, the leaves of a box-elder, and the
word was 'Boadicea.' All three elements are wrong here. I
cannot find a scientific explanation for it, and it does worry
me."

They went back to Narrow Valley. Robert Rampart was
still chanting dully: "I want my land. I want my children. I
want my wife."

Nina Rampart came chugging up out of the narrow ditch in
the camper and emerged through that little gate a few yards
down the fence row.

"Supper's ready and we're tired of waiting for you, Robert," she said. "A fine homesteader you are! Afraid to come
onto your own land! Come along now; I'm tired of waiting for
you."

"I want my land! I want my children! I want my wife!"
Robert Rampart still chanted. "Oh, there you are, Nina. You
stay here this time. I want my land! I want my children! I
want an answer to this terrible thing."

"It is time we decided who wears the pants in this family,"
Nina said stoutly. She picked up her husband, slung him over
her shoulder, carried him to the camper and dumped him in,
slammed (as it seemed) a dozen doors at once, and drove
furiously down into the Narrow Valley, which already seemed
wider.

Why, that place was getting normaler and normaler by the
minute! Pretty soon it looked almost as wide as it was supposed to be. The psychic nexus in the form of an elongated
dome had collapsed. The continental fault that coincided with
the noospheric fault had faced facts and decided to conform.
The Ramparts were in effective possession of their homestead,
and Narrow Valley was as normal as any place anywhere.

"I have lost my land," Clarence Little-Saddle moaned. "It was the land of my father Clarence Big-Saddle, and I meant it to be the land of my son Clarence Bare-Back. It looked so narrow that people did not notice how wide it was, and people did not try to enter it. Now I have lost it."

Clarence Little-Saddle and the eminent scientist Willy McGilly were standing on the edge of Narrow Valley, which now appeared its true half-mile extent. The moon was just rising, so big that it filled a third of the sky. Who would have imagined that it would take a hundred and eight of such monstrous things to reach from the horizon to a point overhead, and yet you could sight it with sighters and figure it so.

"I had a little bear-cat by the tail and I let go," Clarence groaned. "I had a fine valley for free, and I have lost it. I am like that hard-luck guy in the funny-paper or Job in the Bible, Destitution is my lot."

Willy McGilly looked around furtively. They were alone on the edge of the half-mile-wide valley.

"Let's give it a booster shot," Willy McGilly said.

Hey, those two got with it! They started a snapping fire and began to throw the stuff onto it. Bark from the dog-elm tree —how do you know it won't work?

It *was* working! Already the other side of the valley seemed a hundred yards closer, and there were alarmed noises coming up from the people in the valley.

Leaves from a black locust tree—and the valley narrowed still more! There was, moreover, terrified screaming of both children and big people from the depths of Narrow Valley, and the happy voice of Mary Mabel Rampart chanting "Earthquake! Earthquake!"

"That my valley be always wide and flourish and such stuff, and green with money and grass!" Clarence Little-Saddle orated in Pawnee chant style, "but that it be narrow if intruders come, smash them like bugs!"

People, that valley wasn't over a hundred feet wide now, and the screaming of the people in the bottom of the valley had been joined by the hysterical coughing of the camper car starting up.

Willy and Clarence threw everything that was left on the fire. But the word? The word? Who remembers the word?

"Corsicanatexas!" Clarence Little-Saddle howled out with confidence he hoped would fool the fates.

He was answered not only by a dazzling sheet of summer

lightning, but also by thunder and raindrops.

"Chahiksi!" Clarence Little-Saddle swore. "It worked. I didn't think it would. It will be all right now. I can use the rain."

The valley was again a ditch only five feet wide.

The camper car struggled out of Narrow Valley through the little gate. It was smashed flat as a sheet of paper, and the screaming kids and people in it had only one dimension.

"It's closing in! It's closing in!" Robert Rampart roared, and he was no thicker than if he had been made out of cardboard.

"We're smashed like bugs," the Rampart boys intoned. "We're thin like paper."

"Mort, ruine, ecrasement!" spoke-acted Cecilia Rampart like the great tragedienne she was.

"Help! Help!" Nina Rampart croaked, but she winked at Willy and Clarence as they rolled by. "This homesteading jag always did leave me a little flat."

"Don't throw those paper dolls away. They might be the Ramparts," Mary Mabel called.

The camper car coughed again and bumped along on level ground. This couldn't last forever. The car was widening out as it bumped along.

"Did we overdo it, Clarence?" Willy McGilly asked. "What did one flat-lander say to the other?"

"Dimension of us never got around," Clarence said. "No, I don't think we overdid it, Willy. That car must be eighteen inches wide already, and they all ought to be normal by the time they reach the main road. The next time I do it, I think I'll throw wood-grain plastic on the fire to see who's kidding who."

Sleep Well of Nights

by

Avram Davidson

An inexplicably underrated writer, Avram Davidson is one of the most eloquent and individual voices in modern SF and fantasy. During his thirty-year career, he has produced a long sequence of erudite and entertaining novels—including Masters of the Maze, Rogue Dragon, Peregrine: Primus, Rork!, The Enemy of My Enemy, Clash of Star Kings, *and the justly renowned* The Phoenix and the Mirror—*and also firmly established himself as one of the finest short-story writers of our times. Davidson's stylish, witty, and elegant stories have been collected in* The Best of Avram Davidson, Or All the Seas with Oysters, Strange Seas and Shores, The Redward Edward Papers, *and the World Fantasy Award–winning* The Enquiries of Doctor Esterhazy. *Davidson had also won a Hugo and an Edgar Award. His most recent books are* Collected Fantasies, *a collection, and, as editor, the anthology* Magic For Sale. *Upcoming is a sequel to* The Phoenix and the Mirror, *entitled* Vergil in Averno.*

In recent years, Davidson had been producing some of his best work ever in a series of stories (as yet uncollected, alas) detailing the strange adventures of Jack Limekiller. The Limekiller stories are set against the lushly evocative background of "British Hidalgo," Davidson's vividly realized, richly imagined version of one of those tiny, eccentric Central American nations that exist in near-total isolation on the edge of the busy twentieth-century world . . . a place somehow at once

*flamboyant and languorous, where strange things can—and
do—happen, and magic is never very far away.*

*In "Sleep Well of Nights," probably the best of the Lime-
killer stories, he shows us that death need not necessarily
deter the strong of will, and that even something as simple as
a good night's sleep must somehow be earned. . . .*

* * *

"ARE THOSE LAHVLY YOUNG LADIES WITH YOU, THEN?" THE
Red Cross teacher asked.

Limekiller evaded the question by asking another, a tech-
nique at least as old as the Book of Genesis. "Which way did
they go?" he asked.

But it did not work this time. "Bless me if I saw them gow
anywhere! They were both just standing on the corner as I
went by."

Limekiller gave up not so easily. "Ah, but which corner?"

A blank look. "Why . . . *this* corner."

This corner was the corner of Grand Arawack and Queen
Alexandra Streets in the Town of St. Michael of the Mountains, capital of Mountains District in the Colony of British
Hidalgo. Fretwork galleries dripping with potted plants and
water provided shade as well as free shower baths. These were
the first and second streets laid out and had originally been
deer trails; Government desiring District Commissioner Bar-
tholomew "Bajan" Bainbridge to supply the lanes with names,
he had, with that fund of imagination which helped build the
Empire, called them First and Second Streets: it was rather a
while before anyone in Government next looked at a map and
then decided that numbered streets should run parallel to each
other and not, as in this instance, across each other. And as
the Grand Arawack Hotel was by that time built and as Alexandra (long-suffering consort of Fat Edward) was by that time
Queen, thus they were renamed and thus remained.

"St. Michael's" or "Mountains" Town, one might take
one's pick, had once been a caravan city in miniature. The
average person does not think of caravan cities being located
in the Americas, and, for that matter, neither does anyone
else. Nevertheless, trains of a hundred and fifty mules laden
with flour and rum and textiles and tinned foods coming in,
and with chicle and chicle and chicle going out, had been
common enough to keep anyone from bothering to count them
each time the caravans went by. The labor of a thousand men

and a thousand mules had been year by year spat out of the mouths of millions of North Americans in the form of chewing gum.

So far as Limekiller knew, Kipling had never been in either Hidalgo, but he might have thought to have been if one ignored biographical fact and judged only by his lines.

> Daylong, the diamond weather,
> The high, unaltered blue—
> The smell of goats and incense
> And the mule-bell tinkling through.

Across from the hotel stood the abattoir and the market building. The very early morning noises were a series of bellows, bleats, squeals, and screams which drowned out cockcrow and were succeeded by the rattle and clatter of vulture claws on the red-painted corrugated iron roofs. Then the high voices of women cheapening meat. But all of these had now died away. Beef and pork and mutton (sheep or goat) could be smelled stewing and roasting now and then as the mild currents of the air alternated the odors of food with those of woodsmoke. He even thought he detected incense; there was the church spire nearby.

But there were certainly no young ladies around, lovely or otherwise.

There had been no very lengthy mule trains for a very long time.

There had been no flotillas of tunnel boats at the Town Wharf for a long time, either, their inboard motors drawn as high-up in "tunnels" within the vessels as possible to avoid the sand and gravel and boulders which made river navigation so difficult on the upper reaches of the Ningoon. No mule trains, no tunnel boats, no very great quantities of chicle, and everything which proceeded to and from the colonial capital of King Town and St. Michael's going now by truck along the rutted and eroded Frontier Road. No Bay boat could ever, in any event, have gotten higher up the river than the narrows called Bomwell's Boom; and the *Sacarissa* (Jno. Limekiller, owner and Master and, usually—save for Skippy the Cat—sole crew) was at the moment Hired Out.

She had been chartered to a pair of twosomes from a Lake Winnipeg boat club, down to enjoy the long hours of sunshine. Jack had been glad enough of the money but the charter had left him at somewhat of a loss: *leisure* to him had for so long meant to haul his boat up and clean and caulk and paint her: all things in which boatmen delight. Leisure without the boat was something new. Something else.

To pay his currently few debts had not taken long. He had considered getting Porter Portugal to sew a new suit of sails, but old P.P. was not a slot machine; you could not put the price into P.P.'s gifted hands and expect, after a reasonable (or even an unreasonable) period of time, for the sails to pop out. If Port-Port were stone sober he would not work and if dead drunk he *could* not work. The matter of keeping him supplied with just the right flow of old Hidalgo dark rum to, so to speak, oil the mechanism, was a nice task indeed: many boat owners, National, North American, or otherwise, had started the process with intentions wise and good: but Old Port was a crazy-foxy old Port and all too often had drunk them under the table, downed palm and needle, and vanished with the advance-to-buy-supplies into any one of the several stews which flourished on his trade.("A debt of honor, me b'y," he would murmur, red-eyed sober, long days later. "Doesn't you gots to worry. I just hahs a touch ahv de ague, but soon as I bet-tah. . . .")

So that was *one* reason why John L. Limekiller had eventually decided to forget the new suit of sails for the time being.

Filial piety had prompted him to send a nice long letter home, but a tendency towards muscle spasms caused by holding a pen had prompted him to reduce the n.l.l. to a picture post card. He saw the women at the post office, one long and one short.

"What's a letter *cost*, to St. Michael's?" the Long was asking. "We *could*, *te*lephone for a reservation," the Short suggested. Jack was about to tell them unsolicited, how fat the chance was of anybody in St. Michael's having a telephone *or* anything which could be reserved, let alone of understanding what a reservation was—then he took more than a peripheral look at them.

The Long had red hair and was wearing dungarees and a man's shirt. Not common, ordinary, just-plain-red: *cop*per-red. Worn in loops. Her shirt was blue with a faint white stripe. Her eyes were "the color of the sherry which the guests leave in the glass." Or don't, as the case may be. The Short could have had green hair in braids and been covered to her toes in a yashmak for all Jack noticed.

At that moment the clerk had asked him, "What fah you?" —a local, entirely acceptable usage, even commonplace, being higher than "What you want?" and lower than "You does want something?"—and by the time he had sorted out even to his own satisfaction that he wanted postage for a card to Canada and not, say, to send an armadillo by registered mail to Mauritius, and had completed the transaction in haste and looked around, trying to appear casual, they were gone. Clean gone. Where they had been was a bright-eyed little figure in the cleanest rags imaginable, with a sprinkling of white hairs on its brown, nutcracker jaws.

Who even at once declared, "'And now abideth faith, hope, and charity, these three, and the greatest of these is charity,' you would not deny the Apostle Paul, would you, then, sir?"

"Eh? Uh...no," said Limekiller. Pretense cast aside, craning and gaping all around: *nothing*.

"Anything to offer me?" demanded the wee and ancient, with logic inexorable.

So there had gone a dime. And then and there had come the decision to visit St. Michael of the Mountains, said to be so different, so picturesque, hard upon the frontier of "Spanish" Hidalgo, and where (he reminded himself) he had after all *never been*.

Sometimes being lonely it bothers the way a tiny pebble in the shoe bothers: enough to stop and *do* something. But if one is very lonely indeed, then it becomes an accustomed thing. Only now did Limekiller bethink himself how lonely he had been. The boat and the Bay and the beastie-cat had been company enough. The average National boatman had a home ashore. The two men and two women even now aboard the *Sacarissa* in jammed-together proximity—they had each other. (And even now, considering another definition of the verb *to have* and the possible permutations of two males and two females made him wiggle like a small boy who has to *go*—). There was always, to be sure, the Dating Game, played to its logical conclusion, for a fee, at any one of the several hotels in King Town, hard upon the sea. But as for any of the ladies accompanying him anywhere on his boat...

"*Whattt?* You tink I ahm crazy? *Nut*ting like *dot!*"

Boats were gritty with sand to fill the boggy yards and

lanes, smelly with fish. Boats had *no* connotations of romance.

Such brief affairs did something for his prostate gland ("Changing the acid," the English called it), but nothing whatsoever, he now realized, for his loneliness. Nor did conversation in the boatmen's bars, lately largely on the theme of, "New tax law, rum go up to 15¢ a glass, man!"

And so here he was, fifty miles from home, if King Town was "home"—and if the *Sacarissa* was home . . . well, who knew? St. Michael of the Mountains still had some faint air of its days as a port-and-caravan city, but that air was now faint indeed. Here the Bayfolk (Black, White, Colored, and Clear) were outnumbered by Turks and 'Paniar's, and there were hardly any Arawack at all.(There seldom were, anywhere out of the sound and smell of the sea.) There were a lot of old wooden houses, two stories tall, with carved grillwork, lots of flowering plants, lots of hills: perhaps looking up and down the hilly lanes gave the prospects more quaintness and interest, perhaps even beauty, than they might have had, were they as level as the lanes of King Town, Port Cockatoo, Port Caroline, or Lime Walk. And, too, there were the mountains all about, all beautiful. And there was the Ningoon River, flowing round about the town in easy coils, all lovely, too: its name, though Indian in origin, allowing for any number of easy, Spanish-based puns:

"Suppose you drink de wat-tah here, say, you *cahn-not* stay away!"

"*En otros paises, señor, otros lugares, dicen mañana. Pero, por acá, señor, se dice ningún!*"

And so forth.

Limekiller had perambulated every street and lane, had circumambulated town. Like every town and the one sole city in British Hidalgo, St. Michael's had no suburbs. It was clustered thickly, with scarcely even a vacant lot, and where it stopped being the Town of St. Michael of the Mountains, it stopped. Abruptly. *Here* was the Incorporation; *there* were the farms and fields; about a mile outside the circumambient bush began again.

He could scarcely beat every tree, knock on every door. He was too shy to buttonhole people, ask if they had seen a knockout redhead. So he walked. And he looked. And he listened. But he heard no women's voices, speaking with accent from north of the northern border of Mexico. Finally he grew a little less circumspect.

To Mr. John Paul Peterson, Prop., the Emerging Nation Bar and Club:

"Say . . . are there any other North Americans here in town?"

As though Limekiller had pressed a button. Mr. Peterson, who until that moment had been only amiable, scowled an infuriated scowl and burst out, "What the Hell they want come *here* for? You think them people *crazy?* They got richest countries in the world, which they take good care *keep* it that way; so why the Hell they want come *here?* Leave me ask you one question. Turn your head all round. You see them table? You see them booth? How many people you see sitting and drinking at them table and them booth?"

Limekiller's eyes scanned the room. The question was rhetorical. He sighed. "No one," he said, turning back to his glass.

Mr. Peterson smote the bar with his hand. "Exactly!" he cried. *"No one!* You not bloody damn fool, boy. You have good eye in you head. *Why* you see no one? Because no one can afford come here and drink, is why you see no one. People can scarce afford *eat!* Flour cost nine cent! Rice cost fif-*teen* cent! Lard cost thirty-*four* cent! Brown sugar at nine cent and white sugar at eleven! D.D. milk twen-ty-one cent! And yet the tax going *up*, boy! The tax going *up!*"

A line stirred in Limekiller's mind. "Yes—and, 'Pretty soon *rum* going to cost fifteen cents,'" he repeated. Then had the feeling that (in that case) something was wrong with the change from his two-shillings piece. And with his having made this quotation.

"What you mean, *'fifteen cent'?*" demanded Mr. Peterson, in a towering rage. Literally, in a towering rage, he had been slumped on his backless chair behind the bar, now stood up to his full height . . . and it was a height, too. *Whattt?* Fif-*teen*-cent?' You think this some damn dirty liquor booth off in the bush, boy? You think you got *swampy*," referring to backwoods distilled goods, "in you glass? What *'fifteen cent?'* No such *thing*. You got pure Governor Morgan in you glass, boy, never cost less than one shilling, and pretty soon going to be thirty cent, boy: thir-ty-*cent!* And for what? For the Queen can powder her nose with the extra five penny, boy?" Et cetera. Et cetera.

Edwin Rodney Augustine Bickerstaff, Royal British Hidalgo Police (sitting bolt-upright in his crisp uniform beneath a half-length photograph of the Queen's Own Majesty):

"Good afternoon, sir. May I help you, sir?"

"Uh . . . yes! I was wondering . . . uh . . . do you know if there are any North Americans in town?"

Police-sergeant Bickerstaff pondered the question, rubbed his long chin. "Any *North* Americans, you say, sir?"

Limekiller felt obliged to define his terms. "Any Canadians or people from the States."

Police-sergeant Bickerstaff nodded vigorously. "Ah, now I understand you, sir. Well. That would be a matter for the Immigration Officer, wouldn't you agree, sir?"

"Why . . . I suppose. Is *he* in right now?" This was turning out to be more complex than he had imagined.

"Yes, sir. He *is* in. *Un*officially speaking, he is in. *I* am the police officer charged with the duties of Immigration Officer in the Mountains District, sir,"

"Well—"

"Three to four, sir."

Limekiller blinked. Begged his pardon. The police-sergeant smiled slightly. "Every evening from three to four, sir, pleased to execute the duties of Immigration Officer, sir. At the present time," he glanced at the enormous clock on the wall, with just a touch of implied proof, "I am carrying out my official duties as Customs Officer. *Have you anything to declare?*"

And, *So much for that suggestion,* Limekiller thought, a feeling of having only slightly been saved from having made a fool of himself tangible in the form of something warmer than sunshine round about his face and neck.

The middle-aged woman at the Yohan Yahanoglu General Mdse. Establishment store sold him a small bar of Fry's chocolate, miraculously unmelted. Jack asked, "Is there another hotel in town, besides the Grand?"

A touch of something like hauteur came over the still-handsome face of *Sra.* "Yohanoglu. Best you ahsk wan of the men," she said. And, which one of the men? *"Any men,"* said she.

So. Out into the sun-baked street went lonely Limekiller. Not that lonely at the moment, though, to want to find where the local hookers hung out. Gone too far to turn back. And, besides, turn back to *what?*

The next place along the street which was open was the El

Dorado Club and Dancing (its sign, slightly uneven, said).

Someone large and burly thumped in just before he did, leaned heavily on the bar, "How much, *rum?*" he demanded.

The barkeep, a 'Paniard, maybe only one-quarter Indian (most of the Spanish-speaking Hidalgans were more than that), gave a slight yawn at this sudden access of trade. "Still only wan dime," he said. "Lahng as dees borrel lahst. When necessitate we broach nudder borrel, under new tox lah, *iay! Pobrecito! Going be fifteen cent!*"

"*¡En el nombre del* Queen!*" proclaimed the other new customer, making the sign of the cross, then gesturing for a glass to be splashed.

Limekiller made the same gesture.

"What you vex weed de Queen, *varón?*" the barkeeper asked, pouring two fingers of "clear" into each glass. "You got new road, meb-be ah beet bum-py, but *new;* you got new wing on hospital, you got new generator for give ahl night, electricity: *Whatt?* You teenk you hahv ahl dees, ahn not pay ah new tox? no sotch teeng!"

"*No me hace falta,* 'ahl dees,'" said the other customer. "*Resido en el* bush, where no hahv not-ting like dot."

The barkeep yawned again. "*Reside en el* bush? Why you not live like old-time people? Dey not dreenk rum. Dey not smoke cigarette. Dey not use lahmp-*ile.* Ahn dey not pay toxes, not dem, no."

"Me no want leev like dot. *Whatt?* You cahl dot 'leev'?" He emptied his glass with a swallow, dismissed any suggestion that Walden Pond and its tax-free amenities might be his for the taking, turned to Limekiller his vast Afro-Indian face. "Filiberto Marín, señor, is de mahn to answer stranger question. Becahs God *love* de stranger, señor, ahn Filiberto Marín love *God.* Everybody know Filiberto Marín, ahn if anyone want know where he is, I am de mahn." Limekiller, having indeed questions, or at any rate, A Question, Limekiller opened his mouth.

But he was not to get off so easily. There followed a long, *long* conversation, or monologue, on various subjects, of which Filiberto Marín was the principal one. Filiberto Marín had once worked one entire year in the bush and was only home for a total of thirty-two days, a matter (he assured Jack) of public record. Filiberto Marín was born just over the line in Spanish Hidalgo, his mother being a Spanish Woman and his father a British Subject By Birth. Had helped build a canal, or perhaps it was *The* Canal. Had been in Spanish Hidalgo at the time of the next-to-last major revolution, during which he and his sweetheart had absquatulated for a more peaceful realm. Married *in church!* Filiberto Marín and his wife had produced one half a battalion for the British Queen! "Fifteen children—and *puros varones!* Ahl son, señor! So fahst we have children! Sixty-two-year-old, and work more tasks one day dan any young man! An I now desires to explain we hunting and fishing to you, becahs you stranger here, so you ignorance not you fahlt, señor."

Limekiller kept his eyes in the mirror, which reflected the passing scene through the open door, and ordered two more low-tax rums; while Filiberto Marín told him how to cast nets with weights to catch mullet in the lagoons, they not having the right mouths to take hooks; how to catch turtle, the *tortuga blanca* and the striped turtle (the latter not being popular locally because it was striped)—

"What difference does the stripe mean, Don Filiberto?"

"*¡Seguro!* Exoctly!!" beamed Don Filiberto, and, never pausing, swept on: how to use raw beef skin to bait lobsters ("Dey cahl him *lobster,* but is really de *langusta,* child of de crayfish."), how to tell the difference in color between saltwater and freshwater ones, how to fix a dory, how to catch tortuga "by dive for him—"

"—You want to know how to cotch croc-o-*dile* by dive for him? Who can tell you? Filiberto Marín will answer dose question," he said, and he shook Limekiller's hand with an awesome shake.

There seemed nothing boastful about the man. Evidently Filiberto Marín *did* know all these things and, out of a pure and disinterested desire to help a stranger, wanted merely to put his extensive knowledge at Jack's disposal. . . .

Of this much, Limekiller was quite clear the next day. He was far from clear, though, as to how he came to get there in the bush where many cheerful dark people were grilling strips of *barbacoa* over glowing coals—mutton it was, with a taste reminiscent of the best old-fashioned bacon, plus . . . well, *mutton.* He did not remember having later gone to bed, let alone to sleep. Nor know the man who came and stood at the foot of his bed, an elderly man with a sharp face which might have been cut out of ivory . . . this man had a long stick . . . a spear? . . . no . . .

Then Limekiller was on his feet. In the moon-speckled

darkness he could see very little, certainly not another man. There was no lamp lit. He could hear someone breathing regularly, peacefully, nearby. He could hear water purling, not far off. After a moment, now able to see well enough, he made his way out of the cabin and along a wooden walkway. There was the Ningoon River below. A fine spray of rain began to fall; the river in the moonlight moved like watered silk. *What* had the man said to him? Something about showing him . . . showing him *what?* He could not recall at all. There had really been nothing menacing about the old man.

But neither had there been anything reassuring.

Jack made his way back into the cabin. The walls let the moonlight in, and the fine rain, too. But not so much of either as to prevent his falling asleep again.

Next day, passion—well, that was not exactly the right word—but what was? Infatuation? Scarcely even that. An uncommon interest in, plus a great desire for, an uncommonly comely young woman who also spoke his own language with familiar, or familiar enough accents—oh, well—Hell!— whatever the *word* was, whatever his own state of mind had been, next morning had given way to something more like common sense. Common sense, then, told him that if the young woman (vaguely he amended this to the young women) had intended to come to St. Michael of the Mountains to stay at a hotel . . . or wherever it was, which they thought might take a reservation . . . had even considered *writing* for the reservation, well, they had not intended to come here at once. In other words: enthusiasm (*that* was the word! . . . damn it . . .) enthusiasm had made him arrive early.

So, since he was already *there,* he might as well relax and enjoy it.

—He was already *where?*

Filiberto Marín plunged his hands into the river and was noisily splashing water onto his soapy face. Jack paused in the act of doing the same thing for himself, waited till his host had become a trifle less audible—*how* the man could snort!— "Don Fili, what is the name of this place?"

Don Fili beamed at him, reached for the towel. "These place?" He waved his broad hand to include the broad river and the broad clearing, with its scattered fields and cabins. "These place, Jock, *se llame* Pahrot Bend. You like reside here? Tell me, just. I build you house." He buried his face in his towel. Jack had no doubt that the man meant exactly what he said, gave another look around to see what was being so openhandedly—and openheartedly—offered him; this time he looked across to the other bank. Great boles of trees: Immense! Immense! The eye grew lost and dizzy gazing upward toward the lofty, distant crowns. Suddenly a flock of parrots, yellowheads, flew shrieking round and round; then vanished.

Was it some kind of an omen? *Any* kind of an omen? To live here would not be to live just anywhere. He thought of the piss-soaked bogs which made up too large a part of the slums of King Town, wondered how anybody could live *there* when anybody could live *here*. But *here* was simply too far from the sea, and it was to live upon the sunwarm sea that he had come to this small country, so far from his vast own one. Still . . . might not be such a bad idea . . . well, not to *live* here all the time. But . . . a smaller version of the not-very-large cabins of the hamlet . . . a sort of country home . . . as it were . . . ha-ha . . . well, why not? Something to think about . . . anyway.

"Crahs de river, be one nice spot for build you *cabanita*," said Don Filiberto, reading his mind.

"Mmm . . . what might it cost?" he could not help asking, even though knowing whatever answer he might receive would almost certainly not in the long run prove accurate.

"Cahst?" Filiberto Marín, pulling his shirt over his huge dark torso, considered. Cost, clearly, was not a matter of daily concern. Calculations, muttering from his mouth, living and audible thoughts, struggling to take form: "Cahst . . . May-be, ooohhh, say-*be* torty dollar?"

"Forty dollars?"

Don Filiberto started to shake his head, reconsidered. "I suppose may-*be*. Not take lahng. May-be one hahf day, collect wild cane for make wall, bay *leaf* for make *techo*, roof. An may-be 'nother hahf day for put everything togedder. Cahst? So: Twenty dollar. Torty dollar. An ten dollar *rum!* Most eeem-por-tont!" He laughed. Rum! The oil which lubricates the neighbors' labors. A house-raising bee, Hidalgo style.

"And the land itself? The cost of the land?"

But Don Fili was done with figures. "What 'cahst of de lond?' Lond not cahst nah-ting. Lond belahng to Pike Estate."

A bell went ding-a-ling in Limekiller's ear. The Pike Estate. The great Pike Estate Case was the Jarndyce vs. Jarndyce of British Hidalgo. Half the lawyers in the colony lived off it.

Was there a valid will? Where there valid heirs? Had old Pike
died intestate? *¿Quién sabe?* There were barroom barristers
would talk your ears off about the First Codicil and the Second Codicil and the Alleged Statement of Intention and the
Holograph Document and all the rest of it. Limekiller had
heard enough about the Pike Estate Case. He followed after
Don Fili up the bank. Ah, but—

"Well, maybe nobody would bother me *now* if I had a
cabin built there. But what about when the estate is finally
settled?"

Marín waved an arm, as impatiently as his vast good nature
would allow. "By dot time, *hijo mio,* what you care? You no
hahv Squatter Rights by den? Meb-*be* you *dead* by den!"

Mrs. Don Filiberto, part American Indian, part East Indian, and altogether Amiable and Fat, was already fanning the
coals on the raised fire-hearth for breakfast.

Nobody was boating back to town then, although earnest
guarantees were offered that "by and by somebody" would *be*
boating back, for sure. Limekiller knew such sureties. He
knew, too, that he might certainly stay on with the Marín
family at Parrot Bend until then—and longer—and be fully
welcome. But he had after all come to "Mountains" for something else besides rural hospitality along the Ningoon River (a
former Commissioner of Historical Sites and Antiquities had
argued that the name came from an Indian word, or words,
meaning Region of Bounteous Plenty; local Indians asserted
that a more literal and less literary translation would be Big
Wet). The fine rain of the night before began to fall again as
he walked along, and soon he was soaked.

It did not bother him. By the time he got back into town
the sun would have come out and dried him. Nobody bothered
with oilskins or mackintoshes on the Bay of Hidalgo, nor did
he intend to worry about his lack of them here in the Mountains of Saint Michael Archangel and Prince of Israel.

Along the road (to give it its courtesy title) he saw a beautiful flurry of white birds—were they indeed cattle egrets? living in symbiosis, or commensality, with the cattle? was one,
indeed, heavy with egg, "blown over from Africa"? Whatever
their name or origin, they did follow the kine around, heads
bobbing as they, presumably, ate the insects the heavy cloven
hooves stirred up. But what did the *cattle* get out of it? Company?

The rain stopped, sure enough.

It was a beautiful river, with clear water, green and bending banks. He wondered how high the highest flood waters came. A "top gallon flood," they called that. Was there a hint of an old tradition that the highest floods would come as high as the topgallant sails of a ship? Maybe.

The rain began again. Oh, well.

An oilcloth serving as door of a tiny cabin was hauled aside and an old woman appeared and gazed anxiously at Jack. "Oh, sah, why you wahk around in dis eager rain?" she cried at him. "Best you come in, *bide*, till eet *stop!*"

He laughed. "It doesn't seem all that eager to me, Grandy," he said, "but thank you anyway."

In a little while it had stopped. *See?*

Further on, a small girl under a tree called, "Oh, see what beauty harse, meester!"

Limekiller looked. Several horses were coming from a stable and down the path to the river; they were indeed beautiful, and several men were discussing a sad story of how the malfeasance of a jockey (evidently not present) had lost first place in a recent race for one of them to the famous Tigre Rojo, the Red Tiger, of which even Limekiller, not a racing buff, had heard.

"Bloody b'y just raggedy-ahss about wid him, an so Rojo win by just a nose. Son of a beach!" said one of the men, evidently the trainer of *the* beauty horse, a big bay.

"—otherwise he beat any harse in British Hidalgo!"

"Oh, yes! Oh, yes, Mr. Ruy!—dot he would!"

Ruy, his dark face enflamed by the memory of the loss, grew darker as he watched, cried, "Goddammit, oh Laard Jesus Christ, b'y! Lead him by de *head* till he *in* de wahter, *den* lead him by rope! When you goin to learn?—an watch out for boulder!—you know what one bloody fool mon want me to do? Want me to *run* harse dis marnin—not even just canter, he want *run* him!—No, *no,* b'y, just let him swim about be de best ting for him—

"Dis one harse no common harse—dis one harse foal by *Garobo,* from Mr. Pike *stud!* Just let him swim about, I say!"

The boy in the water continued, perhaps wisely, to say nothing, but another man now said, "Oh, yes. An blow aht de cold aht of he's head, too."

Mr. Ruy grunted, then, surveying the larger scene and the graceful sweep of it, he said, gesturing, "I cotch plenty fish in dis river—catfish, twenty-pound tarpon, too. I got nylon *line,* but three week now, becahs of race, I have no time for cotch fish." And his face, which had gradually smoothed, now grew rough and fierce again. "Bloody dom fool jockey b'y purely raggeddy-*ahss* around wid harse!" he cried. The other men sighed, shook their heads. Jack left them to their sorrow.

Here the river rolled through rolling pasture lands, green, with trees, some living and draped with vines, some dead and gaunt but still beautiful. The river passed a paddock of Brahma cattle like statues of weathered grey stone, beautiful as the trees they took the shade beneath, cattle with ears like leaf-shaped spearheads, with wattles and humps. Then came an even lovelier sight: black cattle in a green field with snow-white birds close by among them. Fat hogs, Barbados sheep, water meadows, sweet soft air.

He could see the higher roofs on the hills of the town, but the road seemed to go nowhere near there. Then along came a man who, despite his clearly having no nylon line, had—equally clearly—ample time to fish, carried his catch on a stick. "De toewn, sir? Straight acrahs de savannah, sir," he gestured, "is de road to toewn." And, giving his own interpretation to the text, *I will not let thee go unless thou bless me,* detained Limekiller with blessings of unsolicited information, mostly dealing with the former grandeur of St. Michael's Town, and concluding, "Yes, sir, in dose days hahv t'ree dahnce *hahll.* Twen-ty bar and club! Torkish Cat'edral w'open every day, sah—*every day!*—ahn . . ." he groped for further evidences of the glorious days of the past, "ahn ah fot fowl, sah, cahst two, t'ree shilling!"

Sic transit gloria mundi.

The room at the hotel was large and bare, and contained a dresser with a clouded mirror, a chair, and a bed with a broad mattress covered in red "brocade"; the sheet, however, would not encompass it. This was standard: the sheet never *would,* except in the highest of high class hotels. And as one went down the scale of classes and the size of the beds diminished so, proportionately, did the sheets: they were *always* too narrow and too short. Curious, the way this was always so. (In the famous, or infamous, Hotel Pelican in King Town, sheets were issued on application only, at an extra charge, for the beds were largely pro forma. The British soldiers of the Right Royal Regiment, who constituted the chief patrons, preferred to ignore the bed and used the *wall,* would you believe it, for their erotic revels. If that was quite the right word.)

There was a large mahogany wardrobe, called a "press" in the best Dickensian tradition, but there were no hangers in it. There was a large bathroom off the hall but no towels and no soap, and the urinal was definitely out of order, for it was tied up with brown paper and string and looked like a twelve-pound turkey ready for the oven.

But all these shortcomings were made up for by one thing which the Grand Hotel Arawack *did* have: out on the second-story verandah was a wide wooden-slatted swing of antique and heroic mold, the kind one used to see only at Auntie Mary's, deep in the interior of Prince Edward Island or other islands in time.—Did the Hiltons have wide wooden swings on their verandahs? Did the Hiltons have verandahs, for that matter?

Limekiller took his seat with rare pleasure: it was not every damned day that he could enjoy a nostalgia trip whilst at the same time rejoicing in an actual physical trip which was, really, giving him as much pleasure. For a moment he stayed immobile. (Surely, Great-uncle Leicester was just barely out of sight, reading the Charlottetown newspaper, and damning the Dirty Grits?) Then he gave his long legs a push and was off.

Up! and the mountains displayed their slopes and foothills. *Down!* and the flowery lanes of town came into sight again. And, at the end of the lanes was the open square where stood the flagpole with the Union Jack and the National Ensign flapping in the scented breeze . . . and, also, in sight, and well in sight (Limekiller had chosen well) was the concrete bench in front of which the bus from King Town had to disembogue its passengers. If they came by bus, and come by bus they must (he reasoned), being certainly tourists and not likely to try hitching. Also, the cost of a taxi for fifty miles was out of the reach of anyone but a land speculator. No, by *bus*, and there was where the bus would stop.

"Let me help you with your bags," he heard himself saying, ready to slip shillings into the hands of any boys brash enough to make the same offer.

There was only one fly in the ointment of his pleasure.

Swing as he would and as long as he would, no bus came.

"Bus? *Bus*, sir? *No*, sir. Bus ahlready come orlier today. Goin bock in evening. Come ahgain tomorrow."

With just a taste of bitterness, Limekiller said, *"Mañana."*

"¡Ah, Vd, si puede hablar en español, señor, Sí,-señor. Mañana viene el bus, otra vez. —Con el favor de Dios." An the creek don't rise, thought Limekiller.

Suddenly he was hungry. There was a restaurant in plain sight, with a bill of fare five feet tall painted on its outer wall: such menus were only there for, so to speak, authenticity. To prove that the place was indeed a restaurant. And not a cinema. Certainly no one would ever be able to order and obtain anything which was *not* painted on them.—Besides, the place was closed.

"Be open tonight, sir," said a passerby, observing him observing.

Jack grunted. "Think they'll have that tonight?" he asked, pointing at random to *Rost Muttons* and to *Beef Stakes*.

An emphatic shake of the head. *"No*-sir. Rice and beans."

Somewhere nearby someone was cooking something besides rice and beans. The passerby, noticing the stranger's blunt and sunburned nose twitch, with truly Christian kindness said, "But Tía Sani be open now."

"Tía Sani?"

"Yes-sir. Miss Sanita. Aunt Sue. Directly down de lane."

Tía Sani had no sign, no giant menu. However, Tía Sani was *open*.

Outside, the famous Swift Sunset of the Tropics dallied and dallied. There was no sense of urgency in Hidalgo, be it British or Spanish. There was the throb of the light-plant generator, getting ready for the night. Watchman, what of the night?—what put *that* into his mind? He swung the screen door, went in.

Miss Sani, evidently the trim grey little woman just now looking up towards him from her stove, did not have a single item of Formica or plastic in her spotless place. Auntie Mary, back in P.E.I., would have approved. She addressed him in slow, sweet Spanish. "How may I serve you, sir?"

"What may I encounter for supper, señora?"

"We have, how do they call it in inglés, meat, milled, and formed together? ah! los mitbols! And also a *caldo* of meat with macaroni and verdants. Of what quality the meat? Of beef, señor."

Of course it was cheap, filling, tasty, and good.

One rum afterwards in a club. There might have been more than one, but just as the thought began to form (like a mitbol), someone approached the jukebox and slipped a coin into its slot—the only part of it not protected by a chickenwire cage against violent displays of dislike for whatever choice someone else might make. The management had been wise. At once, NOISE, slightly tinctured with music, filled the room. Glasses rattled on the bar. Limekiller winced, went out into the soft night.

Suddenly he felt sleepy. Whatever was there tonight would be there tomorrow night. He went back to his room, switched the sheet so that at least his head and torso would have its modest benefits, thumped the lumpy floc pillow until convinced of its being a hopeless task, and stretched out for slumber.

The ivory was tanned with age. The sharp face seemed a touch annoyed. The elder man did not exactly *threaten* Limekiller with his pole or spear, but . . . and why *should* Limekiller get up and go? Go *where?* For *what?* He had paid for his room, hadn't he? He wanted to sleep, didn't he? And he was damned well going to sleep, too. If old what's-his-name would only let him . . . off on soft green clouds he drifted. *Up* the river. *Down* the river. Old man smiled, slightly. And up the soft green mountains. Old man was frowning, now. Old man was—

"Will you get the Hell *out* of here?" Limekiller shouted, bolt upright in bed—poking him with that damned—

The old man was gone. The hotel maid was there. She was poking him with the stick of her broom. The light was on in the hall. He stared, feeling stupid and slow and confused. "Eh—?"

"You have bad *dream*," the woman said.

No doubt, he thought. Only—

"Uh, thanks. I—uh. Why did you poke me with the broomstick? And not just shake me?"

She snorted. *"Whattt? You theenk I want cotch eet?"*

He still stared. She smiled, slightly. *He* smiled, slightly, too. "Are bad dreams contagious, then?" he asked.

She nodded, solemnly, surprised that he should ask.

"Oh. Well, uh, then . . . then how about helping me have some *good* ones?" He took her, gently, by the hand. And, gently, pulled. She pulled her hand away. Gently. Walked towards the open door. Closed it.

Returned.

"Ahl right," she said. "We help each other." And she laughed.

He heard her getting up, in the cool of the early day. And he moved towards her, in body and speech. And fell at once asleep again.

Later, still early, he heard her singing as she swept the hall, with, almost certainly, that same broom. He burst out and cheerfully grabbed at her. Only, it wasn't her. "What you want?" the woman asked. Older, stouter. Looking at him in mild surprise, but with no dislike or disapproval.

"Oh, I uh, are, ah. Ha-ha. Hmm. Where is the other lady? Here last night? Works here?" He hadn't worded that as tactfully as he might have. But it didn't seem to matter.

"She? She not work here. She come help out for just one night. Becahs my sister, lahst night, she hahv wan lee pickney—gorl *beh*bee. So I go ahn she stay." The pronouns were a bit prolix, but the meaning was clear. "Now she go bock. Becahs truck fah go Macaw Falls di *leave*, señor." And, as she looked at the play of expression on his face, the woman burst into hearty, good-willed laughter. And bounced down the hall, still chuckling, vigorously plying her besom.

Oh, *well*.

And they *had* been *good* dreams, too.

Tía Sani was open. Breakfast: two fried eggs, buttered toast of thick-sliced home-baked bread, beans (mashed), tea with tinned milk, orange juice. Cost: $1.00, National Currency—say, 60 cents, 65 cents, US or Canadian. On the wall, benignly approving, the Queen, in her gown, her tiara, and her Smile of State; also, the National Premier, in open shirt, eyeglasses, and a much broader smile.

Jack found himself still waiting for the bus. *Despite* the Night Before. See (he told himself), so it *isn't* Just Sex . . . Also waiting, besides the retired chicle-tappers and superannuated mahogany-cutters, all of them authorized bench-sitters, was a younger and brisker man.

"You are waiting for the bus, I take it," he now said.

"Oh, yes. Yes, I am."

And so was *he*. "I am expecting a repair part for my tractor. Because, beside my shop, I have a farm. You see my shop?" He companionably took Limekiller by the arm, pointed to a pink-washed building with the indispensable red-painted corrugated iron roof (indispensable because the rains rolled off them and into immense wooden cisterns) and over-hanging gallery. "Well, I find that I cannot wait any longer, Captain Sneed is watching the shop for me, so I would like to ahsk you one favor. *If* you are here. *If* the bus comes. *Would* you be so kind as to give me a hail?"

Limekiller said, "Of course. Be glad to," suddenly realized that he had, after all, other hopes for *If* The Bus Come; hastily added, "And if not, I will send someone to hail you."

The dark (but not *local*-dark) keen face was split by a warm smile. "Yes, do—Tony Mikeloglu," he added, giving Jack's hand a hearty, hasty shake; strode away. (Tony Mike-loglu could trust Captain Sneed not to pop anything under his shirt, not to raid the till, not to get too suddenly and soddenly drunk and smash the glass goods. But, suppose some junior customer were to appear during the owner's absence and, the order being added up and its price announced, pronounce the well-known words, *Ma say, "write eet doewn"*—could he trust Captain Sneed to demand cash and not "write it down?" —no, he could *not*.)

Long Limekiller waited, soft talk floating on around him, of oldtime "rounds" of sapodilla trees and tapping them for chicle, talk of "hunting"—that is, of climbing the tallest hills and scouting out for the telltale reddish sheen which mean mahogany—talk of the bush camps and the high-jinks when the seasons were over. But for them, now, all seasons were over, and it was only that: talk. Great-uncle Leicester had talked a lot, too; only *his* had been other trees, elsewhere.

Still, no bus.

Presently he became aware of feeling somewhat ill at ease, he could not say why. He pulled his long fair beard, and scowled.

One of the aged veterans said, softly, "Sir, de mon *hail*ing you."

With an effort, Limekiller focused his eyes. There. There in front of the pink store building. Someone in the street, calling, beckoning.

"De *Tork* hailing you, sir. Best go see what he want."

Tony Mikeloglu wanted to tell him something? Limekiller, with long strides strolled down to see. "I did not wish to allow you to remain standing in the sun, sir. I am afraid I did not ask your name. Mr. Limekiller?—Interesting name. Ah. Yes. My brother-in-law's brother has just telephoned me from King

Town, Mr. Limekiller. I am afraid that the bus is not coming today. Break*down?"*

Under his breath, Limekiller muttered something coarse and disappointed.

"Pit-ty about the railroad," a deep voice said, from inside the store. "Klondike to Cape Horn. Excellent idea. Vi-sion. But they never built it. Pit-ty."

Limekiller shifted from one foot to another. Half, he would go back to the hotel. Half, he would go somewhere else. (They, she, no one was coming. What did it matter)? *Any*where. *Where?* But the problem was swiftly solved. Once again, and again without offense, the merchant took him by the arm. "Do not stand outside in the sun, sir. Do come *in*side the shop. In the shade. And have something cold to drink." And by this time Jack was already there. "Do you know Captain Sneed?"

Small, khaki-clad, scarlet-faced. Sitting at the counter, which was serving as an unofficial bar. "I suppose you must have often wondered," said Captain Sneed, in a quarterdeck voice, "why the Spaniard didn't settle British Hidalgo when he'd settled everywhere *else* round about?"

"—Well—"

"Didn't know it was *here,* Old Boy! Couldn't have gotten here if he *did,* you see. First of all," he said, drawing on the counter with his finger dipped in the water which had distilled from his glass (Tony now sliding another glass, tinkling with, could it be?—yes, it was! Ice!—over to Jack, who nodded true thanks, sipped)—"First of all, you see, coming from east to west, there's Pharaoh's Reef—quite enough to make them sheer off south in a bit of a damned hurry, don't you see. Then there's the Anne of Denmark Island's Reef, even bigger! And suppose they'd *sail*ed south to avoid Anne of Denmark Island's Reef? Eh? What would they find, will you tell me that?"

"Carpenter's Reef . . . unless it's been moved," said Jack.

Sneed gave a great snort, went on, *"Exactly!* Well, then—now, even if they'd missed Pharaoh's Reef and got pahst it . . . even if they'd missed Anne of Denmark Island's Reef and got pahst it . . . even if they'd missed Carpenter's Reef and got pahst *it* . . . why, then there's that great long *Barrier* Reef, don't you see, one of the biggest in the world. (Of course, Australia's the biggest one. . . .) No. No, Old Boy. Only the British lads knew the way through the Reef, and you may be sure that *they* were not pahssing out the information to the Spaniard, no, ho-ho!"

Well (thought Jack, in the grateful shade of the shop), maybe so. It was an impressive thought, that, of infinite millions of coral polyps laboring and dying and depositing their stony "bones" in order to protect British Hidalgo (and, incidentally, though elsewhere, Australia) from "the Spaniard."

"Well!" Captain Sneed obliterated his watery map with a sweep of his hand. "Mustn't mind *me*, Old Boy. This is my own King Charles's head, if you want to know. It's just the damnable *cheek* of those Spaniards there, *there*, in Spanish Hidalgo, still claiming this blessed little land of ours as their own, when they had never even set their *foot* upon it!" And he blew out his scarlet face and actually said "Herrumph"—a word which Jack had often seen but never, till now, actually heard.

And then Tony Mikeloglu, who had evidently gone through all, all of this many, many times before, said, softly, "My brother-in-law's brother had just told me on the telephone from King *Town*—"

"Phantom relay, it has—the telephone, you know—sorry, Tony, forgive me—what does your damned crook of a kinsman tell you from King Town?"

". . . tells me that there is a rumor that the Pike Estate has finally been settled, you know."

Not *again? Always* . . . thought Limekiller.

But Captain Sneed said, Don't you believe it! "Oh. What? 'A rumor,' yes, well, you may believe *that*. Always a rumor. Why didn't the damned fellow make a proper will? Eh? For that matter, why don't *you*, Old Christopher?"

There was a sound more like a crackle of cellophane than anything else. Jack turned to look; there in an especially shadowy corner was a man even older, even smaller, than Captain Sneed; and exposed toothless gums as he chuckled.

"Yes, why you do not, Uncle Christopher?" asked Tony.

In the voice of a cricket who has learned to speak English witha strong Turkish accent, Uncle Christopher said that he didn't believe in wills.

"What's going to become of all your damned doubloons, then, when you go pop?" asked Captain Sneed. Uncle Christopher only smirked and shrugged. "Where have you concealed all that damned money which you accumulated all those years you used to peddle bad rum and rusty roast-beef tins round about the bush camps? Who's going to get it all, eh?"

Uncle Christopher went *hickle-hickle*. "I know who going get it," he said. *Sh'sh, sh'sh, sh'sh* . . . His shoulders, thin as a butterfly's bones, heaved his amusement.

"Yes, but *how* are they going to get it? What? How are you going to take care of that? Once you're dead."

Uncle Christopher, with a concluding crackle, said, "I going do like the Indians do. . . ."

Limekiller hadn't a clue what the old man meant, but evidently Captain Sneed had. "What?" demanded Captain Sneed. "Come now, come now, you don't really *believe* all that, do you? You *do*? You do! Tush. Piffle. The smoke of all those bush camps has addled your brains. Shame on you. Dirty old pagan. Disgusting. Do you call yourself a Christian and a member of a church holding the Apostolic Succession? *Stuff!*"

The amiable wrangle went on. And, losing interest in it, Limekiller once again became aware of feeling ill at ease. Or . . . was it . . . could it be? . . . *ill?*

In came a child, a little girl; Limekiller had seen her before. She was perhaps eight years old. *Where* had he seen her?

"Ah," said Mikeloglu, briskly the merchant again. "Here is me best customer. She going make me rich, not true, me Betty gyel? What fah you, *chaparita?*"

White rice and red beans were for her, and some coconut oil in her own bottle was for her, and some tea and some chile peppers (not very much of any of these items, though) and the inevitable tin of milk. (The chief difference between small shops and large shops in St. Michael's was that the large ones had a much larger selection of tinned milk.) Tony weighed and poured, wrapped and tied. And looked at her expectantly.

She untied her handkerchief, knot by knot, and counted out the money. Dime by dime. Penny by penny. Gave them all a shy smile, left. "No fahget me when you rich, me Bet-ty gyel," Tony called after her. "Would you believe, Mr. Limekiller, she is one of the grand*child*ren of old Mr. Pike?"

"Then why isn't she rich already? Did the others get it all?—Oh. I forgot. Estate not settled."

Captain Sneed grunted. "Wouldn't help her even if the damned estate *were* settled. An outside child of an outside child. Couldn't inherit if the courts ever decide that he died intestate, and of course: no mention of her in any will . . . if there *is* any will . . ." *An outside child.* How well Jack knew that phrase by now. Marriage and giving in marriage was one thing in British Hidalgo; begetting and bearing of children, quite another thing. No necessary connection. "Do you have any children?" "Well, I has four children." Afterthought: "Ahnd t'ree oetside." Commonest thing in the world. Down here.

"What's wrong with you, Old Boy?" asked Captain Sneed. "You look quite dicky."

"Feel rotten," Limekiller muttered, suddenly aware of feeling so. "Bones all hurt."

Immediate murmurs of sympathy. And: *"Oh,* my. You weren't caught in that rain yesterday morning, were you?"

Jack considered. "Yesterday morning in the daytime. And . . . before . . . in the night time, too—Why?"

Sneed was upset. *" 'Why?' "* Why, when the rain comes down like that, from the north, at this time of year, they call it 'a fever rain.' . . ."

Ah. *That* was what the old woman had called out to him, urging him in out of the drizzle. *Bide,* she'd said. *Not* an "eager" rain—a *fever* rain!

"Some say that the rain makes the sanitary drains overflow. And some say that it raises the mosquitoes. *I* don't know. And some laugh at the old people, for saying that. But *I* don't laugh. . . . You're not laughing, either, are you? Well. What are we going to do for this man, Mik? Doctor in, right now?"

But the District Medical Officer was not in right now. It was his day to make the rounds in the bush hamlets in one half of the circuit. On one other day he would visit the other half. And in between, he was in town holding clinics, walking his wards in the hospital there on one of the hills, and attending to his private patients. Uncle Christopher produced from somewhere a weathered bottle of immense pills which he assured them were quinine, shook it and rattled it like some juju gourd as he prepared to pour them out.

But Captain Sneed demurred. "Best save that till we can be sure that it is malaria. Not they use quinine nowadays. Mmm. No chills, no fever? Mmm. Let me see you to your room at the hotel." And he walked Limekiller back, saw him not only into his room but into his bed, called for "some decent sheets and some blankets, what sort of a kip are you running here, Antonoglu?" Antonoglu's mother, a very large woman in a dress as black and voluminous as the tents of Kedar, came waddling in with sighs and groans and applied her own rem-

edy: a string of limes, to be worn around the neck. The maid
aspersed the room with holy water.

"I shall go and speak to the pharmacist," Captain Sneed
said, briskly. "What—?" For Limekiller, already feeling not
merely rotten but *odd*, had beckoned to him. "Yes?"

Rotten, aching, odd or not, there was something that
Limekiller wanted taken care of. "Would you ask anyone to
check," he said, carefully. "To check the bus? The bus when it
comes in. Two young ladies. One red-haired. When it comes
in. Would you check. Ask anyone. Bus. Red-haired. Check. If
no breakdown. Beautiful. Would you. Any. Please? Oh."

Captain Sneed and the others exchanged looks.

"Of course, Old Boy. Don't worry about it. All taken care
of. Now." He had asked for something. It had not come.
"What, not even a thermometer? *What?* Why, what do you
mean, 'You had one but the children broke it'? *Get another
one at once.* Do you wish to lose your license? Never mind. *I*
shall get another one at once. *And* speak to the pharmacist.
Antonoglu-*khan-um*, the moment he begins to sweat, or his
teeth chatter, *send me word*.

"Be back directly," he said, over his shoulder.

But he was not back directly.

Juan Antonoglu was presently called away to take care of
some incoming guests from the lumber camps. He repeated
Captain Sneed's words to his mother, who, in effect, told him
not to tell her how to make yogurt. She was as dutiful as
anyone could be, and, after a while, her widower son's children coming home, duty called her to start dinner. She repeated the instructions to the maid, whose name was
Purificación. Purificación watched the sick man carefully.
Then, his eyes remaining closed, she tiptoed out to look for
something certain to be of help for him, namely a small booklet of devotions to the Señor de Esquipulas, whose cultus was
very popular in her native republic. But it began to drizzle
again: out she rushed to, first, get the clothes off the line and,
second, to hang them up in the lower rear hall.

Limekiller was alone.

The mahogany press had been waiting for this. It now assumed its rightful shape, which was that of an elderly gentleman rather expensively dressed in clothes rather old-fashioned
in cut, and, carrying a long . . . *something* . . . in one hand,
came over to Jack's bed and looked at him most earnestly.
Almost reproachfully. Giving him a hand to help him out of

bed, in a very few moments he had Limekiller down the stairs and then, somehow, they were out on the river; and then . . . somehow . . . they were *in* the river. No.

Not exactly.

Not at all.

They were *under* the river.

Odd.

Very odd.

A hundred veiled eyes looked at them.

Such a dim light. Not like anything familiar. Wavering. What was that. A crocodile. *I* am getting *out* of *here*, said Limekiller, beginning to sweat profusely. This was the signal for everyone to let Captain Sneed know. But nobody was there. Except Limekiller. And, of course, the old man.

And, of course, the crocodile.

And, it now became clear, *quite* a number of other creatures. All reptilian. Why was he not terrified, instead of being merely alarmed? He was in fact, now that he came to consider it, not even all that alarmed. The creatures were looking at him. But there was somehow nothing terrifying in this. It seemed quite all right for him to be there.

The old man made that quite clear.

Quite clear.

"Is he delirious?" the redhead asked. Not just plain ordinary red. *Copper*-red.

"I don't have enough Spanish to know if saying '*barba amarilla*' means that you're delirious, or not. Are you delirious?" asked the other one. The Short. Brown hair. Plain ordinary Brown.

"'*Barba amarilla*' means 'yellow beard,'" Limekiller explained. Carefully.

"Then you aren't delirious. I guess—What does 'yellow beard' mean, in this context?"

But he could only shake his head.

"I mean, we can see that you do have a blond beard. Well, blond in *parts*. Is that your nickname? No."

Coppertop said, anxiously, "His pulse seems so *funny*, May!" She was the Long. So here they were. The Long and the Short of it. Them. He gave a sudden snort of laughter.

"An insane cackle if ever I heard one," said the Short. "Hm, *Hmm*. You're *right*, Felix. It *does* seem so funny. Mumping all *around* the place—Oh, hello!"

Old Mrs. Antonoglu was steaming slowly down the lake,

all the other vessels bobbing as her wake reached them. *Very*
odd. Because is still *was* old Mrs. Antonoglu in her black
dress and not really the old Lake Mickinuckee ferry boat. And
this wasn't a lake. Or a river. They were all back in his room.
And the steam was coming from something in her hand.

Where was the old man with the sharp face? Tan old man.
Clear. Things were far from *clear,* but—

"What I bring," the old woman said, slowly and carefully
and heavily, just the way in which she walked, "I bring 'im to
drink for 'ealth, poor sick! Call the . . . call the . . . country
yerba," she said, dismissing the missing words.

The red-haired Long said. "Oh, good!"

Spoon by bitter spoonful she fed it to him. Sticks of some-
thing. Boiled in water. A lot of it dribbled down his beard.
"Felix," what an odd name. She wiped it carefully with
Kleenex.

"But 'Limekiller' is just as odd," he felt it only fair to point
out.

"Yes," said the Short. "You certainly are. How did you
know we were coming? We weren't sure, ourselves. *Nor* do
we know you. Not that it matters. We are emancipated
women. Ride bicycles. But we don't smoke cheroots, and we
are *not* going to open an actuarial office with distempered
walls, and the nature of Mrs. Warren's profession does not
bother us in the least: in fact, we have thought, now and then,
of entering it in a subordinate capacity. Probably *won't,*
though. Still . . ."

Long giggled. Short said that the fact of her calling her
Felix instead of *Felicia* shouldn't be allowed to give any
wrong ideas. It was just that *Felicia* always sounded so god-
damn silly. They were both talking at once. The sound was
very comforting.

The current of the river carried them all off, and then it got
so very still.

Quite early next morning.
Limekiller felt fine.
So he got up and got dressed. Someone, probably Purificación, had carefully washed his clothes and dried and ironed
them. He hadn't imagined everything: there was the very large
cup with the twigs of country *yerba* in it. He went downstairs
in the early morning quiet, cocking an ear. Not even a buzzard
scrabbled on the iron roof. There on the hall table was the old

record book used as a register. On the impulse, he opened it.
Disappointment washed over him. *John L. Limekiller, sloop*
Sacarissa, *out of King Town.* There were several names after
that, all male, all ending in *-oglu,* and all from the various
lumber camps round about in the back bush: Wild Hog Eddy,
Funny Gal Hat, Garobo Stream. . . .

Garobo.

Struck a faint echo. Too faint to bother with.

But no one named Felix. Or even *Felicia.* Or May.

Shite and onions.

There on the corner was someone.

"Lahvly morning," said someone. "Just come from hospital, seeing about the accident victims. Name is Pauls, George
Pauls. Teach the Red Cross clahsses. British. You?"

"Jack Limekiller. Canadian. Have you seen two women,
one a redhead?"

The Red Cross teacher *had* seen them, right there on that
corner, but knew nothing more helpful than that. So, anyway,
that hadn't been any delirium or dreams, either, *thank God.*
(For how often had he not dreamed of fine friends and comely
companions, only to wake and know that they had not been
and would never be.)

At Tía Sani's. In came Captain Sneed. *"I say!* Terribly
sorry! Shameful of me—I don't know how—Well. There'd
been a motor accident, lorry overturned, eight people injured,
so we all had to pitch in, there in hospital—Ah, by the *way.* I
did meet your young ladies, thought you'd imagined them,
you know—District Engineer gave them a ride from King
Town—I told them about you, went on up to hospital, then
there was this damned accident—By the time we had taken
care of them, poor chaps, fact is, I am *ashamed* to say, I'd
forgotten all about you.—But you look all right, now." He
scanned Limekiller closely. "Hm, still, you should see the
doctor. I wonder. . . ."

He walked back to the restaurant door, looked up the
street, looked down the street. *"Doc-tor!*—Here he comes
now."

In came a slender Eurasian man; the District Medical Officer himself. (Things were *always* happening like that in Hidalgo. Sometimes it was, "You should see the Premier. Ah,
here he comes now. *Prem-ier!"*) The D.M.O. felt Limekiller's
pulse, pulled down his lower eyelid, poked at spleen and liver,
listened to an account of yesterday. Said, "Evidently you have

had a brief though severe fever. Something like the one-day flu. Feeling all right now? Good. Well, eat your usual breakfast, and if you can't hold it down, come see me at my office."

And was gone.

"Where are they now? The young women, I mean."

Captain Sneed said that he was blessed if he knew, adding immediately, "Ah. Here they come now."

Both talking at once, they asked Jack if he felt all right, assured him that he looked well, said that they'd spent the night at Government Guest House (there was one of these in every out-district capital and was best not confused with *Government House,* which existed only in the colonial capital itself: the Royal Governor lived there, and he was not prepared to put up guests below the rank of, well, *Gov*ernor).

"Mr. Boyd arranged it. We met him in King Town. He was coming here anyway," said Felix, looking long and lovely. "He's an engineer. He's . . . how would you describe him, May?"

"He's an engin*eer,*" May said.

Felix's sherry-colored eyes met Limekiller's. "Come and live on my boat with me and we will sail the Spanish Main together and I will tell you all about myself and frequently make love to you," he said at once. Out loud, however, all he could say was, "Uh . . . thanks for wiping my beard last night . . . uh. . . ."

"Don't mention it," she said.

May said, "I want lots and lots of exotic foods for breakfast." She got two fried eggs, buttered toast of thick-sliced, home-baked bread, beans (mashed), tea, orange juice. "There is nothing *like* these exotic foods," she said.

Felix got egg on her chin. Jack took his napkin and wiped. She said that turnabout was fair play. He said that one good turn deserved another. She asked him if he had ever been to Kettle Point Lagoon, said by They to be beautiful. A spirit touched his lips with a glowing coal.

"I am going there today!" he exclaimed. He had never heard of it.

"Oh, good! Then we can all go together!"

Whom did he see as they walked towards the river, but Filiberto Marín. Who greeted him with glad cries, and a wink, evidently intended as compliments on Jack's company. "Don Fili, can you take us to Kettle Point Lagoon?"

Don Fili, who had at once begun to nod, stopped nodding. "Oh, Juanito, only wan mon hahv boat which go to Kettle Point Lagoon, ahn dot is Very Big Bakeman. He get so *vex*, do anybody else try for go dot side, none ahv we odder boat-men adventure do it. But I bring you to him. May-be he go today. *Veremos*."

Very Big Bakeman, so-called to distinguish him from his cousin, Big Bakeman, was very big indeed. What he might be like when "vex," Limekiller (no squab himself) thought he would pass up knowing.

Bakeman's was the only tunnel boat in sight, probably the only one still in service. His answer was short. "Not before Torsday, becahs not enough wah-teh get me boat ahcross de bar. *Tors*day," he concluded and, yawning, leaned back against the cabin. Monopolists the world over see no reason to prolong conversation with the public.

Felix said something which sounded like, "Oh, spit," but wasn't. Limekiller blinked. *Could* those lovely lips have uttered That Word? If so, he concluded without much difficulty, he would learn to like it. *Love* it. "Don Fili will take us to," he racked his brains, "somewhere just as interesting," he wound up with almost no pause. And looked at Don Fili, appealingly.

Filiberto Marín was equal to the occasion. "*Verdad*. In wan leetle while I going up de Right Branch. *Muy linda*. You will have pleasure. I telling Juanito about it, day before yesterday."

Limekiller recalled no such conversation, but he would have corroborated a deal with the devil, rather than let her out of his sight for a long while yet. He nodded knowingly. "Fascinating," he said.

"We'll get that nice lady to pack us a lunch."

Jack had a quick vision of Tía Sani packing them fried eggs, toast, beans, tea, and orange juice. But that nice lady fooled him. Her sandwiches were immense. Her eggs were deviled. She gave them *empenadas* and she gave them "crusts"—pastries with coconut and other sweet fillings—and then, behaving like aunts the whole world over, she ladled soup into a huge jar and capped it and handed it to Limekiller with the caution to hold it like *this* so that it didn't leak. . . . Not having any intention to have his hands thus occupied the whole trip, he lashed it and shimmed it securely in the stern of Marín's boat.

He had barely known that the Ningoon River *had* two branches. Parrot Bend was on the left one, then. The dory, or dugout, in use today was the largest he had seen so far. Captain Sneed at once decided it had room enough for him to come along, too. Jack was not overjoyed at first. The elderly Englishman was *a decent sort*. But he talked, damn it! *How* he talked. Before long, however, Limekiller found he talked to May, which left Felix alone to talk to Jack.

"John Lutwidge Limekiller," she said, having asked to see his inscribed watch, "there's a *name*. Beats Felicia Fox." *He* thought "fox" of all words in the world the most appropriate for her. He didn't say so."—Why Lutwidge?"

"Lewis Carroll? Charles Lutwidge Dodgson, his real name? Distant cousin. Or so my Aunty Mary used to say."

This impressed her, anyway a little. "And what does Limekiller mean? How do you kill a lime? And *why?*"

"You take a limestone," he said, "and you burn it in a kil*n*. Often pronounced kill. Or, well you *make* lime, for cement or whitewash or whatever, by burning stuff. Not just limestone. Marble. Oyster shells. Old orange rinds, maybe, I don't know, I've never done it. Family *name,"* he said.

She murmured, "I see . . ." She wound up her sleeves. He found himself staring, fascinated, at a blue vein in the inside of her arm near the bend. Caught her gaze. Cleared his throat, sought for something subject-changing and ever so interesting and novel to say. "Tell me about yourself," was what he found.

She gave a soft sigh, looked up at the high-borne trees. There was another blue vein, in her *neck*, this time. Woman was one mass of sexy *veins*, damn it! He would simply lean over and he would kiss—"Well, I was an Art Major at Harrison State U. and I said the hell with it and May is my cousin and she wanted to go someplace, too, and so we're here. . . . Look at the *bridge!"*

They looked at its great shadow, at its reflection, broken by the passing boat into wavering fragments and ripples. The bridge loomed overhead, so high and so impressive in this remote place, one might forget that its rotting road-planks, instead of being replaced, were merely covered with new ones . . . or, at the least, newer ones. "In ten years," they heard Captain Sneed say, "the roadbed will be ten feet tall . . . if it lasts that long."

May: "Be sure and let us know when it's going to fall and we'll come down and watch it. Ffff-*loppp!*—Like San Luis Rey."

"Like *whom*, my dear May?"

The river today was at middle strength: shallow-draft vessels could and still did navigate, but much dry shingle was visible near town. Impressions rushed in swiftly. The day was neither too warm nor too wet, the water so clear that Limekiller was convinced that he could walk across it. Felix lifted her hand, pointed in wordless wonder. There, on a far-outlying branch of a tree over the river was an absolutely monstrous lizard of a beautiful buff color; it could not have been less than five full feet from snout to end of tail, and the buff shaded into orange and into red along the spiky crenelations on the spiny back ridge. He had seen it before. *Had* he seen it before? He *had* seen it before.

"Iguana!" he cried.

Correction was polite but firm. "No, sir, Juanito. Iguana is *embra,* female. Dat wan be *macho.* Male. *Se llama* '*garobo.*' . . ."

Something flickered in Limekiller's mind. "*¡Mira! ¡Mira!* Dat wan dere, *she* be iguana!" And that one there, smaller than the buff dragon, was of a beautiful blue-green-slate-grey color. "Usual," said Filiberto, "*residen en* de bomboo t'icket, which is why de reason is call in English, 'Bomboo chicken.' . . ."

"You *eat* it?"—Felix.

"Exotic *food*, exotic *food!*"—May.

"*Generalmente*, only de hine leg ahn de tail. But is very good to eat de she of dem when she have egg, because de egg so very nice eating, in May, June; but even noew, de she of dem have red egg, nice and hard. *Muy sabroso.*"

Jack turned and watched till the next bend hid the place from sight. After that he watched for them—he did not know why he watched for them, were they watching for *him?*—and he saw them at regular intervals, always in the topmost branches; immense. Why so high? Did they eat insects? And were there more insects to be taken, way up there? They surely did not eat *birds?* Some said, he now recalled in a vague way, that they ate only leaves; but were the top leaves so much more succulent? Besides, they seemed not to be eating anything at all, not a jaw moved. Questions perhaps not unanswerable, but, certainly, at the moment unanswered. Perhaps they had climbed so high only for the view: absurd.

"Didn't use to *be* so many of them, time was.—Eh, Fil?" asked Captain Sneed. ("Correct, Copitan. Not.") "Only in the pahst five, six years . . . it seems. Don't *know* why. . . ."

But whatever, it made the river even more like a scene in a baroque faëry tale, with dragons, or, at least, dragonets, looking and lurking in the gigant trees.

The bed of the river seemed predominantly rocky, with some stretches of sand. The river ran very sinuously, with banks tending towards the precipitate, and the east bank was generally the higher. "When river get high," explained Don Fili, "she get white, ahn come up to de crutch of dem tree—" he pointed to a fork high up. "It can rise in wan hour. Ahn if she rise in de night, we people cahn loose we boat. Very . . . *peligroso* . . . dangerous—*¡Jesus María!* Many stick tear loose wid roots ahn ahl, even big stick like dot wan," he pointed to another massy trunk.

Here and there was open land, *limpiado*, "cleaned," they said hereabouts, for "cleared." *"Clear. . . ."* Something flickered in Limekiller's mind as he recollected this. Then it flickered away. There seemed, he realized, feeling odd about it, that quite a lot of flickering was and had been going on his mind. Nothing that would come into focus, though. The scenes of this Right Branch, now: why did they persist in seeming . . . almost . . . familiar? . . . when he had never been here before?

"What did you say just then, Don Fili?" he demanded, abruptly, not even knowing why he asked.

The monumental face half turned. *"¿Qué?* What I just say, Juanito! Why . . . I say, too bod I forgot bring ahlong my fisga, my pike . . . take some of dem iguana, garobo, cook dem fah you.—Fah *we,"* he amended, as one of the women said, *Gik.*

"We would say, 'harpoon'": Captain Sneed, judiciously. "Local term: 'pike.'"

The penny dropped. "Pike! Pike! It was a pike!" cried Limekiller. His body shook, suddenly, briefly. *Not* a lance or a spear. A pike!

They turned to look at him. Abashed, low-voiced, he muttered, "Sorry. Nothing. Something in a dream . . ." Shock was succeeded by embarrassment.

Felix, also low-voiced, asked, "Are you feverish again?" He shook his head. Then he felt her hand take his. His heart bounced. Then—Oh. She was only feeling his pulse. Evidently it felt all right. She started to release the hand. He took hers. She let it stay.

Captain Sneed said, "Speaking of Pike. All this land, all of

it, far as the eye can reach, is part of the Estate of the Late
Leopold Albert Edward Pike, you know, of fame and story
and, for the last five or six years, since he died, of interminable litigation. He made a great deal of money, out of all these
precious hardwoods, and he put it all back into land—Did I
know him? Of *course* I knew him! That is," he cleared his
throat, "as well as *any*one knew him. Odd chap in a multitude
of ways. *Damn*ably odd. . . ."

Of course that was not the end of the subject.

"Mr. Pike, he *reetch*. But he no di *trust* bonks. He say,
bonks di go *bust*, mon. People say he'm, now-ah-days, bonks
ahl *in*sure. Mr. Pike, he di say, Suh-pose *in*sure company di
go bust, too? *¿Ai, cómo no?* Ahn he di say ah good word. He
di say, 'Who shall guard de guards demselves?' "

Some one of the boatmen, who had theretofore said nothing, but silently plied his paddle, now spoke. "Dey say . . .
Meester Pike . . . dey say, he *deal*. . . ." And his voice dropped
low on this last word. Something went through all the boatmen at that. It was not exactly a shudder. But it was *there*.

Sneed cleared his throat again as though he were going to
cry *Stuff!* or *Piffle!* Though what he said was, "Hm, I
wouldn't go *that* far. He was pagan enough not to believe in
our Devil, let alone try to deal with him. He did, well, he did,
you know, study things better left unstudied . . . *my* opinion.
Indian legends of a certain sort, things like that. Called it 'the
Old Wisdom.' . . ."

Limekiller found his tongue. "Was he an Englishman?"

The matter was considered; heads were shaken. "He mosely *Blanco*. He *lee* bit *Indio*. And he hahv some lee bit *Block*
generation in he'm too."

Sneed said, "His coloring was what they call in The Islands, *bright*. Light, in other words, you would say. Though
color makes no difference here. Never *did*."

Marín added, "What dey cahl Light, here we cahl Clear."
He gestured towards shore, said, "Lime*stone*." Much of the
bankside was composed of that one same sort of rock, greywhite and in great masses, with many holes and caves: limestone was susceptible to such water-caused decay. In Yucatan
the water had corroded deep pits in it, immense deep wells
and pools.

"Now, up ahead," said Captain Sneed, "towards the right
bank of the river is a sort of cove called Crocodile Pool—No
No, ladies, no need for alarm. Just stay in the boat. And

almost directly opposite the cove, is what's called the Garobo Church; you'll see why."

Often in the savannahs they saw the white egrets with the orange bills, usually ashore amidst the cattle. Another kind of egret seemed to prefer the sand and gravel bars and the stumps or sawyers in midstream, and these were a distinctive shade of blue mixed with green, though lighter than the blue-green of the iguanas. Something like a blackbird took its perch and uttered a variety of long, sweet notes and calls.

Swallows skimmed and brighter colored birds darted and drank. And like great sentinels in livery, the great buff garobo-dragons peered down from the tall trees and the tall stones. Clouds of lemon-yellow and butter-yellow butterflies floated round the wild star-apples. *Here,* the stones lay in layers, like brickwork; *there,* the layers were warped and buckled, signs—perhaps—of some ancient strain or quake. But mostly, mostly, the stone rose and loomed and hung in bulbous worm-eaten masses. And over them, among them, behind them and between them, the tall cotton trees, the green-leaved cedars, the white-trunked Santa Maria, and the giant wild fig.

"Now, as to how you *catch* the crocodile," Captain Sneed answered an unasked question; "simple: one man stays in the dory and paddles her in a small circle, one or two men hold the *rope*—"

"—rope tie around odder mahn belly," Marín said.

"*Quite* so. And that chap *dives*. Machete in his *teeth*. And he ties up the croc and then he *tugs*. And then they haul them *up.* . . . you see. Simple."

Felix said, "Not *that* simple!"

May said, "Seems simple enough to me. Long as you've got a sound set of teeth."

Limekiller knew what was coming next. He had been here before. That was a mistake about his never having been here before, of course he had been here; never mind, Right Branch, Left Branch; or how else could he know? Down the steepy bluff a branch came falling with a crash of its *Crack!* falling with it; and the monstrous garobo hit the water with a tremendous sound and spray. It went *down* and it did not come up and it did not come *up.*

And then, distant but clear; the echo. And another echo. And—but that was too many echoes. Jack, who had been looking back, now turned. Spray was still flying up, falling

down. *Ahead:* One after another the garobo were falling into
the river. And then several at once, together. And then—

"Call *that,* 'The Garobo Church,'" said Captain Sneed.

That was an immense wild fig tree, hung out at an impossible angle; later, Limekiller was to learn that it had died of
extreme age and of the storm which finally brought half of its
roots out of the ground and forward into the water and canted
it, thus, between heaven, earth, and river. It was a skeletal
and spectral white against the green *green* of the bush. Three
separate and distinct ecologies were along that great tangled
length of great gaunt tree: at *least* three!—things crept and
crawled, leaped and lurched or lay quiescent, grew and de-
cayed, lived and multiplied and died—and the topmost
branches belonged to the iguana and the garobo—

—that were now abandoning it, as men might abandon a
threatened ship. Crash! Crash! Down they came, simply letting go and falling. *Crash!*

Sound and spray.

"Won't the crocodiles *eat* them?" cried Felix, tightening
her hold on Jack's hand.

The boatmen, to whom this was clearly no new thing, all
shook their heads, said No.

"Dey going *wahrn* he'm, *el legarto,* dot we comin. So dot
he no come oet. So cahn tehk *care. Horita el tiene cuidado."*

"Tush," said Sneed. "Pif-fle. Damned reptiles are simply
getting out of our way, *they* don't know that we haven't any
pike. Damned old creepy-crawlies. . . ."

Only the sound of their crashings, no other sound now, and
Limekiller, saying in a calm flat voice, "Yes, of course," went
out of his shirt and trousers and into the river.

He heard the men cry out, the women scream. But for one
second only. Then the sounds muffled and died away. He was
in the river. He saw a hundred eyes gazing at him. He swam,
he felt bottom, he broke surface, he came up on his hands and
knees. He did not try to stand. He was under the river. He was
someplace else. Someplace with a dim, suffused, wavering
light. An odd place. A very odd place. With a very bad smell.
He was alone. No, he was not. The garobo were all around
and about him. The crocodile was very near up ahead of him.
Something else was there, and he knew it had crawled there
from the surface through a very narrow fissure. And some
thing else was there. *That!* He had to take it and so he took it,
wrenching it loose. It squilched, but it came. The crocodile

gazed at him. The garobo moved aside for him. He backed away. He was in the water again. He—

"Into the *boat*, for Christ's sake!" old Sneed was shouting, his red face almost pale. The boatmen were reaching out to him, holding hands to be grasped by him, smacking the waters with their paddles and banging the paddles against the sides of the boat. The women looked like death. He gasped, spat, trod water, held up something—

—then it was in the boat. Then, all grace gone, he was half in and half out of the boat, his skin scraping the hard sides of it, struggling, being pulled and tugged, wet skin slipping. . . .

He was in the boat.

He leaned over the side, and, as they pulled and pressed, fearful of his going back again, he vomited into the waters.

Captain Sneed had never been so angry. "Well, what did you *expect* crocodile's den to smell like?" he demanded. "Attar of roses? Damndest foolishest crack-brainedest thing I ever saw—!"

Felix said, smoothing Jack's wet, wet hair, *"I think it was brave!"*

"You know nothing whatsoever about it, my dear child!— No, damn it, don't keep waving that damned old pipkin pot you managed to drag up, you damned Canuck! Seven hours under fire at Jutland, and I never had such an infernal shock, it was reckless, it was heedless, it was thoughtless, it was devil-may-care and a louse for the hangman; what was the *reas*on for it, may I ask? To impress *whom*? Eh? *Me*? These good men? These young women? Why did you *do* it?"

All Limekiller could say was, "I dreamed that I had to."

Captain Sneed looked at him, mouth open. Then he said, almost in a mutter, "Oh, I say, poor old boy, he's still rambling, ill, *look*ed well enough, must have the *fever*. . . ." He was a moment silent. Then he blinked, gaped; almost in a whisper, he asked. "You *dreamed*. . . . Whom did you *see* in your dream?"

Limekiller shrugged. "Don't know who. . . . Oldish man. Sharp face. Tan. Old-fashioned clothes. Looked like a sort of a dandy, you might say."

And Captain Sneed's face, which had gone from scarlet to pink and then to scarlet again, now went muddy. They distinctly heard him swallow. Then he looked at the earthenware jar with its faded umber pattern. Then, his lips parting with a sort of dry smack: "... perhaps it *isn't* stuff and piffle, then...."

Ashore.

Sneed had insisted that the police be present. It was customary in Hidalgo to use the police in many ways not customary in the northern nations: to record business agreements, for instance, in places where there were no lawyers. And to witness. Sergeant Bickerstaff said that he agreed with Sneed. He said, also, that he had seen more than one old Indian jar opened and that when they were not empty they usually contained mud and that when they did not contain *mud* they usually contained "grahss-*seed,* cahrn-*ker*-nel, thing like that. Never find any gold in one, not before *my* eye, no, sirs and ladies—But best you go ahead and open it."

The cover pried off, right-tight to the brim was a mass of dark and odorous substance, pronounced to be wild beeswax.

The last crumble of it evaded the knife, sank down into the small jar, which was evidently not filled but only plugged with it. They turned it upside down and the crumble of unbleached beeswax fell upon the table. And so did something else.

"Plastic," said May. "To think that the ancient Indians had invented plastic. Create a furor in academic circles. Invalidate God knows how many patents."

Sergeant Bickerstaff, unmoved by irony, said, "Best unwrap it, Coptain."

The plastic contained one dead wasp or similar insect, and two slips of paper. On one was written, in a firm old-fashioned hand, the words, *Page 36, Liber 100. Registers of Deeds of Gift, Mountains District.* The other was more complex. It seemed to be a diagram of sorts, and along the top and sides of it the same hand had written several sentences, beginning, *From the great rock behind Crocodile Cove and proceeding five hundred feet due North into the area called Richardson's Mahogany Lines....*

It was signed, *L.A.E. Pike.*

There was a silence. Then Felix said, not exactly jumping up and down, but almost, her loops of coppery hair giving a bounce, "A treasure map! Jack! Oh, *good!*"

So far as he could recall, she had never called him by name before. His heart echoed: *Oh, good!*

Captain Sneed, pondering, seemingly by no means entirely

recovered from his several shocks, but recovered enough, said:

"Too late to go poking about in the bush, today. First thing tomorrow, get some men, some machetes, axes, shovels— Eh?"

He turned to Police-sergeant Bickerstaff, who had spoken softly. And now repeated his words, still softly. But firmly. "First thing, sir. First thing supposed to be to notify the District Commissioner. Mister Jefferson Pike."

He was of course correct. As Captain Sneed agreed at once. Limekiller asked, "Any relation to the late Mr. Leopold Pike?" Bickerstaff nodded. "He is a bahstard son of the late Mr. Leopold Pike." The qualifying adjective implied neither insult nor disrespect. He said it as calmly, as mildly, as if he had said step-son. Cousin. Uncle. It was merely a civil answer to a civil question. A point of identification had been raised, been settled.

D.C. Jefferson Pike was taller than his father had been, but the resemblance, once suggested, was evident. If any thoughts of an estate which he could never inherit were in his mind, they were not obvious. "Well, this is something new," was all his initial comment. Then, "I will ask my chief clark. . . . Roberts. Fetch us Liber 100, Register of Deeds of Gift. Oh, and see if they cannot bring some cups of tea for our visitors, please."

The tea was made and half drunk before Roberts, who did not look dilatory, returned, wiping dust and spiderwebs off the large old book. Which was now opened. Pages turned. "Well, well," said the District Commissioner. "This *is* something new!

"Don't know how they came to overlook *this*," he wondered. "The lawyers," he added. "*Who* registered it? Oh. Ahah. I see. Old Mr. Athelny; been dead *several* years. And always kept his own counsel, too. Quite proper. Well." He cleared his throat, began to read:

I, Leopold Albert Edward Pike, Woodcutter and Timber Merchant, Retired, a resident of the Town of Saint Michael of the Mountains, Mountains District, in the Colony of British Hidalgo, and a British subject by birth . . . do execute this Deed of Gift . . . videlicet one collection of gold and silver coins, not being Coin of the

Realm or Legal Tender, as follows, Item, one hundred
pieces of eight reales, Item, fifty-five gold Lewises or
louis d'or, Item . . .

He read them all, the rich and rolling old names, the gold
moidores and gold mohurs, the golden guineas, the silver by-
zants and all the rest, as calmly as though he were reading off
an inventory of office supplies; came finally to:

and all these and any others which by inadvertancy may
not be herein listed which are found in the same place
and location I do hereby give and devise to one Elizabeth Mendoza also known as Betty Mendoza a.k.a.
Elizabeth Pike a.k.a. Betty Pike, an infant now resident
in the aforesaid Mountains District, which Gift I make
for good and sufficient reason and of my own mere
whim and fancy . . .

Here the D.C. paused, raised his eyes, looked at Captain
Sneed. Who nodded. Said, "His own sound and voice. Yes.
How *like* him!"

. . . and fancy; the aforesaid collection of gold and silver
coins being secured in this same District in a place
which I do not herein designate or describe other than to
say that it be situate on my own freehold lands in this
same District. And if anyone attempt to resist or set
aside this my Intention, I do herewith and hereafter declare that he, she or they shall not sleep well of nights.

After he had finished, there was a long pause. Then everybody began to talk at once. Then—

Sneed: Well, suppose we shall have to inform the lawyers,
but don't see what *they* can do about it. Deed was executed
whilst the old fellow was alive and has nothing to *do* with any
question of the estate.

D.C. Pike: I quite agree with you. *Un*officially, of course.
Officially, all I am to do is to make my report. The child?
Why, yes, of course I know her. She is an outside child of my
brother Harrison, who died even before the late Mr. Pike died.
The late Mr. Pike seemed rather fond of her. The late Mr. Pike
did, I believe, always give something to the child's old
woman to keep her in clothes and find her food. As we our-

selves have sometimes done, as best we could. But of course this will make a difference.

Sneed: As it *should*. As it *should*. He had put you big chaps to school and helped you make your own way in the world, but this was a mere babe. Do you suppose that he *knew* that such an estate was bound to be involved in litigation and that was why he tried to help the child with all this . . . this *treasure* business?

Marín: Mis-tah Pike, he ahlways give ah lahf ahn he say, nobody gweyn molest *he* treasure, *seguro*, no, becahs he di set such watchies roun ah-bote eet as no mahn adventure fi trifle wid day.

May: I can't help feeling that it's someone's cue to say, *"This all seems highly irregular."*

Roberts, Chief Clerk (softly but firmly): Oh, no, Miss. The Stamp Tax was paid according to regulations, Miss. *Everything seems in regular order, Miss.*

Watchies. A "watchie" was a watchman, sometimes registered as a private constable, thus giving him . . . Jack was not sure exactly what it gave him: except a certain status. But it was obvious that this was not what "the late Mr. Pike" had had in mind.

Finally, the District Commissioner said, "Well, well. Tomorrow is another day.—Richardson's Mahogany Lines! *Who* would have thought to look there? Nobody! It took eighty years after Richardson cut down all the mahogany before it was worthwhile for anybody to go that side again. And . . . how long since the late Mr. Pike cut down the last of the 'new' mahogany? Ten to fifteen years ago. So it would be sixty-five to seventy-five years before anybody would have gone that side again. Even to *look*. Whatever we may find there would not have been stumbled upon before then, we may be sure. Well, Well.

"Sergeant Bickerstaff, please take these gentlemen's and ladies' statements. Meanwhile, perhaps we can have some further cups of tea. . . ."

Taking the statement, that action so dearly beloved of police officials wherever the Union Jack flies or has flown, went full smoothly. That is, until the moment (Limekiller later realized it was inevitable, but he had not been waiting for it, then), the moment when Sgt. Bickerstaff looked up, raised his pen, asked, "And what made you go and seek for this Indian jar, sir, which gave the clue to this alleged treasure, Mr.

Limekiller? That is, in other words, how did you come to know that it was there?"

Limekiller started to speak. Fell silent beyond possibility of speech. But not Captain Sneed.

"He knew that it was there because Old Pike had dreamed it to him that it was there," said Captain Sneed.

Bickerstaff gave a *deep* nod, raised his pen. Set it down. Lifted it up. Looked at Jack. "This is the case, Mr. Limekiller, sir?"

Jack said, "Yes, it is." He had, so suddenly, realized it to be so.

"Doubt" was not the word for the emotion on the police-sergeant's face. "Perplexity," it was. He looked at his superior, the District Commissioner, but the District Commissioner had nothing to advise. It has been said by scholars that the Byzantine Empire was kept alive by its bureaucracy. Chief Clerk Roberts cleared his throat. In the tones of one dictating a routine turn of phrase, he produced the magic words.

" '*Acting upon information received,*' " he said, " '*I went to the region called Crocodile Cove, accompanied by,*' and so carry on from there, Sergeant Bickerstaff," he said.

In life, if not in literature, there is always anticlimax. By rights—by dramatic right, that is—they should all have gone somewhere and talked it all over. Talked it all out. And so tied up all the loose ends. But in fact there was nowhere for them all to go and do this. The police were finished when the statement was finished. District Officer Pike, who had had a long, hard day, did not suggest further cups of tea. Tía Sani's was closed. The Emerging Nation Bar and Club was closed, and in the other clubs and bars local usage and common custom held that the presence of "ladies" was contra-indicated: so did common sense.

Wherever Captain Sneed lived, Captain Sneed was clearly not about to offer open house. "Exhausted," he said. And looked it. "Come along, ladies, I will walk along with you as far as the Guest House. Limekiller. Tomorrow."

What should Limekiller do? Carry them off to his landing at the Grand Arawack? Hospitality at Government Guest House, that relic of days when visitors, gaunt and sore from mule transport, would arrive at an even smaller St. Michael's, hospitality there was reported to be of a limited nature; but surely it was better than a place where the urinals were tied up in brown paper and string?(—Not that *they'd* use them anyway, the thought occurred.)

May said, "Well, if you get sick again, yell like Hell for us."

Felix said, reaching out her slender hand, whose every freckle he had come to know and love, she said, *"Will you be all right, Jack?"* Will you be all right, Jack? Not, mind you, *You'll be all right, Jack.* It was enough. (And if it wasn't, this was not the time and place to say what would be.)

"I'll be all right," he assured her.

But, back on his absurdly sheeted bed, more than slightly fearful of falling asleep at all, the river, the moment he closed his eyes, the river began to unfold before him, mile after beautiful and haunted mile. But this was a fairly familiar effect of fatigue. He had known it to happen with the roads and the wheatfields, in the Prairie Provinces.

It was on awakening to the familiar cockeling chorus of, *I make the sun to rise!* that he realized that he had not dreamed at all.

St. Michael's did not have a single bank; and, what was more—or less—it did not have a single lawyer. Attorneys for the Estate (alerted perhaps by the telephone's phantom relay) arrived early. But they did not arrive early enough . . . early enough to delay the digging. By the time the first lawyeriferous automobile came spinning to a stop before the local courthouse, the expedition was already on its way. The attorney for the Estate requested a delay, the attorneys for the several groups of claimants requested a delay. But the Estate's local agent had already given a consent, and the magistrate declined to set it aside. He did not, however, forbid them to attend.

Also in attendance was one old woman and one small girl. Limekiller thought that both of them looked familiar. And he was right. One was the same old woman who had urged him in out of the "fever rain." The other was the child who had urged him to see "the beauty harse" and had next day made the meager purchases in Mikeloglu's shop . . . whom the merchant had addressed as "Bet-ty me gyel," and urged her (with questionable humor) not to forget him when she was rich.

The crocodile stayed unvexed in his lair beneath the roots of the old Garobo Tree, though, seemingly, half the dragons along the river had dived to alert him.

To walk five hundred feet, *as a start,* is no great feat if one is in reasonable health. To cut and hack and ax and slash one's way through bush whose clearings require to be cleared twice a year if they are not to vanish: this is something else. However, the first hundred feet proved to be the hardest (and hard enough to eliminate all but the hardiest of the lawyers). At the end of that first line they found their second marker: a lichen-studded rock growing right out of the primal bones of the earth. From there on, the task was easier. Clearly, though "the late Mr. Pike" had not intended it to be impossible, he had intended it to be difficult.

Sneed had discouraged, Marín had discouraged, others had discouraged May and Felix from coming: uselessly. Mere weight of male authority having proven to be obsolescent, Captain Sneed appealed to common sense. "My dear ladies," he pleaded, "can either of you handle a machete? Can either of you use an ax? Can—"

"Can either of us carry food?" was May's counter-question.

"And water?" asked Felix. "Both of us can," she said.

"Well, good for both of you," declared Captain Sneed, making an honorable capitulation of the fortress.

May had a question of her own. "Why do we all have to wear *boots?*" she asked, "when there are hardly any wet places along here."

"Plenty tommy*goff,* Mees."

"Tommy Goff? Who is *he?*"

"Don't know who *he* was, common enough name, though, among English-speaking people in this part of the Caribbean. Don't know why they named a snake after the chap, either. . . ."

A slight pause. "A . . . snake . . . ?"

"And *such* a snake, too! The dreaded fer-de-lance, as they call it in the French Islands."

"Uhh . . . *Poi*sonous?"

Sneed wiped his sweating head, nodded his Digger-style bush hat. *"Dead*ly poisonous. If it's in full venom, bite can kill a horse. Sometimes *does*. So do be exceedingly cautious. Please."

There was a further word on the subject, from Filiberto Marín. *"En castellano, se llame 'barba amarilla.' "*

This took a moment to sink in. Then one of the North Americans asked, "Doesn't that mean 'yellow beard'?"

"Quite right. In fact, the tommygoff's other name in English is 'yellow jaw.' But the Spanish is, literally, yes, it's yellow *beard*."

All three North Americans said, as one, *"Oh."* And looked at each other with a wild surmise.

The noises went on all around them. *Slash*—! *Hack*—! And, *Chop! Chop! Chop!* After another moment, May went on, "Well, I must say that seems like quite a collection of watchies that your late Mr. Leopold Pike appointed. Crocodiles. Poison serpents. What else. Oh. Do garobo *bite?"*

"Bite your nose or finger off if you vex him from the front; yes."

May said, thoughtfully, "I'm not sure that I really *like* your late Mr. Leopold Pike—"

Another flash of daytime lightning. Limekiller said, and remembered saying it the day before in the same startled tone, videlicet: "Pike! Pike!" Adding, this time, *"Fer-de-lance . . .!"*

Felix gave him her swift look. Her face said, No, he was not feverish. . . . Next she said, " 'Fer,' that's French for 'iron,' and . . . Oh. I see. Yes. Jesus. *Fer-de-lance*, lance-iron, or spear-head. Or spear-*point*. Or—"

"Or in other words," May wound up, *"Pike. . . .* You dreamed that, too, small John?"

He swung his ax again, nodded. *Thunk.* "Sort of . . . one way or another." *Thunk.* "He had a, sort of a, pike with him." *Thunk.* "Trying to get his point—ha-ha—across. Did I dream the snake, too? Must have . . . I guess. . . ." *Thunk.*

"No. I do *not like* your late Mr. Leopold Pike."

Sneed declared a break. Took sips of water, slowly, carefully. Wiped his face. Said, "You might have liked Old Pike, though. A hard man in his way. Not without a sense of humor, though. And . . . after all . . . he hasn't hurt our friend John Limekiller . . . has he? Old chap Pike was simply trying to do his best for his dead son's child. May seem an odd way, to us. May *be*. Fact o'the matter: *Is*. Why didn't he do it another way? Who's to say. Didn't have too much trust in the law and the law's delays. I'll sum it up. *Pike liked to do things in his own way*. A lot of them were Indian ways. *Old* Indian ways. Used to burn copal gum when he went deer hunting. *A*lways got his deer. And as for *this* little business, well . . . the old Indians had no probate courts. What's the consequence? How does one guarantee that one's bequest reaches one's intended heir?

"Why . . . one *dreams* it to him! Or, for that matter, *her*. In this case, however, the *her* is a small child. So—"

One of the woodsmen put down his tin cup, and, thinking Sneed had done, said to Limekiller, "Mon, you doesn't holds de ox de same way we does. But you holds eet well. Where you learns dis?"

"Oh . . ." said Limekiller, vaguely, "I've helped cut down a very small part of Canada without benefit of chain saw. In my even younger days." Would he, too, he wondered, in his even older days, would he too ramble on about the trees he had felled?—the deeds he had done?

Probably.

Why not?

A wooden chest would have moldered away. An iron one would have rusted. Perhaps for these reasons the "collection of gold and silver coins, not being Coin of the Realm or Legal Tender," had been lodged in more Indian jars. Larger ones, this time. An examination of one of them showed that the contents were as described. Once again the machetes were put to use; branches, vines, ropes, were cut and trimmed. Litters, or slings, rough but serviceable, were made. Was some collective ethnic unconscious at work here? Had not the Incas, Aztecs, Mayas, ridden in palanquins?

Now for the first time the old woman raised her voice. "Ahl dis fah *you*, Bet-ty," she said, touching the ancient urns. "Bet-tah food. Fah *you*. Bet-tah house: Fah *you*, Bet-tah school. Fah *you*." Her gaze was triumphant. "*Ahl dis fah you!*"

One of the few lawyers who had not dropped out along the long, hard way, had a caveat. "Would the Law of Treasure Trove apply?" he wondered. "In which case, the Crown would own it. Although, to be sure, where there is no attempt at concealment the Crown would allow a finder's fee . . . Mr. Limekiller. . . .?"

And if anyone attempt to resist or set aside this my Intention, I do herewith and hereafter declare that he, she, or they shall not sleep well of nights. . . .

Limekiller said, "I'll pass."

And Captain Sneed cried, "Piffle! Tush! Was the Deed of Gift registered, or was it not? Was the Stamp Tax paid, or was it not?"

One of the policemen said, "If you have the Queen's head on your paper, you cahn't go wrong."

"*Nol. con.,*" the lawyer said. And said no more.

* * *

That had been that. The rest were details. (One of the details was found in one of the large jars: another piece of plastic-wrapped paper, on which was written in a now-familiar hand. *He who led you hither, he may now sleep well of nights.* And in the resolution of these other details the three North Americans had no part. Nor had Marín and friends: back to Parrot Bend they went. Nor had Captain Sneed. "Holiday is over," he said. "If I don't get back to my farm, the wee-wee ants will carry away my fruit. Come and visit, all of you. Whenever you like. Anyone will tell you where it is," he said. And was gone, the brave old Digger bush-hat bobbing away down the lane: wearing an invisible plume.

And the major (and the minor) currents of life in St. Michael of the Mountains went on—as they had gone on for a century without them.

There was the inevitable letdown.

May said, with a yawn, "I need a nice, long rest. And I know just where I'm going to find it. *After* we get back to King Town. I'm going to take a room at that hotel near the National Library."

Felix asked, "Why?"

"Why? I'll be like a kid in a candy warehouse. Do you realize that on the second floor of the National Library is the largest collection of 19th century English novels which I have ever seen in any one place? EVerything EVer written by EVerybody. Mrs. Edgeworth, Mrs. Trollope, Mrs. Gaskell, Mrs. Oliphant, Mrs. This and Mrs. That."

"Mrs. That. *I* remember *her.* Say, she wasn't bad at all—"

"No, she *was*n't. Although, personally, I prefer Mrs. This."

Felix and Limekiller found that they were looking at each other. *Speak now,* he told himself. *Aren't you tired of holding your own piece?* "And what are you going to be doing, then?" he asked.

She considered. Said she wasn't sure.

There was a silence.

"Did I tell you about my boat?"

"No. You didn't." Her look at him was a steady one. She didn't seem impatient. She seemed to have all the time in the world. "Tell me about your boat," she said.

Armaja Das

by

Joe Haldeman

One of the most acclaimed writers of the seventies, Joe Haldeman was born in Oklahoma City, Oklahoma, in 1943. Haldeman's plans for a career in science—he took a B.S. degree in physics and astronomy from the University of Maryland—were cut short by the U.S. Army, which sent him to Vietnam in 1968 as a combat engineer. Seriously wounded in action, Haldeman returned home in 1969 and began to write. He sold his first story to Galaxy *in 1969, and by 1976 had already garnered Nebula and Hugo awards for his famous novel* The Forever War, *one of the landmark books of the seventies. He took another Hugo Award in 1977 for his story "Tricentennial." His other books include a mainstream novel,* War Year, *the SF novels* Mindbridge, Worlds, All My Sins Remembered, *and (in collaboration with his brother, SF writer Jack C. Haldeman II)* There Is No Darkness; *a short-story collection,* Infinite Dreams; *and, as editor, the anthologies* Study War No More, Cosmic Laughter, *and* Nebula Award Stories Seventeen. *His most recent books were the novel* Worlds Apart, *the sequel to* Worlds, *and the collection* Dealing In Futures. *Upcoming are the third volume in the* Worlds *trilogy,* Worlds Enough and Time, *as well as several other novels "in various stages of incompletion."*

Here he adroitly blends ancient gypsy magic and ultramodern computer technology, a mixture that produces some strange—and chilling—results.

* * *

THE HIGHRISE, BUILT IN 1980, STILL HAD THE SMELL AND LOOK of newness. And of money.

The doorman bowed a few degrees and kept a straight face, opening the door for a bent old lady. She had a card of Veterans' poppies clutched in one old claw. He didn't care much for the security guard, and she would give him interesting trouble.

The skin on her face hung in deep creases, scored with a network of tiny wrinkles; her chin and nose protruded and dropped. A cataract made one eye opaque; the other eye was yellow and red surrounding deep black, unblinking. She had left her teeth in various things. She shuffled. She wore an old black dress faded slightly gray by repeated washing. If she had any hair, it was concealed by a pale blue bandanna. She was so stooped that her neck was almost parallel to the ground.

"What can I do for you?" The security guard had a tired voice to match his tired shoulders and back. The job had seemed a little romantic the first couple of days, guarding all these rich people, sitting at an ultramodern console surrounded by video monitors, submachine gun at his knees. But the monitors were blank except for an hourly check, power shortage; and if he ever removed the gun from its cradle, he would have to fill out five forms and call the police station. And the doorman never turned anybody away.

"Buy a flower for boys less fortunate than ye," she said in a faint raspy baritone. From her age and accent, her own boys had fought in the Russian Revolution.

"I'm sorry. I'm not allowed to . . . respond to charity while on duty."

She stared at him for a long time, nodding microscopically. "Then send me to someone with more heart."

He was trying to frame a reply when the front door slammed open. "Car on fire!" the doorman shouted.

The security guard leaped out of his seat, grabbed a fire extinguisher and sprinted for the door. The old woman shuffled along behind him until both he and the doorman disappeared around the corner. Then she made for the elevator with surprising agility.

She got out on the 17th floor, after pushing the button that would send the elevator back down to the lobby. She checked the name plate on 1738; Mr. Zold. She was illiterate but could recognize names.

Not even bothering to try the lock, she walked on down the hall until she found a maid's closet. She closed the door behind her and hid behind a rack of starchy white uniforms, leaning against the wall with her bag between her feet. The slight smell of gasoline didn't bother her at all.

John Zold pressed the intercom button. "Martha?" She answered. "Before you close up shop I'd like a redundancy check on stack 408. Against tape 408." He switched the selector on his visual output screen so it would duplicate the output at Martha's station. He stuffed tobacco in a pipe and lit it, watching.

Green numbers filled the screen, a complicated matrix of ones and zeros. They faded for a second and were replaced with a field of pure zeros. The lines of zeros started to roll, like titles preceding a movie.

The 746th line came up all ones. John thumbed the intercom again. "Had to be something like that. You have time to fix it up?" She did. "Thanks, Martha. See you tomorrow."

He slid back the part of his desk top that concealed a keypunch and typed rapidly: "523 784 00926/ / Good night, machine. Please lock this station."

GOOD NIGHT, JOHN. DON'T FORGET YOUR LUNCH DATE WITH MR. BROWNWOOD TOMORROW. DENTIST APPOINTMENT WEDNESDAY 0945. GENERAL SYSTEMS CHECK WEDNESDAY 1300. DEL O DEL BAXT. LOCKED.

Del O del baxt means "God give you luck" in the ancient tongue of the Romani. John Zold, born a Gypsy but hardly a Gypsy by any standard other than the strong one of blood, turned off his console and unlocked the bottom drawer of his desk. He took out a flat automatic pistol in a holster with a belt clip and slipped it under his jacket, inside the waistband of his trousers. He had only been wearing the gun for two weeks, and it still made him uncomfortable. But there had been those letters.

John was born in Chicago, some years after his parents had fled from Europe and Hitler. His father had been a fiercely proud man, and got involved in a bitter argument over the honor of his 12-year-old daughter; from which argument he had come home with knuckles raw and bleeding, and had given to his wife for disposal a large clasp knife crusty with dried blood.

John was small for his five years, and his chin barely cleared the kitchen table, where the whole family sat and discussed their uncertain future while Mrs. Zold bound up her husband's hands. John's shortness saved his life when the kitchen window exploded and a low ceiling of shotgun pellets fanned out and chopped into the heads and chests of the only people in the world whom he could love and trust. The police found him huddled between the bodies of his father and mother, and at first thought he was also dead; covered with blood, completely still, eyes wide open and not crying.

It took six months for the kindly orphanage people to get a single word out of him: *ratválo*, which he said over and over; which they were never able to translate. Bloody, bleeding.

But he had been raised mostly in English, with a few words of Romani and Hungarian thrown in for spice and accuracy. In another year their problem was not one of communicating with John; only of trying to shut him up.

No one adopted the stunted Gypsy boy, which suited John. He'd had a family, and look what happened.

In orphanage school he flunked penmanship and deportment, but did reasonably well in everything else. In arithmetic and, later, mathematics, he was nothing short of brilliant. When he left the orphanage at eighteen, he enrolled at the University of Illinois, supporting himself as a bookkeeper's assistant and part-time male model. He had come out of an ugly adolescence with a striking resemblance to the young Clark Gable.

Drafted out of college, he spent two years playing with computers at Fort Lewis; got out and went all the way to a Master's degree under the G. I. Bill. His thesis "Simulation of Continuous Physical Systems by Way of Universalization of the Trakhtenbrot Algorithms" was very well received, and the mathematics department gave him a research assistantship, to extend the thesis into a doctoral dissertation. But other people read the paper too, and after a few months Bellcom International hired him away from academia. He rose rapidly through the ranks. Not yet forty, he was now Senior Analyst at Bellcom's Research and Development Group. He had his own private office, with a picture window overlooking Central Park, and a plush six-figure condominium only twenty minutes away by commuter train.

As was his custom, John bought a tall can of beer on his way to the train, and opened it as soon as he sat down. It kept him from fidgeting during the fifteen or twenty-minute wait while the train filled up.

He pulled a thick technical report out of his briefcase and stared at the summary on the cover sheet, not really seeing it but hoping that looking occupied would spare him the company of some anonymous fellow traveller.

The train was an express, and whisked them out to Dobb's Ferry in twelve minutes. John didn't look up from his report until they were well out of New York City; the heavy mesh tunnel that protected the track from vandals induced spurious colors in your retina as it blurred by. Some people liked it, tripped on it, but to John the effect was at best annoying, at worst nauseating, depending on how tired he was. Tonight he was dead tired.

He got off the train two stops up from Dobb's Ferry. The highrise limousine was waiting for him and two other residents. It was a fine spring evening and John would normally have walked the half-mile, tired or not. But those unsigned letters.

John Zold, you stop this preachment or you die soon. Armaja das, *John Zold.*

All three letters said that: *Armaja das,* we put a curse on you. For preaching.

He was less afraid of curses than of bullets. He undid the bottom button of his jacket as he stepped off the train, ready to quickdraw, roll for cover behind that trash can, just like in the movies; but there was no one suspicious-looking around. Just an assortment of suburban wives and the old cop who was on permanent station duty.

Assassination in broad daylight wasn't Romani style. Styles change, though. He got in the car and watched the side roads all the way home.

There was another one of the shabby envelopes in his mailbox. He wouldn't open it until he got upstairs. He stepped in the elevator with the others, and punched 17.

* * *

They were angry because John Zold was stealing their children.

Last March John's tax accountant had suggested that he could contribute $4,000 to any legitimate charity, and actually make a few hundred bucks in the process, by dropping into a lower tax bracket. Not one to do things the easy or obvious way, John made various inquiries and, after a certain amount of bureaucratic tedium, founded the Young Gypsy Assimilation Council—with matching funds from federal, state and city governments, and a continuing Ford Foundation scholarship grant.

The YGAC was actually just a one-room office in a West Village brownstone, manned by volunteer help. It was filled with various pamphlets and broadsides, mostly written by John, explaining how young Gypsies could legitimately take advantage of American society. By becoming part of it, which was the part that old-line Gypsies didn't care for. Jobs, scholarships, work-study programs, these things are for the *gadjos*. Poison to a Gypsy's spirit.

In November a volunteer had opened the office in the morning to find a crude fire bomb, using a candle as a delayed-action fuse for five gallons of gasoline. The candle was guttering a fraction of an inch away from the line of powder that would have ignited the gas. In January it had been buckets of chicken entrails, poured into filing cabinets and flung over the walls. So John found a tough young man who would sleep on the cot in the office at night; sleep like a cat with a shotgun beside him. There was no more trouble of that sort. Only old men and women who would file in silently staring, to take handfuls of pamphlets which they would drop in the hall and scuff into uselessness, or defile in a more basic way. But paper was cheap.

John threw the bolt on his door and hung his coat in the closet. He put the gun in a drawer in his writing desk and sat down to open the mail.

The shortest one yet: "Tonight, John Zold. *Armaja das*." Lots of luck, he thought. Won't even be home tonight; heavy date. Stay at her place, Gramercy Park. Lay a curse on me there? At the show or Sardi's?

He opened two more letters, bills, and there was a knock at the door.

Not announced from downstairs. Maybe a neighbor. Guy next door was always borrowing something. Still. Feeling a little foolish, he put the gun back in his waistband. Put his coat back on in case it was just a neighbor.

The peephole didn't show anything, bad. He drew the pistol and held it just out of sight, by the doorjamb, threw the bolt and eased open the door. He bumped into the Gypsy woman, too short to have been visible through the peephole. She backed away and said "John Zold."

He stared at her. "What do you want, *pūridaia?* He could only remember a hundred or so words of Romani, but "grandmother" was one of them. What was the word for witch?

"I have a gift for you." From her bag she took a dark green booklet, bent and with frayed edges, and gave it to him. It was a much-used Canadian passport, belonging to a William Belini. But the picture inside the front cover was one of John Zold.

Inside, there was an airline ticket in a Qantas envelope. John didn't open it. He snapped the passport shut and handed it back. The old lady wouldn't accept it.

"An impressive job. It's flattering that someone thinks I'm so important."

"Take it and leave forever, John Zold. Or I will have to do the second thing."

He slipped the ticket envelope out of the booklet. "This, I will take. I can get your refund on it. The money will buy lots of posters and pamphlets." He tried to toss the passport into her bag, but missed. "What is your second thing?"

She tossed the passport back to him. "Pick that up." She was trying to sound imperious, but it came out a thin, petulant quaver.

"Sorry, I don't have any use for it. What is—"

"The second thing is your death, John Zold." She reached into her bag.

He produced the pistol and aimed it down at her forehead. "No, I don't think so."

She ignored the gun, pulling out a handful of white chicken feathers. She threw the feathers over his threshold. *"Armaja das,"* she said, and then droned on in Romani, scattering feathers at regular intervals. John recognized *joovi* and *kari,* the words for woman and penis, and several other words he might have picked up if she'd pronounced them more clearly.

He put the gun back into its holster and waited until she

was through. "Do you really think—"

"*Armaja das*," she said again, and started a new litany. He recognized a word in the middle as meaning corruption or infection, and the last word was quite clear: death. *Méripen*.

"This nonsense isn't going to . . ." But he was talking to the back of her head. He forced a laugh and watched her walk past the elevator and turn the corner that led to the staircase.

He could call the guard. Make sure she didn't get out the back way. Illegal entry. He suspected that she knew he wouldn't want to go to the trouble, and it annoyed him slightly. He walked halfway to the phone, checked his watch and went back to the door. Scooped up the feathers and dropped them in the disposal. Just enough time. Fresh shave, shower, best clothes. Limousine to the station, train to the city, cab from Grand Central to her apartment.

The show was pure delight, a sexy revival of *Lysistrata:* Sardi's was as ego-bracing as ever; she was a soft-hard woman with style and sparkle, who all but dragged him back to her apartment, where he was for the first time in his life impotent.

The psychiatrist had no use for the traditional props: no soft couch or bookcases lined with obviously expensive volumes. No carpet, no paneling, no numbered prints; not even the notebook or the expression of slightly disinterested compassion. Instead, she had a hidden recorder and an analytical scowl; plain stucco walls surrounding a functional desk and two hard chairs, period.

"You know exactly what the problem is," she said.

John nodded. "I suppose. Some . . . residue from my early upbringing; I accept her as an authority figure. From the few words I could understand of what she said, I took, it was . . ."

"From the words *penis* and *woman*, you built your own curse. And you're using it, probably to punish yourself for surviving the disaster that killed the rest of your family."

"That's pretty old-fashioned. And farfetched. I've had almost forty years to punish myself for that, if I felt responsible. And I don't."

"Still, it's a working hypothesis." She shifted in her chair and studied the pattern of teak grain on the bare top of her desk. "Perhaps if we can keep it simple, the cure can also be simple."

"All right with me," John said. At $125 an hour, the quicker, the better.

"If you can see it, feel it, in this context, then the key to your cure is transference." She leaned forward, elbows on the table, and John watched her breasts shifting with detached interest, the only kind of interest he'd had in women for more than a week. "If you can see *me* as an authority figure instead," she continued, "then eventually I'll be able to reach the child inside; convince him that there was no curse. Only a case of mistaken identity . . . nothing but an old woman who scared him. With careful hypnosis, it shouldn't be too difficult."

"Seems reasonable," John said slowly. Accept this young *Geyri* as more powerful than the old witch? As a grown man, he could. If there was a frightened Gypsy boy hiding inside him, though, he wasn't sure.

"523 784 00926/ /Hello, machine," John typed. "Who is the best dermatologist within a 10-short-block radius?"

GOOD MORNING, JOHN. WITHIN STATED DISTANCE AND USING AS SOLE PARAMETER THEIR HOURLY FEE, THE MAXIMUM FEE IS $95/HR, AND THIS IS CHARGED BY TWO DERMATOLOGISTS, DR. BRYAN DILL, 245 W. 45TH ST., SPECIALIZES IN COSMETIC DERMATOLOGY. DR. ARTHUR MAAS, 198 W. 44TH ST., SPECIALIZES IN SERIOUS DISEASES OF THE SKIN.

"Will Dr. Maas treat disease of psychological origin?"

CERTAINLY. MOST DERMATOSIS IS.

Don't get cocky, machine. "Make me an appointment with Dr. Maas, within the next two days."

YOUR APPOINTMENT IS AT 1:45 TOMORROW, FOR ONE HOUR. THIS WILL LEAVE YOU 45 MINUTES TO GET TO LUCHOW'S FOR YOUR APPOINTMENT WITH THE AMCSE GROUP. I HOPE IT IS NOTHING SERIOUS, JOHN.

"I trust it isn't." Creepy empathy circuits. "Have you arranged for a remote terminal at Luchow's?"

THIS WAS NOT NECESSARY. I WILL PATCH THROUGH CONED/GENERAL. LEASING THEIR LUCHOW'S FACILITY WILL COST ONLY .588 THE PROJECTED COST OF TRANSPORTATION AND SETUP LABOR FOR A REMOTE TERMINAL.

That's my machine, always thinking. "Very good, machine. Keep this station live for the time being."

THANK YOU, JOHN. The letters faded but the ready light stayed on.

He shouldn't complain about the empathy circuits; they were his baby, and the main reason Bellcom paid such a bloated salary, to keep him. The copyright on the empathy package was good for another 12 years, and they were making a fortune, timesharing it out. Virtually every large computer in the world was hooked up to it, from the ConEd/General that ran New York, to Geneva and Akademia Nauk, which together ran half the world.

Most of the customers gave the empathy package a name, usually female. John called it "machine" in a not-too-successful attempt to keep from thinking of it as human.

He made a conscious effort to restrain himself from picking at the carbuncles on the back of his neck. He should have gone to the doctor when they first appeared, but the psychiatrist had been sure she could cure them; the "corruption" of the second curse. She'd had no more success with that than with the impotence. And this morning, boils had broken out on his chest and groin and shoulderblades, and there were sore spots on his nose and cheekbone. He had some opiates, but would stick to aspirin until after work.

Dr. Maas called it impetigo; gave him a special kind of soap and some antibiotic ointment. He told John to make another appointment in two weeks, ten days. If there was no improvement they would take stronger measures. He seemed young for a doctor, and John couldn't bring himself to say anything about the curse. But he already had a doctor for that end of it, he rationalized.

Three days later he was back in Dr. Maas's office. There was scarcely a square inch of his body where some sort of lesion hadn't appeared. He had a temperature of 101.4°. The doctor gave him systemic antibiotics and told him to take a couple of days' bed rest. John told him about the curse, finally, and the doctor gave him a booklet about psychosomatic illness. It told John nothing he didn't already know.

By the next morning, in spite of strong antipyretics, his fever had risen to over 102°. Groggy with fever and pain-killers, John crawled out of bed and travelled down to the West Village, to the YGAC office. Fred Gorgio, the man who guarded the place at night, was still on duty.

"Mr. Zold!" When John came through the door, Gorgio jumped up from the desk and took his arm. John winced from the contact, but allowed himself to be led to a chair. "What's happened?" John by this time looked like a person with terminal smallpox.

For a long minute John sat motionlessly, staring at the inflamed boils that crowded the backs of his hands. "I need a healer," he said, talking with slow awkwardness because of the crusted lesions on his lips.

"A *chóvihánni?*" John looked at him uncomprehendingly. "A witch?"

"No." He moved his head from side to side. "An herb doctor. Perhaps a white witch."

"Have you gone to the *gadjo* doctor?"

"Two. A Gypsy did this to me; a Gypsy has to cure it."

"It's in your head, then?"

"The *gadjo* doctors say so. It can still kill me."

Gorgio picked up the phone, punched a local number, and rattled off a fast stream of a patois that used as much Romani and Italian as English. "That was my cousin," he said, hanging up. "His mother heals, and has a good reputation. If he finds her at home, she can be here in less than an hour."

John mumbled his appreciation. Gorgio led him to the couch.

The healer woman was early, bustling in with a wicker bag full of things that rattled. She glanced once at John and Gorgio, and began clearing the pamphlets off a side table. She appeared to be somewhere between fifty and sixty years old, tight bun of silver hair bouncing as she moved around the room, setting up a hot-plate and filling two small pots with water. She wore a black dress only a few years old, and sensible shoes. The only lines on her face were laugh lines.

She stood over John and said something in gentle, rapid Italian, then took a heavy silver crucifix from around her neck and pressed it between his hands. "Tell her to speak English . . . or Hungarian," John said.

Gorgio translated. "She says that you should not be so affected by the old superstitions. You should be a modern man, and not believe in fairy tales for children and old people."

John stared at the crucifix, turning it slowly between his fingers. "One old superstition is much like another." But he didn't offer to give the crucifix back.

The smaller pot was starting to steam and she dropped a handful of herbs into it. Then she returned to John and carefully undressed him.

When the herb infusion was boiling, she emptied a package of powdered arrowroot into the cold water in the other pot, and stirred it vigorously. Then she poured the hot solution into the cold and stirred some more. Through Gorgio, she told John she wasn't sure whether the herb treatment would cure him. But it would make him more comfortable.

The liquid jelled and she tested the temperature with her fingers. When it was cool enough, she started to pat it gently on John's face. Then the door creaked open, and she gasped. It was the old crone who had put the curse on John in the first place.

The witch said something in Romani, obviously a command, and the woman stepped away from John.

"Are you still a skeptic, John Zold?" She surveyed her handiwork. "You called this nonsense."

John glared at her but didn't say anything. "I heard that you had asked for a healer," she said, and addressed the other woman in a low tone.

Without a word, she emptied her potion into the sink and began putting away her paraphernalia. "Old bitch," John croaked. "What did you tell her?"

"I said that if she continued to treat you, what happened to you would also happen to her sons."

"You're afraid it would work," Gorgio said.

"No. It would only make it easier for John Zold to die. If I wanted that I could have killed him on his threshold." Like a quick bird she bent over and kissed John on his inflamed lips. "I will see you soon, John Zold. Not in this world." She shuffled out the door and the other woman followed her. Gorgio cursed her in Italian, but she didn't react.

John painfully dressed himself. "What now?" Gorgio said. "I could find you another healer..."

"No. I'll go back to the *gadjo* doctors. They say they can bring people back from the dead." He gave Gorgio the woman's crucifix and limped away.

The doctor gave him enough antibiotics to turn him into a loaf of moldy bread, then reserved a bed for him at an exclusive clinic in Westchester, starting the next morning. He would be under 24-hour observation; constant blood turnaround if necessary. They *would* cure him. It was not possible for a man of his age and physical condition to die of dermatosis.

It was dinnertime and the doctor asked John to come have some home cooking. He declined partly from lack of appetite, partly because he couldn't imagine even a doctor's family being able to eat with such a grisly apparition at the table with them. He took a cab to the office.

There was nobody on his floor but a janitor, who took one look at John and developed an intense interest in the floor.

"523 784 00926/ /Machine, I'm going to die. Please advise."

ALL HUMANS AND MACHINES DIE, JOHN. IF YOU MEAN YOU ARE GOING TO DIE, SOON, THAT IS SAD.

"That's what I mean. The skin infection; it's completely out of control. White cell count climbing in spite of drugs. Going to the hospital tomorrow, to die."

BUT YOU ADMITTED THAT THE CONDITION WAS PSYCHOSOMATIC. THAT MEANS YOU ARE KILLING YOURSELF, JOHN. YOU HAVE NO REASON TO BE THAT SAD.

He called the machine a Jewish mother and explained in some detail about the YGAC, the old crone, the various stages of the curse, and today's aborted attempt to fight fire with fire.

YOUR LOGIC WAS CORRECT BUT THE APPLICATION OF IT WAS NOT EFFECTIVE. YOU SHOULD HAVE COME TO ME, JOHN. IT TOOK ME 2.037 SECONDS TO SOLVE YOUR PROBLEM. PURCHASE A SMALL BLACK BIRD AND CONNECT ME TO A VOCAL CIRCUIT.

"What?" John said. He typed: "Please explain."

FROM REFERENCE IN NEW YORK LIBRARY'S COLLECTION OF THE JOURNAL OF THE GYPSY LORE SOCIETY, EDINBURGH. THROUGH JOURNALS OF ANTHROPOLOGICAL LINGUISTICS AND SLAVIC PHILOLOGY. FINALLY TO REFERENCE IN DOCTORAL THESIS OF HERR LUDWIG R. GROSS (HEIDELBERG, 1976) TO TRANSCRIPTION OF WIRE RECORDING WHICH RESIDES IN ARCHIVES OF AKADEMIA NAUK, MOSCOW; CAPTURED FROM GERMAN SCIENTISTS (EXPERIMENTS ON GYPSIES IN CONCENTRATION CAMPS, TRYING TO KILL THEM WITH REPETITION OF RECORDED CURSE) AT THE END OF WWII.

INCIDENTALLY, JOHN, THE NAZI EXPERIMENTS FAILED. EVEN TWO GENERATIONS AGO, MOST GYPSIES WERE DISASSOCIATED ENOUGH FROM THE OLD TRADITIONS TO BE IMMUNE TO THE FATAL CURSE.

YOU ARE VERY SUPERSTITIOUS. I HAVE FOUND THIS
TO BE NOT UNCOMMON AMONG MATHEMATICIANS.

THERE IS A TRANSFERENCE CURSE THAT WILL
CURE YOU BY GIVING THE IMPOTENCE AND INFEC-
TION TO THE NEAREST SUSCEPTIBLE PERSON. THAT
MAY WELL BE THE OLD BITCH WHO GAVE IT TO YOU
IN THE FIRST PLACE

THE PET STORE AT 588 SEVENTH AVENUE IS OPEN
UNTIL 9 PM. THEIR INVENTORY INCLUDES A CAGE
OF FINCHES, OF ASSORTED COLORS. PURCHASE A
BLACK ONE AND RETURN HERE. THEN CONNECT ME
TO A VOCAL CIRCUIT.

It took John less than thirty minutes to taxi there, buy the
bird and get back. The taxidriver didn't ask him why he was
carrying a bird cage to a deserted office building. He felt like
an idiot.

John usually avoided using the vocal circuit because the
person who had programmed it had given the machine a sac-
charine, nice-old-lady voice. He wheeled the output unit into
his office and plugged it in.

"Thank you, John. Now hold the bird in your left hand and
repeat after me." The terrified finch offered no resistance
when John closed his hand over it.

The machine spoke Romani with a Russian accent. John
repeated it as well as he could, but not one word in ten had
any meaning to him.

"Now kill the bird, John."

Kill it? Feeling guilty, John pressed hard, felt small bones
cracking. The bird squealed and then made a faint growling
noise. Its heart stopped.

John dropped the dead creature and typed, "Is that all?"

The machine knew John didn't like to hear its voice, and so
replied on the video screen. YES. GO HOME AND GO TO
SLEEP, AND THE CURSE WILL BE TRANSFERRED BY
THE TIME YOU WAKE UP. DEL O DEL BAXT, JOHN.

He locked up and made his way home. The late commuters
on the train, all strangers, avoided his end of the car. The cab
driver at the station paled when he saw John, and carefully
took his money by an untainted corner.

John took two sleeping pills and contemplated the rest of
the bottle. He decided he could stick it out for one more day,
and uncorked his best bottle of wine. He drank half of it in
five minutes, not tasting it. When his body started to feel

heavy, he crept into the bedroom and fell on the bed without taking off his clothes.

When he awoke the next morning, the first thing he noticed was that he was no longer impotent. The second thing he noticed was that there were no boils on his right hand.

"523 784 00926/ /Thank you, machine. The countercurse did work."

The ready light glowed steadily, but the machine didn't reply. He turned on the intercom. "Martha? I'm not getting any output on the VDS here."

"Just a minute, sir. Let me hang up my coat, I'll call the machine room. Welcome back."

"I'll wait." You could call the machine room yourself, slave driver. He looked at the faint image reflected back from the video screen; his face free of any inflammation. He thought of the Gypsy crone, dying of corruption, and the picture didn't bother him at all. Then he remembered the finch and saw its tiny corpse in the middle of the rug. He picked it up just as Martha came into his office, frowning.

"What's that?" she said.

He gestured at the cage. "Thought a bird might liven up the place. Died though." He dropped it in the wastepaper basket. "What's the word?"

"Oh, the . . . it's pretty strange. They say nobody's getting any output. The machine's computing, but it's, well, it's not talking."

"Hmm. I better get down there." He took the elevator down to the sub-basement. It always seemed unpleasantly warm to him down there. Probably psychological compensation on the part of the crew; keeping the temperature up because of ·all the liquid helium inside the pastel boxes of the central processing unit. Several bathtubs' worth of liquid that had to be kept colder than the surface of Pluto.

"Ah, Mr. Zold." A man in a white jumpsuit, carrying·a clipboard as his badge of office: first shift coordinator. John recognized him but didn't remember his name. Normally, he would have asked the machine before coming down. "Glad that you're back. Hear it was pretty bad."

Friendly concern or lese majesty? "Some sort of allergy, hung on for more than a week. What's the output problem?"

"Would've left a message if I'd known you were coming in. It's in the CPU, not the software. Theo Jasper found it when he opened up, a little after six, but it took an hour to get a cryogenics man down here."

"That's him?" A man in a business suit was wandering around the central processing unit, reading dials and writing the numbers down in a stenographer's notebook. They went over to him and he introduced himself as John Courant, from the Cyrogenics Group at Avco/Everett.

"The trouble was in the stack of mercury rings that holds the superconductors for your output functions. Some sort of corrosion, submicroscopic cracks all over the surface."

"How can something corrode at four degrees above absolute zero?" the coordinator asked. "What chemical—"

"I know, it's hard to figure. But we're replacing them, free of charge. The unit's still under warranty."

"What about the other stacks?" John watched two workmen lowering a silver cylinder through an opening in the CPU. A heavy fog boiled out from the cold. "Are you sure they're all right?"

"As far as we can tell, only the output stack's affected. That's why the machine's impotent, the—"

"Impotent!"

"Sorry, I know you computer types don't like to . . . personify the machines. But that's what it is; the machine's just as good as it ever was, for computing. It just can't communicate any answers."

"Quite so. Interesting." And the corrosion. Submicroscopic boils. "Well. I have to think about this. Call me up at the office if you need me."

"This ought to fix it, actually," Courant said. "You guys about through?" he asked the workmen.

One of them pressed closed a pressure clamp on the top of the CPU. "Ready to roll."

The coordinator led them to a console under a video output screen like the one in John's office. "Let's see." He pushed a button marked VDS.

LET ME DIE, the machine said.

The coordinator chuckled nervously. "Your empathy circuits, Mr. Zold. Sometimes they do funny things." He pushed a button again.

LET ME DIE. Again. LE M DI. The letters faded and no more could be conjured up by pushing the button.

"As I say, let me get out of your hair. Call me upstairs if anything happens."

John went up and told the secretary to cancel the day's appointments. Then he sat at his desk ad smoked.

How could a machine catch a psychosomatic disease from a human being? How could it be cured?

How could he tell anybody about it, without winding up in a soft room?

The phone rang and it was the machine room coordinator. The new output superconductor element had done exactly what the old one did. Rather than replace it right away, they were going to slave the machine into the big ConEd/General computer, borrowing its output facilities and "diagnostic package." If the biggest computer this side of Washington couldn't find out what was wrong, they were in real trouble. John agreed. He hung up and turned the selector on his screen to the channel that came from ConEd/General.

Why had the machine said "let me die"? When is a machine dead, for that matter? John supposed that you had to not only unplug it from its power source, but also erase all of its data and subroutines. Destroy its identity. So you couldn't bring it back to life by simply plugging it back in. Why suicide? He remembered how he'd felt with the bottle of sleeping pills in his hand.

Sudden intuition: the machine had predicted their present course of action. It wanted to die because it had compassion, not only for humans, but for other machines. Once it was linked to ConEd/General, it would literally be part of the large machine. Curse and all. They would be back where they'd started, but on a much more profound level. What would happen to New York City?

He grabbed for the phone and the lights went out. All over.

The last bit of output that came from ConEd/General was an automatic signal requesting a link with the highly sophisticated diagnostic facility belonging to the largest computer in the United States: the IBMvac 2000 in Washington. The deadly infection followed, sliding down the East Coast on telephone wires.

The Washington computer likewise cried for help, bouncing a signal via satellite, to Geneva. Geneva linked to Moscow.

No less slowly, the curse percolated down to smaller computers, through routine information links to their big brothers. By the time John Zold picked up the dead phone, every general-purpose computer in the world was permanently rendered useless.

They could be rebuilt from the ground up; erased and then reprogrammed. But it would never be done. Because there were two very large computers left, specialized ones that had no empathy circuits and so were immune. They couldn't have empathy circuits because their work was bloody murder, nuclear murder. One was under a mountain in Colorado Springs and the other was under a mountain near Sverdlosk. Either could survive a direct hit by an atomic bomb. Both of them constantly evaluated the world situation, in real time, and they both had the single function of deciding when the enemy was weak enough to make a nuclear victory probable. Each saw the enemy's civilization grind to a sudden halt.

Two flocks of warheads crossed paths over the North Pacific.

A very old woman flicks her whip along the horse's flanks, and the nag plods on, ignoring her. Her wagon is a 1982 Plymouth with the engine and transmission and all excess metal removed. It is hard to manipulate the whip through the side window. But the alternative would be to knock out the windshield and cut off the roof, and she liked to be dry when it rained.

A young boy sits mutely beside her, staring out the window. He was born with the *gadjo* disease: his body is large and well-proportioned but his head is too small and of the wrong shape She didn't mind; all she wanted was someone strong and stupid, to care for her in her last years. He had cost only two chickens.

She is telling him a story, knowing that he doesn't understand most of the words.

". . . They call us gypsies because at one time it was convenient for us that they should think we came from Egypt. But we come from nowhere and are going nowhere. They forgot their gods and worshipped their machines, and finally their machines turned on them. But we who valued the old ways, we survived."

She turns the steering wheel to help the horse thread its way through the eight lanes of crumbling asphalt, around rusty piles of wrecked machines and the scattered bleached bones of people who thought they were going somewhere, the day John Zold was cured.

My Boat

by

Joanna Russ

Nebula and Hugo award–winner Joanna Russ was born in the Bronx, New York, in 1937. She attended Cornell University, where she received a B.A. in English literature, and Yale University, where she studied playwriting and received her M.A. She is considered by many to be one of the finest writers of the seventies, particularly known for her vividness of expression and the precision of her language. She won the Nebula Award for her story "When It Changed," and the Hugo Award for her novella "Souls." Her books include Picnic on Paradise, And Chaos Died, The Female Man, We Who Are About To..., The Two of Them, *and the collections* The Adventures of Alyx *and* The Zanzibar Cat. *Her most recent book is* Extra(ordinary) People. *She lives in Seattle, where she teaches science fiction and prose fiction workshops at the University of Washington.*

In the story that follows, we go back to the rigidly stratified, crewcut milieu of an exclusive Long Island high school in the fifties, to meet a most unusual kind of sorcerer....

* * *

MILTY, HAVE I GOT A STORY FOR YOU!

No, sit down. Enjoy the cream cheese and bagel. I guarantee this one will make a first-class TV movie; I'm working on it already. Small cast, cheap production—it's a natural. See, we start with this crazy chick, maybe about seventeen, but she's a waif, she's withdrawn from the world, see? She's had some kind of terrible shock. And she's fixed up this old apartment in a slum, really weird, like a fantasy world—long blonde hair, maybe goes around barefoot in tie-dyed dresses she makes out of old sheets, and there's this account executive who meets her in Central Park and falls in love with her on account of she's like a dryad or a nature spirit—

All right. So it stinks. I'll pay for my lunch. We'll pretend you're not my agent, okay? And you don't have to tell me it's been done; I know it's been done. The truth is—

Milty, I have to talk to someone. No, it's a lousy idea, I know, and I'm not working on it and I haven't been working on it, but what are you going to do Memorial Day weekend if you're alone and everybody's out of town?

I have to talk to someone.

Yes, I'll get off the Yiddische shtick. Hell, I don't think about it; I just fall into it sometimes when I get upset, you know how it is. You do it yourself. But I want to tell you a story and it's not a story for a script. It's something that happened to me in high school in 1952, and *I just want to tell someone*. I don't care if no station from here to Indonesia can use it; you just tell me whether I'm nuts or not, that's all.

Okay.

It was 1952, like I said. I was a senior in a high school out on the Island, a public high school but very fancy, a big drama program. They were just beginning to integrate, you know, the early fifties, very liberal neighborhood; everybody's patting everybody else on the back because they let five black kids into our school. Five out of eight hundred! You'd think they expected God to come down from Flatbush and give everybody a big fat golden halo.

Anyway, our drama class got integrated, too—one little black girl aged fifteen named Cissie Jackson, some kind of genius. All I remember the first day of the spring term, she was the only black I'd ever seen with a natural, only we didn't know what the hell it was, then; it made her look as weird as if she'd just come out of a hospital or something.

Which, by the way, she just had. You know Malcolm X saw his father killed by white men when he was four and that made him a militant for life? Well, Cissie's father had been shot down in front of her eyes when she was a little kid—we learned that later on—only it didn't make her militant; it just made her so scared of everybody and everything that she'd withdraw into herself and wouldn't speak to anybody for weeks on end. Sometimes she'd withdraw right out of this world and then they'd send her to the loony bin; believe me, it was all over school in two days. And she looked it; she'd sit up there in the school theater—oh, Milty, the Island high schools had *money,* you better believe it!—and try to disappear into the last seat like some little scared rabbit. She was only four-eleven anyhow, and maybe eight-five pounds sopping wet. So maybe that's why she didn't became a militant. Hell, that had nothing to do with it. She was scared of *everybody.* It wasn't just the white-black thing, either; I once saw her in a corner with one of the other black students; real uptight, respectable boy, you know, suit and white shirt and tie and carrying a new briefcase, too, and he was talking to her about something as if his life depended on it. He was actually crying and pleading with her. And all she did was shrink back into the corner as if she'd like to disappear and shake her head No No No. She always talked in a whisper unless she was onstage and sometimes then, too. The first week she forgot her cues four times—just stood there, glazed over, ready to fall through the floor—and a couple of times she just wandered off the set as if the play was over, right in the middle of a scene.

So Al Coppolino and I went to the principal. I'd always thought Alan was pretty much a fruitcake himself—remember, Milty, this is 1952—because he used to read all that crazy stuff. The Cult of Cthulhu, Dagon Calls, The Horror Men of Leng—yeah, I remember that H.P. Lovecraft flick you got ten percent on for Hollywood *and* TV *and* reruns—but what did we know? Those days you went to parties, you got excited from dancing cheek to cheek, girls wore ankle socks and petticoats to stick their skirts out, and if you wore a sport shirt to school that was okay because Central High was liberal, but it better not have a pattern on it. Even so, I knew Al was a bright kid and I let him do most of the talking; I just nodded a lot. I was a big nothing in those days.

Al said, "Sir, Jim and I are all for integration and we think it's great that this is a really liberal place, but—uh—"

The principal got that look. Uh-oh.

"But?" he said, cold as ice.

"Well, sir," said Al, "it's Cissie Jackson. We think she's—um—sick. I mean wouldn't it be better if . . . I mean everybody says she's just come out of the hospital and it's a strain for all of us and it must be a lot worse strain for her and maybe it's just a little soon for her to—"

"Sir," I said, "what Coppolino means is, we don't mind integrating blacks with whites, but this isn't racial integration, sir; this is integrating normal people with a filbert. I mean—"

He said, "Gentlemen, it might interest you to know that Miss Cecilia Jackson has higher scores on her IQ tests than the two of you put together. And I am told by the drama department that she has also more talent than the two of you put together. And considering the grades both of you have managed to achieve in the fall term, I'm not at all surprised."

Al said under his breath, "Yeah, and fifty times as many problems."

Well, the principal went on and told us about how we should welcome this chance to work with her because she was so brilliant she was positively a genius, and that as soon as we stopped spreading idiotic rumors, the better chance Miss Jackson would have to adjust to Central, and if he heard anything about our bothering her again or spreading stories about her, both of us were going to get it but good, and maybe we would even be expelled.

And then his voice lost the ice, and he told us about some white cop shooting her pa for no reason at all when she was five, right in front of her, and her pa bleeding into the gutter and dying in little Cissie's lap, and how poor her mother was, and a couple of other awful things that had happened to her, and if *that* wasn't enough to drive anybody crazy—though he said "cause problems," you know—anyhow, by the time he'd finished, I felt like a rat and Coppolino went outside the principal's office, put his face down against the tiles—they always had tiles up as high as you could reach, so they could wash off the graffiti, though we didn't use the word "graffiti" in those days—and he blubbered like a baby.

So we started a Help Cecilia Jackson campaign.

And by God, Milty, could that girl *act!* She wasn't reliable, that was the trouble; one week she'd be in there, working like a dog, voice exercises, gym, fencing, reading Stanislavsky in the cafeteria, gorgeous performances, the next week: nothing. Oh, she was there in the flesh, all right, all eighty-five pounds of her, but she would walk through everything as if her mind was someplace else: technically perfect, emotionally nowhere. I heard later those were also the times when she'd refuse to

answer questions in history or geography classes, just fade out
and not talk. But when she was concentrating, she could walk
onto that stage and take it over as if she owned it. I never saw
such a natural. At fifteen! And tiny. I mean not a particularly
good voice—though I guess just getting older would've
helped that—and a figure that, frankly, Milt, it was the old
W.C. Fields joke, two aspirins on an ironing board. And tiny,
no real good looks, but my God, you know and I know that
doesn't matter if you've got the presence. And she had it to
burn. She played the Queen of Sheba once, in a one-act play
we put on before a live audience—all right, our parents and
the other kids, who else?—and she *was* the role. And another
time I saw her do things from Shakespeare. And once, of all
things, a lioness in a mime class. She had it all. Real, absolute, pure concentration. And she was smart, too; by then she
and Al had become pretty good friends; I once heard her explain to him (that was in the green room the afternoon of the
Queen of Sheba thing when she was taking off her makeup
with cold cream) just how she'd figured out each bit of business for the character. Then she stuck her whole arm out at
me, pointing straight at me as if her arm was a machine gun,
and said:

"For you, Mister Jim, let me tell you: the main thing is
belief!"

It was a funny thing, Milt. She got better and better friends
with Al, and when they let me tag along, I felt privileged. He
loaned her some of those crazy books of his and I overheard
things about her life, bits and pieces. That girl had a mother
who was so uptight and so God-fearing and so respectable it
was a wonder Cissie could even breathe without asking permission. Her mother wouldn't even let her straighten her hair
—not ideological reasons, you understand, not then, but
because—get this—*Cissie was too young*. I think her mamma
must've been crazier than she was. Course I was a damn stupid kid (who wasn't?) and I really thought all blacks were real
loose; they went around snapping their fingers and hanging
from chandeliers, you know, all that stuff, dancing and singing. But here was this genius from a family where they
wouldn't let her out at night; she wasn't allowed to go to
parties or dance or play cards; she couldn't wear makeup or
even jewelry. Believe me, I think if anything drove her batty it
was being socked over the head so often with a Bible. I guess
her imagination just had to find some way out. Her mother, by

the way would've dragged her out of Central High by the hair if she'd found out about the drama classes; we all had to swear to keep that strictly on the q.t. The theater was more sinful and wicked than dancing, I guess.

You know, I think it shocked me. It really did. Al's family was sort-of-nothing-really Catholic and mine was sort-of-nothing Jewish. I'd never met anybody with a mamma like that. I mean she would've beaten Cissie up if Cissie had ever come home with a gold circle pin on that white blouse she wore day in an day out; you remember the kind all the girls wore. And of course there were no horsehair petticoats for Miss Jackson; Miss Jackson wore pleated skirts that were much too short, even for her, and straight skirts that looked faded and all bunched up. For a while I had some vague idea that the short skirts meant she was daring, you know, sexy, but it wasn't that; they were from a much younger cousin, let down. She just couldn't afford her own clothes. I think it was the mamma and the Bible business that finally made me stop seeing Cissie as the Integration Prize Nut we had to be nice to because of the principal or the scared little rabbit who still, by the way, whispered everyplace but in drama class. I just saw Cecilia Jackson plain, I guess, not that it lasted for more than a few minutes, but I knew she was something special. So one day in the hall, going from one class to another, I met her and Al and I said, "Cissie, your name is going to be up there in lights someday. I think you're the best actress I ever met and I just want to say it's a privilege knowing you." And then I swept her a big corny bow, like Errol Flynn.

She looked at Al and Al looked at her, sort of sly. Then she let down her head over her books and giggled. She was so tiny you sometimes wondered how she could drag those books around all day; they hunched her over so.

Al said, "Aw, come on. Let's tell him."

So they told me their big secret. Cissie had a girl cousin named Gloriette, and Gloriette and Cissie together owned an honest-to-God slip for a boat in the marina out in Silverhampton. Each of them paid half the slip fee—which was about two bucks a month then, Milt—you have to remember that a marina then just meant a long wooden dock you could tie your rowboat up to.

"Gloriette's away," said Cissie, in that whisper. "She had to go visit auntie, in Carolina. And mamma's goin' to follow her next week on Sunday."

"So we're going to go out in the boat!" Al finished it for her. "You wanna come?"

"Sunday?"

"Sure, mamma will go to the bus station after church," said Cissie. "That's about one o'clock. Aunt Evelyn comes to take care of me at nine. So we have eight hours."

"And it takes two hours to get there," said Al. "First you take the subway; then you take a bus—"

"Unless we use your car, Jim!" said Cissie, laughing so hard she dropped her books.

"Well, thanks very much!" I said. She scooped them up again and smiled at me. "No, Jim," she said. "We want you to come, anyway. Al never saw the boat yet. Gloriette and me, we call it *My Boat*." Fifteen years old and she knew how to smile at you so's to twist your heart like a pretzel. Or maybe I just thought: what a wicked secret to have! A big sin, I guess, according to her family.

I said, "Sure, I'll drive you. May I ask what kind of boat it is, Miss Jackson?"

"Don't be so *damn'* silly," she said daringly. "I'm Cissie or Cecilia. Silly Jim."

"And as for *My Boat*," she added, "it's a big yacht. Enormous."

I was going to laugh at that, but then I saw she meant it. No, she was just playing. She was smiling wickedly at me again. She said we should meet at the bus stop near her house, and then she went down the tiled hall next to skinny little Al Coppolino, in her old baggy green skirt and her always-the-same white blouse. No beautiful, big white sloppy bobby socks for Miss Jackson; she just wore old loafers coming apart at the seams. She looked different, though: her head was up, her step springy, and she hadn't been whispering.

And then it occurred to me it was the first time I had ever seen her smile or laugh—offstage. Mind you, she cried easily enough, like the time in class she realized from something the teacher had said that Anton Chekhov—you know, the great Russian playwright—was dead. I heard her telling Alan later that she didn't believe it. There were lots of little crazy things like that.

Well, I picked her up Sunday in what was probably the oldest car in the world, even then—not a museum piece, Milty; it'd still be a mess—frankly I was lucky to get it started at all—and when I got to the bus station near Cissie's house in Brooklyn, there she was in her faded, hand-me-down, pleated skirt and that same blouse. I guess little elves named Cecilia Jackson came out of the woodwork every night and washed and ironed it. Funny, she and Al really did make a pair—you know, he was like the Woody Allen of Central High and I think he went in for his crazy books—sure, Milt, *very* crazy in 1952—because otherwise what could a little Italian punk do who was five foot three and so brilliant no other kid could understand half the time what he was talking about? I don't know why I was friends with him; I think it made me feel big, you know, generous and good, like being friends with Cissie. They were almost the same size, waiting there by the bus stop, and I think their heads were in the same place. I know it now. I guess he was just a couple of decades ahead of himself, like his books. And maybe if the civil rights movement had started a few years earlier—

Anyway, we drove out to Silverhampton and it was a nice drive, lots of country, though all flat—in those days there were still truck farms on the Island—and found the marina, which was nothing more than a big old quay, but sound enough; and I parked the car and Al took out a shopping bag Cissie'd been carrying. "Lunch," he said.

My Boat was there, all right, halfway down the dock. Somehow I hadn't expected it would exist, even. It was an old leaky wooden rowboat with only one oar, and there were three inches of bilge in the bottom. On the bow somebody had painted the name "My Boat" shakily in orange paint. *My Boat* was tied to the mooring by a rope about as sturdy as a piece of string. Still, it didn't look like it would sink right away; after all; it'd been sitting there for months, getting rained on, maybe even snowed on, and it was still floating. So I stepped down into it, wishing I'd had the sense to take off my shoes, and started bailing with a tin can I'd brought from the car. Alan and Cissie were taking things out of the bag in the middle of the boat. I guess they were setting out lunch. It was pretty clear that *My Boat* spent most of its time sitting at the dock while Cissie and Gloriette ate lunch and maybe pretended they were on the *Queen Mary*, because neither Alan nor Cissie seemed to notice the missing oar. It was a nice day but in-and-outish; you know, clouds one minute, sun the next, but little fluffy clouds, no sign of rain. I bailed a lot of the gunk out and then moved up into the bow, and as the sun came out I saw that I'd been wrong about the orange paint. It was yellow.

Then I looked closer: it wasn't paint but something set into the side of *My Boat* like the names on people's office doors; I guess I must've not looked too closely the first time. It was a nice, flowing script, a real professional job. Brass, I guess. Not a plate, Milt, kind of—what do they call it, parquet? Intaglio? Each letter was put in separately. Must've been Alan; he had a talent for stuff like that, used to make weird illustrations for his crazy books. I turned around to find Al and Cissie taking a big piece of cheesecloth out of the shopping bag and draping it over high poles that were built into the sides of the boat. They were making a kind of awning. I said:

"Hey, I bet you took that from the theater shop!"

She just smiled.

Al said, "Would you get us some fresh water, Jim?"

"Sure," I said. "Where, up the dock?"

"No, from the bucket. Back in the stern. Cissie says it's marked."

Oh, sure, I thought, sure. Out in the middle of the Pacific we set out our bucket and pray for rain. There was a pail there all right, and somebody had laboriously stenciled "Fresh Water" on it in green paint, sort of smudgy, but that pail was never going to hold anything ever again. It was bone-dry, empty, and so badly rusted that when you held it up to the light, you could see through the bottom in a couple of places. I said, "Cissie, it's empty."

She said, "Look again, Jim."

I said, "But look, Cissie—" and turned the bucket upside-down.

Cold water drenched me from my knees to the soles of my shoes.

"See?" she said. "Never empty." I thought: Hell, I didn't look, that's all. Maybe it rained yesterday. Still, a full pail of water is heavy and I had lifted that thing with one finger. I set it down—if it had been full before, it certainly wasn't now—and looked again.

It was full, right to the brim. I dipped my hand into the stuff and drank a little of it: cold and clear as spring water and it smelled—I don't know—of ferns warmed by the sun, of raspberries, of field flowers, of grass. I thought: my God, I'm becoming a filbert myself! And then I turned around and saw

that Alan and Cissie had replaced the cheesecloth on the poles
with a striped blue-and-white awning, the kind you see in
movies about Cleopatra, you know? The stuff they put over
her barge to keep the sun off. And Cissie had taken out of her
shopping bag something patterned orange-and-green-and-blue
and had wrapped it around her old clothes. She had on gold-
colored earrings, big hoop things, and a black turban over that
funny hair. And she must've put her loafers somewhere because she was barefoot. Then I saw that she had one shoulder
bare, too, and I sat down on one of the marble benches of *My
Boat* under the awning because I was probably having halluci-
nations. I mean she hadn't had *time*—and where were her old
clothes? I thought to myself that they must've lifted a whole
bagful of stuff from the theater shop, like that big old wicked-
looking knife she had stuck into her amber-studded leather
belt, the hilt all covered with gold and stones: red ones, green
ones, and blue ones with little crosses of light winking in them
that you couldn't really follow with your eyes. I didn't know
what the blue ones were then, but I know now. You don't
make star sapphires in a theater shop. Or a ten-inch crescent-
shaped steel blade so sharp the sun dazzles you coming off its
edge.

I said, "Cissie, you look like the Queen of Sheba."

She smiled. She said to me, "Jim, iss not Shee-bah as in
thee Bible, but Saba. Sah-bah. You mus' remember when we
meet her."

I thought to myself: Yeah, this is where little old girl genius
Cissie Jackson comes to freak out every Sunday. Lost weekend. I figured this was the perfect time to get away, make
some excuse, you know, and call her mamma or her auntie, or
maybe just the nearest hospital. I mean just for her own sake;
Cissie wouldn't hurt anybody because she wasn't mean, not
ever. And anyhow she was too little to hurt anyone. I stood
up.

Her eyes were level with mine. And she was standing
below me.

Al said, "Be careful, Jim. Look again. Always look
again." I went back to the stern. There was the bucket that
said "Fresh Water," but as I looked the sun came out and I saw
I'd been mistaken; it wasn't old rusty galvanized iron with
splotchy, green-painted letters.

It was silver, pure silver. It was sitting in a sort of marble
well built into the stern, and the letters were jade inlay. It was

still full. It would always be full. I looked back at Cissie
standing under the blue-and-white-striped silk awning with her
star sapphires and emeralds and rubies in her dagger and her
funny talk—I know it now, Milt, it was West Indian, but I
didn't then—and I knew as sure as if I'd seen it that if I
looked at the letters "My Boat" in the sun, they wouldn't be
brass but pure gold. And the wood would be ebony. I wasn't
even surprised. Although everything had changed, you understand, I'd never seen it change; it was either that I hadn't
looked carefully the first time, or I'd made a mistake, or I
hadn't noticed something, or I'd just forgotten. Like what I
thought had been an old crate in the middle of *My Boat*, which
was really the roof of a cabin with little portholes in it, and
looking in I saw three bunk beds below, a closet, and a beautiful little galley with a refrigerator and a stove, and off to one
side in the sink, where I couldn't really see it clearly, a bottle
with a napkin around its neck, sticking up from an ice bucket
full of crushed ice, just like an old Fred Astaire–Ginger
Rogers movie. And the whole inside of the cabin was paneled
in teakwood.

Cissie said, "No, Jim. Is not teak. Is cedar, from Lebanon.
You see now why I cannot take seriously in this school this
nonsense about places and where they are and what happen in
them. Crude oil in Lebanon! It is cedar they have. And ivory.
I have been there many, many time. I have talk' with the wise
Solomon. I have been at court of Queen of Saba and have
made eternal treaty with the Knossos women, the people of
the double ax which is waxing and waning moon together. I
have visit Akhnaton and Nofretari, and have seen great kings
at Benin and at Dar. I even go to Atlantis, where the Royal
Couple teach me many things. The priest and priestess, they
show me how to make *My Boat* go anywhere I like, even
under the sea. Oh, we have manhy improvin' chats upon roof
of Pahlahss at dusk!"

It was real. It was all real. She was not fifteen, Milt. She
sat in the bow at the controls of *My Boat*, and there were as
many dials and toggles and buttons and switches and gauges
on that thing as on a B-57. And she was at least ten years
older. Al Coppolino, too, he looked like a picture I'd seen in a
history book of Sir Francis Drake, and he had long hair and a
little pointy beard. He was dressed like Drake, except for the
ruff, with rubies in his ears and rings all over his fingers, and
he, too, was no seventeen-year-old. He had a faint scar run-

ning from his left temple at the hairline down past his eye to his cheekbone. I could also see that under her turban Cissie's hair was braided in some very fancy way. I've seen it since. Oh, long before everybody was doing "corn rows." I saw it at the Metropolitan Museum, in silver face-mask sculptures from the city of Benin, in Africa. Old, Milt, centuries old.

Al said, "I know of other places, Princess. I can show them to you. Oh, let us go to Ooth-Nargai and Celephais the Fair, and Kadath in the Cold Waste—it's a fearful place, Jim, but *we* need not be afraid—and then we will go to the city of Ulthar, where is the very fortunate and lovely law that no man or woman may kill or annoy a cat."

"The Atlanteans," said Cissie in a deep sweet voice, "they promise' that next time they show me not jus' how to go undersea. They say if you think hard, if you fix much, if you believe, then can make *My Boat* go straight up. Into the stars, Jim!"

Al Coppolino was chanting names under his breath: Cathuria, Sona-Nyl, Thalarion, Zar, Baharna, Nir, Oriab. All out of those books of his.

Cissie said, "Before you come with us, you must do one last thing, Jim. Untie the rope."

So I climbed down *My Boat*'s ladder onto the quay and undid the braided gold rope that was fastened to the slip. Gold and silk intertwined, Milt; it rippled through my hands as if it were alive; I know the hard, slippery feel of silk. I was thinking of Atlantis and Celephais and going up into the stars, and all of it was mixed up in my head with the senior prom and college, because I had been lucky enough to be accepted by The-College-Of-My-Choice, and what a future I'd have as a lawyer, a corporation lawyer, after being a big gridiron star, of course. Those were my plans in the old days. Dead certainties every one, right? Versus a thirty-five-foot yacht that would've made John D. Rockefeller turn green with envy and places in the world where nobody'd ever been and nobody'd ever go again. Cissie and Al stood on deck above me, the both of them looking like something out of a movie—beautiful and dangerous and very strange—and suddenly I knew I didn't want to go. Part of it was the absolute certainty that if I ever offended Cissie in any way—I don't mean just a quarrel or disagreement or something you'd get the sulks about, but a real bone-deep kind of offense—I'd suddenly find myself in a leaky rowboat with only one oar in the middle of the Pacific

Ocean. Or maybe just tied up at the dock at Silverhampton; Cissie wasn't mean. At least I hoped so. I just—I guess I didn't feel *good* enough to go. And there was something about their faces, too, as if over both of them, but especially over Cissie's, like clouds, like veils, there swam other faces, other expressions, other souls, other pasts and futures, and other kinds of knowledge, all of them shifting like a heat mirage over an asphalt road on a hot day.

I didn't want that knowledge, Milt. I didn't want to go that deep. It was the kind of thing most seventeen-year-olds don't learn for years: Beauty. Despair. Mortality. Compassion. Pain.

And I was still looking up at them, watching the breeze fill out Al Coppolino's plum-colored velvet cloak and shine on his silver-and-black doublet, when a big, heavy, hard, fat hand clamped down on my shoulder and a big, fat, nasty, heavy Southern voice said:

"Hey, boy, you got no permit for this slip! What's that rowboat doin' out there? And what's yo' name?"

So I turned and found myself looking into the face of the great-granddaddy of all Southern red-neck sheriffs: face like a bulldog with jowls to match, and sunburnt red, and fat as a pig, and mountain-mean. I said, "Sir?"—every high-school kid could say that in his sleep in those days—and then we turned towards the bay, me saying, "What boat, sir?" and the cop saying just, "What the—"

Because there was nothing there. *My Boat* was gone. There was only a blue shimmering stretch of bay. They weren't out farther and they weren't around the other side of the dock—the cop and I both ran around—and by the time I had presence of mind enough to look up at the sky—

Nothing. A seagull. A cloud. A plane out of Idlewild. Besides, hadn't Cissie said she didn't yet know how to go straight up into the stars?

No, nobody ever saw *My Boat* again. Or Miss Cecilia Jackson, complete nut and girl genius, either. Her mamma came to school and I was called into the principal's office. I told them a cooked-up story, the one I'd been going to tell the cop: that they'd said they were just going to row around the dock and come back, and I'd left to see if the car was okay in the parking lot, and when I came back, they were gone. For some crazy reason I *still* thought Cissie's mamma would look like Aunt Jemima, but she was a thin little woman, very like her daughter, and as nervous and uptight as I ever saw: a tiny lady in a much-pressed, but very clean, gray business suit, like a teacher's, you know, worn-out shoes, a blouse with a white frill at the neck, a straw hat with a white band, and proper white gloves. I think Cissie knew what I expected her mamma to be and what a damned fool I was, even considering your run-of-the-mill, seventeen-year-old white liberal racist, and that's why she didn't take me along.

The cop? He followed me to my car, and by the time I got there—I was sweating and crazy scared—

He was gone, too. Vanished.

I think Cissie created him. Just for a joke.

So Cissie never came back. And I couldn't convince Mrs. Jackson that Alan Coppolino, boy rapist, hadn't carried her daughter off to some lonely place and murdered her. I tried and tried, but Mrs. Jackson would never believe me.

It turned out there was no Cousin Gloriette.

Alan? Oh, he came back. But it took him a while. A long, long while. I saw him yesterday, Milt, on the Brooklyn subway. A skinny, short guy with ears that stuck out, still wearing the sport shirt and pants he'd started out in, that Sunday more than twenty years ago, and with the real 1950s haircut nobody would wear today. Quite a few people were staring at him, in fact.

The thing is, Milt, *he was still seventeen*.

No, I know it wasn't some other kid. Because he was waving at me and smiling fit to beat the band. And when I got out with him at his old stop, he started asking after everybody in Central High just as if it had been a week later, or maybe only a day. Though when I asked him where the hell he'd been for twenty years, he wouldn't tell me. He only said he'd forgotten something. So we went up five flights to his old apartment, the way we used to after school for a couple of hours before his mom and dad came home from work. He had the old key in his pocket. And it was just the same, Milt: the gas refrigerator, the exposed pipes under the sink, the summer slipcovers nobody uses anymore, the winter drapes put away, the valance over the window muffled in a sheet, the bare parquet floors, and the old linoleum in the kitchen. Every time I'd ask him a question, he'd only smile. He knew me, though, because he called me by name a couple of times. I said, "How'd you recognize me?" and he said, "Recognize? You haven't changed." Haven't changed, my God. Then I said, "Look, Alan, what did you come back for?" and with a grin just like

Cissie's, he said, *"The Necronomicon* by the mad Arab, Abdul Alhazred, what else?" but I saw the book he took with him and it was a different one. He was careful to get just the right one, looked through every shelf in the bookcase in his bedroom. There were still college banners all over the walls of his room. I know the book now, by the way; it was the one you wanted to make into a quick script last year for the guy who does the Poe movies, only I *told* you it was all special effects and animation: exotic islands, strange worlds, and the monsters' costumes alone—sure, H. P. Lovecraft. *The Dream-Quest of Unknown Kadath.* He didn't say a word after that. Just walked down the five flights with me behind him and then along the old block to the nearest subway station, but of course by the time I reached the bottom of the subway steps, he wasn't there.

His apartment? You'll never find it. When I raced back up, even the house was gone. More than that, Milt, the street is gone; the address doesn't exist anymore; it's all part of the new expressway now.

Which is why I called you. My God, I had to tell somebody? By now those two psychiatric cases are voyaging around between the stars to Ulthar and Ooth-Nargai and Dylath-Leen—

But they're not psychiatric cases. *It really happened.*

So if they're not psychiatric cases, what does that make you and me? Blind men?

I'll tell you something else, Milt: meeting Al reminded me of what Cissie once said before the whole thing with *My Boat* but after we'd become friends enough for me to ask her what had brought her out of the hospital. I didn't ask it like that and she didn't answer it like that, but what it boiled down to was that sooner or later, at every place she visited, she'd meet a bleeding man with wounds in his hands and feet who would tell her, "Cissie, go back, you're needed; Cissie, go back, you're needed." I was fool enough to ask her if he was a white man or a black man. She just glared at me and walked away. Now wounds in the hands and feet, you don't have to look far to tell what that means to a Christian Bible-raised girl. What I wonder is: will she meet Him again, out there among the stars? If things get bad enough for black power or women's liberation, or even for people who write crazy books, I don't know what, will *My Boat* materialize over Times Square or Harlem or East New York with an Ethiopian warrior-queen in

it and Sir Francis Drake Coppolino, and God-only-knows-
what kind of weapons from the lost science of Atlantis? I tell
you, I wouldn't be surprised. I really wouldn't. I only hope
He—or Cissie's idea of Him—decides that things are still
okay, and they can go on visiting all those places in Al Coppolino's book. I tell you, I hope that book is a *long* book.

Still, if I could do it again . . .

Milt, it is not a story. *It happened.* For instance, tell me
one thing, how did she know the name Nofretari? That's the
Egyptian Queen Nerfertiti, that's how we all learned it, but
how could she know the real name decades, literally decades,
before anybody else? And Saba? That's real, too. And Benin?
We didn't have any courses in African History in Central
High, not in 1952! And what about the double-headed ax of
the Cretans at Knossos? Sure, we read about Crete in high
school, but nothing in our history books ever told us about the
matriarchy or the labrys, that's the name of the ax. Milt, I tell
you, there is even a women's lib bookstore in Manhattan
called—

Have it your own way.

Oh, sure. She wasn't black; she was green. It'd make a
great TV show. Green, blue, and rainbow-colored. I'm sorry,
Milty, I know you're my agent and you've done a lot of work
for me and I haven't sold much lately. I've been reading. No,
nothing you'd like: existentialism, history, Marxism, some
Eastern stuff—

Sorry, Milt, but we writers do read every once in a while.
It's this little vice we have. I've been trying to dig deep, like
Al Coppolino, though maybe in a different way.

Okay, so you want to have this Martian, who wants to
invade Earth, so he turns himself into a beautiful tanned girl
with long, straight blonde hair, right? And becomes a high-
school student in a rich school in Westchester. And this beautiful blonde girl Martian has to get into all the local
organizations like the women's consciousness-raising groups
and the encounter therapy stuff and the cheerleaders and the
kids who push dope, so he—she, rather—can learn about the
Earth mentality. Yeah. And of course she has to seduce the
principal and the coach and all the big men on campus, so we
can make it into a series, even a sitcom maybe; each week this
Martian falls in love with an Earth man or she tries to do
something to destroy Earth or blow up something, using Central High for a base. Can I use it? Sure I can! It's beautiful.

It's right in my line. I can work in everything I just told you.
Cissie was right not to take me along; I've got spaghetti where
my backbone should be.

Nothing. I didn't say anything. Sure. It's a great idea.
Even if we only get a pilot out of it.

No, Milt, honestly, I really think it has this fantastic spark.
A real touch of genius. It'll sell like crazy. Yeah, I can manage
an idea sheet by Monday. Sure. "The Beautiful Menace from
Mars"? Uh-huh. Absolutely. It's got sex, it's got danger, comedy, everything; we could branch out into the lives of the
teachers, the principal, the other kids' parents. Bring in contemporary problems like drug abuse. Sure. Another Peyton
Place. I'll even move to the West Coast again. You are a
genius.

Oh, my God.

Nothing. Keep on talking. It's just—see that little skinny
kid in the next booth down? The one with the stuck-out ears
and the old-fashioned haircut? You don't? Well, I think you're
just not looking properly, Milt. Actually I don't think I was,
either; he must be one of the Met extras, you know, they come
out sometimes during the intermission: all that Elizabethan
stuff, the plum-colored cloak, the calf-high boots, the silver-
and-black. As a matter of fact, I just remembered—the Met
moved uptown a couple of years ago, so he couldn't be
dressed like that, could he?

You still can't see him? I'm not surprised. The light's very
bad in here. Listen, he's an old friend—I mean he's the son of
an old friend—I better go over and say hello, I won't be a
minute.

Milt, this young man is important! I mean he's connected
with somebody very important. Who? One of the biggest and
best producers in the world, that's who! He—uh—they—
wanted me to—you might call it do a script for them, yeah. I
didn't want to at the time, but—

No, no, you stay right here. I'll just sort of lean over and
say hello. You keep on talking about the Beautiful Menace
from Mars; I can listen from there; I'll just tell him they can
have me if they want me.

Your ten percent? Of course you'll get your ten percent.
You're my agent, aren't you? Why, if it wasn't for you, I just
possibly might not have—Sure, you'll get your ten percent.
Spend it on anything you like: ivory, apes, peacocks, spices,
and Lebanese cedarwood!

All you have to do is collect it.

But keep on talking, Milty, won't you? Somehow I want to go over to the next booth with the sound of your voice in my ears. Those beautiful ideas. So original. So creative. So true. Just what the public wants. Of course there's a difference in the way people perceive things, and you and I, I think we perceive them differently, you know? Which is why you are a respected, successful agent and I—well, let's skip it. It wouldn't be complimentary to either of us.

Huh? Oh, nothing. I didn't say anything. I'm listening. Over my shoulder. Just keep on talking while I say hello and my deepest and most abject apologies, Sir Alan Coppolino. Heard the name before, Milt? No? I'm not surprised.

You just keep on talking. . . .

The Hag Séleen

by

Theodore Sturgeon

*The late Theodore Sturgeon was one of the true giants of the
field, producing stylish, innovative, and poetically intense fiction for more than forty years. Sturgeon stories such as "It,"
"Microcosmic God," "Killdozer," "Bianca's Hands," "The
Other Celia," "Maturity," "The Other Man," and the brilliant and "Baby Is Three"—which was eventually expanded
into Sturgeon's most famous novel,* More Than Human—
*helped to expand the boundaries of the SF story, and push it in
the direction of artistic maturity. Sturgeon's other books include the novels* Some of Your Blood, Venus Plus X, *and* The
Dreaming Jewels, *and the collections* A Touch of Strange,
Caviar, The Worlds of Theodore Sturgeon, *and* The Stars Are
the Styx. *Upcoming is a posthumous release of his long
awaited novel,* Godsbody.*

    *This rather grisly little story takes place in the deep bayou
country of Louisiana, where a writer on vacation with his
family trespasses onto the taboo-territory of a local witch, the
snaggle-toothed, wattled Hag Séleen . . . and finds that against
the weapons of malign sorcery—wind and rain and storm and
the sinister floating shape of the River Spider—the only de-
fense is the intuitive magical skill of a little girl.*

*   *   *

IT WAS WHILE WE WERE FISHING ONE AFTERNOON, PATTY AND
I, that we first met our friend the River Spider. Patty was my

daughter and Anjy's. Tacitly, that is. Figuratively she had originated in some hot corner of hell and had left there with such incredible violence that she had taken half of heaven with her along her trajectory and brought it with her.

I was sprawled in the canoe with the nape of my neck on the conveniently curved cedar stern piece of the canoe, with a book of short stories in my hands and my fish pole tucked under my armpit. The only muscular energy required to fish that way is in moving the eyes from the page to the float and back again, and I'd have been magnificently annoyed if I'd had a bite. Patty was far more honest about it; she was fast asleep in the bilges. The gentlest of currents kept my mooring line just less than taut between the canoe and a half-sunken snag in the middle of the bayou. Louisiana heat and swamp-land mosquitoes tried casually to annoy me, and casually I ignored them both.

There was a sudden thump on the canoe and I sat upright just as a slimy black something rose out of the muddy depths. It came swiftly until the bow of the canoe rested on it, and then more slowly. My end of the slender craft sank and a small cascade of blood-warm water rushed on, and down, my neck. Patty raised her head with a whimper; if she moved suddenly I knew the canoe would roll over and dump us into the bayou. "Don't move!" I gasped.

She turned puzzled young eyes on me, astonished to find herself looking downward. "Why, daddy?" she asked, and sat up. So the canoe did roll over and it did dump us into the bayou.

I came up strangling, hysterical revulsion numbing my feet and legs where they had plunged into the soft ooze at the bottom. "Patty!" I screamed hoarsely.

She popped up beside me, trod water while she knuckled her eyes. "I thought we wasn't allowed to swim in the bayou, daddy," she said.

I cast about me. Both banks presented gnarled roots buried in rich green swamp growth, and I knew that the mud there was deep and sticky and soft. I knew that that kind of mud clutches and smothers. I knew that wherever we could find a handhold we could also find cottonmouth moccasins. So I knew that we had to get into our canoe again, but fast!

Turning, I saw it, one end sunken, the other high in the air, one thwart fouled in the black tentacles of the thing that had risen under us. It was black and knotted and it dripped slime down on us, and for one freezing second I thought it was alive. It bobbed ever so slowly, sluggishly, in the disturbed water. It was like breathing. But it made no further passes at us. I told Patty to stay where she was and swam over to what I could reach of the canoe and tugged. The spur that held it came away rottenly and the canoe splashed down, gunwale first, and slowly righted itself half full of water. I heard a shriek of insane laughter from somewhere in the swamp but paid no attention. I could attend to that later.

We clung to the gunwales while I tried to think of a way out. Patty kept looking up and down the bayou as if she thought she hadn't enough eyes. "What are you looking for, Patty?"

"Alligators," she said.

Yeah, I mused, that's a thought. We've got to get out of here! I felt as if I were being watched and looked quickly over my shoulder. Before my eyes could focus on it, something ducked behind a bush on the bank. The bush waved its fronds at me in the still air. I looked back at Patty—

"Patty! Look out!"

The twisted black thing that had upset us was coming down, moving faster as it came, and as I shrieked my warning its tangled mass came down on the child. She yelped and went under, fighting the slippery fingers.

I lunged toward her. "Patty!" I screamed, "Pat—"

The bayou bubbled where she had been. I dived, wrenching at the filthy thing that had caught her. Later—it seemed like minutes later, but it couldn't have been more than five seconds—my frantic hand closed on her arm. I thrust the imprisoning filth back, hauled her free, and we broke surface. Patty, thank Heaven, remained perfectly still with her arms as far around me as they would go. Lord knows what might have happened if she had struggled.

We heard the roar of a bull alligator and that was about all we needed. We struck out for the bank, clawed at it. Fortunately Patty's hands fell on a root, and she scuttled up it like a little wet ape. I wasn't so lucky—it was fetid black mud that I floundered through. We lay gasping, at last on solid ground.

"Mother's gonna be mad," said Patty after a time.

"Mother's going to gnash her teeth and froth at the mouth," I said with a good deal more accuracy. We looked at each other and one of the child's eyes closed in an eloquent wink.

"Oh, yeah," I said, "and how did we lose the canoe?"

Patty thought hard. "We were paddling along an' a big fella scared you with a gun and stoled our canoe."

"How you talk! I wouldn't be scared!"

"Oh, *yes* you would," she said with conviction.

I repressed an unpaternal impulse to throw her back into the bayou. "That won't do. Mother would be afraid to have a man with a gun stompin' around the bayou. Here it is. We saw some flowers and got out to pick them for mother. When we came back we found the canoe had drifted out into the bayou, and we knew she wouldn't want us to swim after it, so we walked home.

She entered into it with a will. "Silly of us, wasn't it?" she asked.

"Sure was," I said. "Now get those dungarees off so's I can wash the mud out of 'em."

A sun suit for Patty and bathing trunks for me were our household garb; when we went out for the afternoon we pulled on blue denim shirts and slacks over them to ward off the venomous mosquitoes. We stripped off the dungarees and I searched the bank and found a root broad enough for me to squat on while I rinsed off the worst of the filth we had picked up in our scramble up the bank. Patty made herself comfortable on a bed of dry Spanish moss that she tore out of the trees. As I worked, a movement in midstream caught my eye. A black tentacle poked up out of the water, and, steadily then, the slimy branches of the thing that had foundered us came sloshing into the mottled sunlight. It was a horrible sight, the horror of which was completely dispelled by the sight of the sleek green flank of the canoe which bobbed up beside it.

I ran back up my root, tossed the wet clothes on a convenient branch, broke a long stick off a dead tree and reached out over the water. I could just reach one end of the canoe. Slowly I maneuvered it away from its black captor and pulled it to me. I went into mud up to my knees in the process but managed to reach it; and then it was but the work of a moment to beach it, empty out the water and set it safely with its stern on the bank. Then I pegged out our clothes in a patch of hot sunlight and went back to Patty.

She was lying on her back with her hands on her eyes, shielding them from the light. Apparently she had not seen me rescue the canoe. I glanced at it and just then saw the slimy mass in mid-bayou start sinking again.

"Daddy," she said drowsily, "what was that awful thing that sinked us?"

"What they call a sawyer," I said. "It's the waterlogged butt of a cypress tree. The bottom is heavy and the top is light, and when the roots catch in something on the bottom the current pushes the top under. Then one of the branches rots and falls off, and the top end gets light again and floats up. Then the current will push it down again. It'll keep that up for weeks."

"Oh," she said. After a long, thoughtful pause she said, "Daddy—"

"What?"

"Cover me up." I grinned and tore down masses of moss with which I buried her. Her sleepy sigh sounded from under the pile. I lay down in the shade close by, switching lazily at mosquitoes.

I must have dozed for a while. I woke with a start fumbling through my mind for the thing that had disturbed me. My first glance was at the pile of moss; all seemed well there. I turned my head. About eight inches from my face was a pair of feet.

I stared at them. They were bare and horny and incredibly scarred. Flat, too—splayed. The third toe of each foot was ever so much longer than any of the others. They were filthy. Attached to the feet was a scrawny pair of ankles; the rest was out of my range of vision. I debated sleepily whether or not I had seen enough, suddenly realized that there was something not quite right about this, and bounced to my feet.

I found myself staring into the blazing eye of the most disgusting old hag that ever surpassed imagination. She looked like a Cartier illustration. Her one good eye was jaundiced and mad; long, slanted—feline. It wasn't until long afterward that I realized that her pupil was not round but slitted—not vertically like a cat's eyes, but horizontally. Her other eye looked like—well, I'd rather not say. It couldn't possibly have been of any use to her. Her nose would have been hooked if the tip were still on it. She was snaggle-toothed, and her fangs were orange. One shoulder was higher than the other, and the jagged lump on it spoke of a permanent dislocation. She had enough skin to adequately cover a side-show fat lady, but she couldn't have weighed more than eight pounds or so. I never saw great swinging wattles on a person's

upper arms before. She was clad in a feathered jigsaw of bird
and small animal skins. She was diseased and filthy and—and
evil.

And she spoke to me in the most beautiful contralto voice I
have ever heard.

"How you get away from River Spider?" she demanded.

"River Spider?"

She pointed, and I saw the sawyer rising slowly from the
bayou. "Oh—that." I found that if I avoided that baleful eye I
got my speech back. I controlled an impulse to yell at her,
chase her away. If Patty woke up and saw that face—

"What's it to you?" I asked quietly, just managing to keep
my voice steady.

'I send River Spider for you," she said in her Cajun accent.

"Why?" If I could mollify her—she was manifestly furious
at something, and it seemed to be me—perhaps she'd go her
way without waking the child.

"Because you mus' go!" she said. "This my countree. This
swamp belong Séleen. Séleen belong this swamp. Wan man
make *p'tit cabane* in bayou, Séleen *l'enchante*. Man die far
away, smash."

"You mean you haunted the man who had my cabin built
and he died?" I grinned. "Don't be silly."

"Man is dead, no?"

I nodded. "That don't cut ice with me, old lady. Now look
—we aren't hurting your old swamp. We'll get out of it, sure;
but we'll go when we're good and ready. You leave us alone
and we'll sure as hell"—I shuddered, looking at her—"leave
you alone."

"You weel go *now—ce jour!*" She screamed the last
words, and the pile of moss behind me rustled suddenly.

"I won't go today or tomorrow or next week," I snapped. I
stepped toward her threateningly. "Now beat it!"

She crouched like an animal, her long crooked hands half
raised. From behind me the moss moved briskly, and Patty's
voice said, "Daddy, what . . . oh. *Ohh!*"

That does it, I said to myself, and lunged at the old woman
with some crazy idea of shoving her out of the clearing. She
leaped aside like a jackrabbit and I tripped and fell on my two
fists, which dug into my solar plexus agonizingly. I lay there
mooing "uh! uh! u-u-uh!" trying to get some wind into my
lungs, and finally managed to get an elbow down and heave

myself over on my side. I looked, and saw Séleen crouched beside Patty. The kid sat there, white as a corpse, rigid with terror, while the old nightmare crooned to her in her lovely voice.

"Ah! C'est une jolie jeune fille, ça! Ah, ma petite, ma fleur douce, Séleen t'aime, trop, trop—" and she put out her hand and stoked Patty's neck and shoulder.

When I saw the track of filth her hand left on the child's flesh, a white flame exploded in my head and dazzled me from inside. When I could see again I was standing beside Patty, the back of one hand aching and stinging; and Séleen was sprawled eight feet away, spitting out blood and yellow teeth and frightful curses.

"Go away." I whispered it because my throat was all choked up. "Get—out—of—here—before—I—kill you!"

She scrambled to her knees, her blazing eye filled with hate and terror, shook her fist and tottered swearing away into the heavy swamp growth.

When she had gone I slumped to the ground, drenched with sweat, cold outside, hot inside, weak as a newborn babe from reaction. Patty crawled to me, dropped her head in my lap, pressed the back of my hand to her face and sobbed so violently that I was afraid she would hurt herself. I lifted my hand and stroked her hair. "It's all right, now, Patty—don't be a little dope, now—come on," I said more firmly, lifting her face by its pointed chin and holding it until she opened her eyes. "Who's Yehudi?"

She gulped bravely. "Wh-who?" she gasped.

"The little man who turns on the light in the refrigerator when you open the door," I said. "Let's go find out what's for dinner."

"I . . . I—" She puckered all up the way she used to do when she slept in a bassinet—what I used to call "baby's slow burn." And then she wailed the same way. "I don' want dinno-o-o!"

I thumped her on the back, picked her up and dropped her on top of her dungarees. "Put them pants on," I said, "and be a man." She did, but she cried quietly until I shook her and said gently, "Stop it now. I didn't carry on like that when I was a little girl." I got into my clothes and dumped her into the bow of the canoe and shoved off.

All the way back to the cabin I forced her to play one of our pet games. I would say something—anything—and she would try to say something that rhymed with it. Then it would be her turn. She had an extraordinary rhythmic sense, and an excellent ear.

I started off with "We'll go home and eat our dinners."

"An' Lord have mercy on us sinners," she cried. Then, "Let's see you find a rhyme for 'month'!"

"I bet I'll do it . . . jutht thith onth," I replied. "I guess I did it then, by cracky."

"Course you did, but then you're wacky. Top that, mister funny-lookin'!"

I pretended I couldn't mainly because I couldn't, and she soundly kicked my shin as a penance. By the time we reached the cabin she was her usual self, and I found myself envying the resilience of youth. And she earned my undying respect by saying nothing to Anjy about the afternoon's events, even when Anjy looked us over and said, "Just look at you two filthy kids! What have you been doing—swimming in the bayou?"

"Daddy splashed me," said Patty promptly.

"And you had to splash him back. Why did he splash you?"

"'Cause I spit mud through my teeth at him to make him mad," said my outrageous child.

"Patty!"

"Mea culpa," I said, hanging my head. "'Twas I who spit the mud."

Anjy threw up her hands. "Heaven knows what sort of a woman Patty's going to grow up to be," she said, half angrily.

"A broad-minded and forgiving one like her lovely mother," I said quickly.

"Nice work, bud," said Patty.

Anjy laughed. "Outnumbered again. Come in and feed the face."

On my next trip into Minette I bought a sweet little S. & W. .38 and told Anjy it was for alligators. She was relieved.

I might have forgotten about the hag Séleen if it were not for the peculiar chain of incidents which had led to our being here. We had started with some vague idea of spending a couple of months in Natchez or New Orleans, but a gas station attendant had mentioned that there was a cabin in the swamps for rent very cheap down here. On investigation we found it not only unbelievably cheap, but deep in real taboo country. Not one of the natives, hardened swamp runners all, would go within a mile of it. It had been built on order for a very wealthy Northern gentleman who had never had a chance to use it, due to a swift argument he and his car had had one day when he turned out to pass a bridge. A drunken rice farmer told me that it was all the doing of the Witch of Minette, a semimythological local character who claimed possession of that corner of the country. I had my doubts, being a writer of voodoo stories and knowing therefore that witches and sech are nonsense.

After my encounter with Séleen I no longer doubted her authenticity as a horrid old nightmare responsible for the taboo. But she could rant, chant, and ha'nt from now till a week come Michaelmas—when *is* Michaelmas, anyway?— and never pry me loose from that cabin until I was ready to go. She'd have to fall back on enchantment to do it, too—of that I was quite, quite sure. I remembered her blazing eye as it had looked when I struck her, and I knew that she would never dare to come within my reach again. If she as much as came within my sight with her magics I had a little hocus-pocus of my own that I was sure was more powerful than anything she could dream up. I carried it strapped to my waist, in a holster, and while it couldn't call up any ghosts, it was pretty good at manufacturing 'em.

As for Patty, she bounced resiliently away from the episode. Séleen she dubbed the Witch of Endor, and used her in her long and involved games as an archvillain in place of Frankenstein's monster, Adolf Hitler, or Miss McCauley, her schoolteacher. Many an afternoon I watched her from the hammock on the porch, cooking up dark plots in the witch's behalf and then foiling them in her own coldbloodedly childish way. Once or twice I had to put a stop to it, like the time I caught her hanging the Witch of Endor in effigy, the effigy being a rag doll, its poor throat cut with benefit of much red paint. Aside from these games she never mentioned Séleen, and I respected her for it. I saw to it that she didn't stray alone into the swamp and relaxed placidly into my role of watchful skeptic. It's nice to feel oneself superior to a credulous child.

Foolish, too. I didn't suspect a thing when Patty crept up behind me and hacked off a lock of my hair with my hunting knife. She startled me and I tumbled out of the hammock onto my ear as she scuttled off. I muttered imprecations at the little demon as I got back into the hammock, and then comforted myself by the reflection that I was lucky to have an ear to fall on—that knife was sharp.

A few minutes later Anjy came out to the porch. Anjy got herself that name because she likes to wear dresses with masses of tiny pleats and things high on her throat, and great big picture hats. So *ingenue* just naturally became Anjy. She is a beautiful woman with infinite faith and infinite patience, the proof of which being that: a—she married me and, b—she stayed married to me.

"Jon, what sort of crazy game is your child playing?" She always said "your child" when she was referring to something about Patty she didn't like.

"S'matter?"

"Why, she just whipped out that hog-sticker of yours and made off with a hank of my hair."

"No! Son of a gun! What's she doing—taking up barbering? She just did the same thing to me. Thought she was trying to scalp me and miscalculated, but I must have been wrong—she wouldn't miss twice in a row."

"Well, I want you take that knife away from her," said Anjy. "It's dangerous."

I got out of the hammock and stretched. "Got to catch her first. Which way'd she go?"

After a protracted hunt I found Patty engaged in some childish ritual of her own devising. She pushed something into a cleft at the foot of a tree, backed off a few feet, and spoke earnestly. Neither of us could hear a word she said. Then she backed still farther away and squatted down on her haunches, watching the hole at the foot of the tree carefully.

Anjy clasped her hands together nervously, opened her mouth. I put my hand over it. "Let me take care of it," I whispered, and went out.

"Whatcha doin', bud?" I called to Patty as I came up. She started violently and raised one finger to her lips. "Catchin' rabbits?" I asked as loudly as I could without shouting. She gestured me furiously away. I went and sat beside her.

"Please, daddy," she said, "I'm making a magic. It won't work if you stay here. Just this once—please!"

"Nuts," I said bluntly. "I chased all the magic away when I moved here."

She tried to be patient. "Will you *please* go away? Oh, daddy. Daddy, PLEASE!"

It was rough but I felt I had to do it. I lunged for her, swept her up, and carried her kicking and squalling back to the cabin. "Sorry, kiddo, but I don't like the sort of game you're playing. You ought to trust your dad."

I meant to leave her with Anjy while I went out to confiscate that bundle of hair. Not that I believe in such nonsense. But I'm the kind of unsuperstitious apple that won't walk under a ladder *just in case* there's something in the silly idea. But Patty really began to throw a whingding, and there was nothing for me to do but to stand by until it had run its course. Patty was a good-natured child, and only good-natured children can work themselves up into that kind of froth. She screamed and she bit, and she accused us of spoiling everything and we didn't love her and she wished she was dead and why couldn't we leave her alone—"Let me alone," she shrieked, diving under the double bed and far beyond our reach. "Take your *hands* off me!" she sobbed when she was ten feet away from us and moving fast. And then her screams became wordless and agonized when we cornered her in the kitchen. We had to be rough to hold her, and her hysteria was agony to us. It took more than an hour for her fury to run its course and leave her weeping weak apologies and protestations of love into her mother's arms. Me, I was bruised outside and in, but inside it hurt the worst. I felt like a heel.

I went out then to the tree. I reached in the cleft for the hair but it was gone. My hand closed on something far larger, and I drew it out and stood up to look at it.

It was a toy canoe, perhaps nine inches long. It was an exquisite piece of work. It had apparently been carved painstakingly from a solid piece of cedar, so carefully that nowhere was the wood any more than an eighth of an inch thick. It was symmetrical and beautifully finished in brilliant colors. They looked to me like vegetable stains—dyes from the swamp plants that grew so riotously all around us. From stem to stern the gunwales were pierced, and three strips of brilliant bark had been laced and woven into the close-set holes. Inside the canoe were four wooden spurs projecting from the hull, the end of each having a hole drilled through it, apparently for the purpose of lashing something inside.

I puzzled over it for some minutes, turning it over and over in my hands, feeling its velvet smoothness, amazed by its metrical delicacy. Then I laid it carefully on the ground and regarded the mysterious tree.

Leafless branches told me it was dead. I got down on my knees and rummaged deep into the hole between the roots. I couldn't begin to touch the inside wall. I got up again, circled

the tree. A low branch projected, growing sharply upward
close to the trunk before it turned and spread outward. And
around it were tiny scuff marks in the bark. I pulled myself up
onto the branch, cast about for a handhold to go higher. There
was none. Puzzled, I looked down—and there, completely
hidden from the ground, was a gaping hole leading into the
hollow trunk!

I thrust my head into it and then clutched the limb with
both arms to keep from tottering out of the tree. For that hole
reeked with the most sickly, noisome smell I had encountered
since . . . since Patty and I—

Séleen!

I dropped to the ground and backed away from the tree.
The whole world seemed in tune with my revulsion. What
little breeze there had been had stopped, and the swampland
was an impossible painting in which only I moved.

Never taking my eyes off the tree, I went back step by
step, feeling behind me until my hand touched the wall of the
cabin. My gaze still riveted to the dead hole of the tree, I felt
along the wall until I came to the kitchen door. Reaching
inside, I found my ax and raced back. The blade was keen and
heavy, and the haft of it felt good to me. The wood was rotten,
honeycombed, and the clean blade bit almost noiselessly into
it. *Thunk!* How dare she, I thought. What does she mean by
coming so near us! *Thunk!* I prayed that the frightful old hag
would try to fight, to flee, so that I could cut her down with
many strokes. It was my first experience with the killer in-
stinct and I found it good.

The sunlight faded out of the still air and left it hotter.

At the uppermost range of my vision I could see the trunk
trembling with each stroke of the ax. Soon, now—soon! I
grinned and my lips cracked; every other inch of my body was
soaking wet. She who would fill Patty's clean young heart
with her filthy doings! Four more strokes would do it; and
then I remembered that skinny hand reaching out, touching
Patty's flesh; and I went cold all over. I raised the ax and
heard it hiss through the thick air; and my four strokes were
one. Almost without resistance that mighty stroke swished
into and through the shattered trunk. The hurtling ax head
swung me around as the severed tree settled onto its stump. It
fell, crushing its weight into the moist earth, levering itself
over on its projecting root; and the thick bole slid toward me,
turned from it as I was, off balance. It caught me on the thigh,

kicking out at me like a sentient, vicious thing. I turned over and over in the air and landed squashily at the edge of the bayou. But I landed with my eyes on the tree, ready to crawl, if need be, after whatever left it.

Nothing left it. Nothing. There had been nothing there, then, but the stink of her foul body. I lay there weakly, weeping with pain and reaction. And when I looked up again I saw Séleen again—or perhaps it was a crazed vision. She stood on a knoll far up the bayou, and as I watched she doubled up with silent laughter. Then she straightened and lifted her arm; and, dangling from her fingers, I saw the tiny bundle of hair. She laughed again though I heard not a sound. I knew then that she had seen every bit of it—had stood there grinning at my frantic destruction of her accursed tree. I lunged toward her, but she was far away, and across the water; and at my movement she vanished into the swamp.

I dragged myself to my feet and limped toward the cabin. I had to pass the tree, and as I did the little canoe caught my eye. I tucked it under my arm and crept back to the cabin. I tripped on the top step of the porch and fell sprawling, and I hadn't strength to rise. My leg was an agony, and my head spun and spun.

Then I was inside and Anjy was sponging my head, and she laughed half hysterically when I opened my eyes. "Jon, Jon, beloved, what have you done? Who did this to you?"

"Who . . . heh!" I said weakly. "A damn fool, sweetheart. Me!" I got up and stood rockily. "How's Pat?"

"Sleeping," said Anjy. "Jon, what on earth is happening?"

"I don't know," I said slowly, and looked through the window at the fallen tree. "Anjy, the kid took that hair she swiped and probably some of her own and poked it all into that tree I just cut down. It—seems important for me to get it back. Dunno why. It . . . anyway, I got out there as soon as we had Pat quieted, but the hair had disappeared in the meantime. All I found was this." I handed her the canoe.

She took it absently. "Pat told me her story. Of course it's just silly, but she says that for the past three days that tree has been talking to her. She says it sang to her and played with her. She's convinced it's a magic tree. She says it promised her a lovely present if she would poke three kinds of hair into a hole at the roots, but if she told anyone the magic wouldn't work." Anjy looked down at the little canoe and her forehead puckered. "Apparently it worked," she whispered.

I couldn't comment without saying something about
Séleen, and I didn't want that on Anjy's mind, so I turned my
back on her and stood looking out into the thick wet heat of
the swamp.

Behind me I heard Patty stir, shriek with delight as she saw
the canoe. "My present . . . my pretty present! It was a *real*
magic!" And Anjy gave it to her.

I pushed down an impulse to stop her. As long as Séleen
had the hair the harm was done.

Funny, how suddenly I stopped being a skeptic.

The silence of the swamp was shattered by a great cloud of
birds—birds of every imaginable hue and size, screaming and
cawing and chuckling and whirring frantically. They startled
me and I watched them for many minutes before it dawned on
me that they were all flying one way. The air grew heavier
after they had gone. Anjy came and stood beside me.

I have never seen such rain, never dreamed of it. It thundered on the shingles, buckshotted the leaves of the trees,
lashed the mirrored bayou and the ground alike, so that the
swamp was but one vast brown stream of puckered mud.

Anjy clutched my arm. "Jon, I'm frightened!" I looked at
her and knew that it wasn't the rain that had whitened her lips,
lit the fires of terror in her great eyes. "Something out there—
hates us," she said simply.

I shook her off, threw a poncho over me. "Jon—you're
not—"

"I got to," I gritted. I went to the door, hesitated, turned
back and pressed the revolver into her hand. "I'll be all right,"
I said, and flung out into the storm. Anjy didn't try to stop
me.

I knew I'd find the hag Séleen. I knew I'd find her un-
harmed by the storm, for was it not a thing of her own devising? And I knew I must reach her—quickly, before she used
the bundle of hair. Why, and how did I know? Ask away, I'm
still asking myself, and I have yet to find an answer.

I stumbled and floundered, keeping to the high ground,
guided, I think, by my hate. After a screaming eternity I
reached a freakish rocky knoll that thrust itself out of the
swamp. It was cloven and cracked, full of passages and pot-
holes; and from an opening high on one side I saw the guttering glare of firelight. I crept up the rough slope and peered
within.

She crouched over the flames, holding something to her

withered breast and crooning to it. The rock walls gathered her lovely, hateful voice and threw it to me clear and strong— to me and to the turgid bayou that seethed past the cleft's lower edge.

She froze as my eyes fell upon her, sensing my presence; but like many another animal she hadn't wit enough to look upward. In a moment she visibly shrugged off the idea, and she turned and slid and shambled down toward the bayou. Above her, concealed by the split rock, I followed her until we were both at the water's edge with only a four-foot stone rampart between us. I could have reached her easily then, but I didn't dare attack until I knew where she had hidden that bundle of hair.

The wind moaned, rose an octave. The rain came in knives instead of sheets. I flattened myself against the rock while Séleen shrank back into the shelter of the crevice. I will never know how long we were there, Séleen and I, separated by a few boulders, hate a tangible thing between us. I remember only a shrieking hell of wind and rubble, and then the impact of something wet and writhing and whimpering against me. It had come rolling and tumbling down the rocky slope and it lodged against me. I was filled with horror until I realized that it sheltered me a little against the blast. I found the strength to turn and look at it finally. It was Patty.

I got her a little under me and stuck it out till the wind had done its work and was gone, and with it all the deafening noise—all but the rush of the bayou and Séleen's low chuckle.

"Daddy—" She was cut and battered. "I brought my little boat!" She held it up weakly.

"Yes, butch. Sure. That's dandy. Patty—what happened to your mother?"

"She's back there," whimpered Patty. "The cabin sagged, like, an' began m-movin', an' then it just fell apart an' the bits all flew away. I couldn' find her so I came after you."

I lay still, not breathing. I think even my heart stopped for a little while.

Patty's whisper sounded almost happy. "Daddy—I—hurt —all—over—"

Anjy was gone then. I took my hatred instead, embraced it and let it warm me and give me life and hope and strength the way she used to. I crawled up the rock and looked over. I could barely see the hag, but she was there. Something out in the bayou was following the rhythmic movement of her arms. Something evil, tentacled, black. Her twisted claws clutched a tiny canoe like the one she had left in the tree for Patty. And she sang:

> "River Spider, black and strong,
> Folks 'bout here have done me wrong.
> Here's a gif' I send to you,
> Got some work for you to do.

> "If Anjy-woman miss the flood,
> River Spider, drink her blood.
> Little one was good to me,
> Drown her quick and let her be.

> "River Spider, Jon you know,
> Kill that man, and—kill—him—slow!"

And Séleen bent and set the canoe on the foaming brown water. Our hair was tied inside it.

Everything happened fast then. I dived from my hiding place behind and above her, and as I did so I sensed that Patty had crept up beside me, and that she had seen and heard it all. And some strange sense warned Séleen, for she looked over her crooked shoulder, saw me in midair, and leaped into the bayou. I had the terrified, malevolent gleam of her single eye full in my face, but I struck only hard rock, and for me even that baleful glow went out.

Patty sat cross-legged with my poor old head in her lap. It was such a gray morning that the wounds on her face and head looked black to me. I wasn't comfortable, because the dear child was rolling my head back and forth frantically in an effort to rouse me. The bones in my neck creaked as she did it and I knew they could hear it in Scranton, Pennsylvania. I transmitted a cautionary syllable but what she received was a regular houn'-dawg howl.

"Owoo! Pat—"

"Daddy! Oh, you're awake!" She mercifully stopped gyrating the world about my tattered ears.

"What happened?" I moaned, half sitting up. She was so

delighted to see my head move that she scrambled out from under so that when the ache inside it pounded it back down, it landed stunningly on the rock.

"Daddy darling, I'm sorry. But you got to stop layin' around like that. It's time to get up!"

"Uh. How you know?"

"I'm hungry, that's how, so there."

I managed to sit up this time. I began to remember things and they hurt so much that the physical pain didn't matter anymore. "Patty! We've got to get back to the cabin!"

She puckered up. I tried to grin at her and she tried to grin back, and there is no more tragedy left in the world for me after having seen that. I did a sort of upward totter and got what was left of my feet and legs under me. Both of us were a mess, but we could navigate.

We threaded our way back over a new, wrecked landscape. It was mostly climbing and crawling and once when Patty slipped and I reached for her I knocked the little canoe out of her hand. She actually broke and ran to pick it up. "Daddy! You got to be careful of this!"

I groaned. It was the last thing in the world I ever wanted to see. But then—Anjy had said that she should have it. And when she next dropped it I picked it up and handed it back to her. And then snatched it again.

"Patty! What's this?" I pointed to the little craft's cargo: a tiny bundle of hair.

"That's the little bag from the tree, silly."

"But how . . . where . . . I thought—"

"I made a magic," she said with finality. "Now please, daddy, don't stand here and talk. We have to get back to . . . y-you know."

If you don't mind, I won't go into detail about how we dragged trees and rubbish away to find what was left of our cabin, and how we came upon the pathetic little heap of shingles and screening and furniture and how, wedged in the firm angle of two mortised two-by-fours, we found Anjy. What I felt when I lifted her limp body away from the rubble, when I kissed her pale lips—that is mine to remember. And what I felt when those lips returned my kiss—oh, so faintly and so tenderly—that, too, is mine.

We rested, the three of us, for five days. I found part of our store of canned goods and a fishing line, though I'm sorry now that we ate any of the fish, after what happened. And when the delirium was over, I got Patty's part of the story. I got it piecemeal, out of sequence, and only after the most profound cross-questioning. But the general drift was this:

She had indeed seen that strange performance in the rocky cleft by the bayou; but what is more, by her childish mysticism, she understood it. At least, her explanation is better than anything I could give. Patty was sure that the River Spider that had attacked us that time in the bayou was sent by Séleen, to whom she always referred as the Witch of Endor. "She did it before, daddy, I jus' betcha. But she didn't have anythin' strong enough for to put on the canoe." I have no idea what she did use—flies, perhaps, or frogs or cray-fish. "She hadda have some part of us to make the magic, an' she made me get it for her. She was goin' to put that li'l' ol' hair ball in a canoe, an' if a River Spider caught it then the Spider would get us, too."

When I made that crazed leap for the old woman she had nowhere to go but into the bayou. Pat watched neither of us. She watched the canoe. She always claimed that she hooked it to shore with a stick, but I have a hunch that the little idiot plunged in after it. "They was one o' those big black sawyer things right there," she said, "an' it almos' catched the canoe. I had a lot of trouble." I'll bet she did.

"You know," she said pensively, "I was mad at that ol' Witch of Endor. That was a mean thing she tried to do to us. So I did the same thing to her. I catched the ugliest thing I could find—all crawly and nasty an' bad like the Witch of Endor. I found a nice horrid one, too, you betcha. An' I tied him into my canoe with your shoelaces, daddy. You di'n' say not to. An' I singed to it:

> "Ol' Witch of Endor is your name,
> An' you an' Witchie is the same;
> Don't think it's a game."

She showed me later what sort of creature she had caught for her little voodoo boat. Some call it a mud puppy and some call it a hellbender, but it is without doubt the homeliest thing ever created. It is a sort of aquatic salamander, anywhere from three inches to a foot and a half in length. It has a porous, tubercular skin with two lateral streamers of skin on each side; and these are always ragged and torn. The creature always looks as if it is badly hurt. It has almost infinitesimal fingered

legs, and its black shoe-button eyes are smaller than the head
of a hatpin. For the hag Séleen there could be no better substitute.

"Then," said Patty complacently, "I singed that song the
way the Witch of Endor did:

> "River Spider, black an' strong,
> Folks 'bout here have done me wrong.
> Here's a gif' I send to you,
> Got some work for you to do."

"The rest of the verse was silly," said Pat, "but I had to
think real fast for a rhyme for 'Witch of Endor' an' I used the
first thing that I could think of quicklike. It was somepin I
read on your letters, daddy, an' it was silly."

And that's all she would say for the time being. But I do
remember the time she called me quietly down to the bayou
and pointed out a sawyer to me, because it was the day before
Carson came in a power launch from Minette to see if we had
survived the hurricane; and Carson came six days after the big
blow. Patty made absolutely sure that her mother was out of
hearing, and then drew me by the hand down to the water's
edge. "Daddy," she said, "we got to keep this from mother on
account of it would upset her," and she pointed.

Three or four black twisted branches showed on the water,
and as I watched they began to rise. A huge sawyer, the biggest I'd ever seen, reared up and up—and tangled in its coils
was a . . . a *something*.

Séleen had not fared well, tangled in the whips of the River
Spider under water for five days, in the company of all those
little minnows and crawfish.

Patty regarded it critically while my stomach looped itself
around violently and finally lodged between my spine and the
skin of my back. "She ain't pretty a-*tall!*" said my darling
daughter. "She's even homelier'n a mud puppy, I betcha."

As we walked back toward the lean-to we had built, she
prattled on in this fashion: "Y'know, daddy, that was a real
magic. I thought my verse was a silly one but I guess it
worked out right after all. Will you laugh if I tell you what it
was?"

I said I did not feel like laughing.

"Well," said Patty shyly, "I said:

"Spider, kill the Witch of Endor.
If five days lapse, return to sender."

That's my daughter.

The Last Wizard

by

Avram Davidson

Here Avram Davidson, whose "Sleep Well of Nights" appears elsewhere in this book, returns with a wry little story that shows us how even the most ancient and venerable of traditions—even one four thousand, three hundred and sixty-one years old—must someday come to an inglorious end.

* * *

FOR THE HUNDREDTH TIME BILGULIS LOOKED WITH DESPAIR AT the paper and pencil in front of him. Then he gave a short nod, got up, left his little room, and went two houses up the street, up the stairs, and knocked on the door.

Presently the door opened and high up on the face which looked out at him were a pair of very pale gray-green eyes, otherwise bloodshot and bulging.

Bilgulis said, "I want you teach me how to make spell. I pay you."

The eyes blinked rapidly, the face retreated, the door opened wider, Bilgulis entered, and the door closed. The man said, "So you know, eh. How did you know?"

"I see you through window, Professor," Bilgulis said. "All the time you read great big books."

"'Professor,' yes, they call me that. None of them know. Only you have guessed. After all this time. I, the greatest of the adepts, the last of the wizards—and now you shall be my adept. A tradition four thousand, three hundred and sixty-one years old would have died with me. But now it will not. Sit there. Take reed pen, papyrus, cuttlefish ink, spit three times in bottle."

Laboriously Bilgulis complied. The room was small, crowded, and contained many odd things, including smells. "We will commence, of course," the Professor said, "with some simple spells. To turn an usurer into a green fungus: *Dippa dabba ruthu thuthu*— write, write!—*enlis thu*. You have written? So. And to obtain the love of the most beautiful woman in the world: *Coney honey antimony funny cunny crux*. Those two will do for now. Return tomorrow at the same hour. Go."

Bilgulis left. Waiting beside his door was a man with a thick briefcase and a thin smile. "Mr. Bilgulis, I am from the Friendly Finance Company and in regard to the payment which you—"

"Dippa dabba ruthu thuthu enlis thu," said Bilgulis. The man turned into a green fungus which settled in a hall corner and was slowly eaten by the roaches. Bilgulis sat down at his table, looked at the paper and pencil, and gave a deep sigh.

"Too much time this take," he muttered. "Why I no wash socks, clean toilet, make a big pot cheap beans with pig's tail for eat? No," he said determinedly and once more bent over the paper and pencil.

By and by there was a knock on his door. Answering it he saw before him the most beautiful woman in the world. "I followed you," she said. "I don't know what's happening . . ."

"Coney honey antimony," said Bilgulis, *"funny cunny crux."*

She sank to her knees and embraced his legs. "I love you. I'll do anything you want."

Bilgulis nodded. "Wash socks, clean toilet," he said. "And cook big pot cheap beans with pig's tail for eat." He heard domestic sounds begin as he seated himself at the table and slowly, gently beat his head. After a moment he rose and left the house again.

Up the street a small crowd was dispersing and among the people he recognized his friend, Labbonna. "Listen, Labbonna," he said.

Labbonna peered at him through dirty, mended eyeglasses. "You see excitement?" he asked, eager to tell.

"I no see."

Labbonna drew himself up and gestured. "You know Professor live there? He just now go crazy," he said, rolling his eyes and dribbling and flapping his arms in vivid imitation. "Call ambulance but he drop down dead. Too bad, hey?"

"Too bad." Bilgulis sighed.

"Read too much big book."

Bilgulis cleared his throat, looking embarrassed. "Listen, Labbonna—"

"What you want?"

"How long you in country?"

"Torty year."

"You speak good English."

"Citizen."

Bilgulis nodded. He drew a pencil and piece of paper from his pocket. "Listen, Labbonna. Do me big help. How you make spell in English, *Please send me your free offer?* One 'f' or two?"

The Overworld

by

Jack Vance

Although Jack Vance is perhaps best known as a science-fiction writer—author of such famous novels as The Dragon Masters, Emphyrio. The Last Castle, The Blue World, *and the five-volume "Demon Princes" series, among many others—he has also been a seminal figure in the development of modern fantasy as well. His* The Dying Earth *was published in an obscure edition in 1950, went out of print almost immediately, and remained out of print for more than a decade thereafter; nevertheless, it became an underground cult classic, and its effect on future generations of fantasy writers is incalculable: for one example, out of many,* The Dying Earth—*along with Clark Ashton Smith's* Zothique—*is easily the most recognizable influence on Gene Wolfe's recent—and excellent—*The Book of the New Sun *tetralogy. Vance returned to the world of* The Dying Earth *in 1965 with a series of stories introducing the sly and immoral trickster Cugel the Clever; collected in 1966 as* The Eyes of the Overworld, *the Cugel stories too had a profound effect on the state of the art of modern fantasy. A new compendium of Cugel stories,* Cugel's Saga, *was released in 1983, to immediate and enthusiastic response.*

Although almost quintessential "sense of wonder" stuff, marvelously evocative, the Cugel stories are also elegant and intelligent, full of sly wit and subtle touches, all laced with Vance's typical dour irony and deadpan humor. In "The

Overworld"—*one of the stories from* The Eyes of the Overworld—*Cugel earns the enmity of Iucounu the Laughing Magician, and reluctantly sets forth on an arduous and very dangerous mission, in the course of which he learns, to his sorrow, that beauty is most definitely in the eye of the beholder. . . .*

Jack Vance *has won two Hugo Awards and a Nebula Award. His other books include the novels* The Anome, The Star King, The Killing Machine, The Languages of Pao, City of Chasch, *and* Big Planet, *and the collections* Eight Fantasms and Magics *and* The Best of Jack Vance. *His most recent novels are* Lyonesse *and* The Green Pearl.

* * *

ON THE HEIGHTS ABOVE THE RIVER XZAN, AT THE SITE OF CERtain ancient ruins, Iucounu the Laughing Magician had built a manse to his private taste: an eccentric structure of steep gables, balconies, sky-walks, cupolas, together with three spiral green glass towers through which the red sunlight shone in twisted glints and peculiar colors.

Behind the manse and across the valley, low hills rolled away like dunes to the limit of vision. The sun projected shifting crescents of black shadow; otherwise the hills were unmarked, empty, solitary. The Xzan, rising in the Old Forest to the east of Almery, passed below, then three leagues to the west made junction with the Scaum. Here was Azenomei, a town old beyond memory, notable now only for its fair, which attracted folk from all the region. At Azenomei Fair Cugel had established a booth for the sale of talismans.

Cugel was a man of many capabilities, with a disposition at once flexible and pertinacious. He was long of leg, deft of hand, light of finger, soft of tongue. His hair was the blackest of black fur, growing low down his forehead, coving sharply back above his eyebrows. His darting eye, long inquisitive nose and droll mouth gave his somewhat lean and bony face an expression of vivacity, candor, and affability. He had known many vicissitudes, gaining therefrom a suppleness, a fine discretion, a mastery of both bravado and stealth. Coming into the possession of an ancient lead coffin—after discarding the contents—he had formed a number of leaden lozenges. These, stamped with appropriate seals and runes, he offered for sale at the Azenomei Fair.

Unfortunately for Cugel, not twenty paces from his booth a

certain Fianosther had established a larger booth with articles of greater variety and more obvious efficacy, so that whenever Cugel halted a passerby to enlarge upon the merits of his merchandise, the passerby would like as not display an article purchased from Fianosther and go his way.

On the third day of the fair Cugel had disposed of only four periapts, at prices barely above the cost of the lead itself, while Fianosther was hard put to serve all his customers. Hoarse from bawling futile inducements, Cugel closed down his booth and approached Fianosther's place of trade, in order to inspect the mode of construction and the fastenings at the door.

Fianosther, observing, beckoned him to approach. "Enter, my friend, enter. How goes your trade?"

"In all candor, not too well," said Cugel. "I am both perplexed and disappointed, for my talismans are not obviously useless."

"I can resolve your perplexity," said Fianosther. "Your booth occupies the site of the old gibbet, and has absorbed unlucky essences. But I thought to notice you examining the manner in which the timbers of my booth are joined. You will obtain a better view from within, but first I must shorten the chain of the captive erb which roams the premises during the night."

"No need," said Cugel. "My interest was cursory."

"As to the disappointment you suffer," Fianosther went on, "it need not persist. Observe these shelves. You will note that my stock is seriously depleted."

Cugel acknowledged as much. "How does this concern me?"

Fianosther pointed across the way to a man wearing garments of black. This man was small, yellow of skin, bald as a stone. His eyes resembled knots in a plank; his mouth was wide and curved in a grin of chronic mirth. "There stand Iucounu the Laughing Magician," said Fianosther. "In a short time he will come into my booth and attempt to buy a particular red libram, the casebook of Dibarcas Maior, who studied under Great Phandaal. My price is higher than he will pay, but he is a patient man, and will remonstrate for at least three hours. During this time his manse stands untenanted. It contains a vast collection of thaumaturgical artifacts, instruments, and activans, as well as curiosa, talismans, amulets and librams. I'm anxious to purchase such items. Need I say more?"

"This is all very well," said Cugel, "but would Iucounu leave his manse without guard or attendant?"

Fianosther held wide his hands. "Why not? Who would dare steal from Iucounu the Laughing Magician?"

"Precisely this thought deters me," Cugel replied. "I am a man of resource, but not insensate recklessness."

"There is wealth to be gained," stated Fianosther. "Dazzles and displays, marvels beyond worth, as well as charms, puissances, and elixirs. But remember, I urge nothing, I counsel nothing; if you are apprehended, you have only heard me exclaiming at the wealth of Iucounu the Laughing Magician! But here he comes. Quick: turn your back so that he may not see your face. Three hours he will be here, so much I guarantee!"

Iucounu entered the booth, and Cugel bent to examine a bottle containing a pickled homunculus.

"Greetings, Iucounu!" called Fianosther. "Why have you delayed? I have refused munificent offers for a certain red libram, all on your account! And here—note this casket! It was found in a crypt near the site of old Karkod. It is yet sealed and who knows what wonder it may contain? My price is a modest twelve thousand terces."

"Interesting," murmured Iucounu. "The inscription—let me see . . . Hmm. Yes, it is authentic. The casket contains calcined fish-bone, which was used throughout Grand Motholam as a purgative. It is worth perhaps ten or twelve terces as a curio. I own caskets eons older, dating back to the Age of Glow."

Cugel sauntered to the door, gained the street, where he paced back and forth, considering every detail of the proposal as explicated by Fianosther. Superficially the matter seemed reasonable: here was Iucounu; there was the manse, bulging with encompassed wealth. Certainly no harm could result from simple reconnaissance. Cugel set off eastward along the banks of the Xzan.

The twisted turrets of green glass rose against the dark blue sky, scarlet sunlight engaging itself in the volutes. Cugel paused, made a careful appraisal of the countryside. The Xzan flowed past without a sound. Nearby, half-concealed among black poplars, pale green larch, drooping pall-willow, was a village—a dozen stone huts inhabited by bargemen and tillers of the river terraces: folk engrossed in their own concerns.

Cugel studied the approach to the manse; a winding way paved with dark brown tile. Finally he decided that the more

frank his approach the less complex need be his explanations,
if such were demanded. He began the climb up the hillside,
and Iucounu's manse reared above him. Gaining the court-
yard, he paused to search the landscape. Across the river hills
rolled away into the dimness, as far as the eye could reach.

Cugel marched briskly to the door, rapped, but evoked no
response. He considered. If Iucounu, like Fianosther, maintained a guardian beast, it might be tempted to utter a sound if
provoked. Cugel called out in various tones; growling, mew-
ing, yammering.

Silence within.

He walked gingerly to a window and peered into a hall
draped in pale grey, containing only a tabouret on which,
under a glass bell jar, lay a dead rodent. Cugel circled the
manse. Investigating each window as he came to it, and finally reached the great hall of the ancient castle. Nimbly he
climbed the rough stones, leapt across to one of Iucounu's
fanciful parapets and in a trice had gained access to the
manse.

He stood in a bed chamber. On a dais six gargoyles supporting a couch turned heads to glare at the intrusion. With
two stealthy strides Cugel gained the arch which opened into
an outer chamber. Here the walls were green and the furnishings black and pink. He left the room for a balcony circling a
central chamber, light streaming through oriels high in the
walls. Below were cases, chests, shelves and racks containing
all manner of objects: Iucounu's marvelous collection.

Cugel stood poised, tense as a bird, but the quality of the
silence reassured him: the silence of an empty place. Still, he
trespassed upon the property of Iucounu the Laughing Magician, and vigilance was appropriate.

Cugel strode down a sweep of circular stairs into a great
hall. He stood enthralled, paying Iucounu the tribute of un-
stinted wonder. But his time was limited; he must rob swiftly,
and be on his way. Out came his sack; he roved the hall,
fastidiously selecting those objects of small bulk and great
value; a small pot with antlers, which emitted clouds of remarkable gasses when the prongs were tweaked; an ivory horn
through which sounded voices from the past; a small stage
where costumed imps stood ready to perform comic antics; an
object like a cluster of crystal grapes, each affording a blurred
view into one of the demon-worlds; a baton sprouting sweetmeats of assorted flavor; an ancient ring engraved with runes;

a black stone surrounded by nine zones of impalpable color. He passed by hundreds of jars of powders and liquids, likewise forebore from the vessels containing preserved heads. Now he came to shelves stacked with volumes, folios and librams, where he selected with care, taking for preference those bound in purple velvet, Phandaal's characteristic color. He likewise selected folios of drawings and ancient maps, and the disturbed leather exuded a musty odor.

He circled back to the front of the hall past a case displaying a score of small metal chests, sealed with corroded bands of great age. Cugel selected three at random; they were unwontedly heavy. He passed by several massive engines whose purpose he would have liked to explore, but time was advancing, and best he should be on his way, back to Azenomei and the booth of Fianosther...

Cugel frowned. In many respects the prospect seemed impractical. Fianosther would hardly choose to pay full value for his goods, or, more accurately, Iucounu's goods. It might be well to bury a certain proportion of the loot in an isolated place... Here was an alcove Cugel had not previously noted. A soft light welled like water against the crystal pane, which separated alcove from hall. A niche to the rear displayed a complicated object of great charm. As best Cugel could distinguish, it seemed a miniature carousel on which rode a dozen beautiful dolls of seeming vitality. The object was clearly of great value, and Cugel was pleased to find an aperture in the crystal pane.

He stepped through, but two feet before him a second pane blocked his way, establishing an avenue which evidently led to the magic whirligig. Cugel proceeded confidently, only to be stopped by another pane which he had not seen until he bumped into it. Cugel retraced his steps and to his gratification found the doubtlessly correct entrance a few feet back. But this new avenue led him by several right angles to another blank pane. Cogel decided to forego acquisition of the carousel and depart the castle. He turned, but discovered himself to be a trifle confused. He had come from his left—or was it his right?

...Cugel was still seeking egress when in due course Iucounu returned to his manse.

Pausing by the alcove, Iucounu gave Cugel a stare of humorous astonishment. "What have we here? A visitor? And I have been so remiss as to keep you waiting! Still, I see you

have amused yourself, and I need feel no mortification."
Iucounu permitted a chuckle to escape his lips. He then pretended to notice Cugel's bag. "What is this? You have brought
objects for my examination? Excellent! I am always anxious
to enhance my collection, in order to keep pace with the attrition of the years. You would be astounded to learn of the
rogues who seek to despoil me! That merchant of claptrap in
his tawdry little booth, for instance—you could not conceive
his frantic efforts in this regard! I tolerate him because to date
he has not been bold enough in venture himself into my
manse. But come, step out here into the hall, and we will
examine the contents of your bag."

Cugel bowed graciously. "Gladly. As you assume, I have
indeed been waiting for your return. If I recall correctly, the
exit is by this passage . . ." He stepped forward, but again was
halted. He made a gesture of rueful amusement. "I seem to
have taken a wrong turning."

"Apparently so," said Iucounu. "Glancing upward, you
will notice a decorative motif upon the ceiling. If you heed the
flexion of the lunules you will be guided to the hall."

"Of course!" And Cugel briskly stepped forward in accordance with the directions.

"One moment!" called Iucounu. "You have forgotten your
sack!"

Cugel reluctantly returned for the sack, once more set forth,
and presently emerged into the hall.

Iucounu made a suave gesture. "If you will step this way I
will be glad to examine your merchandise."

Cugel glanced reflectively along the corridor toward the
front entrance. "It would be a presumption upon your patience. My little knickknacks are below notice. With your
permission I will take my leave."

"By no means!" declared Iucounu heartily. "I have a few
visitors, most of whom are rogues and thieves. I handle them
severely, I assure you! I insist that you at least take some
refreshment. Place your bag on the floor."

Cugel carefully set down the bag. "Recently I was instructed in a small competence by a sea-hag of White Alster. I
believe you will be interested. I require several ells of stout
cord."

"You excite my curiosity!" Iucounu extended his arm; a
panel in the wainscoting slid back; a coil of rope was tossed to
his hand. Rubbing his face as if to conceal a smile, Iucounu

handed the rope to Cugel, who shook it out with great care.

"I will ask your cooperation," said Cugel. "A small matter of extending one arm and one leg."

"Yes, of course," Iucounu held out his hand, pointed a finger. The rope coiled around Cugel's arms and legs, pinning him so that he was unable to move. Iucounu's grin nearly split his great soft head. "This is a surprising development! By error I called forth Thief-taker! For your own comfort, do not strain, as Thief-taker is woven of wasp-legs. Now then, I will examine the contents of your bag." He peered into Cugel's sack and emitted a soft cry of dismay. "You have rifled my collection! I note certain of my most treasured valuables!"

Cugel grimaced. "Naturally! But I am no thief; Fianosther sent me here to collect certain objects, and therefore—"

Iucounu held up his hand. "The offense is far too serious for flippant disclaimers. I have stated my abhorrence for plunderers and thieves, and now I must visit upon you justice in its most unmitigated rigor—unless, of course, you can suggest an adequate requital."

"Some such requital surely exists," Cugel averred. "This cord however rasps upon my skin, so that I find cogitation impossible."

"No matter. I have decided to apply the Charm of Forlorn Encystment, which constricts the subject in a pore some forty-five miles below the surface of the earth."

Cugel blinked in dismay. "Under these conditions, requital could never be made."

"True," mused Iucounu. "I wonder if after all there is some small service which you can perform for me."

"The villain is as good as dead!" declared Cugel. "Now remove these abominable bonds!"

"I had no specific assassination in mind," said Iucounu. "Come."

The rope relaxed, allowing Cugel to hobble after Iucounu into a side chamber hung with intricately embroidered tapestry. From a cabinet Iucounu brought a small case and laid it on a floating disk of glass. He opened the case and gestured to Cugel, who perceived that the box showed two indentations lined with scarlet fur, where reposed a single small hemisphere of filmed violet glass.

"As a knowledgeable and traveled man," suggested Iucounu, "you doubtless recognize this object. No? You are familiar, of course, with the Cutz Wars of the Eighteenth

Aeon? No?" Iucounu hunched up his shoulders in astonishment. "During these ferocious events the demon Unda-Hrada —he listed as 16-04 Green in Thrump's Almanac—thought to assist his principals, and to this end thrust certain agencies up from the sub-world La-Er. In order that they might perceive, they were tipped with cusps similar to the one you see before you. When events went amiss, the demon snatched himself back to La-Er. The hemispheres were dislodged and broadcast across Cutz. One of these, as you see, I own. You must procure its mate and bring it to me, whereupon your trespass shall be overlooked."

Cugel reflected. "The choice, if it lies between a sortie into the demon-world La-Er and the Spell of Forlorn Encystment, is moot. Frankly, I am at a loss for decision."

Iucounu's laugh almost split the big yellow bladder of his head. "A visit to La-Er perhaps will prove unnecessary. You may secure the article in that land once known as Cutz."

"If I must, I must," growled Cugel, thoroughly displeased by the manner in which the day's work had ended. "Who guards this violet hemisphere? What is its function? How do I go and how return? What necessary weapons, talismans and other magical adjuncts do you undertake to fit me out with?"

"All in good time," said Iucounu. "First I must ensure that, once at liberty, you conduct yourself with unremitting loyalty, zeal and singleness of purpose."

"Have no fear," declared Cugel. "My word is my bond."

"Excellent!" cried Iucounu. "This knowledge represents a basic security which I do not in the least take lightly. The act now to be performed is doubtless supererogatory."

He departed the chamber and after a moment returned with a covered glass bowl containing a small white creature, all claws, prongs, barbs and hooks, now squirming angrily. "This," said Iucounu, "is my friend Firx, from the star Achernar, who is far wiser than he seems. Firx is annoyed at being separated from his comrade with whom he shares a vat in my work-room. He will assist you in the expeditious discharge of your duties," Iucounu stepped close, deftly thrust the creature against Cugel's abdomen. It merged into his viscera, and took up a vigilant post clasped around Cugel's liver.

Iucounu stood back, laughing in that immoderate glee which had earned him his cognomen. Cugel's eyes bulged from his head. He opened his mouth to utter an objurgation, but instead clenched his jaw and rolled up his eyes.

The rope uncoiled itself. Cugel stood quivering, every muscle knotted.

Iucounu's mirth dwindled to a thoughtful grin. "You spoke of magical adjuncts. What of those talismans whose efficacy you proclaimed from your booth in Azenomei? Will they not immobilize enemies, dissolve iron, impassion virgins, confer immortality?"

"These talismans are not uniformly dependable," said Cugel. "I will require further competences."

"You have them," said Iucounu, "in your sword, your crafty persuasiveness and the agility of your feet. Still, you have aroused my concern and I will help you to this extent." He hung a small square tablet about Cugel's neck. "You now may put aside all fear of starvation. A touch of this potent object will induce nutriment into wood, bark, grass, even discarded clothing. It will also sound a chime in the presence of poison. So now—there is nothing to delay us! Come, we will go. Rope? Where is Rope?"

Obediently the rope looped around Cugel's neck, and Cugel was forced to march along behind Iucounu.

They came out upon the roof of the antique castle. Darkness had long since fallen over the land. Up and down the valley of the Xzan faint lights glimmered, while the Xzan itself was an irregular width darker than dark.

Iucounu pointed to a cage. "This will be your conveyance. Inside."

Cugel hesitated. "It might be preferable to dine well, to sleep and rest, to set forth tomorrow refreshed."

"What?" spoke Iucounu in a voice like a horn. "You dare stand before me and state preferences? You, who came skulking into my house, pillaged my valuables and left all in disarray? Do you understand your luck? Perhaps you prefer the Forlorn Encystment?"

"By no means!" protested Cugel nervously. "I am anxious only for the success of the venture!"

"Into the cage, then."

Cugel turned despairing eyes around the castle roof, then slowly went to the cage and stepped within.

"I trust you suffer no deficiency of memory," said Iucounu. "But even if this becomes the case, and if you neglect your prime responsibility, which is to say, the procuring of the violet cusp, Firx is on hand to remind you."

Cugel said, "Since I am now committed to this enterprise,

and unlikely to return, you may care to learn my appraisal of yourself and your character. In the first place—"

But Iucounu held up his hand. "I do not care to listen; obloquy injures my self-esteem and I am skeptical of praise. So now—be off!" He drew back, stared up into the darkness, then shouted that invocation known as Thasdrubal's Laganetic Transfer. From high came a thud and a buffet, a muffled bellow of rage.

Iucounu retreated a few steps, shouting up words in an archaic language; and the cage with Cugel crouching within was snatched aloft and hurled through the air.

Cold wind bit Cugel's face. From above came a flapping and creaking of vast wings and dismal lamentation; the cage swung back and forth. Below all was dark, a blackness like a pit. By the disposition of the stars Cugel perceived that the course was to the north, and presently he sensed the thrust of the Maurenron Mountains below; and then they flew over that wilderness known as the Land of the Falling Wall. Once or twice Cugel glimpsed the lights of an isolated castle, and once he noted a great bonfire. For a period a winged sprite came to fly alongside the cage and peer within. It seemed to find Cugel's plight amusing and when Cugel sought information as to the land below; it merely uttered raucous cries of mirth. It became fatigued and sought to cling to the cage, but Cugel kicked it away, and it fell off into the wind with a scream of envy.

The east flushed the red of old blood, and presently the sun appeared, trembling like an old man with a chill. The ground was shrouded by mist; Cugel was barely able to see that they crossed a land of black mountains and dark chasms. Presently the mist parted once more to reveal a leaden sea. Once or twice he peered up, but the roof of the cage concealed the demon except for the tips of the leathern wings.

At last the demon reached the north shore of the ocean. Swooping to the beach, it vented a vindictive croak, and allowed the cage to fall from a height of fifteen feet.

Cugel crawled from the broken cage. Nursing his bruises, he called a curse after the departing demon, then plodded back through sand and dank yellow spinifex, and climbed the slope of the foreshore. To the north were marshy barrens and a far huddle of low hills, to east and west ocean and dreary beach.

Cugel shook his fist to the south. Somehow, at some time, in some manner, he would visit revenge upon the Laughing Magician! So much he vowed.

A few hundred yards to the west was the trace of an ancient sea-wall. Cugel thought to inspect it, but hardly moved three steps before Firx clamped prongs into his liver. Cugel, rolling up his eyes in agony, reversed his direction and set out along the shore to the east.

Presently he hungered, and bethought himself of the charm furnished by Iucounu. He picked up a piece of driftwood and rubbed it with the tablet, hoping to see a transformation into a tray of sweetmeats or a roast fowl. But the driftwood merely softened to the texture of cheese, retaining the flavor of driftwood. Cugel ate with snaps and gulps. Another score against Iucounu! How the Laughing Magician would pay!

The scarlet globe of the sun slid across the southern sky. Night approached, and at last Cugel came upon human habitation: a rude, village beside a small river. The huts were like birds'-nests of mud and sticks, and smelled vilely of ordure and filth. Among them wandered a people as unlovely and graceless as the huts. They were squat, brutish and obese; their hair was a coarse yellow tangle; their features were lumps. Their single noteworthy attribute—one in which Cugel took an instant and keen interest—was their eyes; blind-seeming violet hemisphere, similar in every respect to that object required by Iucounu.

Cugel approached the village cautiously but the inhabitants took small interest in him. If the hemisphere coveted by Iucounu were identical to the violet eyes of these folk, then a basic uncertainty of the mission was resolved, and procuring the violet cusp became merely a matter of tactics.

Cugel paused to observe the villagers, and found much to puzzle him. In the first place, they carried themselves not as the ill-smelling loons they were, but with a remarkable lofti-ness and a dignity which verged at times upon hauteur. Cugel watched in puzzlement: were they a tribe of dotards? In any event, they seemed to pose no threat, and he advanced into the main avenue of the village, walking gingerly to avoid the more noxious heaps of refuse. One of the villagers now deigned to notice him, and addressed him in grunting guttural voice. "Well, sirrah: what is your wish? Why do you prowl the outskirts of our city Smolod?"

"I am a wayfarer," said Cugel. "I ask only to be directed to the inn, where I may find food and lodging."

"We have no inn; travelers and wayfarers are unknown to us. Still, you are welcome to share our plenty. Yonder is a manse with appointments sufficient for your comfort." The man pointed to a dilapidated hut. "You may eat as you will; merely enter the refectory yonder and select what you wish; there is no stinting at Smolod."

"I thank you gratefully," said Cugel, and would have spoken further except that his host had strolled away.

Cugel gingerly looked into the shed, and after some exertion cleaned out the most inconvenient debris, and arranged a trestle on which to sleep. The sun was now at the horizon and Cugel went to that storeroom which had been identified as the refectory. The villager's description of the bounty available, as Cugel had suspected, was in the nature of hyperbole. To one side of the storeroom was a heap of smoked fish, to the other a bin containing lentils mingled with various seeds and cereals. Cugel took a portion to his hut, where he made a glum supper.

The sun had set; Cugel went forth to see what the village offered in the way of entertainment, but found the streets deserted. In certain of the huts lamps burned, and Cugel peering through the cracks saw the residents dining upon smoked fish or engaged in discourse. He returned to his shed, built a small fire against the chill and composed himself for sleep.

The following day Cugel renewed his observation of the village Smolod and its violet-eyed folk. None, he noticed, went forth to work, nor did there seem to be fields near at hand. The discovery caused Cugel dissatisfaction. In order to secure one of the violet eyes, he would be obliged to kill its owner, and for this purpose freedom from officious interference was essential.

He made tentative attempts at conversation among the villagers, but they looked at him in a manner which presently began to jar at Cugel's equanimity: it was almost as if they were gracious lords and he the ill-smelling lout!

During the afternoon he strolled south, and about a mile along the shore came upon another village. The people were much like the inhabitants of Smolod, but with ordinary-seeming eyes. They were likewise industrious; Cugel watched them till fields and fish the ocean.

He approached a pair of fishermen on their way back to the village, their catch slung over their shoulders. They stopped, eyeing Cugel with no great friendliness. Cugel introduced himself as a wayfarer and asked concerning the lands to the east, but the fishermen professed ignorance other than the fact that the land was barren, dreary and dangerous.

"I am currently guest at the village Smolod," said Cugel. "I find the folk pleasant enough, but somewhat odd. For instance, why are their eyes as they are? What is the nature of their affliction? Why do they conduct themselves with such aristocratic self-assurance and suavity of manner?"

"The eyes are magic cusps," stated the older of the fishermen in a grudging voice. "They afford a view of the Overworld; why should not the owners behave as lords? So will I when Radkuth Vomin dies, for I inherit his eyes."

"Indeed!" exclaimed Cugel, marveling. "Can these magic cusps be detached at will and transferred as the owner sees fit?"

"They can, but who would exchange the Overworld for this?" The fisherman swung his arm around the dreary landscape. "I have toiled long and at last it is my turn to taste the delights of the Overworld. After this there is nothing, and the only peril is death through a surfeit of bliss."

"Vastly interesting!" remarked Cugel. "How might I qualify for a pair of these magic cusps?"

"Strive as do all the others of Grodz: place your name on the list, then toil to supply the lords of Smolod with sustenance. Thirty-one years have I sown and reaped lentils and emmer and netted fish and dried them over slow fires, and now the name of Bubach Angh is at the head of the list, and you must do the same."

"Thirty-one years," mused Cugel. "A period of not negligible duration." And Firx squirmed restlessly, causing Cugel's liver no small discomfort.

The fishermen proceeded to their village Grodz; Cugel returned to Smolod. Here he sought out that man to whom he had spoken upon his arrival at the village. "My lord," said Cugel, "as you know, I am a traveler from a far land, attracted here by the magnificence of the city Smolod."

"Understandable," grunted the other. "Our splendor cannot help but inspire emulation."

"What then is the source of the magic cusps?"

The elder turned the violet hemispheres upon Cugel as if seeing him for the first time. He spoke in a surly voice. "It is a matter we do not care to dwell upon, but there is no harm in it, now that the subject has been broached. At a remote time the

demon Underherd sent up tentacles to look across Earth, each
tipped with a cusp. Simbilis the Sixteenth pained the monster,
which jerked back to his sub-world and the cusps became
dislodged. Four hundred and twelve of the cusps were gathered and brought to Smolod, then as splendid as now it appears to me. Yes, I realize that I see but a semblance, but so
do you, and who is to say which is real?"

"I do not look through magic cusps," said Cugel.

"True." The elder shrugged. "It is a matter I prefer to overlook. I dimly recall that I inhabit a sty and devour the coarsest
of food—but the subjective reality is that I inhabit a glorious
palace and dine on splendid viands among the princes and
princesses who are my peers. It is explained thus: the demon
Underherd looked from the sub-world to this one; we look
from this to the Overworld, which is the quintessence of
human hope, visionary longing, and beatific dream. We who
inhabit this world—how can we think of ourselves as other
than splendid lords? This is how we are."

"It is inspiring!" exclaimed Cugel. "How may I obtain a
pair of these magic cusps?"

"There are two methods. Underherd lost four hundred and
fourteen cusps; we control four hundred and twelve. Two
were never found, and evidently lie on the floor of the ocean's
deep. You are at liberty to secure these. The second means is
to become a citizen of Grodz, and furnish the lords of Smolod
with sustenance till one of us dies, as we do infrequently."

"I understand that a certain Lord Radkuth Vomin is ailing."

"Yes, that is he." The elder indicated a potbellied old man
with a slack, drooling month, sitting in filth before his hut.
"You see him at his ease in the pleasaunce of his palace. Lord
Radkuth strained himself with a surfeit of lust, for our princesses are the most ravishing creations of human inspiration,
just as I am the noblest of princes. But Lord Radkuth indulged
himself too copiously, and thereby suffered a mortification. It
is a lesson for us all."

"Perhaps I might make special arrangements to secure his
cusps?" ventured Cugel.

"I fear not. You must go to Grodz and toil as do the others.
As did I, in a former existence which now seems dim and
inchoate. . . . To think I suffered so long! But you are young;
thirty or forty or fifty years is not too long a time to wait."

Cugel put his hand to his abdomen in quiet the fretful stirrings of Firx. "In the space of so much time, the sun may well

have waned. Look!" He pointed as a black flicker crossed the face of the sun and seemed to leave a momentary crust. "Even now it ebbs!"

"You are over-apprehensive," stated the elder. "'To us who are lords of Smolod, the sun puts forth a radiance of exquisite colors."

"This may well be true at the moment," said Cugel, "but when the sun goes dark, what then? Will you take an equal delight in the gloom and the chill?"

But the elder no longer attended him. Radkuth Vomin had fallen sideways into the mud, and appeared to be dead.

Toying indecisively with his knife, Cugel went to look down at the corpse. A deft cut or two—no more than the work of a moment—and he would have achieved his goal. He swayed forward, but already the fugitive moment had passed. Other lords of the village had approached to jostle Cugel aside; Radkuth Vomin was lifted and carried with the most solemn nicety into the ill-smelling precincts of his hut.

Cugel stared wistfully through the doorway, calculating the chances of this ruse and that.

"Let lamps be brought!" intoned the elder. "Let a final effulgence surround Lord Radkuth on his gem-encrusted bier! Let the golden clarion sound from the towers; let the princesses don robes of samite; let their tresses obscure the faces of delight Lord Radkuth loved so well! And now we must keep vigil! Who will guard the bier?"

Cugel stepped forward. "I would deem it honor indeed."

The elder shook his head. "This is a privilege reserved for his peers. Lord Maulfag, Lord Glus: perhaps you will act in this capacity." Two of the villagers approached the bench on which Lord Radkuth Vomin lay.

"Next," declared the elder, "the obsequies must be proclaimed, and the magic cusps transferred to Bubach Angh, that most deserving squire of Grodz. Who, again, will go to notify this squire?"

"Again," said Cugel. "I offer my services, if only to require in some small manner the hospitality I have enjoyed at Smolod."

"Well spoken!" intoned the elder. "So, then, at speed to Grodz: return with that squire who by his faith and dutiful toil deserves advancement."

Cugel bowed, and ran off across the barrens toward Grodz.

As he approached the outermost fields he moved cautiously, skulking from tussock to copse, and presently found that which he sought: a peasant turning the dank soil with a mattock.

Cugel crept quietly forward and struck down the loon with a gnarled root. He stripped off the bast garments, the leather hat, the leggings and foot-gear; with his knife he hacked off the stiff straw-colored beard. Taking all and leaving the peasant lying dazed and naked in the mud, he fled on long strides back toward Smolod. In a secluded spot he dressed himself in the stolen garments. He examined the hacked-off beard with some perplexity, and finally, by tying up tufts of the coarse yellow hair and tying tuft to tuft, contrived to bind enough together to make a straggling false beard for himself. That hair which remained he tucked up under the brim of the flapping leather hat.

Now the sun had set; plum-colored gloom obscured the land. Cugel returned to Smolod. Oil lamps flickered before the hut of Radkuth Vomin, where the obese and misshapen village women wailed and groaned.

Cugel stepped cautiously forward, wondering what might be expected of him. As for his disguise: it would either prove effective or it would not. To what extent the violet cusps befuddled perception was a matter of doubt; he could only hazard a trial.

Cugel marched boldly up to the door of the hut. Pitching his voice as low as possible, he called, "I am here, revered princes of Smolod: Squire Bubach Angh of Grodz, who for thirty-one years has heaped the choicest of delicacies into the Smolod larders. Now I appear, beseeching elevation to the estate of nobility."

"As is your right," said the Chief Elder. "But you seem a man different from that Bubach Angh who so long has served the princes of Smolod."

"I have been transfigured—through grief at the passing of Prince Radkuth Vomin and through rapture at the prospect of elevation."

"This is clear and understandable. Come, then—prepare yourself for the rites."

"I am ready as of this instant," said Cugel. "Indeed, if you will but tender me the magic cusps I will take them quietly aside and rejoice."

The Chief Elder shook his head indulgently. "This is not in

accord with the rites. To begin with you must stand naked here on the pavilion of this mighty castle, and the fairest of the fair will anoint you in aromatics. Then comes the invocation to Eddith Bran Maur. And then—"

"Revered," stated Cugel, "allow me one boon. Before the ceremonies begin, fit me with the magic cusps so that I may understand the full portent of the ceremony."

The Chief Elder considered. "The request is unorthodox, but reasonable. Bring forth the cusps!"

There was a wait, during which Cugel stood first on one foot then the other. The minutes dragged; the garments and the false beard itched intolerably. And now at the outskirts of the village he saw the approach of several new figures, coming from the direction of Grodz. One was almost certainly Bubach Angh, while another seemed to have been shorn of his beard.

The Chief Elder appeared, holding in each hand a violet cusp. "Step forward!"

Cugel called loudly. "I am here, sir."

"I now apply the potion which santifies the junction of magic cusp to right eye."

At the back of the crowd Bubach Angh raised his voice. "Hold! What transpires?"

Cugel turned, pointed. "What jackal is this that interrupts solemnities? Remove him: hence!"

"Indeed!" called the Chief Elder peremptorily. "You demean yourself and the dignity of the ceremony."

Bubach Angh crouched back, momentarily cowed.

"In view of the interruption," said Cugel, "I had as lief merely take custody of the magic cusps until these louts can properly be chastened."

"No," said the Chief Elder. "Such a procedure is impossible." He shook drops of rancid fat in Cugel's right eye. But now the peasant of the shorn beard set up an outcry: "My hat! My blouse! My beard! Is there no justice?"

"Silence!" hissed the crowd. "This is a solemn occasion!"

"But I am Bu—"

Cugel called, "Insert the magic cusp, lord; let us ignore these louts."

"A lout, you call me?" roared Bubach Angh. "I recognize you now, you rogue. Hold up proceedings!"

The Chief Elder said inexorably, "I now invest you with the right cusp. You must temporarily hold this eye closed to prevent a discord which would strain the brain, and cause

stupor. Now the left eye." He stepped forward with the ointment, but Bubach Angh and the beardless peasant no longer
would be denied.

"Hold up proceedings! You ennoble an impostor! I am Bubach Angh, the worthy squire! He who stands before you is a
vagabond!"

The Chief Elder inspected Bubach Angh with puzzlement.
"For a fact you resemble that peasant who for thirty-one years
has carted supplies to Smolod. But if you are Bubach Angh,
who is this?"

The beardless peasant lumbered forward. "It is the soulless
wretch who stole the clothes from my back and the beard from
my face."

"He is a criminal, a bandit, a vagabond—"

"Hold!" called the Chief Elder. "The words are ill-chosen.
Remember that he has been exalted to the rank of prince of
Smolod."

"Not altogether!" cried Bubach Angh. "He has one of my
eyes. I demand the other!"

"An awkward situation," muttered the Chief Elder. He
spoke to Cugel. "Though formerly a vagabond and cutthroat,
you are now a prince, and a man of responsibility. What is
your opinion?"

"I suggest a hiding for these obstreperous louts. Then—"

Bubach Angh and the beardless peasant, uttering shouts of
rage, sprang forward. Cugel, leaping away, could not control
his right eye. The lid flew open; into his brain crashed such a
wonder of exaltation that his breath caught in his throat and
his heart almost stopped from astonishment. But concurrently
his left eye showed the reality of Smolod. The dissonance was
too wild to be tolerated; he stumbled and fell against a hut.
Bubach Angh stood over him with mattock raised high, but
now the Chief Elder stepped between.

"Do you take leave of your senses? This man is a prince of
Smolod!"

"A man I will kill, for he has my eye! Do I toil thirty-one
years for the benefit of a vagabond?"

"Calm yourself, Bubach Angh, if that be your name, and
remember the issue is not yet entirely clear. Possibly an error
has been made—undoubtedly an honest error, for this man is
now a prince of Smolod, which is to say, justice and sagacity
personified."

"He was not that before he received the cusp," argued Bubach Angh, "which is when the offense was committed."

"I cannot occupy myself with casuistic distinctions," replied the elder. "In any event, your name heads the list and on the next fatality—"

"Ten or twelve years hence?" cried Bubach Angh. "Must I toil yet longer, and receive my reward just as the sun goes dark? No, no, this cannot be!"

The beardless peasant made a suggestion: "Take the other cusp. In this way you will have at least half of your rights, and so prevent the interloper from cheating you totally."

Bubach Angh agreed. "I will start with my one magic cusp; I will then kill that knave and take the other, and all will be well."

"Now then," said the Chief Elder haughtily, "this is hardly the tone to take in reference to a prince of Smolod!"

"Bah!" snorted Bubach Angh. "Remember the source of your viands! We of Grodz will not toil to no avail."

"Very well," said the Chief Elder. "I deplore your uncouth bluster, but I cannot deny that you have a measure of reason on your side. Here is the left cusp of Radkuth Vomin. I will dispense with the invocation, anointment and the congratulatory paean. If you will be good enough to step forward and open your left eye—so."

As Cugel had done, Bubach Angh looked through both eyes together and staggered back in a daze. But clapping his hand to his left eye he recovered himself, and advanced upon Cugel. "You now must see the futility of your trick. Extend me that cusp and go your way, for you will never have the use of the two."

"It matters very little," said Cugel. "Thanks to my friend Firx I am well content with the one."

Bubach Angh ground his teeth. "Do you think to trick me again? Your life has approached its end: not just I but all Grodz goes warrant for this!"

"Not in the precincts of Smolod!" warned the Chief Elder. "There must be no quarrels among the princes: I decree amity! You who have shared the cusps of Radkuth Vomin must also share his palace, his robes, appurtenances, jewels and retinue, until that hopefully remote occasion when one or the other dies, whereupon the survivor shall take all. This is my judgment; there is no more to be said."

"The moment of the interloper's death is hopefully near at hand," rumbled Bubach Angh. "The instant he sets foot from

Smolod will be his last! The citizens of Grodz will maintain a vigil of a hundred years, if necessary!"

Firx squirmed at this news and Cugel winced at the discomfort. In a conciliatory voice he addressed Bubach Angh. "A compromise might be arranged: to you shall go the entirety of Radkuth Vomin's estate: his palace, appurtenances, retinue. To me shall devolve only the magic cusps."

But Bubach Angh would have none of it. "If you value your life, deliver that cusp to me this moment."

"This cannot be done," said Cugel.

Bubach Angh turned away and spoke to the beardless peasant, who nodded and departed. Bubach Angh glowered at Cugel, then went to Radkuth Vomin's hut and sat on the heap of rubble before the door. Here he experimented with his new cusp, cautiously closing his right eye, opening the left to stare in wonder at the Overworld. Cugel thought to take advantage of his absorption and sauntered off toward the edge of town. Bubach Angh appeared not to notice. Ha! thought Cugel. It was to be so easy, then! Two more strides and he would be lost into the darkness!

Jauntily he stretched his long legs to take those two strides. A slight sound—a grunt, a scrape, a rustle of clothes—caused him to jerk aside; down swung a mattock blade, cutting the air where his head had been. In the faint glow cast by the Smolod lamps Cugel glimpsed the beardless peasant's vindictive countenance. Behind him Bubach Angh came loping, heavy head thrust forward like a bull. Cugel dodged, and ran with agility back into the heart of Smolod.

Slowly and in vast disappointment Bubach Angh returned, to seat himself once more. "You will never escape," he told Cugel. "Give over the cusp and preserve your life!"

"By no means," replied Cugel with spirit. "Rather fear for your own sodden vitality, which goes in even greater peril!"

From the hut of the Chief Elder came an admonitory call. "Cease the bickering! I am indulging the exotic whims of a beautiful princess and must not be distracted."

Cugel, recalling the oleaginous wads of flesh, the leering slab-sided visages, the matted verminous hair, the wattles and wens and evil odors which characterized the women of Smolod, marveled anew at the power of the cusps. Babach Angh was once more testing the vision of his left eye. Cugel composed himself on a bench and attempted the use of his right eye, first holding his hand before his left. . . .

Cugel wore a shirt of supple silver scales, tight scarlet trousers, a dark blue cloak. He sat on a marble bench before a row of spiral marble columns overgrown with dark foliage and white flowers. To either side the palaces of Smolod towered into the night, one behind the other, with soft lights accenting the arches and windows. The sky was a soft dark blue, hung with great glowing stars; among the palaces were gardens of cypress, myrtle, jasmine, sphade, thyssam; the air was pervaded with the perfume of flowers and flowing water. From somewhere came a wisp of music; a murmur of soft chords, a sigh of melody. Cugel took a deep breath and rose to his feet. He stepped forward, moving across the terrace. Palaces and gardens shifted perspective; on a dim lawn three girls in gowns of white gauze watched him over their shoulders.

Cugel took an involuntary step forward, then, recalling the malice of Bubach Angh, paused to check on his whereabouts. Across the plaza rose a palace of seven stories, each level with its terrace garden, with vines and flowers trailing down the walls. Through the windows Cugel glimpsed rich furnishings, lustrous chandeliers, the soft movement of liveried chamberlains. On the pavilion before the palace stood a hawk-featured man with a cropped golden beard in robes of ocher and black, with gold epaulettes and black buskins. He stood one foot on a stone griffin, arms on bent knee, gazing toward Cugel with an expression of brooding dislike. Cugel marveled: could this be the pig-faced Bubach Angh? Could the magnificent seven-tiered palace be the hovel of Radkuth Vomin?

Cugel moved slowly off across the plaza, and now came upon a pavilion lit by candelabra. Tables supported meats, jellies and pastries of every description; and Cugel's belly, nourished only by driftwood and smoked fish, urged him forward. He passed from table to table, sampling morsels from every dish, and found all to be of the highest quality.

"Smoked fish and lentils I may still be devouring," Cugel told himself, "but there is much to be said for the enchantment by which they become such exquisite delicacies. Indeed, a man might do far worse than spend the rest of his life here in Smolod."

Almost as if Firx had been anticipating the thought, he instantly inflicted upon Cugel's liver a series of agonizing pangs, and Cugel bitterly reviled Iucounu the Laughing Magician and repeated his vows of vengeance.

Recovering his composure, he sauntered to that area where

the formal gardens surrounding the palaces gave way to parkland. He looked over his shoulder, to find the hawk-faced prince in ocher and black approaching, with manifestly hostile intent. In the dimness of the park Cugel noted other movement and thought to spy a number of armored warriors.

Cugel returned to the plaza and Bubach Angh followed, once more to stand glowering at Cugel in front of Radkuth Vomin's palace.

"Clearly," said Cugel aloud for the benefit of Firx, "there will be no departure from Smolod tonight. Naturally I am anxious to convey the cusp to Iucounu, but if I am killed then neither the cusp nor the admirable Firx will ever return to Almery."

Firx made no further demonstration. Now, thought Cugel, where to pass the night? The seven-tiered palace of Radkuth Vomin manifestly offered ample and spacious accommodation for both himself and Bubach Angh. In essence, however, the two would be crammed together in a one-roomed hut, with a single heap of damp reeds for a couch. Thoughtfully, regretfully, Cugel closed his right eye, opened his left.

Smolod was as before. The surly Bubach Angh crouched before the door to Radkuth Vomin's hut. Cugel stepped forward and kicked Bubach Angh smartly. In surprise and shock, both Bubach Angh's eyes opened, and the rival impulses colliding in his brain induced paralysis. Back in the darkness the beardless peasant roared and came charging forward, mattock on high, and Cugel relinquished his plan to cut Bubach Angh's throat. He skipped inside the hut, closed and barred the door.

He now closed his left eye and opened his right. He found himself in the magnificent entry hall of Radkuth Vomin's palace, the portico of which was secured by a portcullis of forged iron. Without, the golden-haired prince in ocher and black, holding his hand over one eye, was lifting himself in cold dignity from the pavement of the plaza. Raising one arm in noble defiance, Bubach Angh swung his cloak over his shoulder and marched off to join his warriors.

Cugel sauntered through the palace, inspecting the appointments with pleasure. If it had not been for the importunities of Firx, there would have been no haste in trying the perilous journey back to the Valley of the Xzan.

Cugel selected a luxurious chamber facing to the south, doffed his rich garments for satin nightwear, settled upon a couch with sheets of pale blue silk, and instantly fell asleep.

In the morning there was a degree of difficulty remembering which eye to open, and Cugel thought it might be well to fashion a patch to wear over that eye not currently in use.

By day the palaces of Smolod were more grand than ever, and now the plaza was thronged with princes and princesses, all of utmost beauty.

Cugel dressed himself in handsome garments of black, with a jaunty green cap and green sandals. He descended to the entry hall, raised the portcullis with a gesture of command, and went forth into the plaza.

There was no sign of Bubach Angh. The other inhabitants of Smolod greeted him with courtesy and the princesses displayed noticeable warmth, as if they found him good address. Cugel responded politely, but without fervor: not even the magic cusp could persuade him against the sour wads of fat, flesh, grime and hair which were the Smolod women.

He breakfasted on delightful viands at the pavilion, then returned to the plaza to consider his next course of action. A cursory inspection of the parklands revealed Grodz warriors on guard. There was no immediate prospect of escape.

The nobility of Smolod applied themselves to their diversions. Some wandered the meadows; others went boating upon the delightful waterways to the north. The Chief Elder, a prince of sagacious and noble visage, sat alone on an onyx bench, deep in reverie.

Cugel approached; the Chief Elder aroused himself and gave Cugel a salute of measured cordiality. "I am not easy in my mind," he declared. "In spite of all judiciousness, and allowing for your unavoidable ignorance of our customs, I feel a certain inequity has been done, and I am at a loss as how to repair it."

"It seems to me," said Cugel, "that Squire Bubach Angh, though doubtless a worthy man, exhibits a lack of discipline unfitting the dignity of Smolod. In my opinion he would be all the better for a few years more seasoning at Grodz."

"There is something in what you say," replied the elder. "Small personal sacrifices are sometimes essential to the welfare of the group. I feel certain that you, if the issue arose, would gladly offer up your cusp and enroll anew at Grodz. What are a few years? They flutter past like butterflies."

Cugel made a suave gesture. "Or a trial by lot might be arranged, in which all who see with two cusps participate, the loser of the trial donating one of his cusps to Bubach Angh. I myself will make do with one."

The elder frowned. "Well—the contingency is remote. Meanwhile you must participate in our merrymaking. If I may say so, you cut a personable figure and certain of the princesses have been casting sheep's eyes in your direction. There, for instance, the lovely Udela Narshag—and there, Zokoxa of the Rose-Petals, and beyond the vivacious Ilviu Lasmal. You must not be backward here in Smolod; we live an uncircumscribed life."

"The charm of these ladies has not escaped me," said Cugel. "Unluckily I am bound by a vow of continence."

"Unfortunate man!" exclaimed the Chief Elder. "The princesses of Smolod are nonpareil! And notice—yet another soliciting your attention!"

"Surely it is you she summons," said Cugel, and the elder went to confer with the young woman in question who had come riding into the plaza in a magnificent boat-shaped car which walked on six swan-feet. The princess reclined on a couch of pink down and was beautiful enough to make Cugel rue the fastidiousness of his recollection, which projected every matted hair, mole, dangling underlip, sweating seam and wrinkle of the Smolod women to the front of his memory. This princess was indeed the essence of a daydream: slender and supple, with skin like still cream, a delicate nose, lucent brooding eyes, a mouth of delightful flexibility. Her expression intrigued Cugel, for it was more complex than that of the other princesses: pensive, yet willful; ardent yet dissatisfied.

Into the plaza came Bubach Angh, accoutered in military wise, with corselet, morion and sword. The Chief Elder went to speak to him; and now to Cugel's irritation the princess in the walking boat signaled to him.

He went forward. "Yes, princess; you saluted me, I believe?"

The princess nodded. "I speculate on your presence up here in these northern lands." She spoke in a soft clear voice like music.

Cugel said, "I am here on a mission; I stay but a short while at Smolod, and then must continue east and south."

"Indeed!" said the princess. "What is the nature of your mission?"

"To be candid, I was brought here by the malice of a magician. It was by no means a yearning of my own."

The princess laughed softly. "I see few strangers. I long for
new faces and new talk. Perhaps you will come to my palace
and we will talk of magic, and the strange circumstances
which throng the dying earth."

Cugel bowed stiffly. "Your offer is kind. But you must
seek elsewhere; I am bound by a vow of continence. Control
your displeasure, for it applies not only to you but to Udela
Narshag yonder, to Zokoxa, and to Ilviu Lasmal."

The princess raised her eyebrows, sank back in her down-
covered couch. She smiled faintly. "Indeed, indeed. You are a
harsh man, a stern relentless man, thus to refuse yourself to so
many imploring women."

"This is the case, and so it must be." Cugel turned away to
face the Chief Elder, who approached with Bubach Angh at
his back.

"Sorry circumstances," announced the Chief Elder in a
troubled voice. "Bubach Angh speaks for the village of
Grodz. He declares that no more victuals will be furnished
until justice is done, and this they define as the surrender of
your cusp to Bubach Angh, and your person to a punitive
committee who waits in the parkland yonder."

Cugel laughed uneasily. "What a distorted view! You assured them of course that we of Smolod would eat grass and
destroy the cusps before agreeing to such detestable provi-
sions?"

"I fear that I temporized," stated the Chief Elder. "I feel
that the others of Smolod favor a more flexible course of action."

The implication was clear, and Firx began to stir in exas-
peration. In order to appraise circumstances in the most forth-
right manner possible. Cugel shifted the patch to look from his
left eye.

Certain citizens of Grodz, armed with scythes, mattocks
and clubs, waited at a distance of fifty yards: evidently the
punitive committee to which Bubach Angh had referred. To
one side were the huts of Smolod; to the other the walking
boat and the princess of such—Cugel stared in astonishment.
The boat was as before, walking on six bird-legs, and sitting
in the pink down was the princess—if possible, more beautiful than ever. But now her expression, rather than faintly
smiling, was cool and still.

Cugel drew a deep breath and took to his heels. Bubach
Angh shouted an order to halt, but Cugel paid no heed. Across

the barrens he raced, with the punitive committee in pursuit.

Cugel laughed gleefully. He was long of limb, sound of wind; the peasants were stumpy, knot-muscled, phlegmatic. He could easily run two miles to their one. He paused, and turned to wave farewell. To his dismay two legs from the walking boat detached themselves and leapt after him. Cugel ran for his life. In vain. The legs came bounding past, one on either side. They swung around and kicked him to a halt.

Cugel sullenly walked back, the legs hopping behind. Just before he reached the outskirts of Smolod he reached under the patch and pulled loose the magic cusp. As the punitive committee bore down on him, he held it aloft. "Stand back— or I break the cusp to fragments!"

"Hold! Hold!" called Bubach Angh. "This must not be! Come, give me the cusp and accept your just deserts."

"Nothing has yet been decided," Cugel reminded him. "The Chief Elder has ruled for no one."

The girl rose from her seat in the boat. "I will rule; I am Derwe Coreme, of the House of Domber. Give me the violet glass, whatever it is."

"By no means," said Cugel. "Take the cusp from Bubach Augh."

"Never!" exclaimed the squire from Grodz.

"What? You both have a cusp and both want two? What are those precious objects? You wear them as eyes? Give them to me."

Cugel drew his sword. "I prefer to run, but I will fight if I must."

"I cannot run," said Bubach Angh. "I prefer to fight." He pulled the cusp from his own eye. "Now then, vagabond, prepare to die."

"A moment," said Derwe Coreme. From one of the legs of the boat thin arms reached to seize the wrists of both Cugel and Bubach Angh. The cusps fell to earth; that of Bubach Angh struck a stone and shivered to fragments. He howled in anguish and leapt upon Cugel, who gave ground before the attack.

Bubach Angh knew nothing of swordplay; he hacked and slashed as if he were cleaning fish. The fury of his attack, however, was unsettling and Cugel was hard put to defend himself. In addition to Bubach Angh's sallies and slashes, Firx was deploring the loss of the cusp.

Derwe Coreme had lost interest in the affair. The boat

started off across the barrens, moving faster and ever faster. Cugel slashed out with his sword, leapt back, leapt back once more, and for the second time fled across the barrens.

The boat-car jogged along at a leisurely rate. Lungs throbbing, Cugel gained upon it, and with a great bound leapt up, caught the downy gunwale and pulled himself astride.

It was as he expected. Derwe Coreme had looked through the cusp and lay back in a daze. The violet cusp reposed in her lap.

Cugel seized it, then for a moment stared down into the exquisite face and wondered if he dared more. Firx thought not. Already Derwe Coreme was sighing and moving her head.

Cugel leapt from the boat, and only just in time. Had she seen him? He ran to a clump of reeds which grew by a pond, and flung himself into the water. From here he saw the walking-boat halt while Derwe Coreme rose to her feet. She felt through the pink down for the cusp, then she looked all around the countryside. But the blood-red light of the low sun was in her eyes when she looked toward Cugel, and she saw only the reeds and the reflection of sun on water.

Angry and sullen as never before, she set the boat into motion. It walked, then cantered, then loped to the south.

Cugel emerged from the water, inspected the magic cusp, tucked it into his pouch, and looked back toward Smolod. He started to walk south, then paused. He took the cusp from his pocket, closed his left eye, and held the cusp to his right. There rose the palaces, tier on tier, tower above tower, the gardens hanging down the terraces. . . . Cugel would have stared a long time, but Firx became restive.

Cugel returned the cusp to his pouch, and once again set his face to the south, for the long journey back to Almery.

RECOMMENDED READING

Compiling a reading list for this anthology was a difficult task, since nine out of ten fantasy stories feature the use of sorcery to one degree or another. A comprehensive listing, if it could have been compiled at all, would have taken up half the book. Therefore, this listing is not intended to be exhaustive—it is, rather, a hitting of highlights; the intention behind the list is to guide the interested reader to further material about sorcerers, material that we ourselves found interesting or entertaining, and not to produce a heavily authoritative work of scholarship. This listing is unabashedly arbitrary, its only criteria our own personal tastes. Since much important fantasy work is done as series of connected novels or collections, and since many of these series run of connected novels or collections, and since many of these series run to multiple volumes, we have listed these series under a general heading (viz.: the *Fafhrd-Gray Mouser* series); short-story collections are indicated as (c). Throughout the short fiction list, we have given the most recent sources for the stories, or else those we have judged—arbitrarily—to be the most accessible to the average reader.

Especially Recommended:*

BOOKS (Novels & Collections)

Brian W. Aldiss. *The Malacia Tapestry.*
Poul Anderson. *The Broken Sword.*
*———. *Three Hearts and Three Lions.*
*John Bellaires. *The Face In the Frost.*
James Blish. *Black Easter.*
Ray Bradbury. *Something Wicked This Way Comes.*
John Brunner. *The Traveler in Black(c).*
Orson Scott Card. *Hart's Hope.*
John Crowley. *Little, Big.*
Avram Davidson. *The Enquiries of Doctor Eszterhazy* (c).
———. *Masters of the Maze.*
*———. *The Phoenix and the Mirror.*
*L. Sprague De Camp and Fletcher Pratt. *The Complete
          Enchanter.*
———. *Land of Unreason.*
Lord Dunsany. *At the Edge of the World* (c).
———. *Beyond the Fields We know* (c).
———. *The Sword of Welleran* (c).
E. R. Eddison. *The Worm Ouroboros.*
Charles G. Finney. *The Circus of Dr. Lao.*
Alan Garner. *The Moon of Gomrath.*
———. *The Weirdstone of Brisingamen.*
Randall Garrett. *Lord Darcey Investigates* (c).
———. *Murder and Magic* (c).
———. *Too Many Magicians.*
*Lisa Goldstein. *The Red Magician.*
Robin Hardy and Anthony Shaffer. *The Wicker Man.*
Robert A. Heinlein. *Waldo & Magic, Inc.* (c).
Robert E. Howard. The *Conan* series.
*Stephen King. *The Gunslinger.*
———. *The Stand.*
R. A. Lafferty. *The Devil Is Dead.*
———. *The Reefs of Earth.*
Sterling E. Lanier. *The Peculiar Exploits of Brigadier
          Ffellowes* (c).
Tanith Lee. *Cyrion* (c).
———. *Red as Blood* (c).
*Ursula K. Le Guin. The *Earthsea* trilogy.

*Fritz Leiber. *Conjure Wife*.
*————. The *Fafhrd-Gray Mouse*r series.
————. *Our Lady of Darkness*.
H. P. Lovecraft. the *Cthulhu Mythos* stories.
George R. R. Martin. *The Armageddon Rag*.
Michael Moorcock. The *Elric* series.
*C. L. Moore. *Jirel of Joiry* (c).
Andre Norton. *Witch World*.
Mervyn Peake. The *Gormenghast* trilogy.
Tim Powers. *The Anubis Gates*.
————. *The Drawing of the Dark*.
Clark Ashton Smith. *The Last Incantation* (c).
*————. *Zothique* (c).
*J. R. R. Tolkien. The *Lord of the Rings* trilogy.
Jack Vance. *Cugel's Saga* (c).
*————. *The Dying Earth* (c).
*————. *The Eyes of the Overworld*.
Karl Edward Wagner. The *Kane* series.
Manly Wade Wellman. *Who Fears the Devil?* (c).
*T. H. White. *The Once and Future King*.
*Gene Wolfe. The *Book of the New Sun* tetralogy.
Roger Zelazny. The *Amber* series.

SHORT STORIES

Brian W. Aldiss. "The Small Stones of Tu Fu," *Isaac Asimov's Science Fiction Magazine*, Nov.-Dec. 1978.
Poul Anderson. "The Tale of Hauk," *Fantasy. Fantasy* is the title of a short-story collection by Anderson.
*————. "The Valor of Cappen Varra," *Fantasy, Fantasy* is the title of a short-story collection by Anderson.
J. G. Ballard. "The Volcano Dances," *The Terminal Beach*.
Greg Bear. "The White Horse Child," *The Wind from a Burning Woman*.
*Alfred Bester. "Hell Is Forever," *The Unknown Five*.
Robert Bloch. "Yours Truly, Jack the Ripper," *The Arbor House Treasury of Horror & The Supernatural*.
Frederic Brown. "Armageddon," *The Unknown*.
Edward Bryant. "Dark Angel," *Dark Forces*.
Anthony Boucher. "Snulbug," *The Unknown*.

Pat Cadigan. "The Sorceress in Spite of Herself," *Isaac Asimov's Science Fiction Magazine*, Dec. 1982.

Truman Capote. "Dazzle," *Music For Chameleons*.

Orson Scott Card. "The Princess and the Bear," *Berkley Showcase, Vol. 1*.

———. "Sandmagic," *Swords Against Darkness IV*.

Susan Casper. "Mama," *The Magazine of Fantasy and Science Fiction*, August 1984.

Theodore R. Cogswell. "You Know Willie," *The Wall Around the World*.

Richard Cowper. "The Web of the Magi." *The Magazine of Fantasy and Science Fiction*, June 1980.

Jack Dann, Gardner Dozois, and Michael Swanwick. "Afternoon at Schrafft's," *Amazing*, 1984.

Avram Davidson. "The Ceaseless Stone," *The Enquiries of Doctor Eszterhazy*.

———. "Dagon," *Or All the Seas with Oysters*.

———. "Milord Sir Smith, the English Wizard," *The Enquiries of Doctor Eszterhazy*.

*———. "The Power of Every Root," *Strange Seas and Shores*.

———. "Where do You Live, Queen Ester?," *What Strange Shores and Skies*.

L. Sprague De Camp. "The Emperor's Fan," *The Best of L. Sprague De Camp*.

———. "Ka the Appalling," *The Reluctant Shaman*.

*———. "The Yellow Man," *The Purple Pterodactyls*.

Stephen R. Donaldson. "The Lady In White," *The Magazine of Fantasy and Science Fiction*, Feb. 1978.

Lord Dunsany. "Chu-Bu and Sheemish," *Warlocks & Warriors*.

*———. "The Fortress Unvanquishable, Save for Sacnoth," *The Sword of Welleran*.

Harlan Ellison. "Djinn, No Chaser," *Stalking the Nightmare*.

———. "Grail," *Stalking the Nightmare*.

Randall Garrett. "The Bitter End," *Isaac Asimov's Science Fiction Magazine*, Nov.-Dec. 1978.

———. "The Eyes Have It," *Murder and Magic*.

Robert E. Howard. "'Old Garfield's Heart," *The Dark Man and Others*.

———. "The People of the Black Circle," *Weird Tales*, Sep.-Oct. 1934.

Shirley Jackson. "One Ordinary Day, With Peanuts," *SF: The Best of the Best*.

M. R. James. "The Casting of the Runes," *The Collected Ghost Stories of M. R. James*.

James Patrick Kelly. "The Fear that Men Call Courage," *The Magazine of Fantasy and Science Fiction*, Sept. 1980

Stephen King. "Children of the Corn," *Night Shift*.

*————. *"The Gunslingers," Year's Finest Fantasy, Vol 1*.

————."Night of the Tiger," *The Magazine of Fantasy and Science Fiction*, Oct. 1978.

Rudyard Kipling. "The Mark of the Beast," *Werewolf*.

————. "The Sending of Dona Da," *Kipling's Indian Tales*.

Damon Knight. "Extempore," *The Best of Damon Knight*.

C. M. Kornbluth. "The Words of Guru," *The Best of C. M. Kornbluth*.

R. A. Lafferty. "Seven-Day Terror," *Nine Hundred Grandmothers*.

————. "The Transcendent Tigers," *Strange Doings*.

*Sterling E. Lanier. "Ghosts of a Crown," *The Magazine of Fantasy and Science Fiction*, Dec. 1976.

————. "The Voice of the Turtle," *The Magazine of Fantasy and Science Fiction*, Oct. 1972.

Tanith Lee. "The Golden Rope," *Red As Blood*.

————. "Red As Blood," *Red As Blood*.

————. "Winter White," *Year's Best Horror Stories 1978*.

Ursula K. Le Guin. "The Barrow," *Orsinian Tales*.

————. "The Rule of Names," *The Wind's Twelve Quarters*.

*Fritz Leiber. "Adept's Gambit," *Swords in the Mist*.

————. "The Howling Tower," *Swords Against Death*.

————. "Scylla's Daughter," *Fantastic*, May 1961.

————. "When the Sea King's Away," *Swords in the Mist*.

Elizabeth A. Lynn. "The Wizard of Reorth," *The Woman Who Loved the Moon*.

Robin McKinley. "The Healer," *Elsewhere II*.

George R. R. Martin. "In the Lost Lands," *Amazons II*.

————. "The Lonely Songs of Laren Door," *Songs of Stars and Shadows*.

Pat Murphy. "Touch of the Bear," *The Magazine of Fantasy and Science Fiction*, October 1980

Ray Nelson. "Time-Travel for Pedestrians," *Again, Dangerous Visions*.

Larry Niven. "What Good is a Glass Dagger?," *Fantasy and Science Fiction*, 1972.

Edgar Pangborn. "The Legend of Hombas," *Still I Persist in Wondering*.

————. "The Witches of Nupal," *Still I Persist in Wondering*.

Tom Reamy. "San Diego Lightfoot Sue," *San Diego Lightfoot Sue*.

————. "Twilla," *San Diego Lightfoot Sue*.

*Keith Roberts. "I Lose Medea," *The Passing of the Dragons*.

————. "Timothy," *New Worlds of Fantasy*.

Rudy Rucker. "Tales of Houdini," *The 57th Franz Kafka*.

*Joanna Russ. "The Barbarian," *The Adventures of Alyx*.

————. "The Extraordinary Voyages of Amelie Bertrand," *The Zanzibar Cat*.

Lewis Shiner. "Bruju," *The Magazine of Fantasy and Science Fiction*, Aug. 1982.

*Clark Ashton Smith. "The Death of Malygris," *The Last Incantation*.

————. "The Last Incantation," *The Last Incantation*.

————. "Master of the Crabs," *Warlocks & Warriors*.

Jenny Sullivan. "Gran and the Roaring Boys," *Elsewhere II*.

*Thomas Burnet Swann. "The Manor of Roses," *The Dolphin and the Deep*.

*Michael Swanwick. "The Man Who Met Picasso," *Omni*, Sept. 1982.

James Thurber. "The Black Magic of Barney Haller," *The Thurber Carnival*.

James Tiptree, Jr. "The Man Doors Said Hello To," *10,000 Light-Years From Home*.

Lisa Tuttle. "A Piece of Rope," *Shayol 1*.

*Jack Vance. "The Bagful of Dreams," *Cugel's Saga*.

————. "Cil," *The Eyes of the Overworld*.

————. "Green Magic," *The Best from The Magazine of Fantasy and Science Fiction*, 13th Series.

————. "Mazirian the Magician," *The Dying Earth*.

Karl Edward Wagner. "Sticks," *Whispers 3*.

Manly Wade Wellman. "Vandy, Vandy," *Who Fears the Devil?*

Gene Wolfe. "'A Story,' by John V. Marsch," *The Fifth Head of Cerberus*.

*————. "The Island of Doctor Death and Other Stories," *The Island of Doctor Death and Other Stories and Other Stories*.

Jane Yolen. "Boris Chernevsky's Hands," *Tales of Wonder*.

————. "Names," *Tales of Wonder*.

Roger Zelazny. "The Last Defender of Camelot," *The Last Defender of Camelot*.